I0527703

CHAMPAGNE PROMISES

DORIS LEMCKE

CHAMPAGNE PROMISES
Copyright © 2020 by Doris Lemcke

ISBN: 978-1-68046-869-4

Published by Satin Romance
An Imprint of Melange Books, LLC
White Bear Lake, MN 55110
www.satinromance.com

Names, characters, and incidents depicted in this book are products of the author's imagination or are used fictitiously. Any resemblance to actual events, locales, organizations, or persons, living or dead, is entirely coincidental and beyond the intent of the author or the publisher. No part of this book may be reproduced or transmitted in any form or by any means, electronic or mechanical, including photocopying, recording, or by any information storage and retrieval system, without permission in writing from the publisher except for the use of brief quotations in a book review or scholarly journal.

Published in the United States of America.

Cover Design by Caroline Andrus

No one writes a book alone. It's the shared experience of "inventing" that breathes life into an idea until it becomes characters to care about, lives to be shared, and a world to remember. I have many people to thank for helping me write books that readers ask, "Did that really happen?"

Thank you to my publisher, Nancy Schumacher, for accepting this adventure into a little-known, oft-forgotten—and world-changing—war that put America onto the path of becoming a world power. To Joan Samipieri, my mentor, writing partner and friend, for keeping me focused with her "get 'er done" philosophy of life. And as always, my dear friends and authors Karen Auriti (writing as Kerryn Reid) and Karen Benson from the Southwest Florida Romance Writers for enduring the starts, stops and many drafts of this book for more than a decade.

I'm also grateful for the support of my new friends in a new town—Maurine Nelson, Dick Dice, and the very special and supportive, CADDY Quilters group in Chelsea, MI, who listened to my ramblings about "the book" and provided me with a new character. Thank you. Pat Kraska for inspiring me to invent the sweet, gentle soul of Ailish, O'Malley.

And most of all, a special thanks to my husband John, for 49 years of telling me, "You can do it!"

CHAPTER 1

Tampa, FL – December 31, 1897

"Where's the net, Victor?"

Lily Champagne stopped pacing in tight circles on the portable stage to peer between the curtains. The Tampa Bay Hotel's massive dining room was packed. Nearly six hundred people—including Joseph Pulitzer, publisher of the *New York World*—awaited her portrayal of Lady Liberty descending from the room's starlit dome.

Without success, she'd been submitting stories to Pulitzer for three years in hopes of being hired as a reporter. Her idol, Nellie Bly, Pulitzer's correspondent in Mexico, had gotten his attention by posing as an inmate in a women's asylum for a story. At the very least, she hoped this performance dramatizing the cause for Cuban independence would gain her an introduction.

Gulping back nausea at the thought of dangling nearly seventy feet in the air, she touched her husband's arm beneath a loose-fitting Cuban peasant costume. "What if the cable breaks? Or the harness? You said I'd have a net. Even Ringling uses nets."

He looked down at her, his lips tight beneath a pencil-thin mustache. Long, elegant fingers cupped her chin as he leaned over her like a parent with a petulant child. "A net will spoil the effect. This hotel is only seven years old. Everything here is top-of-the-line. Pull yourself together. You'll be as safe up there as in your mama's arms. And your future is riding on this."

The warning in Victor's voice raised gooseflesh on her arms while the rest of her body broiled under a canvas harness covered by a silk leotard and diaphanous Grecian gown. His smile softened his classic, Roman features as he stroked her cheek. "Darling, it's you they paid twice the ticket price to see. Lady Liberty's flight for Cuba's freedom will make you more famous than that cow, Nellie Bly's, few days in a madhouse. Pulitzer will beg you to write stories of your adventures on our upcoming tour of the island."

Lily stared into the smoldering amber eyes that always set her blood on fire. Victor's lips and fingers had brought her body to life in ways she'd never thought possible—and he'd brought her to the right place at the right time. With Florida's Key West only ninety miles from Cuba, American outrage over Spanish General Valeriano Weyler's atrocities against native Cubans imprisoned in his *reconcentrado* camps, was growing by the day. Despite his having been called back to Spain, thousands of prisoners still held behind his walled trenches were dying from torture, starvation, and disease. Stories about their plight would be critical in helping free them—if she could find a publisher.

Businessmen heavily invested in Cuban tobacco and sugar plantations, filled the hotel's dining room, along with politicians and journalists. She recognized the tall, lean, Joseph Pulitzer, owner of the *New York World,* by his thick dark hair and pince-nez eyeglasses dangling from a drop chain pinned to his lapel. She'd also glimpsed Richard Harding-Davis, the famous author and journalist for Pulitzer's competitor, William Randolph Hearst's *New York Journal.*

If it took descending from a seventy-foot dome to help free Cuba—and gain introductions to New York's biggest publisher and most famous war correspondent—she'd do it, but she needed to live to tell the tale.

She straightened her shoulders. "I want a net."

Victor's hand again cupped her chin and squeezed it this time. "You're only going as far up as the gallery, at least a dozen feet below the dome. Don't be a coward."

"Coward?" She pulled away and jabbed a finger into his chest. "How dare you call me a coward. I broke horses when I was twelve years old. I lied about my age to attend the Conservatory of Music and moved to New York alone at sixteen. And have you forgotten that I left it all behind to marry you, using my savings to support us after you were robbed in St. Louis? Or that when you asked me to, I sang and danced for tips from riverboat gamblers on the way to down the Mississippi? I even slept on the deck of a cattle boat to get here—and never questioned you until now. But this time you're asking too much. I'm not ready. I can't control the swinging and could crash into the gallery railings. Without a net, a fall from fifty or twenty feet onto a marble floor will…"

"Are you blind as well as tiresome?" The anger in his voice felt like a blow.

He opened the end of the stage curtain. "Look around you. Those are electric lights in the chandeliers, and Thomas Edison's incandescent footlights around the stage. Elevators go up to all five floors to rooms with electric lights and telephones. What makes you think the masters who built this monument to modern technology couldn't devise a harness and pulley system to keep a hundred-pound girl aloft for three minutes?"

She admitted to the extravagant amenities Henry Plant had built into what he called the jewel of his railroad and shipping empire. But even the florists who perfumed the air with magnolias, orange blossoms, and jasmine couldn't cover the stench of decay from the swamps and marshes surrounding the tiny city of Tampa. And Victor, not the masters who built the hotel, had designed the harness and pulley system.

She lifted the thick velvet curtain a few inches from the floor, revealing two inches of mildew clinging to the hem. "No, you look around." Dropping it, she pointed to the mold creeping up the walls of the painted backdrop. "Nothing escapes this hellish heat and humidity. Did you even check those seven-year-old pulleys and wire cables for rust?"

Fury ignited his eyes as he yanked her against him, his breath hot against her ear. "My dear Princess Lily, if you want to make news instead of reporting it, you must take risks. We need this performance to pay for our passage to Cuba. I've booked you for a concert at the Captain-General's palace. It will open doors to all the major Spanish cities. And if you don't do this…"

3

The clash of cymbals and a drumroll overrode his voice to announce the final magic trick by the Wildstar Theatrical Group's illusionist, Merlyn Drake. "And now, Ladies and Gentlemen," the old magician shouted above catcalls from the impatient audience. "For my final exhibition, I will make hair appear on a barren skull."

It was too late to walk away. Lily's dream of reporting on the political powder keg Cuba had become, rested on this performance. In exactly four minutes, after Merlyn completed his famous "hat trick," she'd risk her life to become Joseph Pulitzer's first female foreign correspondent in Cuba.

"Abracadabra," came from the other side of the curtain.

She didn't have to look to know he'd stopped at the table of one of America's richest scions of business, planted his top hat on the man's bald head, and waved a glittering wand. After a few more gibberish incantations, he'd lift the hat to reveal an old hare sitting on the man's head—and use the distraction to steal the robber baron's wallet.

Three minutes! She fought her revulsion to the odors of stage makeup, oiled ropes, and sweat that Victor referred to as the "perfume" of the theater. *God, please don't let me vomit above Joseph Pulitzer.* Unable to look up at the rigging or out at the excited crowd, she stared at her husband of only four months. His skin was dry, his thick, black hair pressed smoothly against his perfectly shaped head while he breathed easily in the hot, moist air. Even in peasant clothes with a red kerchief around his neck, he looked as elegant— and arrogant—as he did in the tuxedo on his pasteboard cutouts.

"Observe. Nothing up my sleeve." Merlyn's voice rose above an audience chanting, "Lily, Lily, Lily."

Reasoning she could only die once; she wagged a finger at Victor's nose. "No more risqué costumes and swinging from ceilings. I want first class travel to Havana. And a suite at the Inglaterra Hotel."

One side of his mouth raised in a sly smile. "My, aren't you the feisty one. I suggest you harness your courage for the flight instead of haranguing me with outrageous demands."

He nodded to the stagehands who approached to connect her to the rigging, raising his voice enough for them to hear, "You are the embodiment of the Angel of Liberty, my love. The audience will worship you." Smoothing her waist-length silver-blonde hair, he traced the line of her cheek with the back of his hand, then leaned close and said with a voice as sweet as warm honey, "You'll be in Cuba before you know it. Trust me."

She wanted to, but with Victor, it was often impossible to tell where the actor ended, and the man began. Every inch the besotted cavalier and successful theater promoter in New York, he'd called her his golden-haired princess, promising her the moon and all the stars. But after he was robbed in St. Louis, he had spells of dark moods and a short temper. She told herself it was shame for having to borrow money from her.

"No more flights," she pressed again. "I'm a serious journalist."

His head cocked. "Serious? Do you call those penny-dreadful Western novels you churn out, serious? And what will you do, Lily, if I ask you to fly again? Go back to the conservatory and teach vacant-headed debutantes to play "Fur Elise" at tea parties? Or will you crawl back to that backwoods plantation you couldn't wait to escape? Perhaps you misled me into thinking you have what it takes to succeed as both an actress and a correspondent."

"How dare you!" It no longer mattered that she was drenched with sweat while her mouth felt like it was stuffed with sawdust. She would have slapped him except his hands imprisoned hers at her side. "Langesford is the premier plantation and horse-breeding stable in Georgia. It was *you* who misled *me*. I gave you everything I had and would have given you my trust fund if it was yet mine to give. I *believed* you through everything—until now. From now on you'll have to earn my trust."

Unaffected by her threat, he kissed her fingers. "You're mistaken, my little Rebel princess. You invested your meager funds with me to make you famous, and I fully intend to do that."

Thunderous applause announced the end of Merlyn's act and hundreds of voices again raised to chant, "Lily, Lily, Lily."

One minute! The musical introduction to her flight began. Victor was right about one thing. She couldn't allow a Florida swamp to kill her dream. She stepped back for him to drape a floor-length satin flag over her shoulders.

He kissed her cheek. "I knew you'd see things my way."

Victor threaded two cables, each as thin as a child's finger, through the back of her gown, hooking them to her harness, and ignoring her wince at the tug when he tested the tension. After securing the flag around her shoulders with a braided cord at her neck, his palm lingered over her hammering heart. He smiled and kissed the tip of her nose before stepping away and nodding for the stagehand to raise Lady Liberty to the heavens.

Another drumroll and Thomas Edison's stage lights blinked out, one by one, followed by each of the six massive chandeliers, until only the moon and stars above the glass dome illuminated the room in a soft, silver glow. Lily gasped as her feet left the floor. Following the advice of their aging, acrobat/shape artist, Wilhelmina (Willie) Malloy, she chanted, "Don't look down. Don't look down."

With every turn of the winch, she heard Willie's voice in her head. "Jest stretch out like a bird in the wind and enjoy the ride. But hold yer body tight," she added with a gap-toothed grin. "Or ye'll end up danglin' like a wishbone from yer belt."

Liberty's papier-mâché torch was attached to the second cable as a counterweight, and Lily stretched her legs out behind her like Willie's bird, rising slowly through the maze of hemp and spun-steel cables above the stage. Pretending she was only a stepladder away from a down-filled mattress, she fixed her gaze on the stars until she was centered under the dome.

She swayed like a feather in the breeze until the orchestra struck up John Philip Sousa's new march, "The Stars and Stripes Forever". Approving cheers rushed up to her like a warm gust of wind scented with the intoxicating aromas of Cuban cigars and expensive perfume. Her anger with Victor, her doubts, and the fear that had choked her backstage disappeared. She'd never felt so alive.

The music accompanied her slow descent toward the lone spotlight in the center of the dining room floor. Feeling like the true Angel of Liberty, she forgot her fear of heights and raised her free hand to wave and throw kisses to her adoring subjects nearly three stories below. At the second balcony, still thirty feet from the floor, the wire holding the torch snapped, tearing it from her hand. Both arms grasped at thin air and her scream was lost in the screech of metal on metal as she dropped like a stone toward the polished marble floor.

A sudden, body-wrenching stop at chandelier-level saved her from falling into the hot glass and metal spotlight below her. She hung by one thin wire on the back of her harness, the room swirling below her like a whirlpool until she became the wishbone Willie had foretold.

The audience fell silent as Lily hung facedown from the waist of her harness, her thick hair shielding her eyes from the blinding light below. The belt on the harness felt like a knife slowly slicing her in half, but she managed a few shallow breaths and slowly raised her head.

The crowd cheered, then gasped as the heavy flag broke the fragile clasp at her neck and drifted to the floor. It took the sheer gown with it, leaving her exposed in only a skintight leotard and corset harness.

Bedlam erupted. Tables crashed, scattering glasses and dinnerware onto the floor while men shouted, "Let go, Sweetie... Jump...I'll catch you."

"Help me Victor!" she cried through tears of pain and fear as the faceless male chorus outside the circle of light chanted for her jump into its maw. But she couldn't hear her husband's voice or see his face in the darkness.

Her head pounding, vision blurred, and certain she was going to die, she remembered Willie's advice—"*If you get into trouble, look up, not down.*"

She freed her arms from the harness shoulder straps and with strength she didn't know she had, pulled her legs up, away from the grasping hands, then twisted to grasp the rough braided steel rope until her palms were slippery with blood. Feeling every muscle in her body tense, she hooked her arms around the cable, stretched out her legs, and lay back as far as she could onto Willie's imaginary magic carpet of air.

Pretending the cacophony below was the sound of waves crashing against the shore, she looked up at the stars, waiting for either rescue or death. Then the pulleys screamed again. The harness jerked, and the world went dark.

The spotlight switched off and Victor stood by a lone footlight on the edge of the stage, his back to the audience, arms outstretched, to receive the slain Lady Liberty. When she was within reach, he nodded for a stagehand to release the cable and a hushed crowd watched her fall into his embrace.

He wasn't acting when he turned slowly to face the audience, his face contorted in horror and anger. It wasn't supposed to happen this way. He'd counted on Lily's fear of heights to make her swoon as soon as the track pulled her out over the crowd. His blank gunshot would have coincided with her faint and he'd have caught her lifeless body as it floated gently down from the heavens. Then he'd lay her on the stage floor beneath a stuffed effigy of the evil Spanish General Weyler.

It was supposed to be a poignant, dramatic tableau—not the bloody fiasco her silly bravado created. He had to improvise, cutting the wire to the torch and making sure she dropped to within a safe distance of the floor. She could have released the harness and fallen into the arms of one of the wealthy captains of industry in the audience. She'd have been safe, the rich guest would be a hero, and the crowd would have emptied their pockets to ensure her well-being.

"Instead, you made yourself a bloody mess and I had to haul you in like a goddamned mackerel on a line," he hissed when she moaned in his arms. "Keep your mouth shut and don't move until I tell you to."

He strode to the edge of the stage where the footlight highlighted the sharp angles of his features and the stains of Lady Liberty's blood on his shirt. Raising his face to the starlit sky, he called out in a baritone that carried through the now-open doors to the hotel lobby, "Lady Liberty has fallen to the Spanish rule of terror. Can anyone save her? Now who will free Cuba?"

But instead of cheers and applause, members of the audience muttered among themselves, asking if it was real, or part of the mysterious finale touted to be "heart-stopping and exciting in the extreme."

A new round of murmurs began when a man in a white suit rose from a table for one and said a few words to a waiter before approaching the stage. The puzzled crowd in the ravaged dining room parted to let him through.

Sweat finally beaded on Victor's forehead when he recognized the man approaching him with measured steps. He'd been at every performance, center table, second row, with one tall drink. He'd watched with quiet attention and was always gone by the time they took their bows. Who was he? Police? Government agent? Or a private investigator sent by one of his other so-called wives?

He took a deep breath and calmed, knowing that in the last five years, he'd eluded all of them more times than he could count. And if the police knew he had two filibuster boats in the Hillsboro River ready to load crates of .44 Russian and Smith & Wesson pistols, Mexican Krag-Jorgenson carbines, and three hundred rifles stolen from the Springfield Armory in '65, they wouldn't have sent one man—or waited until the end of the show.

Still, he worried that this man who walked with military bearing, his bootheels loud on the marble floor of the now-silent room, was more than a besotted admirer of the talented little chit he'd chosen to finance the last phase of his gun-smuggling operation to Cuba.

The chap took the stage steps two at a time, meeting him in front of the footlight. Slightly shorter than Victor's nearly six feet, he stood straight, his gaze steady, even under the actor's menacing glare. He held out his hand. "I'm a doctor. May I be of service?"

Victor's mouth went dry. Anticipating this very circumstance, he'd bribed a porter to call the hotel doctor out to a false emergency on the river…but he didn't check for vacationing doctors. Now, two hours away from closing the deal of a lifetime with the leader of the Cuban Liberation Movement in Ybor City, he had to improvise.

"At last!" he shouted, "America has come to save Lady Liberty from a fate worse than death!"

With perfect timing, the curtains closed, lights dimmed, and fireworks joined the stars above the dome, ushering in the new year of 1898. Cheers and applause erupted from an audience convinced they'd all been part of a grand finale that had fulfilled its purpose to be "heart-stopping in the extreme".

"Are you planning a curtain call, Champagne?" the stranger asked. "Or you gonna put her down so I can help her?"

They were in front of a fainting couch used in the previous skit when the curtains parted and a young waiter stepped in, handing the stranger a tattered medical bag. He disappeared backstage after catching his silver dollar tip and Victor dropped Lily unceremoniously onto the faded red-velvet divan.

He faced the intruder, demanding, "Who are you?"

The clean-shaven man in white answered with a smile that didn't meet his eyes. "Doctor Colin Winters. At your service."

Amid the noise of fireworks, a chorus demanding an encore captured Victor's attention. He stabbed the doctor's chest with a finger. "Stay right where you are. If you lay a hand on her before I get back, I'll kill you."

He grabbed Merlyn's top hat, threw back the curtains, and stepped into the light of six electric chandeliers. Arms open wide, he swept the hat in front of his bloodied shirt and wiped imaginary tears from his cheek before stepping down from the stage.

"We thank you all for your appreciation of our never-before-seen grand finale," he shouted above the din. "While Lady Liberty is in fine health, the strain of the performance has exhausted my poor darling. She has taken to her bed; however, your admiration may be shown in other ways to cheer her and speed her recovery."

He circulated the hat among Lily's adoring admirers, taking more bows as he accepted bank notes and gold coins from men, and jewelry from over-accessorized dowagers. The hat was full when he bounded back up to the stage for his final bow. "Thank you, patriots for freedom. Further tokens of your good wishes will be received by Georges St. James at the front desk."

Now he had to get rid of the doctor and clean Lily up for his final performance as a loving husband.

CHAPTER 2

*V*ictor's threatening glare stopped Merlyn, Willie, and a dog trainer named Esther, in their rush toward Lily. Willie leaned against the magician and Esther gathered her puppies to her breasts, crying into their soft fur. None of them dared help the battered young woman.

While Victor separated a room full of professional liars, cheats, and corrupt politicians from their cash, Dr. Colin Winfield, aka Dr. Colin Winters, a former US Army surgeon, opened the battered Army medical bag he hadn't used in nearly eight years.

To honor his oath as a healer, he continued to read the medical journals, observe surgeries at Johns Hopkins Hospital, and join patient rounds with his old friends. He also remembered everything that Harvard Medical School and five years in the US Cavalry, four of them among the Lakota Sioux, had taught him. But he hadn't touched a patient since his wife died eight years ago. But this time he seemed to have no choice. No one else had stepped forward and the girl needed help. He knelt beside Lily's motionless frame now covered with the magician's satin-lined cape, sensing the other performers hovering over him—silent, macabre angels praying for her with voices only the heart could hear.

Willie stepped between him and the fainting couch, arms crossed over her chest, eyes brimming with tears.

He pulled a bottle of smelling salts from the medical bag and handed it to her. "Hold this. If she doesn't come around in a few minutes, we'll use them." Then to Merlyn, "I need more light. Open the curtain and bring me a bucket of cool water. And something for bandages if I need them."

Light and sound poured through the open curtains and Colin seethed at hearing Victor profit from his wife's injuries. Likely she wouldn't see a dime of it. If he hadn't vowed to do no harm, he'd show the bastard how the Sioux treated a man who mistreated his wife.

Merlyn's return with two ice buckets and several linen tablecloths pulled Colin back from a past that often seemed more real than the present. He wiped sweat from his brow and examined the cuts on Lily's hand. Minor, he concluded, but she was still unconscious, and the possibility of broken ribs concerned him. The jarring trip back to the stage and Victor's careless handling could have caused internal bleeding. He couldn't move her until he knew how badly she was hurt.

"I need to examine her in private," he told the motley gathering.

Willie ordered the dog trainer, "Take yer dogs off, Esther. They ain't healthy 'round wounds." She sent Merlyn for more water, then ripped a tablecloth into strips, dipping it into one of the ice buckets. Her gray eyes challenged Colin. "I ain't leavin' her."

He picked up one of Lily's flayed hands. "I know. I need more light. Bring one of the lanterns over here."

Willie's rye-whiskey breath assailed him in small puffs while he carefully cleaned the wounds on Lily's palms. She was an extraordinary pianist. He couldn't let anything happen to them. Satisfied they were free of any metal or rust from the cable, he left them to dry in the air instead of wrapping them, then gave Willie a jar of ointment. "Aloe vera," answered her raised eyebrows. "It has healing powers beyond anything from the apothecary. Apply it every few hours to keep the skin soft until the cuts are fully healed."

His main concern was why Lily was still unconscious. It had been more than a half-hour since the fall, yet her breathing was still shallow, her skin pale as parchment.

"The rag's gettin' hot," Willie warned.

He sat back on his heels, realizing that while his own suit was soaked with sweat, and it dripped generously from Willie's brow, Lily's skin was dry. "When did she last eat or drink?"

"Early, I guess. Poor dear was terrified of the flight. Stayed near the privy until setup. Missed dinner. Supper too."

Another look at a satin-lined cape covering a silk leotard told him the problem. He tossed the cape to the floor. "She's overheated. Get more water," he shouted at a winded Merlyn. "As cold as you can. And more ice if you can find it. And find a fan—somewhere."

He pressed his ear against Lily's chest, relieved to feel a strong heartbeat, then doused his own jacket into one of champagne buckets of melted ice, tucking it behind her neck before tossing his pocketknife to Willie. "Cut her out of this," he ordered. "Her skin needs to breathe."

Her nude body now covered by a linen tablecloth, Colin sponged Lily's face and waved the smelling salts under her nose while Willie massaged her arms and legs. "Come on back, girl," he urged. "I saw courage in your eyes when you were hanging from that cable. You're a fighter. You won't let that bastard, no matter what name he's going by, stop you."

Still nothing. She reminded him of the fairy-tale princess, Snow White; her perfect, pale features serene, long, black eyelashes resting on luminescent fair skin. If only a kiss could wake her, he thought. *But I'm no Prince Charming.*

Tears clouded his eyes as he relived hovering over another beautiful young woman—one with shining, onyx-black hair, dark, almond-shaped eyes, and sun-kissed golden skin. He'd also begged her to open her eyes and look at him—one last time. But she didn't, and when the last breath escaped her pale lips, it took his soul with it.

Lost in the eight-year-old memory of finding his Sioux wife mortally wounded in her father's lodge at Wounded Knee, South Dakota, he begged, "Don't leave me, Winona."

"Lily."

It was little more than a sigh. Then her cheeks flushed, and eyes the color of a New England autumn sky opened. Willie let out a whoop of joy and Colin blinked away the image of his dead wife to straighten the linen square over Lily's naked body. How small she is, he realized. How fragile. And yet, how strong. He touched her cool forehead and stood.

"Welcome back," he said. "You'll…"

"Get your hands off my wife." Victor's baritone assaulted Colin's eardrum and the muzzle of a gun pressed into his back. "What the hell do you think you're doing?"

"She has heat prostration," Colin explained. "She's severely dehydrated.

The rise in her body temperature could have killed her, regardless of her injuries."

The gun pressed harder against his spine. "I don't believe you."

"How do you think the headlines will read, Champagne? 'Husband of the Fallen Angel of Liberty refuses medical treatment for injured wife.' I dare say the police might want to investigate, since you were likely the last one to check those cables."

It was a guess, but when the pressure of the gun eased, Colin knew it was true. Victor had caused his wife's accident. Why?

Precious seconds ticked by and Lily's eyes closed again. Her chest barely rose with each breath, but at least it was steady. With her head and feet propped up for better circulation, and Willie sponging her face, she still had a chance. But they had to get some fluids into her—fast.

"Damn it, man. Think about it," Colin hissed. "Heat rises. After she spent the day vomiting, you sent her up to the ceiling squeezed into a corset and covered with a suffocating cape. If she doesn't pull through, it's as good as murder."

Gun notwithstanding, he turned, stepping close to Victor's face. "And I'll personally see you hang."

The actor's breath smelled like stale brandy, his gold eyes as soulless as a diamondback snake. Like most snakes, Colin bet Champagne would rather slither away than fight. A long moment later, Victor broke eye contact, stepped aside, and tucked the pistol in the waist of his trousers. With a last, venomous glare at Willie, he ran his fingers through hair that finally looked mussed. "Do what you have to do, but if you value your life, you'll keep this *fainting spell* to yourself. Both of you."

Willie nudged Colin. "She's awake."

He turned to see gooseflesh rippling the skin of Lily's arms and shoulders amid an array of fresh and old bruises while her dry mouth tried to form words. He knelt beside her to whisper "Good girl. Don't try to speak. We'll take you to your room and get some water into you."

When he looked for Victor's help, the cad was gone. Willie's hand stopped him from leaving his patient to give him the thrashing he deserved. Her lips trembled and she diverted her gaze and nodded at the bruises. "They're from the harness."

He doubted that. Old bruises had already faded to shades of green and yellow, but that was a conversation for another time. Swallowing his rage, he asked his patient, "Can you take a deep breath?"

"Of course, I…," she whispered without trying it. "I'm fine. I just fainted. Oooh." She lay back, her gaze fixed on Colin. "I…just need to rest. Who…are…you?"

Her bravado after a near-fatal fall and waking up naked under a skimpy tablecloth in front of a strange man, surprised him. But her color was returning. He took her at her word, at least until he could properly examine her.

"My name is Colin Win…ters." He winced at lying to her. The name Winfield was widely known in Boston and New York society. He needed to change it if he was going to catch the confidence man currently known as Victor Champagne. But he didn't know how deeply Lily was involved in the man's latest gun-running scheme. Was she a victim, or an accomplice? It didn't matter. If his luck held, he'd deposit her in her room under Willie's watchful care and catch the bastard in the act of selling stolen US Army guns to Cuban rebels at an Ybor City club.

"You took quite a jolt," he told her. "If you don't mind, I'd like to check for broken ribs before we move you."

"No!" Holding the tablecloth in place, she winced and tried to sit up. "I've had broken ribs. They hurt a lot more than this. Where are my clothes?"

Willie stepped between them to help her into a lavender silk robe embroidered with pink butterflies. "Let him help you, girl. He's done good so far. I had my own share o' tumbles in my time an' this one was a whopper. Let 'im check."

She glared at Colin, "And I ain't going nowhere."

Her body properly covered, Lily lay back, closed her eyes, and took a few shallow breaths. "All right, but in my room, not here. This couch stinks."

Colin smiled at her spirit. Since she'd been able to raise her head and nearly sit up without fainting, he didn't have much of an argument. And she was right. Sitting up in bed would be better for her lungs than lying on the musty couch. "Deal. We'll get you back in your bed as soon as we can."

He turned to Merlyn. "Scare up one of those indoor Chinese rickshaws Henry Plant uses for his guests. If she can sit up, it'll get her to her room faster."

"You bet, boss." Merlyn clicked his heels and exited stage left, his footsteps echoing in the ruined dining room.

"I've seen you before," Lily said, a little stronger than before.

"Yes, I'm an admirer of your...work. You and your *husband* are very talented." It was an understatement. If she was involved in Victor's schemes, her talent and his cunning would make a perfect partnership. As much as he hoped it wasn't true, it was a possibility. "Now open your mouth."

He stuffed a thermometer into her mouth, mostly to stop her from asking more questions. Her temperature was nearly normal, and she only winced a little when he ran his fingers along her rib cage beneath the thin silk robe. She was so thin he had no trouble determining that each fragile bone was still intact.

After placing the stethoscope against her chest and back, he told her, "Your lungs are clear and your ribs are likely only bruised, but that can be more painful than broken ones. I'm not in favor of binding bruised ribs, or prolonged bed rest, so I advise you to simply take it easy for a few days." He lifted her easily to transfer her to the rickshaw Merlyn had found. "Let's get you up to your room."

She raised her palm to her nose. "Is that aloe vera?"

How did she know about aloe vera? While Western doctors recognized the plant's curative powers, physicians east of the Mississippi still scoffed at using it as anything other than a laxative. Rather, they smeared bear grease and even strips of raw bacon over scrapes and burns, wrapping them with linen that crept inside the healing wounds. It was a combination that caused infections and thick scarring.

"The scrapes are shallow and should be fine in a week or so if you keep them clean and moist. You're a magnificent pianist. Move your fingers as much as you can without opening the wounds, so they stay limber. With proper care they should be right as rain."

"I haven't been right as rain for some time."

An odd comment for a blushing bride, he thought. Did she know her husband seduced and swindled wealthy women for a living? If she was a victim, she didn't fit the profile. Most of Victor's marks were rich widows or spinsters near the end of their child-bearing years.

He pulled the rickshaw through the hotel's labyrinth of service corridors to her first-floor room near the kitchen. With no sign of a male occupant, the bed was neatly made. Simple gowns hung on hooks in a small wardrobe and a battered steamer trunk stenciled with L. O'Grady on the side, sat at the foot of the bed.

O'Grady? Colin recalled whispered stories about a shirttail family relationship to a senator named Patrick O'Grady, from the wrong side of the sheets. No, he told himself. O'Grady was as common in Boston as Smith is in New York, and he hadn't noticed any trace of the South in Lily's speech. But then, she *was* an actress.

"You can put me down now," she whispered against his neck.

"What? Oh, yes, of course," he said. He laid her gently on the feather tick mattress.

She moaned as she tried to find a comfortable position for her battered body, while Willie pulled the sheet up over her and turned to Colin. "You done here?"

Lily's eyes were already closed, her breathing even. With some effort, Colin pulled his gaze from her to face deep lines the harsh life of the circus had carved into Willie's. "Yes, I suppose I am. See that she applies the ointment at least four times a day, and every time she washes. And don't let her use lye soap. Only Castile. If you need to buy it, charge it to me."

He reached back into his bag, handing her a tiny black bottle labeled, *Doctor Clark Johnson's Indian Blood Syrup.* If she's in pain, give her two drops of this, but no more than twice a day, and only for two days."

Willie's eyes narrowed at the tiny vial of dark liquid and handed it back to him. "Laudanum is the Devil's sugar."

"You're right about that, but it isn't laudanum. It's a special tonic made with herbs and tree sap." He omitted the rattlesnake venom. "It's safe."

Willie's eyes narrowed. "I'll see she don't take more'n she needs."

He nodded toward the trunk. "Is that hers?"

"Don't know who else's it'd be. Why?"

"Just curious. I know an O'Grady family in Georgia. Is she from there?"

"Yes" flickered in Willie's eyes before her face closed. "I don' ask. An' you don' need to know."

No, he supposed he didn't, and time was wasting. "Where does Champagne…relax?"

Willie's wise eyes widened. "How did you know?"

"The room is too neat for a man's regular occupancy."

She sighed and crossed herself as if was a blessing. "Ybor City. Merlyn followed him one night. Ain't a place for no decent man. A private club called Gaspar's."

Damn. The bastard had nearly an hour's head start on him. Ybor City was only nine miles away, outside Port Tampa, but the road was rough, and the surrounding swamp teemed with alligators, snakes, and panthers. As much as Colin liked the idea of catching him in an alley, slicing his throat with a scalpel, and dumping him in a swamp, it would be too easy. Victor had committed too many crimes and hurt too many people. He needed to be alive when federal agents took him—hopefully to a noose.

He decided to forego the effort, telling himself he'd be better off getting a good night's rest. Willie and Merlyn were taking turns sitting with Lily, but their frowns told him they were worried about what would happen when Victor returned. "I'm on the third floor," he told Willie. "Room 303. I have a telephone in my room. Call me if you need me."

CHAPTER 3

Colin paced his room, trying to outthink his enemy. Victor was an expert at the game of cat and mouse. Among his many alias identities, he'd used the name Robert Carter to marry Colin's widowed sister, Amanda Winfield Smythe. And like his other victims, when her money was gone, he seemed to disappear from the face of the earth.

Devastated, Amanda tried to hang herself from the second-floor balustrade in the Smythe mansion. But she was not a slight woman. The railing broke and she dropped onto an overstuffed couch in the foyer. She sold the house to pay for Robert/Victor's debts and became a recluse at Waverly, the Winfield family's Boston estate. The police did their best, but even a private investigator, posters, and ads in all the major New England newspapers failed to turn up a clue—until two months ago.

Colin became involved after meeting an old family friend, Theodore Roosevelt, in Baltimore. He dined with the new Assistant Secretary of the Navy at Baltimore's exclusive Maryland Club and after the small talk about "Teedy's" growing family and menagerie of wild animals, the former New York City Police commissioner smoothed an old Wanted poster on the table.

As usual, Theodore went right to the point. "This is William Carter, our prime suspect in the robbery of the Springfield, Massachusetts Armory in March of '65. He was night foreman at the armory and got away with a dozen crates of new Springfield repeating rifles, plus ammunition. But it was close to the end of the war and his buyers must have backed out because three months later, he went back to fishing out of Boston Harbor. Without the guns or a money trail, we had no real evidence to charge him. Pinkerton agents watched him for ten years, but nothing surfaced. He was a drunk and barely made a living. In '75, his boat went missing in clear weather and calm seas with both Carter and his ten-year-old son, Lionel, aboard."

Colin stared at the faded, nearly thirty-year-old likeness of Victor Champagne, then glared across the table at his old friend. "What is this?"

Roosevelt stabbed a finger at the old Wanted poster and set the one Colin's father had commissioned next to it. "Is this the man who ruined your sister?"

"The resemblance is uncanny," Colin admitted. "But they can't possibly be the same man—or even twin brothers."

Theodore employed a toothy, politician grin. "No, but your man could be my man's son, Lionel Carter."

"That's quite a reach, Teedy. A lot of fishing boats go missing off the North Atlantic coast."

"Agreed. But Carter's showed up after a week, washed up on a barrier island near St. Mary's, Georgia with only a ten-year-old boy on board. After days adrift, he was barely coherent, but managed to disappear a few days later." Theodore sat back as if to make his final point. "Not a lot of lobsters in those waters, but plenty of caves to stash a fortune's worth of guns. All Carter needed was a war and a buyer. Back then, after seven years of war with Spain, the Cuban rebels were short on arms."

"What do you think happened?"

"Maybe he had a meet set up with his customers and it went bad. A falling out among thieves. Either way, the guns never showed up and the case is still open. He stabbed the newer poster. That boy is a man now and he is the only person who knows what happened to them."

Colin nodded to his brilliant, highly energetic, and imaginative old friend. "I'll admit that if the man who swindled my sister is Carter's son, the rotten fruit didn't fall far from the tree, but saying he's waited all these years to dig up and sell a pile of rusty old guns is too far-fetched."

"Not so far-fetched," Roosevelt countered. "The guns were wrapped in canvas in tin boxes and packed in straw. If the caves didn't flood, they could pass for new—on the outside. And you said yourself. The fruit doesn't fall far from the tree."

Colin bristled. He was proud that he was nothing like his own elitist father. "What are you saying?"

Theodore leaned across the table and squinted through his thick spectacles. "Six months ago, rumors about the guns surfaced among the Cuban Liberation Party in New York. With things in Cuba heating up again, even as old as they are, they could be worth a fortune to General Gómez and his rebels. I reopened the case this spring, when I saw your father's poster. And I'll admit I was taken aback a few weeks later when I met the spitting image of the man in New York, at a recital by New York's Conservatory of Music. I made a few inquiries and found that he was going by the name 'Victor Champagne.' He seemed especially smitten with a talented and stunning blonde music instructor. I assigned someone to watch them, but after some serious courting, they both seemed to disappear into thin air."

"Not even the Sioux can disappear into thin air," Colin said. "And they can blend in with most barren badlands of South Dakota."

"Well, Lionel Carter did. Twice." Roosevelt sipped his white wine and sparkling water and ordered Colin another scotch.

"The bastard can smell an agent a mile away," he said. "It's likely he's moved the guns. And I'll bet they aren't the only ones he's selling. Spanish pistols and Russian rifles are funneling up from Mexico City through Texas and New Orleans. There's more profit in them than horses these days. And I hear the barrier islands between Matanzas and Ciego de Avila are easy to negotiate—if you know the right people."

Roosevelt's fist hit the table in the center of Victor Champagne's smarmy likeness. "It's of utmost importance that we find him, sooner rather than later. I heard about your tracking and…other…exploits after Wounded Knee. Your family wants him caught and so do I. I need your help."

The thrill of the hunt shone from Roosevelt's nearsighted eyes. A devoted family man with six children, he had compensated for his sickly childhood by becoming as aggressive as a bull and wasn't shy about his political ambition to become President. He also knew the best way to do that was to be on the right side of a war. But Colin had seen the ravages of war on American soil and was inclined to agree with President McKinley's more diplomatic approach to Spain.

He also knew reality when it stared him in the face. It had been three decades since the end of the Civil War, and eight years since the massacre at Wounded Knee killed the fighting spirit of the native tribes. With no more enemies to fight on American soil, Spain's tenuous hold on nearby Cuba held the best odds for an ambitious politician.

Waving away his second drink, he leaned forward. "Are you saying that with the possibility of war, those old rifles could be worth more now than when they were new, even after being hidden somewhere off the coast of Georgia for upward of thirty years? If Lionel Carter is the man who defrauded my sister, and Victor Champagne is Lionel Carter, I'm more than happy to help."

Big white teeth again showed beneath Roosevelt's handlebar mustache. "Bully! Everything happens for a reason, my friend. He leaned back and tossed his napkin over what was left of his chicken and white gravy. "It looks like sitting through that recital at the Conservatory of Music wasn't a waste of time after all."

It took Colin four months to track down the man who caused his sister's ruin but his job was only half done. He didn't have the guns. He stopped pacing at three o'clock to lay down and woke at seven to the sun streaming through the window overlooking manicured lawns surrounded by dense swamps home to some of Mother Nature's most dangerous creatures. Lily would likely sleep through breakfast, he thought, and Willie hadn't alerted him that Victor was back. Probably passed out from too much Bacardi rum in Ybor City, he surmised, looking forward to seeing Victor's face when he stumbled through the hotel's Moorish doors to face a gun pointed at his chest and a warrant for his arrest.

Georges St. James, the hotel concierge, was already at his post, looking fresh after spending hours cleaning up the mess from the fiasco in the dining room.

"Champagne show up yet?" Colin asked in what he hoped was a noncommittal voice.

"You mean last night with Doc Holloway, or this mornin' with that lovely little wife of his?"

"Doc Holloway?"

Georges rolled his big dark eyes. "Hotel doctor. He gets free room and board for fixin' bumps an' bruises and keepin' the ladies in smellin' salts." He leaned across the counter. "Personally, I wouldn't go to him for a hangnail."

Colin ignored his attempt at humor. "When did they come in?"

Georges again looked toward the hand-painted ceiling fresco, remembering. "Not long after you left the little lady, Champagne come back

22

with the doc and went to her room. Won't long after, the doc went upstairs. I got off at one o'clock and passed Champagne on his way out again. Seemed in a hurry."

"Not to worry," answered Colin's quiet oath. "Lady Liberty must be fine. They checked out together this mornin'."

"Checked out!" Colin's raised voice turned heads in the carpeted lobby overcrowded with overstuffed furnishings and overdressed people. He leaned close to Georges and lowered his voice. "Where did they go?"

"The train for Port Tampa."

It was a quarter mile walk to Henry Plant's train that made the nine-mile run between the hotel and the Tampa Bay Harbor twice a day. He doubted Lily could make even that distance on foot and Georges hadn't mentioned them renting a rickshaw. He spun a five-dollar gold piece on the polished mahogany counter. "Tell me everything you know. How she looked, what she was wearing, where they were going, and for how long."

Georges scooped up the coin. "The Missus didn't look none the worse for wear. Smart in a flowered hat with a gray veil an' a long, white shawl." The old Creole from New Orleans stroked his gray-speckled handlebar mustache and narrowed his obsidian eyes. "It was odd, though. She's always friendly to me, wishin' me good day, sayin' please and thanks. She barely looked at me and never even nodded when I wished 'em a safe voyage." He shrugged. "Then again it was early, and she had a rough night."

An understatement, Colin thought. But why hadn't Willie called him when Victor came back? He pumped his questions like bullets. "Voyage? Where? When—exactly—did they check out? Were they alone?"

Now Georges looked concerned and answered his questions out of order. "It was jest the two of 'em. 'Course, it was early. 'Round six-thirty."

"Six-thirty? Don't you ever sleep?"

Georges produced a hesitant smile. "Sleep is only for the young and innocent."

Colin didn't disagree. He couldn't remember sleeping a night through since…had it really been eight years? He stopped the direction of his thoughts to ask, "What ship and where are they going?"

"Mr. Plant's ship, *Olivette*. To Havana. When Champagne left the dining room last night, he asked me when the first ship was due out. It steams to Havana the first Sunday of the month for…supplies. Always takes a few tourists along. Sails around ten."

His gaze again rolled up to recall the conversation. "Champagne won't happy when I tol' him there's no rush. Sometimes it's a couple hours late getting' goin'. Depends on if Cap'n Tait's had too much Cap'n Morgan the night before, if ya know what I mean. An' with all the shenanigans goin' on over Havana way, ain't that many folks headed there these days. Mos'ly reporters and such."

"You're sure it's the *Olivette?*"

He nodded. "No other choice. The Ward Line ship, *City of Washington*, is still in dry-dock and the *Mascotte* is on its way back from Havana."

Colin took a deep breath. Unlike the filibuster boats like William Randolph Hearst's *Vamoose,* that could run between Key West and Havana in a single day, it would take nearly three days for the *Olivette* to get there. But where were Willie and Merlyn? And Esther, the lady with the dogs?

He couldn't imagine Willie allowing even the Devil himself to spirit Lily away until she could safely travel. And a few hours of drugged sleep certainly didn't qualify. Another question nagged at him. "Was Mrs. Champagne wearing gloves?"

Georges rubbed his chin. "Yup. They looked puffed up. Like mittens."

Colin's fists clenched. *Damn Doc Holloway.* He probably wrapped them in linen up to her elbows. The open scrapes would heal around the cloth and stiffen her fingers. She'd never reach an octave again.

He reached for his wallet. "I think I'd like to see Havana for myself. But I'm not a patient man. What will it take to beat the *Olivette?*"

Georges smiled back. "I can think of one or two boats for hire. *The Three Friends* is the fastest. Used to filibuster supplies to Cuba, 'til the Navy beefed up patrols. Now, when Cap'n Broward ain't picking up salvage, he's for hire. He's moored on the Hillsboro, leavin' today for a wreck outside Key West. He may be open to a side trip."

A gray-flecked eyebrow rose. "I hope you don't get seasick. Broward's been known to beat the *Vamoose.*

Colin nodded. "Perfect. I'll be ready in fifteen minutes." He handed Georges another five-dollar gold piece. "Have a motorcar waiting for me. And keep my room until I return. It may be a while."

At the foot of the broad staircase flanked by giant, carved horses' heads, he turned down the corridor to Lily's room, determined to find Willie. The door was locked but he heard knocking sounds coming from the inside. It wasn't hard to pick the lock and he followed the muffled sounds to the wardrobe. A walking stick ran through the twin handles, holding it shut against whatever—or whoever—was imprisoned inside.

He pulled out the stick and Willie tumbled out, hands tied behind her back, a gag covering one side of her mouth. "He took her!" she screeched then grabbed the wide lapels of his white jacket. "He took her. An' he'll kill her. I know he'll kill her."

He held her close until she quieted enough for him to tell her, "I won't let Champagne hurt her. They left for the docks in Tampa. Georges said she was standing and walking on her own. So far, she's fine. Tell me what happened."

She hiccupped and took a deep breath, holding it while she wiped her face with Colin's handkerchief. "You don't understand. Victor...he, he, come up here in the wee hours this mornin' with that so-called doctor." She touched a swollen eyelid already turning purple. "When I wouldn't let 'em near her, Victor knocked me out cold. I woke up an' saw the hotel doc puttin' bear grease on her hands and wrappin' 'em like one o' them Egyptian mummies in a museum.

"Then the doc left an' Victor locked me up in the wardrobe. He said if I made a sound, he'd kill her. I heard him wake her up and git her dressed. She sounded confused but went along with him."

Angry with himself for underestimating Doc Holloway's stupidity and Victor's cruelty, Colin asked, "Where was Merlyn?"

"He come to take my place sittin' with her, but Victor run him off. Then he grabbed some dresses and forced me into the closet at the point of a knife."

"Did Lily protest?"

She gripped his arm. "I think she was drugged. I heard him say they was sailing this morning. We got to find out what ship. Lily needs our help."

His hand covered hers. "Yes, she does. I know where they're going, but you and Merlyn aren't going anywhere. I am. Alone."

CHAPTER 4

*L*ily leaned against the rail of the *Olivette* as it approached the ancient port of Havana, Cuba. She'd been raised in southeast Georgia, visited New Orleans and Savannah, and lived in New York City, but she'd never smelled sea air that wasn't tainted with soot, cinders, and dead fish. Breathing deeply, she looked through the morning mist at a foreign land guarded by three forbidding, ancient forts.

She should have been terrified of a world so foreign to her, but she'd never felt so alive. She was finally beginning the life she'd dreamed of on her family's remote cotton plantation. A life of travel and adventure—and excitement.

As a child, she'd devoured the ancient Greek epics her tutors required, but the American Western dime novels her brother Sean left lying around, captured her heart and soul. The exciting tales of brave cowboys and fierce Indians, of mountains rising from the floor of long-dead oceans, and caves filled with treasure, drew her like a moth to a flame.

After her brother Sean married Elena Santiago, a half-Apache ward of her parents' friends, and moved to New Mexico, his letters inspired her to write her own Western novels. Using the pseudonym Lucas Stone, she vicariously lived the adventures denied by her gender—until at fifteen, she found Nellie Bly's, *Around the World in 72 Days*.

At sixteen she convinced her parents to enroll her in New York's

Conservatory of Music rather than a Boston finishing school—because it was only a few blocks from the biggest newspapers in the country. She added two years to her age to meet the enrollment qualifications for the exclusive conservatory. By the age of twenty, she supported herself on the sales of her popular Western Adventures and tutoring debutantes—until Victor convinced her that showcasing her talents on the stage would introduce her to New York's social elite that included prominent publishers and journalists.

Now, the playful Caribbean breeze tugged at her bleached, silver-blonde hair as she the thought of her colossal failure in Tampa. After Victor paid the hotel for damages, their only hope to recover was the concert for the new Captain-General of Cuba, Ramon Balnco—if her hands healed in time.

"Lily!" came from the direction of their on-deck stateroom. She turned her back to the brooding, Castle El Morro guarding the entrance to Havana Harbor. Victor's frown marred the symmetry of his handsome face when he called, "There you are," above the squeals of seabirds and waves lapping against the ship's metal hull. "How did you get out here?"

His hand cupped her elbow and squeezed painfully. "You'll catch a chill. Go back inside."

She pulled away, the swift movement sending a sharp pain through her rib cage. Disguising her gasp as surprise, she met his angry, golden gaze. "You startled me. I'm fine. The salt air is healthful to me. It clears my head."

It was true. The fresh morning breeze from their stateroom window had roused her early, her mind finally clear of the haze she'd felt since her fall. Truth be told, she remembered little of that night after falling into Victor's arms: the first doctor's gentle touch, the fresh, green scent of aloe vera, Willie cooling her forehead with cool, wet cloths. Then Victor's angry voice and another doctor forcing her to drink a noxious, bitter-tasting liquid, followed by…nothing. It was still dark when Victor shook her awake and prodded her to get dressed. But she couldn't without his help. Her hands were wrapped in white strips of linen up to her elbows. She barely recalled the walk to the ship.

"I feel fine now," she protested. "Where are Willie and the others?"

"Patience," he scolded. "Come with me. It's time for your medication and we need to discuss your performance for Captain-General Blanco."

He reached for her and noticed her bare hands. "You removed your bandages."

"Yes," confirmed the obvious. She flexed her long, talented fingers. "The first doctor said to leave them uncovered and rub them with aloe vera to keep the skin flexible. It's only been three days and they feel better already."

"And speaking of three days," she added. "I've spent the days in our cabin alone. Where have *you* been?"

He looked over her shoulder, at the harbor. "I've had…things…to deal with."

"Yes, poker is a serious business," acknowledged his favorite pursuit. "Please tell me you won."

He smiled in the way that made women in their audiences reach for their smelling salts. "Ah, now there's my practical Lily." He fished a neatly rolled wad of bank notes from his pocket. "Five hundred dollars. Not bad for two nights."

It was more than enough for a quality hotel and new dresses to replace those Victor left behind. She smiled. "Not bad at all. Now, tell me about this concert for Captain-General Blanco."

He pulled her close to his side. "After this performance, you will be an international sensation. In fact, we have rooms at the famous Inglaterra Hotel, and I booked you at Havana's Tacôn Theater in advance of the concert, to announce our upcoming world tour."

World Tour. Could it really happen? She again forgave Victor and turned to watch the ancient and exotic Spanish city come into view. Perhaps it truly was the humiliation and worry about money that had turned him into such a mulish boor. She leaned against him to return to their cabin and prepare for their arrival.

Once inside, he pulled her close and threaded his fingers through her hair, whispering against her cheek, "We're so close, darling." His lips traced a path down her neck while his nimble fingers opened the buttons on her shirtwaist. "Soon all our dreams will come true."

As usual, his touch sent her pique—and her common sense—out the window. He knew every place that ached for his touch. Her breasts woke to his teasing lips as he laid her gently onto the bed. Naked beneath him, his fingers traced the multicolored bruises on her shoulders, massaging her strained muscles until she felt as if she was floating, unable to move of her own volition.

Still fully clothed, he opened his fly and entered her. Slowly rocking inside her, he focused his smoldering eyes on hers. "Ah, Lily," he whispered, "You never disappoint."

As always, he fit her perfectly, filling her until her only thought was to pull him deeper inside, but before reaching the point of no return, she dropped her arms and met his gaze. "So, you'll keep your word. No more saloons, no more exotic dancing, and no more flying. And while we're here, you'll get me access to the camps to interview the *reconcentrados*."

His jaw tightened and he pulled away, leaving her body aching with need. "Why do you never trust me?" He traced the fading bruises on her neck. "Everything I do is for you. For us. But to answer your questions, yes, to everything, my love. Once Captain-General Blanco hears you sing and listens to the magic of your fingers on the ivory keys of his gilded grand piano, the whole of Cuba will bow to you, followed by Spain."

She laughed at the absurdity of the statement while he whispered other silly romantic fantasies into her ear. She moaned when his body pressed against her bruised ribs, and again when his fingers found the moist center of her soul. Breathless, she whispered, "But my hands. They're not ready yet."

"Not to worry," he whispered back. "Your concert at the palace is on the fifteenth. The next two weeks will be the honeymoon we never had. We can enjoy every day as if it will be our last, and every night as if it's our first."

From your lips to God's ears, she prayed and let her body overrule her doubts.

Two hours after docking in Havana, their hansom cab drove past the Captain-General's palace on the Plaza de Armas, on their way to Paseo del Prado and the Inglaterra Hotel. Lily marveled at the wide, tree-lined avenue stretching through central Havana, and gaped at the hotel's thick limestone façade and full-length glass windows. Thinking of her upcoming concert for General Weyler's replacement, she was finally grateful for her uncanny and often burdensome musical talents.

The Inglaterra Hotel was also the meeting place for the cadre of competing journalists following Cuba's never-ending revolution. She squeezed Victor's arm. "It was all worth it, wasn't it? The riverboats, the clubs in New Orleans. Even the cattle boat and flight as Lady Liberty. I'm so sorry for doubting you."

He nodded. "It was indeed worth it, my love. And all is forgiven. I hope you have learned your lesson."

She ignored the transparent threat as the carriage halted in front of the hotel occupying a full city block. Enormous, even by New York City standards, she looked up at three stories, with walk-out balconies on the top two floors and imagined enjoying the sea breezes through open French doors and wide windows. A valet with a trolley met them at the curb.

The understated European elegance of the Inglaterra made The Tampa Bay Hotel look like a gaudy frontier trollop, compared to a Spanish Contessa. If the Inglaterra was just a hotel and Cuba was just a Spanish colony, she wondered what splendors might exist in the Captaion-General's Palace—and in Spain itself. But most of all, her heart thrilled at the possibility of meeting some of the world's most influential correspondents, including Richard Harding Davis and Pulitzer's star correspondent, Harry Scovel.

Victor helped her descend from the cab, leaning close to caution. "I'll do the talking, and you do as I say."

Her temper flared at the implication that she needed his help to communicate. She was fluent in Spanish, while he could barely pronounce the word "*gracias*."

Along with an ear for music, Lily had a gift for dialects. She'd learned Spanish and some Apache from Sean's wife, Elena, who mesmerized her with stories of magical mountains and deserts in the West, and native medicines that included aloe vera. In New York, she polished her dialect with both Spanish students, and servants who had escaped the violence in Cuba. The students praised General Weyler for his suppression of the rebels while the servants' tales of his atrocities broke her heart. Their stories about the heroic deeds of the legendary guerilla leader/martyr, José Martí, inspired her dream to become a journalist and report the truth.

She nodded without meeting Victor's eyes. Perhaps it was better he didn't know her grasp of the language. When he was absent, as he often was, she intended to learn about Captain-General Blanco's plans for the thousands of Cuban peasants still in Weyler's prison camps.

Victor's fractured Spanish while registering at the hotel desk made her blush with embarrassment, but she kept her silence. "The hotel is nearly full," he told her on their way up the grand staircase to the third floor. But she'd understood the concierge to say they were the cheapest rooms, not yet equipped with electricity or private baths. What other lies had Victor told her since leaving Tampa?

Still, she was impressed with the cleanliness of the small, inexpensive room; a sturdy double bed was made up with fine linen sheets and a French lace spread. A porcelain sink and chamber pot were curtained off for privacy. The room filled with light and air freshened by sea breezes when she opened the French doors to the balcony and music rose to them from the cafes and cantina's lining the Prado below them. Once again, she forgave her husband for his past sins.

Victor stepped onto the balcony and looked down at the street like an emperor surveying the peasants below. Still not fond of heights, she sat in one of the wicker chairs near the door and opened the fan in her reticule to accelerate the breeze.

"What do we do next?" she asked. "And when will Willie and the others arrive? Did you make sure they have lodging? Will they be performing for the Captain-General too? And the Tacôn? I can't wait to see their surprise at the wonderful venue we have. When will my trunk be delivered? It wasn't in our—my—cabin on the *Olivette...*"

"Stop!"

Victor glared at her. "I don't mean to be sharp darling, but you shouldn't bother yourself will all those mundane things. We came here early to have our honeymoon. But to answer your *many* questions, the Captain-General requested only your performance. And since you brought them up, I must break the news to you that the troupe will not accompany us. Esther feared for her mangey mutts. Willie is afraid of water, and Merlyn was thrown out of Havana years ago for using his nimble fingers in non-magical ways."

"But you told me...why have I never heard of these things? Willie never mentioned a fear of...well, anything..."

"Are you calling me a liar?" He pointed a finger at her nose. "We are doing this for you. For the fame and fortune that means so much to you. You'll be a headliner after this, both in the newspapers and theaters. When will you understand that *everything* I've done has been for you?"

She almost believed him, but the last line was from one of their skits in Natchez—a drunken husband blaming his ungrateful wife for making him beat her. And while Esther's concern for her dogs could be true. And Merlyn's checkered past. But Willie had been an acrobat, tightrope walker, and high diver for P. T. Barnum. She wouldn't be afraid of sailing on an ocean liner.

"But what will they do? Did you pay them before we left?"

"I'm not a monster, Lily. They received their due—with a bonus for their help after your...accident. Unfortunately, your trunk was lost between the hotel and the ship."

He turned and held out his hand. "Come, darling. You need to eat, and we need to buy you a new wardrobe. One fit for the Captain-General's palace."

CHAPTER 5

January 11, 1898

*L*ily thrived after a week of shopping along the tree-lined Paseo del Prado and touring the ancient city, including the historic Church of the Holy Spirit and opulent Palacio de los Capitanos, where the new Captain-General lived. Victor was nearly as attentive and amusing as when they'd first met while they sampled the shops and enjoyed the mix of Spanish and Cuban cuisine. In the evenings, they strolled by the Tacón Theater on nearby Raphael Street, where Victor had booked her "international" debut.

Three days before the theater concert, Lily's fingers were nimble enough to fasten her corset by herself and she was eager to test them on the keyboard. As they prepared for dinner in the Inglaterra dining room, she said, "I've chosen my music for the theater and the Captain-General's recital and need to practice. Can we get into the Tacón early to test the acoustics and rehearse?"

"Impossible, darling," he told her in a patronizing voice. "The theater is booked until our performance."

But she wouldn't be denied. "I've been doing finger exercises, but it's critical to test them on the keyboard. She touched his arm to emphasize, "If I'm going to be a success at the at the theater or the palace, I need to practice. Perhaps I could use the piano in the lobby here. It's nearly empty in the afternoon."

"And spoil your debut by playing for free? Absolutely not." The cold gleam in his eyes told her the honeymoon was over—if it had ever truly begun. Despite playing the adoring escort on their tours of Havana, Matanzas, and Santiago de Cuba, most nights Victor didn't return to their room until nearly dawn. When she asked where he'd been, he snapped that he was making the connections they needed, then fell on the bed to sleep in his clothes.

His eyes glowed in the light of the vanity's kerosene lamp while he adjusted his crimson ascot. "Trust me, our future will be made here."

"Then I need to rehearse."

As usual, he ignored any question he didn't want to answer and turned to her, the epitome of a fashionable gentleman. He reminded her of the journalist Richard-Harding Davis, who was rumored to be the model for artist Charles Dana Gibson's *Gibson Man*. And though Victor had complained about the cost of the gown she'd purchased for the Palace, he sported a new diamond stick pin.

"You may be right, darling," he answered with a dazzling smile. "Perhaps you *should* practice here. After the fiasco you caused in Tampa, it won't be good to fumble the keyboard in front of the Captain-General of Cuba. And your practice sessions here could whet the guests appetites for the theater performance and boost ticket sales."

She winced at the callous reference to her near-fatal accident, and ignored the greed shining in his eyes. "I want the governor's recital to be perfect as much as you do. I have so many questions for him now that Spain has approved Cuba's transition to autonomy. First and foremost, about his plans to free the *reconcentrados*. There are…"

Victor's hand squeezed her cheeks to silence her. "I've shown enough patience in allowing you to write your little stories about the Wild West. But you won't insult our host with talk of the insurrectionists. You should be writing about the *true* citizens of Cuba. The Spanish who carved this star of civilization out of the swamps, not the children of slaves and savages living like animals in the jungle.

"We can't afford another fiasco like Tampa. Our posters were delayed by the autonomy announcements, but they should be up any day now. I will announce your international debut this evening at a private dinner with some of Havana's most prominent citizens—Spanish sugar and tobacco barons. Men who can usher us into the top social echelons on the Spanish mainland."

He brushed the back of his hand across the marks of his fingers on her cheeks and purred into her ear, "In two days, you will become the darling of the Spanish elite. Do *exactly* as I say, and we'll be in Madrid by the end of the month."

This wasn't the first time he'd mentioned Madrid. He'd promised it six months ago, when she believed he would make all her dreams come true and eloped with him. And despite his increasing moodiness, lies, and ill-fated insistence that she fly in Tampa, she stayed—because, like Nelly Bly's dangerous trip around the world, it meant she could write about her adventures. She didn't want to write little columns about entertaining European society when what was happening in Cuba was front page news.

Living in New York City had exposed her to the realities of the world— to political posturing, the plight of immigrants, women, and orphans from every corner of the world. The portrait of tyranny and oppression opened her eyes to the larger, hidden world of poverty existing even in America, the "land of opportunity". Now in Havana, seeing suffering she'd never imagined in her sheltered life, and hearing conversations people didn't think she understood, she knew she couldn't save the world, but held more firmly to writing stories that would help stop the slaughter of innocents in Cuba.

She stepped out of Victor's reach. "Madrid? Haven't you read the headlines? America and Spain are on the brink of war. If not for President McKinley's restraint, Theodore Roosevelt and his cronies would already have us at each other's throats. Spanish society will never welcome us now. Reporting from Cuba is the only way for me to be taken seriously as a journalist. To help a just cause. I'm not going anywhere."

He frowned at this new, defiant Lily. A feral light flashed in his eyes and his voice lowered. "You forget you are my wife, Lily. As such, you will do whatever I say and go wherever I tell you. You may think Havana is all wide boulevards and charming shops, but believe me, you do *not* want to be a woman alone in this country. Make your entrance downstairs in fifteen minutes—and mind your manners as if your life depends upon it."

The door closed quietly behind him, but if he'd slammed it, she wouldn't have heard it over her pounding heart. Sadly, it wasn't his temper that shook her to the core. She'd seen it too often lately to be moved. It was the fact that he was right. As his wife, she had virtually no legal rights. When she received her trust fund on her 23rd birthday, it would be under Victor's control.

Hands clenched at her sides, she paced the room, and everything became perfectly clear. He married her for her trust fund. Why on earth did she tell him about it? Oh yes, because she loved him—and thought he loved her. She remembered the surprise on his face when he saw her correct age of 21instead of 23 on the marriage certificate, though she'd turned 22 shortly after. He'd hidden his disappointment well on the first leg of their journey to St. Louis, until he was robbed at the train station. Was it true, she wondered, or was it a ruse to get the money early with her parents' consent? But Patrick and Camilla O'Grady were on a world tour, leaving him stuck with her—without her money.

Anger followed her shock and horror at being used. She cared little about the trust fund, had rarely thought of it. But she'd be no man's slave.

Fifteen minutes later, she stood on the third-floor landing of the hotel's elegant, curving staircase. The hotel's open lobby, dining room, and bar were teeming with local Spanish Cubans, tourists from around the world, and a dozen or more American reporters who had flocked to Havana after Spain granted Cuba autonomy on New Year's Day.

Many of the heated conversations she'd overheard on the streets came from Spanish loyalists claiming Spain had abandoned them and clamoring for the return of Spanish rule. Others supported the still-active rebels who, demanded self-rule over Spanish-controlled autonomy. No matter the outcome, Cuba had the world's attention, and somehow, with or without Victor, she'd write about it.

Heads turned her way when she slowly descended the staircase wearing a low-cut Nile-green gown with a sheer, beaded bodice and narrow skirt flaring at the hem. At the second-floor landing, her slender hands covered by white silk, elbow-length gloves, snapped open an ostrich-feather fan. Victor met her at the bottom, playing the part of devoted husband by kissing her on both cheeks.

"A slight change in plans, darling," he whispered during their brief embrace. "It seems our dinner partners have been called away. It will be just the two of us."

Normally, that smile, the warmth of his breath on her skin, and the touch of his hand on her arm, would melt her anger, but tonight she wondered if his high-powered "partners" were simply a ploy to display her to the hotel guests and generate ticket sales for the theater concert. Would he ever tell her the truth?

No matter, she thought. This time she'd make sure she got a share of the ticket sales. Stepping into her role of adoring bride, she took his arm and smiled. "I understand, darling."

From the top of the stairs, Lily had noticed two men sitting at a corner table in the bar. She recognized Harry Scovel from his photo in Pulitzer's *New York World*. She'd seen the other man on New Year's Eve in Tampa. Richard Harding-Davis.

Her attention focused on the table of New York reporters, she continued to play the charming, dutiful, subservient spouse. It wasn't easy. Her mother, Camilla Langesford O'Grady was fiercely independent. While still in her teens, she ran Langesford Plantation alone during the last two years of the War. And before Lily was born, she survived nearly a year in a Comanche camp before a harrowing escape.

Lily flushed at realizing Victor had made her forget that she'd been raised to be an independent woman. They took a table for two, facing the bar, and ordered their meals. Richard Harding-Davis, tall, broad-shouldered, with a clean-shaven, square jaw, sandy hair and dark blue eyes, approached Victor with his hand extended. "I say, are you the man who masterminded that magnificent New Year's Eve performance at the Tampa Bay Hotel?"

Victor ignored his hand to nod. "The same."

His low voice masked the sound of the chair pushing away from the table. He'd taught Lily that move in Memphis, in case they had to exit hastily. She ignored the hint.

"Bravo, my man," the seasoned war correspondent gushed. "I was spellbound. Positively spellbound. A brilliant drama."

He finally turned to Lily with a charming smile that challenged Victor's. "And this must be our lovely Angel of Liberty." His gaze focused on her bosom when he drawled, "Whenever I behold our new Statue of Liberty, I will always see your beautiful face."

And wonder what's beneath the robe, Lily thought.

Still, he was *the* Richard Harding-Davis. She returned his smile. "I've read your work in the *Herald,* as well as your books, *The Princess Aline* and *Soldiers of Fortune.*"

Davis smiled as if waiting for praise, but she wouldn't lie to feed his arrogance by saying the saccharine, melodramatic tales were to her taste. In the end, it didn't matter. He seemed surprised that an actress could even read his so-called literary masterpieces.

She took advantage of his conceit to ask, "What do you hear about the Spanish Loyalist reaction to autonomy?"

Victor squeezed her fingers so hard tears welled in her eyes. "My dear wife is terrified of an insurgence. Please assure her that she has nothing to be concerned about."

Davis nodded and lowered his voice as if speaking to a child. "My dear Mrs. Champagne. There is nothing to worry your beautiful head about." He sounded disappointed to add, "I'm certain both parties will soon learn the benefit of a negotiated peace."

Before taking his leave, Davis changed the subject and spoke to Victor. "I've heard rumors of a concert on Saturday. I'll want a front row seat of course."

Victor squeezed Lily's hand and forced a smile. "And...*we*...look forward to seeing your friendly face," he said.

When their orders of *ropa vieja* arrived and Davis returned to his table, Victor freed her hand to take a deep draft of a Bacardi rum while she sipped her sparkling water. "You could have damaged my hand," she accused when the waiter left their table.

"Then stop defying me," he said before stabbing a slice of shredded flank steak smothered in tomato sauce.

She ignored her plate of the same spicy food. "We had an agreement that I would write about Cuba while we're here. Davis could be an important connection. It's why I agreed to fly at the hotel. Remember?"

He dropped his fork, splashing tomato sauce dangerously close to her new gown. "And look how that turned out. As a result of your disastrous actions, the terms of our bargain have changed. You are my wife. Get used to the fact that I own you. Now smile and convince these rubes to buy tickets to our concert."

He stood then, tapping a fork against his glass and calling, "Ladies and gentlemen, you're attention please."

All heads turned toward his smooth, deep voice, while Lily obediently smiled and nodded when he announced the upcoming concert and that she would be happy to provide them with a preview, "This very evening." The applause was enthusiastic, and Lily followed him to the grand piano in the center of the lobby.

"Why are you doing this now?" she whispered. "It's too risky to perform without practice. What will I play?"

He glared at her. "Davis may be a pompous ass, but he knows everybody who's anybody. Half these people are drunk, and the other half don't speak English. They won't know if you miss a note."

He leaned in to kiss her cheek with cold, dry lips, then whispered, "If you can't do as you're told, I can find a comely Spanish girl with a good voice to replace you any time. Or would you prefer a permanent tour of the *reconcentrado* camps?"

Too shocked to respond, and knowing he meant every word, she sat at the mahogany piano bench. Miraculously, her healing fingers had no problem playing the more popular songs of the day. Her first rendition of "The Sidewalks of New York" received a standing ovation while Victor sold tickets for their concert.

People danced in the spaces between the tables and the audience joined in the choruses, humming over lyrics they didn't understand. Victor disappeared during a brief break and Davis took advantage of his absence to introduce her to the famous Western artist, Frederick Remington, and Stephen Crane, author of *The Red Badge of Courage*. Crane had only recently arrived and looked shockingly peaked compared to his hardy companions.

While Davis ordered drinks from the bar, Harry Scovel introduced himself and his wife Frances, whose published journals of her experiences in the Klondike had also inspired Lily's professional aspirations.

One face near Davis looked familiar, but the lighting was dim, and the room was filled with smoke and moving bodies. She told herself that after facing so many crowds in the last few months, all the men began to look alike.

By midnight, Victor hadn't returned, and her fingers were aching from the forced exercise. "One more song," she offered the dwindling crowd, and the man she thought she'd recognized rose to approach the piano, asking, "Do you know 'Sweet Rosie O'Grady'?"

She didn't remember much of the night of her accident, but she remembered that voice. Low, with a Boston twang tinted by a hint of the West. It was the doctor who treated her after her accident. She smiled. "How could I not? It's my maiden name. And my father, Patrick O'Grady's favorite song."

His smile dimmed beneath a neat, dark brown mustache she didn't remember from New Year's Eve. "Then I'd be honored to have you sing a verse or two."

He put a five-dollar bill in the champagne glass Victor had placed on the piano for tips and sat at a nearby table, tapping his foot without participating in the enthusiastic final chorus:

"And when we are married,
How happy we'll be;
I love sweet Rosie O'Grady,
And Rosie O'Grady loves me."

By half-past midnight, most of the crowd had stumbled out through the hotel's wide glass doors. The stiffness in her fingers hit Lily first, then her back and finally, her dry throat. She longed to return to what she considered *her* room, gargle a gallon of saltwater, then soak her hands in a warm Epsom-salt bath before applying more aloe vera. It worried her. She would play longer, far more complicated pieces at her palace recital, as well as the concert. What if her fingers locked? Too tired to rise, she swayed on the piano bench.

Frances Scovel placed a gentle hand on her shoulder. "You look exhausted. Harry, get this poor woman a water," she ordered, and offered, "Please join us until your husband returns."

Lily was too tired to care why Victor hadn't returned, and with or without him, she didn't think she could make it up the stairs. She accepted the kind woman's invitation and took Harry Scovel's arm, gratefully accepting the water waiting for her at their table.

The journalists seemed to enjoy her company. Promising to be her protectors until Victor returned, they shared their stories while she switched drinks from water to iced sweet tea. After an hour, Harry Scovel raised a hand to the doctor who had requested her last song.

"Colin," he shouted. "What brings you from Boston to the jungle? Come join us and this charming young woman who, besides singing like an angel, is also a budding journalist."

The man named Colin hesitated a moment, then relented, leaving a half-finished drink on the bar. "Mrs. Victor Champagne," Scovel said with a flourish. "May I present an old friend and Harvard classmate, Doctor Colin…"

"Winters," he interjected with a stern look at his classmate. Then to Lily, "You are an exceedingly talented young woman."

She nodded, surprised to flush at the compliment. "Thank you, though I believe we've met before…in rather…uncomfortable circumstances. While I remember little of my accident in Tampa, your voice is familiar. I haven't had a chance to thank you for your help Doctor Winters."

"Colin, please," he answered. "It was no trouble, I assure you. I'm pleased to see you doing so well…so soon."

All eyes at the table seemed to be staring at them and she felt no choice but to say, "Please join us. I'm sure Victor will return shortly. He'll want to thank you as well."

The mention of her husband's name hardened the doctor's gentle, brown-eyed gaze when he nodded and took a chair next to Davis. For the next hour, Lily lost herself in the reporters' opinions on the possibility of war with Spain.

Scovel shared the less lurid details of his imprisonment at the medieval Castle El Morro where he was charged with abetting rebel leaders, Josef Martí and Máximo Gómez. It was only by Mr. Pulitzer's influence that he'd escaped a firing squad. While Lily's mind reeled at the dangers involved in reporting Cuba's fight for freedom, her heart raced at the exciting lives these journalists lived.

Only Dr. Winters seemed to notice her exhaustion. "Your husband must be delayed, Mrs. Champagne," he said. "Please allow me to escort you to your room."

Davis rose, echoing, "We'll all escort you. Franny, you come too."

Mrs. Scovel winked. "I think Colin can handle the climb better than any of us."

The others nodded their agreement and Lily took Colin's his extended arm to slowly ascend the wide mahogany staircase to the third floor. They stopped in front of her door and she turned to him. "Thank you again, Dr. Winters, for helping me after my accident."

"I didn't think you would recognize me," he answered, "I hope it doesn't upset you to see me again."

"On the contrary. I'm thrilled to have the chance to extend my gratitude.

You saved my life. I think it was your voice that brought me back. I don't know how I can ever repay you."

She gasped at being so forward with a man who was a stranger—despite his having likely seen her naked. The flush coursing up her neck to her cheeks had nothing to do with the stuffy third-floor hallway. "I...really must go."

He didn't protest and she took some comfort knowing he'd wait until she was safely inside her room before leaving. Once there, she breathed a heavy sigh of relief at finding no sign of Victor and she was too tired to wonder where he'd gone—or why.

CHAPTER 6

She opened her eyes slowly, still groggy from the long evening. She was alone in her bed, with no sign that Victor had been there. It didn't surprise her. He'd collected a great deal of money for tickets that looked oddly like the ones they'd used for shows on their way down the Mississippi.

She quenched her parched throat with a tall glass of water from the pitcher on the dresser before checking her pendant watch. Nearly nine-thirty. Her fingers had stiffened during the night and she exercised them before dressing in a simple white skirt and shirtwaist. She smiled at her reflection in the mirror, thrilled to make her own decision about how to spend her day.

Shouts from the street below stopped her at the door and she ignored her fear of heights to rush out onto the open the balcony. The Prado, normally filled will people strolling the brick walk or sitting on benches and tables outside cafes, was in chaos. Pedestrians and mounted men ran wildly in every direction amid a cacophony of unintelligible languages that only added to the panic.

Above it all on the third floor, she watched an ambulance and fire truck race toward Old Havana and shivered, despite the warm Caribbean breeze. Had something happened at the harbor? Was that why Victor hadn't returned? Oddly, she wasn't worried about him. He seemed to have nine lives, but his warning about the danger facing a woman alone in Havana tightened her stomach. Then a second ambulance followed the fire tanker and she saw smoke.

Grabbing her reticule, fat with the contents of Victor's champagne glass on the piano, a notepad and pencil, she bolted from the room. Men on the street shouted, "Down with Blanco. Long Live Weyler! Death to Blanco. *Viva España!*"

"*Que pasa?*" she asked a young man in a white planter's suit. He stared blankly at her and she repeated in English, "What happened?"

"The newspaper," he shouted above the din. "The office of *La Discuscion* has been destroyed."

He sprinted past her to follow the fire trucks and Lily looked up and down the Prado teeming with angry, shouting people—but no police.

"*Donde esta la policia?*" she asked a young boy in a peasant shirt.

He shrugged. "*No se,*" then ran away.

The conspicuous absence of the police or members of the elite Spanish Guardia told her what was happening. The police were paid by the Spanish government. They weren't interested in saving a newspaper that promoted the unpopular notion of sharing autonomy with what Spanish Loyalists considered ignorant peasants, mixed-race *mestizos*, and former slaves. As for the Cuban side of the argument against it, she couldn't conceive that any of them thought such a one-sided compromise after centuries of Spanish domination—including tens of thousands of deaths caused by General Weyler, could ever work.

She followed the surging crowd toward the *El Dairio de la Marina*, the second newspaper office to be attacked. While the police had finally arrived, they did nothing to calm the Spanish loyalists and rebel supporters. Lily stopped to jot notes into her journal.

She jumped when shots rang out ahead of them and the procession froze as one, then reversed course, stampeding madly toward her. Lily and those behind her turned and tried to outrun the human tidal wave. Clutching her reticule and journal to her breast, she managed to keep up until she turned her foot on a loose cobblestone and her ankle-length skirt tangled between her legs.

The heat and crush of people caught up, bouncing her like a piece of driftwood on a wave, while the deafening hoofbeats of mounted soldiers warned that she was about to be trampled. Instead, someone slammed into her back, pushing her face forward, toward the bricks lining the Prado. The journal flew from her grasp. She stretched her arms out to break her fall when a man's arm caught her at the waist and dragged her toward an alley. More frightened of the monster squeezing the life out of her than the terrifying mob, she kicked, screamed and waved her arms, trying to connect with anything solid.

"Stop fighting. I'm not going to hurt you," finally found its way from her ears to her brain.

"Then let go of me, you brute. My husband will kill you for this—if I don't do it first."

"Are you sure you want me to do that here?"

"Yes, you bastard. Let me go *now!*"

"Brace yourself."

"What?" was barely out of her mouth when he let her go. She landed on the garbage-strewn cobblestones of the alley between the dress shop and the café she'd visited the day before. On her knees, her nose inches from a dried horse-pile, she closed her eyes and tried to catch her breath. Hoping her assailant/savior had run away into whatever rathole he occupied, she rolled back to lean against the alley's cool, stucco walls and took inventory of herself between shallow breaths. Her white shirtwaist was ripped at the shoulder and pulled out of her skirt, now soiled with stains she'd rather not identify.

Her notebook was gone, but the reticule filled with cash still hung from her wrist. Satisfied that she'd live, her fingers closed around a broken brick on the alley floor. She pushed back hair that had wrestled free of its pins with her other hand and raised her head to face her attacker—or savior—depending on one's perspective.

"You," she whispered to an angry...Dr. Winters.

She rejected his outstretched hand to inch her way up the rough stucco wall to her feet, wobbling a little on the broken heel of her shoe.

"Yes," he said, the tension lines in his face easing. "I'm sorry if I frightened you, but there wasn't much time to think. You could have been trampled."

While his concern seemed sincere, he somehow always managed to appear unexpectedly. She was grateful for his help after her accident in Tampa, and he was amiable with the reporters the night before, including his offer to escort her to her room. Now, she wondered if he was following her.

She dodged his hand when he reached out for her, wincing at the pain in her twisted ankle. "No, don't...don't touch me. I'm fine...Doctor Winters."

The amused lift of one side of his new mustache made her angry. She didn't need a knight in a white linen suit to rescue her every time she tripped. Using the wall to steady herself, she limped toward the street and looked down the Prado toward the Hotel Inglaterra. "The crowd is clearing and I'm close to the hotel. My husband will be concerned about my absence and I need to...compose myself. Thank you for your help, in Tampa...and now here. Good day."

"Lily, we need to talk," came from behind her.

She refused to turn. "Leave me alone or I'll call the police."

She felt the heat of his body close behind her. "The police are a bit busy right now. I won't force you to talk to me, but you need to know that Victor is not who you think he is. You're in great danger."

"Please leave me alone." Tears of panic filled her eyes and she took a deep breath to compose herself. When she turned, he was gone.

What did he mean about being in danger? And about Victor? She was painfully aware that her husband was an opportunist, a master at manipulating the truth to suit his own purposes, and had a wicked mean streak, but he was also brilliant, mercurial, and tempestuous. Qualities she'd once found irresistible. What else could there be?

She limped back to the hotel, taking deep, cleansing breaths and concluding that Dr. Colin Winters was one of those strange men who formed imaginary relationships with performers they admired. Fanatics, they were called. Fans. It was best to treat them gently, while not encouraging their possessive behavior.

Stepping into the safety of the famous hotel, she told herself she had more important things to consider and hoped the unrest would settle by the time she performed for Captain-General Blanco. She told herself that after the Tacón concert and her interview with Blanco, she'd leave the theater—and Victor—for good. Dr. Winters would have to find another performer to follow.

She ordered an ice pack and limped up the stairs, breathing easier now that she had a plan. She didn't come to Cuba to sit in a hotel dining room, making up stories from rumors and secondhand accounts like far too many reporters taking up space at the Inglaterra. She wanted to hear how the

Cuban people, both native and Spanish, felt about their country's future—in their own words—in their own language.

Dressed in a split, calf-length skirt, she propped her ankle on the ice pack and watched from her balcony as the street slowly cleared. When the Prado became negotiable in late afternoon, she put on comfortable shoes and left the room.

Instead of following the masses toward the *Plaza de Armas* and the Captain-General's palace, she kept watch for the interfering Dr. Winters and made her way through the littered streets to the *La Discuscion* newspaper office.

The publisher, Señor Moran, and a young man were rooting through the carnage, moaning the loss of their new press and destruction of their livelihood. Moran's face was bruised and a nasty cut along his cheek was crusted with dried blood.

"No, no!" he shouted when she stepped inside. He tried to close a door hanging by one hinge in her face. "*Cerrado.*"

"*Si,*" she nodded, then stepped around the battered door into what, only hours earlier, had been a working newspaper releasing its afternoon edition. One crumpled paper lay alongside the editor's upturned desk. It bore the headline, "*Viva Autonomía Para Cuba.*"

Apparently, the paper supported the shared autonomy proposition. She picked it up and asked in fluent Spanish, "Why are the people of Cuba fighting against their own independence? Granted it's weak at best, but at least they'll have a voice in government."

Apparently comfortable conversing with her in his own language, the seasoned publisher shook his head and sat on the wreckage of his desk to explain that the morning's miniature uprising was only the beginning of what he predicted to be the end for Cuba. As a staunch Spanish Loyalist, he told her that while he was not favorable to Spain's abdication under pressure from the US and renegade guerillas, he had faith Captain-General Blanco could work with them to ease the horrific conditions in the countryside, at least until a better solution was found.

"If not," he said, "it is only a matter of time before the US takes advantage of Spain's weakness and becomes the new ruler of Cuba" Tears welled in his battered eyes. "Using the island for its own expansionist purposes."

As the *Criollo*, a white Cuban of pure Spanish descent, detailed the decades of brutal jungle warfare for Cuban independence, Lily put down her notes and picked up a broom. She lost track of time listening and learning the truth about the volatile history of the island from a man whose family had lived it.

As the late afternoon shadows lengthened, rumors of mobs demanding Blanco's resignation reached them and the evening promised to be as chaotic as the afternoon. Lily set the broom aside. Armed with the background of the demonstrations and insight into Cuban temperament toward autonomy, she still had time to wire her eyewitness account to Pulitzer before the other reporters returned from a pointless vigil at Blanco's palace.

Since she'd missed her introduction to Mr. Pulitzer in Tampa, she signed her dispatch "Lucas Stone," referencing her previously published works, and sent it by wire to make the deadline for the morning edition of the *New York World.*

She found a note from Victor on her pillow when she returned to their room. He was going to the wharf to await the delayed shipment of props for the Tacón concert. She didn't believe it for a moment. He more likely found a friendly cantina and was flirting with one of the "comely" Spanish girls he said were so easy to find. But he'd been gone more than twenty-four hours. It was unusual, even for him. She remembered the derringer attached to his wrist, as well as the stiletto tucked in his boot and told herself not to worry.

As the moon rose and shadows shrouded the evidence of the day's violence, she cautiously stepped up to the balcony railing, where the clear night allowed her a view of the lights of the old city, including the Captain-General's palace. Beyond that, in the darkness of the bay, tiny dots of lights from the newly arrived Spanish warship, *Alphonse II,* and the steamship, *City of Washington,* winked in the gentle swell and sway of ocean. It brought her comfort. If things got out of hand, the Ward Liner would offer a quick escape.

The cooling breeze reminded her she hadn't eaten since taking a peeled orange from the hotel dining room in the morning. She splashed water on her face, smoothing her hair and skirt to go downstairs for dinner.

"Are you telling me that I must starve to death because my husband isn't here to escort me to table?" caught her attention and she turned to see Frances Scovel pointing a finger at the maître d'.

He pulled back to avoid losing an eye. "I am so sorry, Senora Scovel," he groveled. "We cannot allow an unaccompanied woman to dine alone. I am happy to send something to your room."

Slender as a reed, though taller than him by a head, Frances leaned closer. "I don't want to eat alone in my room. And I will not be treated like a prisoner because of the lack of a man's arm. I *will* dine here…in this dining room…this evening…or there will be…"

"Frances?" Lily interrupted.

She turned so quickly Lily flinched.

"Oh, Lily." Her voice softened when she smiled and said, "What a marvelous coincidence. It seems a woman needs a companion in order to eat in this establishment. I dare say you'll meet the same fate if you ask for a table." She cast a sly glance at the cringing maître d'. "Perhaps we could dine together. I would love to have you join me. After all, without help, how on earth would we know how to place our order?"

Lily laughed. "I'm sure between the two of us we will be able to solve the problem. And I'm famished. I may order everything on the menu—to avoid confusion, of course."

Arm in arm, they moved toward an empty table by a window facing the Prado. Once seated, Frances ordered a sherry for each of them. Despite her bravado, her doe-brown eyes showed her concern for her husband, who was likely on the other side of town, in the middle of a throng of angry Spanish loyalists demanding action from Captain-General Blanco.

Frances removed her gloves and laid them on the table. "What a mess, all this, don't you think? Men. With a Queen in charge of the Spanish empire, a better solution should have been determined years ago."

Lily nodded. Her father and brothers excluded, she shared her companion's disdain for the male of the species' tendency to fight wars in the name of "freedom for all," but treated their wives like imbeciles, children, or slaves.

"The queen is so far away," she answered. "If she has to depend on a passel of old generals like Weyler for information, she's in trouble."

Frances raised her glass. "Amen to that, my dear. Harry is at the palace. Where's your keeper?"

Keeper?" Lily should have been offended, but sadly, that was exactly the role Victor had chosen to play, with her cast as submissive concubine. And it was her fault. She'd failed to see the trap in his false gallantry and fell into it.

Where was the girl who dreamed of adventure in the Wild West? The girl who pretended to be her brother's fiancé so he could escape the law and capture a murderer. Even the sixteen-year-old who moved to New York City seemed to have more spine than the adult Lily. And though she'd supported herself by teaching and on the meager proceeds of her novels, it took a man's name to get them published.

"Yes," Frances chuckled. "They all think we're helpless. While we can often use it for our own purposes, it is very tedious, don't you think?"

The waiter approached them cautiously, asking if they were waiting for their escorts to order. Both women assured him they could read a menu— even in Spanish.

"My treat," Frances insisted and ordered *Arroz con Pollo*, a spicy chicken dish Lily recognized from her sister-in-law Elena's first visit to Langesford nearly ten years ago and ordered the same thing. Immersed in their conversation about newspapers, politics, and the vagaries of the male species, they dined slowly, interrupted only by a few customers asking Lily when she would play again, or about purchasing tickets for her concert.

She was surprised at her immediate rapport with Mrs. Scovel. An only daughter on a rural plantation, she'd grown up competing with her two brothers, from breaking horses to picking cotton, and had never gotten on easily with other women. And in New York, her independent attitude hadn't endeared her to the other girls focused on making a good marriage. But she felt comfortable with Frances.

As a woman who shared the life of a journalist with her husband, including traveling alone in the Klondike, Frances laughed often and loud, smiling at the other patrons' disapproving stares. "I was a nurse before marrying Harry," she said. "He was beginning his career and we traveled the world. But he was also gone much of the time, to war zones and dangerous places forbidden to a woman.

"I turned to writing to keep from worrying about him. Poetry mostly. Then I began writing about my own adventures during Harry's absences. That led to a few women's columns and I got lucky with my journal about the Klondike. We were on our way to Europe for a delayed honeymoon when Pulitzer asked Harry to come here."

She gazed out the window as if looking for him, then sighed. "We've been here since November. At first it was like an adventure. We covered nearly every inch of the island."

"Every inch?" Lily asked. So much of the island was occupied by rebels, including the cunning veteran of the Ten Years War, General Máximo Gómez. "What about the *insurrectos*? I've heard the rebels are brutal to prisoners."

Frances leaned in and lowered her voice. "Harry is one of those people who can fit in everywhere, from the Captain-General's palace to a rebel camp." Her patient smile gave way to a worried frown. "But now, with Spain stepping back, the horror of Weyler's atrocities, and the feeding frenzy between Pulitzer and Hearst, it's only a matter of time before Theodore Roosevelt and his friends coerce President McKinley into declaring war."

"How do you know all this?"

For the next hour, Lily listened to Frances describe the insurgent camps tucked into the jungle landscape hidden between Cuba's pristine, white sand beaches and sun-kissed sugar plantations. It was a vastly different Cuba than the New York papers reported. A tiny country, less than 800 miles long and 200 miles at its widest, its largest population consisted of recently freed Negroes, native Indians, and racial mixes that included Spanish blood. And for nearly three centuries, Spain had been at war with one or more of them.

It was nearly nine o'clock when they finished their dessert of flan with fresh fruit, followed by strong Cuban coffee. When their dishes were taken away, Frances suggested, "Let's take a walk."

For all their talk of food, war, peace, and even the growing cause for women's suffrage, Frances Scovel's increasing worry about her husband was evident. It made Lily feel guilty about her own lack of concern for Victor. Married only a few months, she was still a bride. Her husband had been gone nearly twenty-four hours without word, but instead of worry, she felt relief.

She jumped when Frances gripped her hand and screamed, "Harry!"

"Franny," came from the shadows near the alley where Lily had confronted Dr. Winters. Frances ran to her husband's arms while Lily fought sudden tears.

CHAPTER 7

*A*fter saving Lily from being trampled, Colin watched her limp back into the Inglaterra, her loosened hair a silver-blonde halo in the bright sun. Her back was straight, and with one hand holding her torn and soiled skirt, a silly black velvet purse dangled from the other wrist. Every time he saw her, she seemed more a mystery. She was a trained musician with a voice that rivaled Jenny Lind. So why did she run into the middle of an angry mob of political protesters when even the adventurous Frances Scovel had kept to the safety of her room?

And where was Victor? The night before, Colin had watched the bastard use his beautiful wife as a shill to pick the pockets of the hotel guests. Then, when he'd gotten all he could, he'd melted into the crowd. Colin had followed him but half-way through the crowded streets of the old town, he disappeared into what seemed thin air. Likely to meet his filibuster of guns in one of the many smuggler coves along Havana's coastline, Colin thought. He could be in Matanzas or Santa Clara by now, meeting General Gómez. Unfortunately, the seventy-year-old former officer of the Spanish Army was as cunning as a fox and never stayed in one place very long. They could be anywhere.

Promising to apologize to Lily for his rough handling, he headed to the cable office to wire Theodore Roosevelt. The small adobe building was already teeming with reporters waiting to wire hastily jotted snippets of gossip and rumors as their stories. With one of them looking over his shoulder, Colin wrote in code, *"Eggs lost in the woods, stop. Rooster has left the coop, stop. Hen is in the nest, stop."* It told Roosevelt that the guns were still missing, along with Victor, but Lily was still in Havana.

While the amused cable agent sent the nonsensical message, Colin scrawled a separate wire to his distant cousin, Senator Ambrose Stainsby, in Boston. *"Please advise location of Patrick O'Grady et al., stop."*

He hailed a cab to the new Captain-General of Cuba's palace, where he found Richard Harding-Davis and Frederick Remington amid the angry mob demanding Blanco's resignation and General Weyler's return. Blanco remained secure in his palace, though his own guard did little to turn the mob away.

Darkness fell, and word that General Arolas was on his way with two thousand Spanish Guardia troops convinced the crowd to disburse. With no further sign of Victor, Colin returned to the Inglaterra, hoping the bastard still had a use for Lily—if only as a way out of Havana.

He fought his way through panicked civilians fleeing Arolas' soldiers who, dressed in gray uniforms with red facing on the collar, white shirts, and straw hats, lived up to their reputation of brutality by clubbing the slow-moving crowd. He followed the soldiers as they took control of the main thoroughfares to guard the ransacked newspaper offices and the Hotel Inglaterra.

The hotel boasted the largest contingent, including the vicious Pavîa Hussars, an elite division of Spanish cavalry whose surly tempers and razor-sharp sabers testified to their barbaric European origins. Their sole purpose was to guard the American and British consuls staying at the hotel, as well as the property of the Cuban-American owner.

Before being granted entry into the hotel, Colin's American identification was scrutinized by several puffed-up Hussar petty functionaries. Once inside, he faced another crowd, this one terrified by both the angry mob and ruthless soldiers outside. The hotel concierge and a Hussar First Sergeant shouted and waved their arms to move the guests back from the glass windows and doors. Since most of the guests were English-speaking, their well-meaning efforts only caused more panic. Then a female voice floated down from the mezzanine, turning all heads.

The high, domed ceiling above the lobby amplified the clear soprano that sounded like an angel from heaven, singing, "Amazing Grace, how great thou art..."

Her voice drew the crowd toward the safety of the staircase and those who knew the words joined in, creating an island of calm inside the hotel. Colin didn't need to look up to know it was Lily O'Grady's voice.

"Damn," he whispered. Could she never stay away from danger?

After the last verse, the crowd followed English and Spanish instructions to return to the safety of their rooms. Several were only steps from the staircase when the walls of the hotel shuddered from an explosion. Screams filled the room as people fell to the floor, taking cover under tables to avoid dust and chunks of plaster falling from the frescoed ceiling. Colin stepped over several screaming patrons to reach Lily, now huddled on the top landing of the staircase.

"Don't move!" he called from half-way up. When the shuddering foundation settled, he slowly climbed toward her, carefully testing each stair until he reached her. An arm's length from him, her hair and face dusted with plaster, she looked like a wraith in her white shirtwaist and skirt. Only the bright blue sheen in her eyes told him she was human.

"You again," she said, not sounding pleased at his chivalrous attempt to climb the still-stable staircase. "Forever the knight in shining armor, I see."

He flashed his own dusty grin at his overreaction and handed her his handkerchief. "At your service, my lady."

They looked down at the wreckage in the lobby. Other than thin sheets of plaster, broken windows and statuary, most of the damage to the first floor was caused by the panicked crowd seeking cover. Colin stood, extended his arm, and cleared his throat. "The stairs appear to be solid. Would you care to join me for a breath of fresh air?"

Once outside, Lily pulled her arm free of Colin's to shield her eyes from the smoky glow of the Teatro Tacón across the alley from the hotel. The wall facing the Inglaterra was nearly completely collapsed, smoke billowing from its open lobby doors while flames reached for the soot-colored moon.

"Oh my God, no!" she cried out. "It can't be." She drew her own handkerchief from her pocket, muttering, "Soot," as she wiped tears from her eyes. Lips trembling, she said, "This is the beginning, isn't it?"

He led her to a bench across the Prado, and amid the cacophony of sirens, screams, and orders shouted by soldiers who now outnumbered the crowd, he asked, "The beginning of what?"

Her tear-filled eyes reflected the glow of the flames. "Don't be coy. The beginning of the end of everything. This lovely country. Peace. Life as we know it." Like a fighter rising from a blow, she straightened and tucked the handkerchief embroidered with lilies of the valley up her sleeve.

He took her hand in his. "Perhaps, and this may not be the right time, but you need to know that Victor is…"

"Lily, my darling," came from behind them. They stood and Victor pulled his wife into his arms. His amber eyes glinting with victory, he said loud enough for other bystanders to hear, "I've been looking for you everywhere, my darling. I'm so glad you're safe."

Colin noticed Lily's fists close against Victor's chest before he set her aside, curled his hand around her wrist, and tugged. "I've been told it's safe to go inside. See, the flames are under control. Come along, my sweet."

Lily jerked free of her husband's grasp. First relief, then anger, colored her voice. "Victor! Where were you?"

He silenced her with a long kiss.

Colin should have turned away from the intimate moment, but something about their exchange was "off." It was like a scene in a play. The suit Victor had worn during Lily's recital looked impeccable for a man who'd been wearing it more than twenty-four hours during a city-wide riot. And when he kissed his wife, she stood stiff as a board.

A closer look at Victor's boots showed dried mud, as if he'd hastily changed into the suit before returning to the hotel. He remembered Victor's peasant costume in Tampa. A perfect disguise. Wearing the loose homespun trousers and shirt with a wide-brimmed straw hat, he'd blend into the crowd like a snake on the desert floor. Even if he wasn't fluent in Spanish, he could get by with the standard, "*No se.*"

Perhaps he'd underestimated the foppish actor and confidence man.

"Don't worry, darling," Victor soothed Lily, again tugging her hand. "The fire is only a small setback. Though our performance at the palace is postponed, our room at the hotel is undamaged."

Lily stepped back from hiss embrace. "Postponed? Are you certain? Because of what happened today? I thought things were settled down now that General Arolas' troops are here. When will it be rescheduled?" A pale arm motioned to the destroyed theater. "With the fire, the Captain-General's performance is all we have."

Victor again pulled her into his arms, glaring at Colin over her shoulder before steering her toward the hotel saying, "Not to worry, my darling. Soon all our dreams will come true."

Colin's blood boiled at the bold-faced lies. The Captain-General's palace would have more guards than Fort Knox, and martial law, enforced by the iron fist of General Arolas and his Hussars' sabers, was already in effect.

He also knew General Gómez would take advantage of the sudden withdrawal of two-thousand Spanish troops from the field to advance up the coast toward Matanzas. President McKinley would have to choose which side of the fence to sit on when it came to Cuba—soon.

But there was nothing he could do now, about anything. Legal husband or not, Lily went with the bastard willingly. He followed them inside. When they turned toward their room at the top of the stairs, he paid Martin, the doorman, to alert him when they emerged; and if he wasn't in, to follow them. A few words to the concierge ensured Martin's job if he had to leave quickly.

Colin woke after a few hours of fitful sleep, still feeling crushed under the weight of his concern that Lily was part of Victor's scheme and wondering how much fuel the riots would add to the United States' fire to become a world power. But while he couldn't stop what was looking like an inevitable war, he could bring Victor Champagne, aka Lionel Carter, to justice.

With no message from Martin, he stepped outside where a light sea breeze stirred the palms lining the Prado. A purifying early morning shower had calmed the smoldering ashes from the fire and drops glinted like diamonds between the bricks. He glanced toward the ruins of the Tacón theater. The fire had nearly gutted it, but all the other businesses on the plaza were open.

The telegraph office bustled with tourists wiring worried relatives, while reporters filed updates and waited for further instructions. Harry Scovel sat at his usual seat by the window. He looked exhausted when he nodded and tipped a finger to the brim of his Panama hat. Returning the salute, Colin sat next to him. It wasn't surprising that Scovel looked like death warmed over. While the Hearst's *Journal* had seven men in Havana, and the *Herald* and *Sun* had four, Scovel was Pulitzer's only correspondent. Yet while the others, including novelist Stephen Crane, lounged at the Inglaterra, reporting gossip and rumors as gospel, Scovel scooped them all—despite being nearly executed three times and surviving malaria twice.

He was about to suggest the exhausted journalist get some rest when the clerk called for Dr. Winters with responses to both his wires from the previous day.

Roosevelt responded in kind to Colin's cryptic message, "*Forget hen. Get rooster and eggs, stop.*"

The crisp response indicated that Victor's current victim wasn't important to Roosevelt's mission. But Lily O'Grady was more than an innocent stranger to Colin. She could be family. His second wire was from his cousin. Senator Ambrose Stainsby II had confirmed that Congressman Patrick O'Grady was Colin's great-uncle Ambrose's illegitimate half-brother. The congressman and his wife were currently on a world tour. His oldest son, Sean, was in New Mexico, and the second son, Clay, ran Langesford and Rosewood plantations. Patrick's daughter, Lily, lived in New York City."

His cousin's confirmation that Lily O'Grady was a distant, illegitimate relation to the Stainsby/Winfield dynasty, muddied the waters. And while the blood tie between them was so thin it was nearly transparent; she was an innocent young woman in danger.

CHAPTER 8

*V*ictor dropped Lily in their room and left without telling her where he was going. He returned only a few hours before dawn and climbed into bed smelling of whisky and stale perfume. When he passed out on top of her without finishing his climax, she rolled him over, washed, and spent the rest of the sleepless night on the tiny settee in the corner of their room.

She wondered if there had ever been a concert scheduled at the Captain-General's palace—and the Tacón booking as well. *Would Victor have set fire to a theater to cover his lie?* But it was no use in confronting him. She'd learned the hard way that when challenged, his lies only got bigger and his temper hotter. Her head pounded and her stomach ached. *Then why are we here?*

He was in and out the days that followed—more out than in—professing to be booking another concert while she spent time with Frances Scovel, whose husband was absent nearly as much as Victor. Conversely, Richard Harding-Davis, who had been urged by Hearst to, "Wait for the war," spent his time lounging in the private dining room behind the bar with a circle of other writers and the illustrator, Frederick Remington.

They generally agreed that it was only a matter of time until the US intervened, though Lily wasn't foolish enough to think it was out of concern for American citizens in Havana. She'd been in New York long enough to know that everything was about money. Cuba was too close to the Unites States to be allowed to disintegrate into anarchy.

Even Germany had smelled the weakness in Spain's hold on its empire, spending much of the previous year tormenting Haiti and the Danish West Indies. Now, with America's hesitation, rumors circulated that four German war ships were engaged in "training maneuvers" off the coast of Santiago de Cuba, while eight more circled the Philippines like vultures. It seemed the whole world was waiting to see when, and to whom, Spain would lose its empire. And sooner, rather than later, President McKinley would be forced to decide which European power to fight for control of the strategic island— a nearly bankrupt Spain, or the more powerful and brutal Germany.

Frances had told her about unconfirmed rumors that the Battleship *Maine* was waiting in Key West for orders to sail for Cuba. And General Gómez was continuing his campaign to shut down all the island's remaining sugar mills and tobacco farms. In the face of Spanish retaliation against them, villagers were joining the rebels every day.

Victor had been gone three days on the morning of January 19 and Lily had stopped feeling guilty for enjoying his absence more than his presence. She knew he'd show up eventually. Probably when he ran out of money. Fortunately, he hadn't discovered where she hid her purse with her tip money.

She went downstairs for breakfast and found Colin sitting at the bar with Davis, Remington, and a scattering of reporters from the lesser, regional newspapers. Harry and Frances were at a table in the dining room. Frances wore a crisp white traveling dress with an ostrich feather in her stylish boater hat. Harry looked pale and pounds lighter since she'd last seen him.

"Franny," Lily called, happy to sidestep the others at the bar "Thank goodness I found you before you leave. I shall miss you both so much."

Frances stood to embrace Lily. Tears glittered in her eyes. "Sadly, only I will be leaving," she said, "Harry's malaria has returned, and the trip would be dangerous for him."

She smiled at Lily's gasp. "He's recovering, but he also suffers from seasickness. It's best if he doesn't travel until the fever and chills subside entirely. He'll join me in a few weeks."

"Don't worry," Lily offered. "I'll check on him regularly and make sure he takes care of himself."

Her new friend smiled. "I wish you luck in that endeavor, my dear. Taking care of himself is not one of my husband's talents. But he keeps his promises and he's promised to return to New York within the month." She winked. "Who knows what fireworks that will unleash?"

Lily didn't see the humor in the statement. "Do you mean war?"

"Not yet perhaps, but there are rumors of what some are predicting a 'political explosion' that will change everything over the next few weeks. Whatever it is, it may finally force McKinley into a decision. Rumors are that the warships *Texas* and *New York* are preparing to leave their ports in the coming weeks."

Frances glanced toward her husband, who had walked a tightrope as correspondent, liaison to the rebels, emissary to the Spaniards, and US spy for nearly ten years. "Don't worry, Harry will survive this, but I will miss him terribly."

Harry reached for his wife's hand and their eyes met in a moment of silent affection that made Lily's heart skip a beat. How beautiful, she thought. And how brave. She recalled the trials her own parents had endured. The things they rarely spoke of—her father's career as a Pinkerton Agent for the Yankees, her mother's imprisonment with the Comanche, her father's rescue and their harrowing escape with her infant brother Sean. Unlike Lily's marriage, it was a story of true love and sacrifice followed by "happily ever after."

Harry took Frances' arm, his blue eyes bright with affection rather than fever. "Time to go, my love."

It alerted the others that there was an adventure in the offing. The gaggle of idle reporters determined to follow the couple to Port Havana and see them off on the *Olivette.*

"May I offer you a ride?" came from behind Lily.

Dr. Winters—again. She turned to face him. "No. Thank you, Doctor. I have an appointment. It's right up the street." It was a lie, but it seemed every time he showed up, her world turned upside down. Or maybe it was the other way around. No matter, his presence confused her and his insistence that Victor harbored deep, dark secrets unnerved her.

"It's no bother," he insisted, his hand already cupping her elbow. "It's a beautiful day for a stroll. Perhaps we could talk along the way."

Talking was exactly what she did *not* want to do with this man. His soulful brown eyes saw too much. Knew too much. "I'm sorry, Doctor Winters, but I don't need—or want—an escort. Now if you'll excuse me, I don't want to be late."

She set off blindly in the direction she was facing and stepped into a milliner's shop, pretending to examine the brilliant feathers: peacock, ostrich, parrot, and pigeon, displayed for custom orders. The wholesale slaughter of the beautiful creatures for their feathers—sometimes entire wings or bodies —disgusted her. She nearly dropped a hat featuring the corpse of a baby owl.

A venomous glare from the shop owner sent her to the window, where a cautious glance showed that the good doctor had taken her rebuff seriously. Turning back to the shopkeeper, she pointed to the murdered owl, calling it the crime it was, then stepped outside and turned in the direction of *El Diario*.

She hoped to find the affable Señor Moran working to restore his office and have another lively discussion about what was really happening in Cuba. Instead, she found the office shuttered, two uniformed Hussars guarding the door. The buttons on their neatly pressed uniforms gleamed in the sunlight and she saw that their swords were sheathed, but ready to be drawn in an instant.

"*Cerrado,*" the tallest of the two Guardia in front of the locked door shouted before spitting on the ground in front of her. "*Dejar puta Americana.*"

Furious at being called an American whore and frustrated with having a here-again-gone-again husband, as well as the departure of her only friend on the island, she responded in Spanish, "I am a friend of Señor Moran, editor of this newspaper. Why is it closed? Where is he? I must speak with him. It is urgent."

Both men frowned and stepped forward, hands shifting toward their swords. Choosing wisdom over bravado, she turned on her heels, muttering under her breath, "Cuba Libre indeed."

She returned to her room to discover an eviction notice beneath her door. It seemed Victor hadn't paid for any of their stay and what she had left in her reticule wouldn't make a dent in the bill. She explained to the concierge that she hadn't seen her husband in three days, and he surprised her by saying, "My apologies, Senora Champagne, but there was a...clerical error at the desk. Your bill has been paid in full."

"What do you mean?" Who would do such a thing? She turned toward the lobby bar where the reporters spent so much of their time. As if he'd felt her gaze, Dr. Winters looked up from his conversation with Stephen Crane. Eyes as dark as Georgia peat met hers and his slight nod told her it was him.

She swayed on her feet and the concierge rushed to steady her. "Senora, what is wrong? Do you need a doctor?"

"No!" burst from her lungs as she pulled her arm free. "I…I'm just so relieved that my debt is paid." Her mind altered the memory of the doctor's smile into a lascivious leer. She'd be no man's whore.

"Señor Lopez," she said. "I seem to be currently at a disadvantage due to my husband's…absence, and I fear he may have met with foul play. Is there a place you and I can talk? Privately?"

"Of course, Señora." He smiled in a grandfatherly way and ushered her into the private office behind the bar. Leaving the door ajar, he stepped behind his desk. "What is it you wish to discuss?"

Fifteen minutes later, Lily left the room with a written contract to perform for the Inglaterra guests in the dining room. Her compensation covered little more than her room and meals, but she could keep her tips. *It's only temporary*, she told herself, admitting for the first time that Victor could be gone for good.

Feeling the heat of Dr. Winters' gaze, she left the hotel for the Guardia office to report her husband missing.

The next day, she met Dr. Winters at his usual barstool. "I'd like to speak with you," she said, struggling to keep her voice steady. "Privately."

"Of course, Mrs. Champagne," he answered and rose to escort her to a table by the window. "Let me preface our conversation with my apology," he said. "I should never have inserted myself into your affairs. But you've had to deal with so much lately, and with Victor…missing, well, I thought I was helping."

Her anger melted at the sincerity in his voice. Whatever his motives, he'd kept her from being thrown to the curb. "How did you know our bill hadn't been paid?"

"A Lucky guess. I've been following him for the last six months. He has a string of unpaid hotel bills and more, from Boston to Chicago."

"Six months?" She struggled to take in air. That meant he'd been following *them*. "Why?"

"First, let me tell you that while I am a doctor, my name is Colin Winfield." He caught her wrist as she rose. "Please let me explain."

She felt dead inside when he finished his story about Victor's many identities and the trail of broken hearts and empty bank accounts. She couldn't stop a shudder when he told her about his sister's attempted suicide and descent into melancholy. Then it registered that she wasn't legally married. Though it was without her knowledge, she was still ruined for any respectable union in the future. *So be it*, she thought, realizing she didn't want…or need…a man to lead her through life like a horse on a tether. Her cheeks heated with the excitement of knowing she would be her own woman.

Misunderstanding the flush, Colin reached out for her hand. "Are you alright?"

She pulled away and straightened her spine, one vertebra at a time until her legs were steady enough to stand. "I'm fine. Thank you, Doctor Win…field." As if outside her body, she heard herself speak calmly, rationally—cordially—as if he'd returned a lost glove from the street. "I appreciate your *current* honesty, and of course your recent generosity. Please be assured that since I'm now employed, you will be repaid with interest. Now if you'll excuse me, I have some…arrangements to make."

Those arrangements included changing the lock on her hotel door and ransacking the trunk of costumes that had managed to arrive, while her personal one was lost. Slowly, methodically, she shredded every lascivious costume Victor had bought with her money. She was about to cut the waist-length hair he'd convinced her to lighten with peroxide, ammonia, and bleach, when her humiliation turned vengeful. Rather than cutting her hair like a widow in mourning, she imagined plunging the shears into his arrogant chest.

Between the evening concerts, she arduously read the American newspapers brought by ships from Tampa and Key West and Havana. Most of it was old news. And much of it was skewed, or completely fictionalized—like Frederick Remington's sketch of Spanish soldiers strip-searching a naked Clemencia Arango aboard the *Olivette*.

Reading between the lines, she felt America's increasing hostility toward

Spain. Yet President McKinley maintained his cautious stance. How much longer, she wondered. Newrly two weeks after the riots, the *El Discuscion* and other papers still hadn't reopened. Rebels had wasted no time taking advantage of the troops diverted to Havana, looting the trains running through Havana, Batabano, and Matanzas.

In a macabre game of "tit for tat," Spain increased the presence of their Army and Navy on and around the island and the *USS Texas* joined the North Atlantic squadron in Hampton Roads, awaiting orders to join the *USS Maine* at Key West. It was all blatant political posturing, of course, with both countries using the standard political tools—rumors, threats and finger-pointing.

Victor had been gone more than a week now. She'd reported him missing to the uninterested Guardia more to create a legitimate reason for her unescorted presence in the city than expecting them to look for him. Deep down, she didn't believe any harm had come to him. The last of his many lives was reserved for her to take. In the meantime, as she read the papers and listened to the reporters talk about places, she, as a woman, couldn't go. She asked so many questions that they called her, "The Inquisitor."

She was about to put a week-old *New York World* down when she saw Lucas Stone's insightful interview with the Spanish owner and editor of the shuttered newspaper, *El Diario de la Marina*. It was on page three, followed by another piece by the same author, detailing the continued censorship of Havana's newspapers after the riots.

"Yes!" Her exclamation caused heads to turn in the reading room otherwise occupied by men. "The *Texas and New York* have set sail for Key West," explained her outburst. Heads nodded, and the parlor returned to muted conversations and rattling newspapers, while her heart raced. Joseph Pulitzer had published her stories!

Her invasion of the reading room had been grudgingly accepted after she commiserated with Richard Harding-Davis about Hearst's salacious fictionalization of the now-infamous strip search. Incensed by the license Hearst took with his story, Davis resigned to join Pulitzer's *New York World*. Considering her now a kindred spirit, he invited her to join him in the all-male reading room. She wished she could tell him they were also colleagues on the same newspaper.

In the days that followed, she also paid close attention to rumors about rebel activity from the few escaped *reconcentrados* who made it to Havana.

Her heart raced when Pulitzer published two more of her dispatches detailing the horrors of thousands of peasants still dying of malnourishment, disease, and abuse by Spanish soldiers in the *reconcentrado* camps.

On January 24, they learned that the *USS Maine* had been dispatched to Havana.

CHAPTER 9

*C*olin kept his distance, letting the news that she'd been duped by Victor sink in. He expected her to run for the nearest ticket office for passage back to New York or her home in South Georgia. But she stayed, living on tips and room and board, playing the role of a dutiful wife waiting for her husband to return from a business trip.

He admitted she could be right. In his experience, parasites didn't leave their victims until they'd sucked every ounce of strength from them. And while Victor had taken all of Lily's money, she still had a wealthy family. It wouldn't be beyond the cad to fake a kidnapping—or manage a real one—if he had a chance. So, he became her shadow.

He took comfort from the fact that she was rarely alone. The dinner crowd loved her as she played requests for old favorites, along with popular ragtime and blues tunes—even the occasional Spanish ballad. Her grasp of the Spanish language and Cuban dialects amazed him. She was an excellent mimic. *The perfect actress.*

This morning, as he had every morning since Victor left, he watched her descend the stairs for a breakfast of *café con leche* and a *tostada*. With her small frame, nearly silver hair, and pale skin against a white shirtwaist and skirt, he again compared her to an ethereal being. But her straight back, bright, sapphire-blue eyes, and rose-tinted lips spoke of a vitality at odds with her fragile appearance.

His, "Good morning, Mrs. Champagne," supported her charade. "May I join you?"

Without waiting for an answer, he pulled out a chair at her table by the window and she frowned, looking like she might bolt. But rather than make a scene, she acknowledged his request with a nod. A few heads turned when he said loud enough to be heard, "Congratulations for another grand performance last night."

She unnecessarily smoothed her skirt. "Thank you, Dr. Winfield, but you needn't flatter me. I simply do what I can."

It was an understatement. When she wasn't performing or hidden behind a newspaper, he followed her through city streets and alleys where no white American woman, with or without an escort, should be. Places where the displaced survivors of the *reconcentrado* camps slept in sewage-strewn alleys and begged in front of restaurants catering to American tourists.

The starving natives of the island were mostly ignored, like stray cats or dogs scratching around garbage in gutters. But not by Lily O'Grady. Colin had come close to stepping from the shadows more than once, to pull her away from the clawing hands of a human skeleton asking, "*Ayuadame?*"

Instead of stepping back in revulsion and refusing their plea for help, she handed them a coin or a piece of bread from the Inglaterra wrapped in a napkin inside her big tapestry purse. Often, she helped them lean against a sun-drenched adobe wall, or take a shaky step. Sometimes she risked ruining one of her few dresses by sitting beside the withered remnant of a human being and opening her journal to write notes, nodding her head as she recorded their stories.

Every day, after her strong Cuban coffee, she stood in line at the telegraph office. The operator wasn't as dedicated to the privacy of his customers as his position would assume and he readily accepted Colin's bribe to reveal that her wires were to Joseph Pulitzer at the *World* in New York, from a man named Lucas Stone.

He knew the name. A reclusive new reporter from Havana who had struck a chord with the bleeding hearts of America's Christian heartland. Apparently, he preferred keeping out of sight to becoming the toast of the town and kept his identity a mystery. Few, if any, of the reporters Colin knew were interested in the plight of starving Cuban peasants and some of the details in Stone's articles seemed shockingly familiar. Was Lily Lucas Stone? There was no time like the present to find out.

He smiled. "I'd say your evening entertainment, reading room marathons, and roaming the alleys in old Havana are a little more than simply, 'what you can'. Do you ever sleep? It's as essential to life as food, you know."

Instead of preening at his praise for her unselfish acts of kindness, she glared at him. "How is it you seem to know so much about my daily activities?"

He suspected he deserved her derision. No matter his motives, he'd lied to her the moment he met her and brought her nothing but heartache since.

"I'm a doctor. I care about my patients' well-being."

"I am not your patient!" Her sharp voice caused a few heads to turn their way, then she lowered her gaze to the uneaten buttered bread on a plate next to her coffee. "As you know, my hands and…other…injuries have healed properly. And I've already thanked you for your help in Tampa…as well as your financial assistance here. What more do you want of me?"

She reached into her oversized bag and pulled out an envelope with his name written on it. "I've been waiting for an opportunity to give you this. It should cover the expenses you so kindly paid when…Victor left…plus interest. I know your motives are honorable, but I can manage for myself. You owe me nothing and I owe you nothing. So please stop following me. It hampers my mission."

Apparently, he was not as stealthy as he thought. He cocked his head. "Mission?"

"To find Victor, of course."

She smiled coyly at his surprise, carefully spreading fresh butter over her tostada and taking a small bite, savoring it with a roll of her eyes. "The food here is delicious. I must take more advantage of it. With a sleight of hand only an accomplished magician could manage, she scooped the remaining slices of bread into a napkin before dropping them into the bag. "Good day," she said and stood.

Colin grasped her hand. "Are you out of your mind? You can't run around the city looking for him. By now you must be aware of the types of places he frequents. It isn't safe…"

"My so-called marriage isn't safe," cut him off. "*Life* isn't safe. Yet here I am. My life belongs to *me*, Dr. Winfield. And I shall live it as I please. Now let me go."

His grip loosened but his hand remained on her wrist. "What about your family? They think you're in New York. How will your parents feel if they return from Europe to find that you went missing in Cuba? I know you won't take money from me, but can someone, your brother Clay perhaps, send you enough for passage back to Georgia?"

Her cheeks flushed and she fell back into her chair. "How do you know about my brother, and where I'm from? And where my parents are? I thought you wanted to find Victor—to avenge what he did to your sister. If so, you don't seem to be trying very hard." Her voice lowered. "Or was that a lie too? Now let me go before I scream."

"Promise me you won't bolt, and I'll tell you the truth."

Satisfied by a faint nod he suspected was prompted more by curiosity than fear, he released her. "I recognized the name O'Grady on your trunk and made some inquiries. Your father, Patrick O'Grady, is related to me, or more specifically to my third cousin, Ambrose Stainsby II."

Her jaw dropped at the revelation, but she recovered quickly. "Ah yes, the mighty Stainsby dynasty. Daddy told us about them. Pirates, slavers, liars, and thieves. My grandmother was one of their indentured servants. One of their victims."

This was not going the way Colin intended. Judging by the taut line of her lips and cold stare, she obviously painted the Winfield and Stainsby families with the same brush. He tried to explain, "Our families aren't close. You have a slight drawl. It was just a hunch. I'm told your father has reconciled with Ambrose, both being legislators and all. And while the bloodline is thin, I felt obligated…"

She held up a hand to stop him. Her eyes could have been icebergs reflecting a clear arctic sky, her skin carved from ancient ivory. "To what? Protect me? Please, don't bother. While I appreciate your medical attention, what happened in Tampa was an accident and as I've said numerous times, I can take care of myself."

Aching to tell her that she had no idea the depth of her danger, he offered an olive branch. "How about we call a truce and take a cab to the waterfront to see the *Maine* come in. I saw it once up in Baltimore. Very impressive."

"How could I possibly want to ride with you to the waterfront?" should have silenced him, but a slight smile and a glint of humor in her gaze told him she was testing him.

"Because I saved your life—three times. And you know all my family secrets."

"Twice," she corrected him. "The stairwell after the explosion doesn't count, Doctor Winfield."

"Please call me Colin." He nodded toward the bag with the napkin full of bread. "Do you think you'll need what's in there?"

"Yes, we may see someone in need of food along the way."

The truth in her statement knotted his stomach. While Havana and every large city in Cuba was teeming with starving refugees from the prison camps, they were the lucky ones. Thousands remained behind the trenches and wire fences, too sick to be moved or refused entry into the towns. If a piece of buttered bread would see a starving child through another day, he wouldn't argue the point.

"A penny for your thoughts," she asked when they'd settled into a cab for the trip to the ancient harbor.

He shrugged. "It wouldn't be worth it. What say we enjoy the ride—and the spectacle?"

The harbor was already filling with citizens of Havana anxious to see the approaching American warship make its way through the channel into the harbor. As always, the Spanish Guardia were easily recognizable. It wasn't surprising. Captain-General Blanco was out of town for two weeks, touring the island. The unannounced arrival of an American warship during such an absence was most incongruous—and troubling—to Colin's way of thinking. The ship could easily be met with the harbor's guns. Fortunately, in Blanco's absence, his assistant, General Parrado, had substituted a confrontation with a chilly charade of hospitality.

The crowd's eerie silence seemed charged with electricity when the ship appeared in the distance. How different it must look from those the sixteenth century fortresses were built to repel. More than three hundred feet long, with modern smokestacks amidships and more traditional tall masts fore and aft, the giant white behemoth muscled its way into the channel, dwarfing the other vessels moored in the harbor—including the *City of Washington*.

Lily clutched Colin's arm at the magnificent display of engineering, beauty, and lethal power. She said, "I was right about this being the beginning of the end."

"What makes you think that? This could just be a show of power to throw the Germans off the scent," he said.

She looked up at him, shading her eyes from the bright sun. "I'm not stupid…Colin. Mr. Roosevelt has campaigned for a war that will bring more pain, suffering, and death to this beautiful island. And for what? Freedom? Do you really believe they will be free of tyranny if we chase the Spanish out? America may be a kinder master than Spain or Germany, but a master nonetheless—all in the name of power—and of course, money."

He looked away when he repeated the government propaganda. "No, it's a diplomatic visit to ease the tensions between the two countries."

She stabbed a finger into his chest. "If we're going to work together, to find Victor, don't *ever* patronize me again. At best, it's the dance before the beginning of the war we all know is coming. At worst, it's a finger in the eye of the last of the great Colonial empires and a warning to Germany."

The passion in her voice, her bright eyes, and flushed cheeks mesmerized him. And he'd spent too many years of his life serving America's insatiable hunger for power—that destroyed the country's indigenous people—to disagree. His hand caught her finger before she could pull away and he leaned in close enough to smell the faint scent of lily of the valley in her hair.

"I would never underestimate you, but I don't recall agreeing to the 'we' part of finding Victor."

CHAPTER 10

W hen they returned to the hotel, Colin asked, "Are you free to attend a welcome reception at the Captain-General's palace tomorrow evening?"

Thinking he was making a cruel joke, taunting her with Victor's empty promise of a recital there, she was about to unleash her temper when he produced an envelope bearing the seal of the US Consulate-General William Henry Fitzhugh Lee.

She examined the seal that looked real. "How did you get this?"

"There may not be a Winfield in Congress, but I too, have connections in high places. The *Maine* arrived unexpectedly, allegedly on its tour to New Orleans. While the Spanish aren't thrilled to have an American warship moored in their harbor, they've apparently decided to play the role of gracious host. No doubt hoping it will leave quickly."

But Lily was still staring at the invitation. "Fitzhugh Lee is Robert E. Lee's son and was a Confederate General. You're Yankee to the bone. What kind of connection could you possibly have with him?"

"Don't look a gift horse in the mouth," he answered harshly. "No reporters are invited. I thought you, or should I say Lucas Stone, would jump at the chance for a story."

"What do you mean by that?"

"I mean that I know about your dispatches to the *World*. And the dime novels. Truth be told, I've read some of them and find them quite entertaining. I was most intrigued by the lost gold in Sierra Madre Mountains. It was so realistic. Almost as if it happened."

She could barely breathe. If he exposed her real identity, she'd be dead in the journalism world. Her mind reeled. Frances wrote society and travel articles for Pulitzer under her maiden name, and while Nellie Bly was a pseudonym for Elizabeth Cochran, she also wrote about women's issues. But a woman reporting a war would never be accepted.

"Are you alright?" he asked with little sympathy in his voice. "Do you need smelling salts?"

She took a deep breath. Whatever the consequences, a story from the palace was too good to pass up. Though it would be hosted by the Acting Captain-General, she'd have the exclusive opportunity to speak with Lee and his former enemy and commander of the *USS Maine*, Yankee Captain Charles Sigsbee,

As US Consul-General, Lee had the authority to order the *Maine* to Cuba. Was he expecting trouble? Or was the ship's show of force for Germany and not Spain? As a fellow Southerner, she felt a regional connection to him, and he, as a former member of the US House of Representatives, likely knew her father. It was a card she didn't want to play, but she wasn't too proud to revive her Southern drawl to catch his attention. Her skin tingled at "havin' a little chat" with him about America's plans for the future of Cuba.

The brief reception's cuisine consisted of rarely seen beef, combined with Spanish and Cuban dishes and generous portions of wine from Barcelona. It was likely that Blanco, who was scouring the interior of the island for Máximo Gómez, wasn't even aware of the *Maine's* presence. And his substitute, while experienced in diplomacy, seemed uncomfortable entertaining his powerful neighbors in his superior's absence.

The only two other women at the reception were the Acting Captain-General Parrado's wife and Senora Engracia Blanco, wife of the Captain-General. Both women hid their disapproval behind fake smiles and whispered comments, followed by giggles and sneers.

Without sharing her fluency in Spanish, Lily learned more about the tattered state of the Spanish empire and the secret activities of the Spanish loyalists, from them than Parrado or Lee. But it gave her no pleasure to have her suspicions confirmed that Cuba's autonomy was a sham intended to placate the restless and trigger-happy United States.

Dinner conversation from former Confederate General Lee was less informative, but she overheard him whisper to Sigsbee that he was shocked at the unexpected arrival. Her stomach tightened at knowing something else had triggered the hasty voyage. Was it the German ships?

At the close of the interminable and awkward evening, Lily's mind was bursting with information for her next dispatch to Pulitzer. This time, the story was so big that she struggled with the decision to use her real name. When Parrado's interpreter extended an invitation to join him at the Sunday bullfight in the Regla Arena across the harbor from Havana, Senora Blanco's obsidian black eyes challenged Lily.

She ignored Colin's frown and shake of his head. "*Con mucho gusto*," she accepted in halting Spanish.

"Are you sure?" Colin whispered in her ear. "It can be very…brutal."

She tossed her head. "I've read about bullfights. And I've been out West. I think I'm capable of coping."

Lee accepted as well, but Captain Sigsbee's nod was less than enthusiastic.

Once outside, Colin scolded, "Do you ever stop to think that you may have bitten off more than you can chew?"

With a smile she'd been told could charm a canary out of its cage, she answered, "I just keep chewing. Besides, I can't resist a dare."

"I'll remember that in the future, but a Spanish bullfight is more savage than a rodeo. While we'll be safe in the *Barrera*, I wouldn't advise wearing white."

She wanted to shout that she wasn't stupid. She'd seen playbills for bullfights when she visited her brother Sean in New Mexico and knew it wasn't all pageantry, music, and glittering costumes. The bulls always died after fighting savagely to kill the teasing, taunting matador. But they were not helpless. Weighing over a thousand pounds, with horns as sharp as swords, if given the chance, they could easily kill him. She told herself they were only cattle, ultimately destined for the slaughterhouse. But to her dismay, occasionally a horse, whose purpose was to distract the bull from the matador, was injured. It was a dangerous game—but still a game.

On Sunday, after talking with a few of the Inglaterra maids, she understood why Colin advised her to not wear white. The *Barrera* was reserved for special dignitaries and the city's wealthy patrons. Well shaded, with benches instead of stone ledges, it was close to the action. Only a wooden fence separated them from the charging bulls. Second thoughts made her stomach quiver, but she reasoned that if the miniature dragon, Senora Blanco, could stomach it, she could.

Dressed in a light blue shirtwaist and navy skirt, she met Colin in the lobby and boarded their cab for the ferry across the harbor to the two-hundred-year-old settlement of Regla. As usual, the streets were bustling on the warm January afternoon and the docks were busy. Like New York City and New Orleans, the chaotic bustle was part of the city's charm.

Normally, she would have enjoyed losing herself in the anonymity offered by the noise and crowds, but since Victor's disappearance, she often felt someone watching her. Not like Colin, who was so pitifully obvious in his surveillance, it felt comforting. This felt sinister. Like Victor. Sometimes it was a tall, thin shadow that quickly disappeared in the sunlight, or the scent of his hair pomade rising above the smell of dried horse dung, urine, and human sweat. Or the hum of a familiar tune coming from a dark alley. Whenever she turned or tried to follow it, she found only faded colors on ancient adobe, broken bricks, trash, and lost, dying people.

While Colin tried to convince her that Victor had likely fled to the mainland, she disagreed. Sometimes, when she woke up, she'd smell his cinnamon cologne for just an instant before it disappeared in the morning breeze. And in the evening, when she performed in a room shrouded in clouds of pungent Cuban tobacco smoke, she thought she heard his laugh. Even on the public Paseo del Prado, gooseflesh rose on her arms when footsteps behind her matched his pace; yet when she turned, she saw only strangers.

Even at the harbor with Colin, she drew a deep breath at glimpsing a tall, slender man dressed in a common peasant shirt and baggy trousers. A ragged straw hat shadowed his face but the jaunty knot of the red kerchief around his neck caught her eye, and the wide blue sash at this waist.

Victor's peasant costume from Tampa! She blinked and he was lost in the sea of people on their way to see the famous Spanish matador, Don Luis Mazzantini.

She jumped when Colin touched her arm before boarding the ferry. Concern showed in his narrowed eyes. "You have nothing to prove. Regla is a charming little town. We don't need to go to the arena."

Still shaken by the sight of a man who looked so much like Victor that she'd *felt* him, she looked up at Colin. "Why are you trying to help me?" she asked. "Really?"

"Because I like you."

She stepped back from his gentle smile and kind eyes. "I don't need a friend."

"It's not your choice. I know you're brave and self-sufficient, but you have to understand that you can't do this alone."

He was right for so many reasons. It was dangerous for a woman to be alone in a foreign land, especially an American woman in Cuba. Nellie Bly may have felt safe traveling the world, but she wasn't in countries hostile to her own—and she didn't know Victor Champagne—no—Lionel Carter.

"I'm fine," she said. "Come, we don't want to miss the ferry."

Once aboard, she stood with Colin at the ship's rail, appreciating the tiny, sun-kissed island city of Regla coming into view. "I'm not fool enough to think I can beat Victor at his own game," she admitted. "But I know him better than his previous…victims. He wanted my trust fund and hates me because he can't bully me into getting my parents to turn it over to him. He won't leave Havana until I pay for my defiance.

"So, while I'm grateful for your invitation to the reception and this… event, I'm capable of luring Victor out of whatever cave he's been hiding in —for you to arrest, of course. But I'll never do it with you hovering over me. I really can take care of myself."

Colin's answer was lost in the riot of cheers as they approached the ancient harbor's docks. They hung back from the crowd rushing to disembark, and Lily scanned the crowd for the man with the red bandana and blue sash. But if he was there, he blended in with the crowd all dressed in the same style clothing and similar colors. Still, the tense muscles in her shoulders told her he was watching her. Like a mountain lion—quiet, patient, blending into the background, waiting to pounce when she least expected it.

"Do you see him?"

She jumped at Colin's hand on her shoulder. How did he know? "Yes. No! I mean, when we boarded, I thought I saw someone who moved like Victor. I must have been wrong."

His smile was patient. "I know the feeling. The Sioux were masters at blending into the scenery. It confuses their prey until they don't trust their own instincts. Makes them careless. In the Western Campaigns, more than a few veteran soldiers shot each other based on a shadow or broken twig. The native tribes may have even prevailed if not for the Army's superior numbers —and the Gatling gun."

His jaw set as he too scanned the milling throng. Then he looked down at her, a sad smile barely curving his lips. "Don't let it get to you. Keep your head clear. Watch and listen, but don't jump at everything you see." He nudged her. "We better get going. Parrado said he'd have a coach waiting for us."

She wanted to ask how the kind, mild-mannered doctor knew so much about war tactics, the Northern tribes—and Gatling guns—but he was right about staying calm. It wouldn't do for Victor to catch her alone and unaware in a strange city, though she doubted he'd try anything while she was in the company of the Acting Captain-General of Cuba, the commander of an American warship, and the US Consulate-General. Reassured for the moment, she threaded her arm through Colin's. "Well, Dr. Winfield, we mustn't keep our hosts waiting. I'm sure Señora Blanco is looking forward to seeing me swoon."

He patted his jacket pocket. "I brought plenty of smelling salts."

"I won't need them," she answered with more confidence than she felt and opened her parasol to shield her face from the growing crowd of strangers shouting, *"Death to the Americans, Death to autonomy. Long Live Weyler,"* at the unpopular Captain-General's carriage. Captain Sigsbee and General Lee were already inside, leaving little space for the two of them.

Lee grumbled, "Rabble,"

"I was afraid of this." Sigsbee worried. "I'd hoped to keep our public presence low and let the ship speak for us."

CHAPTER 11

he *Plaza de Toros* was an open circular stone amphitheater six
stories high. It reminded Lily of the Roman Colosseum where
gladiators fought lions and each other in front of thousands of roaring,
blood-thirsty spectators. Second thoughts gave her chills under the warm sun
and she was suddenly grateful for Colin's smelling salts.

They followed Parrado's guards to the Governor-General's box near the
fence behind the corridor that Colin explained was an escape route for the
matadors if the bull got too close. They approached their box seats behind
the General, his wife, and Señora Blanco. Lily leaned close to Colin. "What
if the bull makes it through the fence and into the corridor?"

He shrugged. "It's the mystique of the bullfight. The audience becomes
part of the spectacle, sharing the danger with the matadors."

She breathed easier when he nudged her up to the second level when
Captain Sigsbee and Fitzhugh Lee filled the front row with Parrado's party.

"Less dust up here," he said, signaling for her to sit behind Parrado,
whose tall body would block some of her view.

"Don Luis Mazzantini, known as the 'Gentleman Bullfighter of Spain', is
the main attraction," Parrado explained to the little group of foreigners,
though his posters were plastered on the stucco walls along the Prado and on
nearly every building in Regla.

Lily looked behind and above them, noting that nearly all six thousand seats were filling up, including the *andanadas* that were so high she wondered how people could even see the arena. A thousand other questions were queued up in her mind when the band in a gallery above them signaled the beginning of the event.

She shared the thrill surging through the excited crowd and cheered with them when a horseman astride a magnificent Lusitano stallion rode up to the box and asked Parrado for a key. The cheering heightened when he caught the toss and ceremoniously opened a gate to the arena, admitting a parade of matadors, banderilleros and picadors. They were all dressed in bright, colorful costumes decorated with silk tinsel and thick gold braiding shimmering in the afternoon sunlight. The embroidery alone was worth a fortune, Lily calculated—and added weight to the load the strong, Spanish horses bore.

She recognized the stunningly beautiful Andalusian stallions her father bred at Langesford Plantation's, Morning Bird Stables. Her grandfather, Anthony Langesford, had begun breeding Andalusians before he married her Creole grandmother from New Orleans. When Lily's parents imported wild mustangs from New Mexico, people laughed at their efforts to breed the smaller, faster breed's agility into Georgia's thinning, show horse bloodlines while keeping the Andalusian and Lusitano bloodlines pure.

Her heart skipped a beat at the sight of the noble line of warhorses, and she cheered at the ancient spectacle of pomp and pageantry. When it was over and the gate closed behind the last mounted matador, everyone in the arena turned toward a huge set of doors beneath the orchestra gallery. The arena went silent when the doors opened and the largest, meanest bull Lily had ever seen charged out.

The terrifying beauty of the animal's raw power took her breath away, until she realized the bright ribbons hanging from its neck were fastened by barbs embedded in its shoulder. Colin took her hand, his frown telling her this was only the beginning.

The creature, dazed from pain and the sudden light, shook its massive head and snorted, pawing the ground and biting itself to dislodge the barbs —to no avail. Lily fought nausea at the blood pouring from its neck while the crowd cheered, and a mounted *picador* rode into the arena. Carrying a lance, he shouted and charged the bull, stabbing it repeatedly for the sole purpose of further enraging the already deranged animal. When the *picador* tired, he jumped over the fence to safety and another took his place.

The crowd went crazy. Ladies, including the ones in their party, threw handkerchiefs onto the sand-covered floor, shouting for more blood; while the men seemed to have lost their minds, screaming for the animal's death and dismemberment.

Lily managed to remain on her feet by clutching Colin's arm. Tears fell unchecked down her cheeks as another *picador* stabbed his lance into the wounded bull. When the rider charged the raging beast, Lily saw the blindfold across his horse's eyes.

Her scream of horror was lost in the cheering crowd and when the bull struck the magnificent mount on the flank, pulling it down, she threw herself toward the Acting Captain-General's back, nearly pushing him into the questionable safety of the matador passageway. Screaming for him to stop the barbaric spectacle, she'd have gone after the horseman herself if Colin hadn't pulled her back, still screaming and waving her arms.

"Do you want to get us both killed?" he barked into her ear.

"*Primera vez*," he shouted an apology to the Spanish dignitary, explaining through his interpreter that it was her first time and she was overpowered by the spectacle.

Parrado turned his attention back to the barbaric blood sport and the others accepted her outburst as exhilaration for the fight—and the kill. Lily's body suddenly felt like a bowl of jelly left out in the sun too long and melted into her seat. Oblivious to her swollen eyes, wet cheeks, and running nose, she leaned close to Colin and stuttered, "Wh-what do you mean...get us killed?"

He faced her, his pleasant face dark with anger. "I told you this was no rodeo. You need to pay better attention to me if you plan to survive here."

Raising eyes crusted by drying tears, she repeated, "What do you mean?"

He nodded toward Parrado and spoke into her ear. "The danger from Victor can't hold a candle to the man in front of you. Women suspected of spying or inciting insurgency are not immune to El Morro Castle. If you want to stay alive here, you need to learn how to play both sides of the fence. You're a good actress and this is far from over. I suggest you prepare for the performance of a lifetime."

The warning in his voice brought her out of her horrified stupor, not the threat of El Morro Castle, so close to Havana that when the breezes blew the right way, shots from executions could be heard as far as the Inglaterra.

"But..."

"Quiet!"

A sudden hush descended on the arena and Lily risked a peek over Parrado's shoulder. The injured horse had been removed, leaving only a dark stain where he'd fallen in the sand. The bull now lay writhing near the doors he'd been forced from only a short time ago. While she'd been having her tantrum, three unmounted *banderilleros* had confused the crippled bull by stabbing it with more darts covered by more bright ribbons. The more the beast struggled to right itself, the more the blood-crazed audience screamed for more gore.

With the bull mad from pain, fear, and rage, Parrado signaled for what Colin told her was "the kill." A bugle blast silenced the crowd and with the bull already half-dead, the great Spanish matador, Don Luis Mazzantini, finally stepped onto the stage. In his tight, glittering pants, short jacket, and ridiculously indescribable hat, he pranced and preened in front of the cheering crowd, his back bravely turned on the blind, stumbling bull. Then he turned toward it, making a few fancy swirls of his red cape in front of the color-blind animal. It charged at the movement and the Great Mazzantini plunged the blade into it.

The foundation of the arena seemed to shudder with the animal's fall. A moment's hush followed as the famous matador slit the behemoth's throat with a dagger. Hats and handkerchiefs, even canes, rained down on the victorious hero of the day, and he bowed before leaving the arena. The band played while festively decorated mules came out to haul the mutilated animal away, and Lily vomited, barely missing the Acting Captain-General of Cuba.

Parrado and his entourage were escorted from the arena amid more cheers. Captain Sigsbee's frown and pallor told Lily that his opinion of bullfighting matched hers, though his military background had kept him from reacting. Colin's similar bearing made her wonder if he'd been in the military as well. There was so much she didn't know about him.

Lee and Sigsbee were invited back to the Governor's palace, but after Senora Parrado whispered something in her husband's ear, he spoke to a Lieutenant in the Spanish Guardia. Lily's heart beat fast when the man blocked their exit to speak to Colin. She took deep breaths but the heat, the smell of blood, sweat, and Spanish whiskey threatened to again humiliate her. She fought the bile rising in her throat by vowing not to eat meat—or anything else—for a long time.

Was the building still ringing with shouts and animals screaming in pain, or was it her blood pounding in her ears? All she caught of the lieutenant's conversation with Colin was, "*loco*" and "*gringa*," followed by, "*Investigación.*"

Investigation?

She missed Colin's response when she turned to dry heave onto the stone floor behind their seats. Fortunately, the episode was brief. Colin touched her arm and asked, "Are you alright?"

She held a scented handkerchief to her mouth. "It must be the heat."

He whispered something in the Guardia's ear, who nodded in what seemed to be understanding before motioning them to follow him outside. Clutching her parasol and bag in one hand and clinging to Colin's arm with the other, they exited into the blinding Caribbean sunlight.

The fresh sea air calmed her stomach and lifted her spirits, though she felt as if she'd just escaped Dante's famous inferno. Colin helped her into their cab, then exchanged a few more words with the Guardia while Lily took a deep breath, tucked her hair back up under her hat, and opened her bag for a fresh handkerchief. Instead, she found a folded piece of Hotel Inglaterra stationery.

"Are you still sick?" Colin asked when he saw her stricken expression.

She handed him the note. "Yes, but not for the reason you think."

He took it from her as if it might bite him. "It's from Victor, isn't it?"

At her nod, he unfolded it for them both to read:

You belong to me and I am not finished with you—yet. And when I am, you won't be worth having.

Colin crushed the note in his fist. "The bastard won't get away with this —or whatever else he's planning. The Guardia is already looking for him."

She shivered at the realization that she really had seen Victor at the harbor. He *was* following her. It was entirely possible that only Colin's presence had kept him from taking her...where? And why? Perhaps Victor was truly the Devil. Somehow, like a phantom, he'd managed to place a note in her purse under the very noses of the Guardia. She was a fool to think she could escape him.

"Why are they looking for him—us?" came out in an unfamiliar thin, tiny voice.

He took her shaking hand. "The Guardia wouldn't tell me the details, only that they're looking for him and want to talk to you. I told him you're my sister and Victor lured you into a false marriage, brought you here, and deserted you when he found out you were *embarazada.*"

"*Pregnant?* You told him I'm pregnant?" Neither her mind nor her mouth could form anything more than "Why?"

His dark eyes glittered with mischief in the shadowed cab. "I had to say something to cover the vomiting. Thankfully, the Guardia didn't know I told Parrado you were my fiancée."

"Fiancée!" She choked again. "How dare you!" She'd have slapped…no… punched him if she had room to swing—and the strength to raise a hand.

"I had to think fast. Parrado was furious with your outburst and… digestive upset. Apparently, like you and Spanish, he knows far more English than he lets on."

"What makes you think…?"

"I followed you, remember. You seemed very fluent in the language during your alley interviews and with your new friend, the editor of *El Diario de la Marina.*"

How did she not notice him following her from the beginning? A stupid question. For the same reason she believed Victor's lies. She couldn't trust her own judgement. She'd once believed Victor to be an honorable man. And Colin appeared to be one as well. If she was wrong about one, what about the other?

She shifted away from him and mustered as much bravado as she could. "I hardly think the esteemed Acting Captain-General of Cuba will put me in El Morro prison for disliking a barbaric bullfight that was no fight at all." Then, more doubtful, "Do you?"

Without looking, she felt the warmth of his smile.

CHAPTER 12

*L*ily sat at the Inglaterra's grand piano, tapping out a new ragtime tune from sheet music Richard Harding-Davis had brought back from his last trip to New York. The syncopated beat reminded her of the African and Haitian music of the former slaves who had accepted offers of homesteads on Langesford after the War. The music touched something primal inside her, lifting her spirits after the debacle at Regla.

After being tied to the classics for so long and attending so many stuffy operas escorted by stuffier old men, she'd almost forgotten how much she loved the music of Lillian Russell operettas and bawdy vaudeville burlesque shows. Her fingers plucked out Fred Stone's "Ma Rag Time Baby," thinking that perhaps she was seduced as much by the glitter and excitement of the popular theater, as by Victor's suave mystique. Sadly, she'd learned the dangers of both the hard way.

"Señora Champagne," made her miss a note and she swiveled on the stool, to meet the stern, steel-gray gaze of the Guardia officer from Regla. He bowed slightly, hat in hand, and lowered his voice to speak in halting English. "I am Lieutenant Abela. A moment of your time, *por favor?*"

She wasn't surprised to see him, only that he'd taken three days to make his appearance. She took a deep breath and nodded. "Of course."

He bowed again, gesturing toward a young civilian man next to him who translated in heavily accented English, "We apologize for interrupting your…practice, but we have matters of utmost importance to discuss with you." An impatient glare from the officer prompted him to add, "Privately. There is an…office…behind the dining room for our…conversation."

"You mean interrogation," Lily muttered and stood. Ignoring Abela, she turned to the nameless Spanish interpreter. For a moment, she reveled in playing the outraged American diva saying loud enough for others to hear, "I will certainly *not* accompany two men alone to an *office* behind a bar."

Abela's angry flush told her he understood her tone, if not her words. Remembering Colin's warning about baiting an officer of the elite Spanish assassins, she smiled at the interpreter. "Perhaps we can enjoy a sweet tea in the courtyard… sometime tomorrow. If you'll excuse me, I need to prepare for a performance."

Abela's hand gripped her arm as she took a step. "*Ahora*," he ordered, followed by his companion's longer, "Our apologies, Señora, but we must speak to you right away. It is most urgent."

"Lily! There you are," cut off her angry retort and Lieutenant Abela released her arm as Colin approached them, hand extended. "Lieutenant Abela. What a surprise," Then in Spanish, "To what do we owe this pleasure?"

There was a low exchange between the officer and his minion, ending in the man's hasty departure. Abela was all business when he told Colin, "I need to speak with your sister. Please convince her of the *wisdom* of cooperating."

Lily's throat went dry at the obvious threat. If the piano wasn't against her back, she'd have run—no doubt with disastrous consequences.

Colin gave her a quick wink before nodding, "I believe my sister is simply unnerved by your sudden appearance in your official capacity. Perhaps some fresh air would be helpful after all."

Abela's eyes narrowed but he stepped aside as Colin unnecessarily took Lily's elbow to guide them into the courtyard. He ordered sweet teas all around and explained that Lily was still emotionally shaken and humiliated by Victor's betrayal—as well as dealing with her delicate condition. Then he unnecessarily repeated it to her in English.

She couldn't fight the blush at having two men openly discuss even an imaginary pregnancy. Abela misread it and spoke through Colin, "I will be discreet."

Though Abela's mouth had softened, his question was blunt. "Where is your husband?"

Colin translated the words slowly, giving her time to prepare her answer. Her eyes clear, she answered Colin honestly. "I have no idea." Then she turned an accusing glare at Abela. "I reported him missing, but neither the Havana police or the Spanish Guardia seemed interested."

Crocodile tears filled her eyes and Colin handed her a handkerchief. Sniffling appropriately and dabbing at her eyes, she held Colin's hand and avoided the Guardia's intense stare. "I'm so frightened. I didn't want to leave until he was…found…and…was using my musical training to exist until you, my dear brother, arrived."

A limp hand dropped to her lap as she faced the Lieutenant while still speaking to Colin. "I…don't understand why *he* is asking me where Victor is when I reported him missing."

A few more sniffles into the handkerchief and Abela's jaw relaxed.

Colin nodded and addressed Abela. "I think my sister deserves to know why she's being interrogated like a common criminal." Then he took a risk. "She doesn't know that Victor is wanted in the US for bigamy and fraud against several women. The news would devastate her. I think it would be better if you told her why Spain is looking for him."

Abela sipped his tea and shared that a filibuster boat leaving Ciego de Ávila had been seized with American weapons onboard. Under threat of execution, the captain had named Victor Champagne as the mastermind.

Abela and Lily both jumped when Colin slammed his fist on the mosaic tabletop. "Guns you say? The blackguard! He's a traitor. I'll see him hang."

With a concerned look at Lily, he apologized for his language and pulled her into a brotherly embrace, whispering, "Trust me."

He pulled away to touch her cheek tenderly, then turned to Abela. "As her brother, I should never have allowed her to see him, though I wouldn't have guessed the fop was a smuggler. I must confess, I'm curious. What kind of guns?"

"*Antigua fusiles.*" Abela answered. "*Doche* Springfields. *Treinta Años. Casi nuevo.*" Twelve thirty-year old Springfield rifles, like new.

Colin rushed in with a translation to cover Lily's, "Ooh, no," as she realized that besides a swindler and bigamist, she'd run away with a thief and smuggler. She wasn't acting when she pressed a hand to her racing heart.

"I'm suddenly feeling unwell," she said, dabbing Colin's handkerchief against her forehead and lips. "Perhaps it was the eggs I ate earlier today. I must go to my room." She stood and faced Colin. "Will you please convince the Lieutenant to let me go?"

He used her obvious discomfort to convince Abela she was an innocent dupe in Victor's scheme, assuring the officer he'd notify the authorities if Champagne returned. A long moment later, Abela rose, bowed stiffly to Lily and when Colin stood, shook his hand, whispering something in his ear before departing.

"What did he tell you?" Lily asked when Abela was gone.

He winked. "The good Lieutenant has entrusted your care to me. I am now your official guardian."

"What?" Her shout startled scavenging pigeons. "What do you mean *guardian*? I don't need a guardian." Her eyes narrowed "Why? Does he still suspect me of being an accomplice?"

He sat back down, ordering a Madeira for him and another tea for her. "You're a better actress than you think. If he thought you were involved, you'd be on your way to tour El Morro already. But we need to be careful."

The sudden softness in his voice drew her attention, though the creases in his forehead and tightness around his lips told her his mind was somewhere else. Somewhere painful. She covered his hand with hers, surprised at how natural the small gesture felt. "You think I'm really pregnant, don't you?"

"What?" He shook his head as if to clear it but didn't smile. "Are you?"

She almost put a hand on her stomach. When was her last period? A week after their arrival in Cuba. She'd barely been in Victor's company after that, and the last time he showed an interest in her, he passed out.

"No," she answered. "God wouldn't be that cruel." She raised a hand to the waiter, ordering a Madeira for herself before asking Colin, "Do you have any cigarettes?"

He should have been shocked that someone as gently reared as Lily O'Grady would ask for a smoke, but it seemed she was always surprising him. She was a warrior—an *amazona*, as the Cubans would say. She had a rebel soul, a steel spine, and was as stubborn as that bull in Regla. It was up to him to make sure she stayed alive.

He pulled a pack of Dukes' Best Turkish tobacco cigarettes from his breast pocket.

"Maybe there's some good news in this," she said after sharing his match, taking a deep draw, and exhaling with her eyes closed and a satisfied sigh. "Abela believes I'm not involved—which I most certainly am not. And Victor has his money for the guns. Maybe he was just jealous of you and now that the Guardia is after him, he'll leave me alone."

"Do you really believe that?" Colin answered, taking a long, second drag on his smoke. "The guns the Spanish captured were likely defective rejects from the rebels. Old guns like that, no matter where they were stored, misfire. His Mexican guns—the ones with smokeless powder and worth the big money—were seized a week ago when the filibuster's engine blew up trying to outrun a US Navy cutter. All he had left were the rest of the Springfields.

"Now, Victor is wanted by both the United States and the Spanish government for smuggling and selling US rifles to the Cuban rebels. You could say he's between the Devil and the deep blue sea. Perhaps quite literally."

He leaned toward her. "Abela said there were a dozen on the boat they found. Three hundred were stolen from the armory. He must have sold them already. But they won't net as much as the others. With two countries looking to hang him, he can't take a cruise ship off the island. And no smuggler is likely to risk transporting him—at any price."

"But why stalk me?" Lily asked. "He knows I don't have any money."

He crushed the stub of his smoke under the heel of his boot. "He's a desperate man, but your father is a wealthy US Congressman. A prime subject for ransom, which I'm sure Victor considered when he took the risk of duping a woman of childbearing age. He must have been facing a deadline then. And now he's running for his life."

He didn't tell her that most kidnapping victims didn't generally survive after the ransom was paid. For the time being, performing in a crowded hotel would make it difficult for Victor to find her alone. But she was prone to roam the streets for her stories, and he couldn't be with her all the time. Somehow, he had to flush the bastard out—without endangering Lily.

They finished their Madeira and smoked the last of the cigarettes until Lily exhaled into the soft sea breeze and sighed, "These are wonderful."

"You've done this before."

"Yes, but I had to roll my own at Langesford." She crushed the stub out with her heel and leaned toward him. "So, how are we going to find my errant husband? It's getting late and I'm performing new songs tonight."

Colin stared into sky-blue eyes with thick lashes a harlot would envy, set in a face as innocent as an angel, on a body a Greek sculptor could only imagine. "I think you should go home—to Georgia."

Her eyes widened and she shook her head. "Why? He's the criminal. I won't let him make me a prisoner."

Was she testing his patience or trying to wear down his resistance? "You don't seem to understand the danger you're in. You know how good he is at disguises. He could pose as anyone, including a member of the hotel staff, and even I could pick the new lock on your door. I need to find a safe place for you."

She stood, her face flushed with either anger or the effects of the wine and tobacco—or both. "Do I need to remind you that you are not really my guardian?"

Looking down at him, one hand on her hip, she leaned so close he could smell the earthy scent of the wine on her breath. "The last thing I need is *another* man telling me what to do. I'm perfectly capable of taking care of myself. Maybe I'll move to another room. On the ground floor...and..."

She opened the exotic tapestry bag. "...I have this."

He swallowed hard when she pointed a Ballard single-shot Rimfire Derringer at him. He rose slowly his arm extended. "Okay, I'm impressed, but you should understand that those things have a hair trigger. You're more likely to shoot yourself in the foot than someone attacking you."

Diverting her attention by looking over her shoulder, he took the gun from her and pulled her into his embrace to whisper into her ear, "Have you ever killed a human being?"

Breathing deeply of her jasmine-scented hair, he felt a slight tremor run through her when she shook her head and whispered, "No. but I will if I have to."

He ended the stalemate by stepping back, emptying the derringer's chamber, and placing the it on the table. "Your courage is commendable, but Victor is a predator. He'll do anything to stay alive, including killing you if he doesn't get what he wants."

He waved a hand at the impotent weapon. "You won't even have a chance to reach for this."

The sound of sea birds and a soft Southern breeze seemed incongruous as they both stared at the gun. But instead of reaching for it or sitting down with a case of the vapors, Lily stepped toward him, so close the heat from her body set his nerves tingling—until he felt the tip of a knife below the waist of his trousers.

"You're quick, Dr. Winfield, but that's not my only weapon. Willie once worked with a knife thrower and she taught me a few tricks."

He stepped back. "Impressive. But Victor won't likely give you a second chance. My sister is...was...a formidable woman. Tall, strong. A champion skeet shooter. She could even fence. But when she started to catch on to his scheme, Victor drugged her food to keep her docile until she signed all her assets over to him. The drugs left her mind permanently damaged and her body a withered shell. So, for now, I suggest you put both your weapons away and we go inside."

CHAPTER 13

*C*olin kept Lily's gun and Lily paced her room after they separated. Once again, he'd proven she wasn't as adept at taking care of herself as she liked to believe, and revealed that Victor, after running from the law since he was a child, was ruthless, amoral, and clinically insane. Still, quitting wasn't in her vocabulary.

She suspected it wasn't in Colin Winfield's nature either, but all she really knew about him was that he was a healer and a vengeful brother, with the social standing to be invited to the Captain-General's palace—and a distant relative of hers. At least he believed she had nothing to do with the guns, but with Victor in hiding, why was Colin still following her?

She took a deep breath and checked the time. Nine o'clock. The dining room would be full of people waiting for her to perform. She rubbed her throbbing temple and opened her door, wondering if Victor might be in the shadows, stalking her, planning to kidnap her and very likely kill her.

For all her doubts about Colin, the thought that he'd be in the audience comforted her. She paused at the second landing to gape at the standing-room only crush of bodies filling the lobby, the bar and dining room. Their attention was focused on the hotel's open front doors, as if waiting for something—or someone.

She finished her descent and pushed her way through the crowd to the front desk to ask Martin, "*Que paso*"

"Clara Barton," he answered. "*Ella esta viniendo.*"

Clara Barton? Coming here? Only two years ago, the famous heroine-nurse of the War Between the States, and the Franco-Prussian War, had helped forge a peace between the Ottoman government and the Armenian provinces in Turkey. As a child, Lily had dreamed of traveling the world like her, bringing peace and comfort. Then the dream changed to writing about wars instead of stopping them.

She'd heard rumors that Miss Barton had offered assistance from Red Cross to help Captain-General Blanco and the new autonomous government reduce the rising *reconcentrado* death tolls—especially among women and children. She wondered if he'd finally accepted. If so, she hoped the coincidental arrival of the battleship *Maine* wouldn't hamper Miss Barton's peaceful mission.

A sudden excited murmur in the crowded room sent her attention to the newly replaced glass doors as they swung open to admit a tiny old woman dressed in black, on the arm of—Colin Winfield. Her breath caught at the sight of her first female idol with the man who, only a short time ago, had taken her gun from her. She stayed at the desk, watching him lower his head to hear the diminutive woman speak.

The room fell into a hush and a path appeared to a table near the center of the room. Four well-dressed men, obviously prominent Havana business or civic leaders, treated her with a deference akin to Queen Victoria herself.

After seeing Miss Barton safely to her meeting, Colin approached Lily, his gaze fixed on her as if she was the only person in the room. His voice raised above the chatter, "You better get your pad. When the crowd thins, you'll only have a few minutes to interview Aunt Clara."

"Aunt Clara?"

The light touch of his finger on her chin closed her gaping mouth and brought her out of her shock. Would the mysteries surrounding Dr. Colin Winfield never end? "There's no need. I have an excellent memory. Did you say *Aunt* Clara?"

Affection for his aunt lit his eyes when he smiled. "She's my great-aunt. On my mother's side. And one of the reasons I went into medicine."

He mesmerized Lily with a list of her accomplishments during what he called the Civil War. Stories of the pain, suffering, lack of supplies and proper medical knowledge that killed as many—or more—soldiers on both sides of the conflict, as the battles. And how, though he was groomed to become a military officer, he'd bargained with his father to join the Army as a surgeon.

An hour later, "Colin, there you are," came from behind Lily. She started, then turned to face a diminutive woman, barely over five feet tall, with kind, dark brown eyes, not unlike her great-nephew's, and a mischievous smile that belied her seventy-seven years. She was accompanied by a young man with a neatly trimmed beard and crooked pince-nez glasses.

"Aren't you going to introduce me to this lovely young woman?" she asked Colin.

He flushed like a schoolboy and introduced her as Lily O'Grady. Miss Barton's eyebrows rose at the name, then she clasped Lily's hands, saying, "What a lovely young woman you are. Tell me, what brings you to this beautiful and tragic country?"

It was a simple question, but not easily answered. "She's a reporter," Colin offered. "For Joseph Pulitzer. She's been canvassing the survivors of the *reconcentrado* camps filtering in from Matanzas and Jaruco."

Lily gaped at how simple he made it sound and Miss Barton smiled at her. "A woman journalist. How fascinating…and exciting, I'm certain. We simply must talk."

"Of course, but not now," the man with Clara interjected. "It's been a very long day."

Miss Barton touched his arm and smiled up at him. "Please excuse my manners. This is my assistant, Mr. J. K. Elwell, a physician, and nephew of a dear friend of mine. His skills at organization, negotiation, and distribution are critical to the success of our mission." Her blue eyes sparked with affection when she said. "Without him I would be everywhere at once and get nothing done at all."

The journalist inside Lily blurted, "Is the Red Cross finally approved to help these poor people? Do you have President McKinley's authority to press for Captain-General Blanco's cooperation? Starvation and sickness are so widespread, how will you go about organizing it? I know it isn't the first time you've done this, but I'd love to hear the process. And will the arrival of the *Maine* complicate things?"

Miss Barton's kind smile never wavered at Lily's barrage of questions, but Colin's nudge brought her attention to the lines of fatigue around the older woman's eyes and the way she clung to Mr. Elwell's arm, as if drawing strength from him.

"I am so sorry," Lily gushed. "You must be exhausted from the voyage and the carriage ride from the harbor. But I'd be ever so grateful if you could find some time—later in the week perhaps—for a short interview."

Miss Barton raised a cautionary eyebrow at her overprotective assistant. "I'm never too tired to talk about our work, Miss O'Grady, but I have received news that the ship, *Vigilancia,* from the New York Committee, has recently arrived with fifty tons of supplies. We'll be off to the docks in the morning to oversee the unloading. If you care to join us, I'd be happy to answer your questions along the way."

She nodded toward Colin. "Unless you have other plans for her, of course."

No one, not even kings and emperors, refused Clara Barton. Unnerved that Colin had been included, Lily answered, "No, no, he...I...we...have no other plans."

Colin grinned at Lily like a schoolboy getting away with a prank. "Well, if you insist. I'll make the arrangements." He held his arm out to one of the most famous and powerful women in the world, leading her and her faithful assistant upstairs.

The next morning, Lily took copious notes during the drive through the ancient city. As always, the forbidding presence of Castle El Morro gave her chills, especially after her narrow escape from Lieutenant Abela. But there was little time to dwell on it as she tried to keep up with the tiny woman old enough to be her grandmother.

Clara moved quickly, overseeing the unloading of small boats called "lighters" as they moved back and forth between the dock and the freighter to unload the life-saving cargo. It was midday when they left with the wagons for the warehouse in San Jose. Once there, Clara toured the run-down old warehouses currently holding the sick and elderly *reconcentrados* who were unable to survive on the streets.

Colin pulled Lily aside at the first one. "Aunt Clara has been dealing with illness, death, and disasters for a half-century," he told her in the same warning tone he'd used about the bullfight. "She's tireless when it comes to this, but you can't have had more than a couple hours' sleep after last night's performance, and you have another one tonight. Are you sure you want to finish the tour? It won't be pretty."

How could he think her so shallow as to put a piano performance for wealthy tourists above Clara Barton's work with the Red Cross? Work that the wealthiest empires in the world seemed unable—or unwilling—to perform. As well-intentioned as his offer of an easy escape from reality was, her response was sharp. "Thank you for your deference to my sensibilities, but this is the reason I came here. I'll be fine." Then her voice softened. "How can they—Spain—abandon their own people like this?"

His jaw set. "Most native Cubans are descended from ancient Indian tribes or former slaves. It's common for a conquering nation to destroy or enslave the native population in order to supplant its own culture. It only took America three generations to accomplish it."

Anger darkened his warm brown eyes to nearly black. "You're from Georgia. Did the cruelty to former slaves end at Appomattox?"

His anger was misplaced. The fate of Native Americans and continued repression of the children of former slaves angered Lily as well. And she could add women to the list. "Slavery ended well before Appomattox with my family," she answered defensively. "My ancestors stopped buying and selling slaves while yours were still trading in them. And my grandfather was the first to provide decent living conditions and wages to his…workers. Their eventual freedom was guaranteed in his will and before Sumter, he offered many of them a chance to own a plot of land."

"Well good for him," he conceded grimly and changed the subject. "Come, Aunt Clara is ready to go to Los Fosos." He stopped a few paces from the open cab. "I'll ask again," he said, giving her a second chance to back out. "It won't be pretty. And once you see it, you'll never be the same."

Instead of answering, she pushed past him to climb in on her own.

As if sensing the tension between them, Clara said, "Colin darling, you and Lily mustn't feel obligated to accompany us. There are plenty of taxis available. We'll likely spend most of the day touring Los Fosos and the other shelters, then finish up at the warehouse. It may well be evening before we return."

Lily was surprised to see him grapple with the decision and recalled his opposition to her helping the poor in the alleys. He was a doctor. What was it about the *reconcentrados* that revolted him so? And how could he be so callous? Was that the chink in her knight's shining armor?

A long moment later, he sighed and met his aunt's worried gaze. "No, Auntie, it's been a long time. I'm happy to help—with the food."

Lily felt a moment's remorse at considering him another selfish member of the elite who preferred writing checks to dirtying their hands. Then she recognized her own hypocrisy. Langesford Plantation and Morning Bird Stables were among the most successful businesses in the state, and she'd wanted for nothing. When she moved to New York City, she saw the need in dozens of faces on the streets every day. And while she did what she thought she could, it grieved her that the need was so great. Colin had obviously been in the West. Had what he'd seen overwhelmed him to a point of surrendering both his calling and his compassion?

The sun was melting into a golden puddle across the bay when they returned to the Inglaterra. They'd been to the three warehouses, none of them more than rotting shacks serving as crude shelters to hundreds more than they could serve. Even Miss Barton was alarmed by the suffering and illness they found.

The contrast with the opulent and exclusive hotel was almost too startling for Lily to absorb when they returned to find it teeming with more people than the evening before. But this time it wasn't Havana dignitaries and American tourists. People living in the streets had heard about Clara Barton bringing supplies and money for food. Police were posted at the doors to keep them at bay.

Colin and Mr. Elwell parted the crowd for Lily and Miss Barton, and once inside, Lily marveled at the elderly woman's stamina. Like a general visiting the hospitals after a battle, she had smiled, visited, touched, and prayed with many patients who wouldn't live out the day. Deep lines from worry and fatigue on her face testified to the tragedies she'd seen in her lifetime when she told Lily, "This compares to the massacres in Armenia. It seems the world learned little from the experience. And the innocents pay the price."

Lily thought of Miss Barton's words as she stripped off clothes reeking of illness, death, and decay. She tried to scrub the experience away, but Colin was right. Nothing would erase the images of hollow-eyed, starving women holding the tiny bones of their dying babies to their empty breasts. And she would never be the same again.

She finally understood Colin's reticence. If he'd seen suffering like this before, it was no wonder he didn't speak of it. But while Miss Barton continued the fight around the world, he'd turned his back to it. Why? Overwhelmed by fatigue, grief, and horror, she lowered her head to her hands and cried until her ribs hurt. Then she rose to dress for her performance.

CHAPTER 14

*L*ily followed Clara Barton around like a puppy for the next four days, filling journal after journal, recording the woman's every move and hanging on every word she said. She'd watched in awe as Miss Barton lobbied for, and received, Captain-General Blanco's acceptance of the American food, then organized its distribution. Mr. Elwell even found a baker with one of the few ovens in Havana, and convinced him to turn their flour into bread.

Colin was nowhere to be seen, but Lily was too busy handing out food tickets to the hundreds of people lined up at the hotel's elegant entrance every morning, to ask. She ignored her exhaustion to entertain in the evenings, encouraging wealthy patrons to contribute to the Red Cross. The more patriotic sing-alongs she played, the faster the coins and bills flowed into her donation jar atop the piano. And since Pulitzer was paying her for her articles now, she could donate the proceeds.

She'd confessed her real identity in her first dispatch to Mr. Pulitzer about Miss Barton's mission and upcoming tour of Cuba's major cities. While not pleased with her deception, he told her to continue her daily reports detailing the famous humanitarian's efforts. He even increased her pay, though it was still less than a man's. And after more than a week without any more notes from Victor, she breathed easier.

On Saturday, the twelfth of February, she was with Clara and her new assistants at the San Jose warehouse when she finally broached the topic of Colin. "Your nephew," she began, "We haven't seen him in days. He seemed hesitant about visiting the hospitals at Las Fosos. I'm surprised since he's a physician."

The older woman looked up from her inventory ledger and sighed. "Colin is a complicated man. He has experienced horrors and personal grief beyond what any person should endure." She patted Lily's hand. "It makes me happy that he cares for you. You should ask him about it."

Surprised about the suggestion that there was a romantic interest between them, Lily, stammered, "No, no. It isn't like that. I'm so sorry to pry. I…just wondered where he is."

The older woman shrugged. "I see. Whatever he's about, I'm sure it's important. He'll show up when he's needed. He always does."

What did that mean? Lily returned to counting cans of milk until Miss Barton leaned back and rubbed her eyes. "Did I tell you Consul-General Lee has asked us to set up an orphanage?"

Lily recalled the forlorn glances from the sad, empty eyes of starving children in the warehouses. Children who couldn't stand on their bird-like legs while the mothers who tried to carry them collapsed on the way to collect their food. Some never rose again, leaving their dying babies orphans. At night, their faces flashed through her dreams. As horrifying as it was, she hoped she'd never become accustomed to the inhumanity. Now, she thrilled at the ray of hope an orphanage provided.

"That sounds wonderful. Where?"

Clara's world-weary eyes brightened with both hope and passion, giving Lily a glimpse of how, at seventy-four years-old, she'd convinced the Ottoman Emperor to allow—and protect—Red Cross humanitarian efforts in Armenia. She reached out for Lily's hand. "I have a favor to ask."

Without thinking, Lily answered, "Anything. What can I do?"

A mischievous smile softened the older woman's features. "Saying yes before knowing what I'm being asked to do, is a habit of mine as well. Perhaps you should hear me out before accepting the challenge." She took a deep breath. "Mr. Elwell will be quite consumed by adding the search for a location and staff, in addition to his current duties. I've seen how bright and efficient you are and would like to offer you a position as my assistant."

At Lily's prolonged silence, she added, "Of course, I'll try not to interfere with your career as a journalist, or musician. I'm very pleased with your news stories and the donations they've generated for the New York Committee. While I can't pay you much, when we find proper housing, it will include room and board—until the end of the crisis, of course."

Lily's silence was from shock, not compensation. Clara Barton was offering her a job—while allowing her to continue reporting about the Red Cross work for Pulitzer. She almost pinched herself to make sure she wasn't dreaming. Her mind raced, deciding she could limit her concerts to weekends and still raise money for the orphanage. Tears filled her eyes and her throat constricted with emotion. All she could do was nod.

When Miss Barton stood, Lily embraced her generous benefactor, noting that despite appearing as fragile as a bird, Clara Barton's iron will, and pure heart made her seem invincible.

"Ahem," came from the open warehouse doors. Lily wiped at happy tears when they both faced to a uniformed messenger from Consul-General Fitzhugh Lee. He gave Clara a formal bow, handing her an envelope bearing the seal of the US Government. She opened it with the tip of her pen and read it before looking at Lily. "It's an invitation to lunch tomorrow, aboard the *USS Maine* with Commander Sigsbee and Consul-General Lee.

The Sunday morning sun rose bright and warm, as always, accompanied by church bells calling rich and poor alike to the city's cathedrals to worship and give thanks. In old Havana City, people who by many standards had precious little reason to be thankful, dressed in white and filled the broad avenues and ancient cobblestone streets to worship their God.

Lily stood on her balcony and breathed deeply of the fresh ocean breeze before meeting Miss Barton and Mr. Elwell in the hotel lobby. It surprised her to see Colin with them. After only a week, he looked thinner, tired. His face was tanned, as if he'd been sailing or working a field. Since farming wasn't allowed outside the deep, wire-rimmed trenches General Weyler ordered dug around the cities, she assumed he'd been on or near the ocean. Perhaps he'd taken a ship back to Key West or Tampa. If so, why hadn't he told her?

"Colin, what a surprise," was met by a silent, sober nod and the grim set of his jaw in the company of his dear aunt worried her.

The arrival of Consul-General Lee's coach saved them from an awkward silence, and they boarded for the short trip to the harbor. It took longer than expected to thread their way through crowds that grew larger nearer their destination. All around them, Spanish Loyalists and Cuban Nationalists joined forces to carry signs and shout for the American warship to go home.

General Lee's guard escorted them to the pier to meet the admiral's launch. To Lily, the *Maine,* with its glittering white hull, enormous black stacks, and rows of massive guns mounted on steel turrets directed toward the city, seemed as frightful a monster as the brooding El Morro Castle. Like an impatient, tethered sea monster, the massive ship tested the buoys between the Spanish cruiser, *Alfonso II,* on one side, and the Ward liner, *The City of Washington,* on the other. Its sheer, lethal power, so blatantly on display inside a foreign country's harbor made her shiver under the warm sun.

"Murder from a distance," came from Colin, now standing beside her.

"What do you mean?" Lily asked, still focused on the massive ship.

"Modern warfare," he explained. "Bigger guns with longer range are thought to shorten wars by inflicting more casualties with less personal contact. More faulty logic to justify indiscriminate destruction in the never-ending pursuit of conquest."

She'd never heard his voice so foreboding, so...empty. "But you said yourself that this is only for show? Flexing America's muscles to prevent a war. Right or wrong, it seems to be working. The Spanish are being civil, and the German warships haven't been seen since it arrived."

"Yes, the Germans," he said as if the word left a bad taste in his mouth. "Hopefully we can leave that war to another generation."

The arrival of Sigsbee's launch cut off her questions and a sailor wearing a smart navy-blue uniform held out his hand to help them aboard. Fifteen minutes later, after the launch was hoisted up to deck level of the *USS Maine.* Captain Sigsbee, slender and elegant in his full-dress uniform and a neatly trimmed handlebar mustache, greeted them most cordially. With his tiny round spectacles, he looked more like a college professor than the commander of a warship, when he thanked Miss Barton for her heroic services to her country and led the party of eight on a tour of the impressive weapon of destruction.

After the tour, they enjoyed a delicious meal on deck with polished tables, fine china, and crystal glassware. Colin ate little and spoke less, while Lily picked at her food, imagining the carnage the ship could inflict on the already critically injured island. She forced herself to applaud with the others after the band played, but couldn't bring herself to cheer when the crew demonstrated a gun drill for their benefit. She noticed that Colin also refrained from applauding the demonstration of the human power to destroy civilizations.

≈

Two days later, Colin offered to share a cab with Lily to the hospital in Los Fosos. They stepped from the hotel to find streets that had echoed with the cries of angry citizens a short time ago, were now filled with music, laughter and people dressed in exotic costumes and masks, dancing and singing their way along the Paseo del Prado.

"It's the beginning of Carnival," Colin explained, and she marveled at the resiliency of the human spirit amidst poverty, oppression, and never-ending war.

"I thought Carnival was banned years ago."

A young woman danced by them, the bright colors of her twirling skirt shimmering like a rainbow, beads dancing over her peasant blouse glinting like stars in the sunlight. Two boys followed her with brightly colored maracas. A third kept the beat on two small drums slung over his shoulders. The rhythm again reminded her of the music the workers on Langesford played in their little village near the ruins of the former slave quarters. And again, it spoke to her. She tapped her feet, longing to join them.

Colin smiled and tapped his own foot. "Some rules are impossible to enforce."

The scent of the woman's Jasmine perfume lingered, tempting Lily to follow the laughter and music down the wide avenue.

"Will you join me this evening?" startled her and she turned to find that Colin had stepped up close, smelling of salt air and sunshine, his dark eyes warm and gentle, drawing her in.

"To what?"

"Carnival, of course."

Oh yes. Carnival. Someone bumped her, sending her into the safe enclosure of his arms. Her cheek rested a moment too long against his chest and when she looked up at his mischievous smile, she said, "Yes."

She took longer to fix her hair than normal, smoothing the folds of her burgundy silk dress too many times. The sounds of revelry had increased, echoing down the avenue, and the now-familiar beat of bongos, maracas, singing and laughter beckoned. She felt guilty for enjoying herself while surrounded by so much misery but could barely remember when she'd last laughed—really laughed. The vanity mirror showed that while in the dim lamplight, her skin remained smooth, unmarred by age and worry, up close, the suffering she'd seen lingered in the faint shadows beneath her eyes and tiny lines alongside her mouth. Colin was right. She'd never be the same.

She pulled away, telling herself that tonight was for laughing. For dancing. Even the poor who lived in Havana's alleys, ran in the streets, banging sticks on broken pottery, singing and smiling with toothless grins beneath masks fashioned from discarded items. She glanced at her grandmother's pendant watch. Eight o'clock. Colin would be waiting.

He smiled from the bottom of the staircase, looking relaxed, if not carefree. She returned his smile when he held out a delicate, black lace mask shaped like a cat's face and mounted on the end of a sequin-studded wand. Puzzled for a moment, she noticed that most everyone in the lobby also carried or wore masks.

"It's lovely," she said raising it to her eyes. The feeling of anonymity was strangely exhilarating, beyond anything she'd felt on the stage. "Where is yours?"

His smile faded. "My whole life has been a masquerade." He held out his hand. "We best hurry. The Scovels and George Rae are meeting us at the café by Parque Central."

"*The* George Bronson Rae? The infamous propagandist who continues to deny the realities of atrocities in the *reconcentrado* camps?" While she was thrilled to see Frances after her return from Washington, and she hadn't seen Harry since he recovered from his bout of malaria, she had to ask, "How can Harry even manage being in the same room with that man?"

Colin chuckled. "Journalism, like politics, is a business. In both cases, it's wise to keep your friends close, and wiser still to keep your enemies closer. And Rae isn't all bad. Sadly, like so many deluded people, he believes what he wants to believe. The problem is that if enough people believe *him*, it could prove disastrous. That's why your stories are so important."

The weight of the printed word suddenly gripped her, followed by doubt in her ability to fight those who fought so hard to hide the truth; as well as the consequences of bringing it to the front. "But what if, truthful as it is, what I write encourages a war?"

He squeezed her hand. "A great many people already want this war—for a lot of reasons—politically, socially, and most of all, economically. Unfortunately, it's Spain, not you, that's handing it to them on a silver platter."

"You seem to know a lot about politics," she fished, hoping his good humor would loosen his tongue about his shadowed past.

They stepped outside and he waved a cab away to walk the short distance to the café. "Like you, I come from a political family," told her what she already knew. "My choice of medicine over a career in the military and… other things, will forever be a bone of contention for them."

The sadness in his voice tugged at Lily's heart and the sounds of music, dancing, and traffic noise faded into the background as she became lost in the pain shimmering in his dark eyes. She couldn't probe for more. Then he brightened. "Ah, here we are."

He raised a hand to the trio of Harry, Frances, and George, already seated at a table facing Parque Central. The humid evening air was still, with light clouds obscuring all but the brightest stars. Lanterns were already lit, and luminaries lined the curbs, creating a glittering path for people to dance and sing.

Lily embraced Frances, knowing better than to ask about the contents of the dispatch she'd carried to President McKinley—or the response she'd likely brought back. They ordered drinks while Harry tried to convince George Rae of the error of his ways. The discussion was heating up when their crystal wineglasses began to tremble.

"Get down!" Colin shouted.

He threw an arm around Lily and pulled her under the table, while Harry did the same with Frances mere seconds before the windows exploded, raining thousands of knife-sharp glass chards into the café. Outside, revelers ducked under tables, carriages, and into filthy alleys to escape the raging glass storm.

All the electric lights in the city went out, followed by a stunned silence as heads cautiously rose above their cover to see what an eerie halo of white surrounding the battleship *Maine*. What seemed barely a heartbeat later, a violent yellow glow rose from the sea as the ammunition aboard the ship exploded.

"Stay here," all three men ordered Frances and Lily, but they refused to be left behind, gathering their skirts to follow the three men into a cab for the harbor. Hundreds of people were already there, silent and spellbound and helpless as the ship consumed itself.

Rae convinced the Guardia that he and Colin were officers from the ship and reached the end of the dock in time to see the fires amidships. The towering smokestacks were already gone, the bow an unrecognizable tangle of twisted steel. It was an unforgettable image of red flames dancing on the surface of the bay amid exploding six-pound shells until, like the bull at Regla, it slowly conceded to death and settled on its side.

Lifeboats and lighters from the *City of Washington* and the *Alfonso II* circled the mangled, smoking wreck. Like small birds following a hawk, yachts, fishing lorries and pleasure boats, followed; their pilots using screams and smoke from burned bodies as beacons to search for survivors in the water. The Chief of Police commandeered a rowboat and signaled for Harry, Rae, and Colin to help him row out to the carnage.

Lily and Frances became separated amid the confusion and horror as bodies and pieces of bodies from the dead ship floated to shore. Lily turned in tight circles to maintain her place in the pushing, shoving crowd, calling, "Frances," over and over.

With no luck distinguishing Frances' response from the surrounding chaos, she stepped toward the dock. Something tugged her skirt, but before she could turn, an arm grasped her around the waist and a hand covered her mouth.

"Alone at last," growled into her ear. "Fight me and I'll break your neck in one quick twist."

Victor! She'd looked everywhere for him, but again, he'd found her first. He stuffed a sickly-sweet smelling cloth over her nose and into her mouth. She gagged until darkness replaced the billowing smoke and ash in front of her eyes and the world went silent.

CHAPTER 15

*R*ae stayed with the rescuers and Harry rushed off to cable New York while Colin promised to collect Frances and Lily. When he returned to where they'd separated, both women were gone. The only evidence they'd been there was Lily's black lace mask waving like a distress signal between planks on the wharf.

He shouted her name until he was hoarse, but his voice was lost in the wails of the horrified crowd as bodies of sailors floated to shore like so many dead fish, their gray, lifeless eyes already bulging. But they weren't fish. They were the crew of an American war vessel peacefully moored in Havana's harbor.

Colin froze as images of another tragedy haunted him. Lodge poles steaming in the cold winter air, black smoke, the charred bodies of women, children, and old men of the defeated Sioux tribe at Wounded Knee, South Dakota. But these were white men. Members of an emerging nation's military force. No matter who, or what, caused this explosion, Spain would be punished—but Cuba would suffer.

He held Lily's mask, turning circles on the dock to scan the few remaining tear-stained faces of furloughed American seamen trying to understand the senseless deaths of their comrades.

"Colin! There you are," came from a female voice behind him that was too shrill to be Lily's. He turned as Frances Scovel fell into his arms. "Where is Harry?"

Her terrified eyes reflected torches from the rescue boats bobbing up and down in the dark, oil-slicked water. He held her tight, saying, "Harry is fine," over and over until she calmed. "He's gone to submit the story. He said to tell you he'd find you back at the Inglaterra."

She pulled away, a tiny smile curving her still trembling lips. She wiped her face with a sooty sleeve and forced a weak smile. "Of course, he did. He knows I can take care of myself."

So like Lily, Colin thought. And maybe it was true for Frances, but Frances wasn't being hunted by Victor Champagne.

Once back in control of her emotions, Frances took Colin's free hand. "I can't find Lily. We were standing right here. I left her for just a minute to get closer to the rescue boats. When I returned, she was gone. I've been looking everywhere." Tears again filled her eyes and she stomped her foot. "She wouldn't have left without us. Something happened to her. There was so much screaming and confusion, I wouldn't have heard if she called out for me. But I swear I was only gone a—well—a few, minutes."

She looked at Colin's free hand. "What is that? Is that Lily's mask?" Panic again set her to trembling. "So, it's true. Someone took her."

"Yes," he choked. "And I know who."

She surprised him by saying, "Victor? Lily didn't talk about him much, but his absence has been conspicuous. And I could tell she was afraid of him."

Apparently the two women were closer than Colin thought. "What did she tell you about him?"

Frances took a deep breath and coughed as smoke and smoldering embers from the *Maine* settled around them. "I know he's a charlatan who married her to get her trust fund, thinking she'd already reached her majority."

"Anything else?"

Frances tipped her head as if gauging his motives. "Only that he's a cad of the first degree. When I was in Washington, I caught up with your cousin, Ambrose. Since he lost the last election, he's been a lobbyist. And you know what gossips they are."

She patted Colin's arm. "Your poor sister. Don't worry, your secret is safe with me."

Her eyes narrowed and she cocked her head. "He said you were following the man who swindled her. Is it Victor? Is that why you're here? To bring him to justice and save the family name?" Her voice turned sly. "Or is there something more?"

Colin sighed and ran his fingers through his hair. He noted the harbor was nearly cleared of bystanders. After a half hour with no call of survivors, the crowd had followed the ambulances to nearby San Ambrosio Hospital. The few remaining, exhausted rescuers were charged with the grisly task of sorting the remains of the dead sailors, many of whom would never be identified.

"They seem to have this under control," he barked at Frances. "I have to find Lily. Can you get back to the Inglaterra without me?"

She nodded. "I knew it. You're in love with her. I told Harry, but he put me off. Said all you cared about was medicine. We both wondered why you were even here. When your Aunt Clara arrived, we assumed you were the advance guard for the Red Cross. But Ambrose said you'd left the Army and had given up medicine. You are quite the mystery, you know."

"No, I'm an open book," he countered, trying to sound glib. "As you said, I'm here to help. And Lily needs help—now. How long since you last saw her?"

"Not long. Counting this conversation, maybe twenty minutes."

Long enough to disappear in the clog of traffic and pedestrians on most of Havana's streets, he thought. But she wouldn't have gone willingly.

"Colin, look!" Frances shouted, pointing to a white handkerchief stuck on a nearby piling.

He plucked it off the exposed spike. Squinting in the fading light of dying torches, he saw the initials "VC" embroidered in one corner. To Frances' disgust, he held it up to his nose. Chloroform. The sequined handle of the mask snapped in his hand. *I led her right into his hands.*

Frances reached for it. "What is it? Is it Lily's?"

He stuffed the handkerchief into his pocket. "No, it isn't," he said trying to keep his voice steady. "On second thought, I'll take you back to the hotel."

They took a cab as far as they could through the congested streets, then sidestepped shards of glass the size of small windows, overturned furniture, and wounded people. Here and there, he saw his great-aunt's artistry with a bandage. She'd been in her room when he left with Lily and had no doubt rushed to help after the explosion. By now, she was probably at St. Ambrose Hospital.

Inside the Inglaterra, waiters again mopped up spilled liquor from the bar shelves, while the concierge swept broken glass amid toppled furniture. Irritated at the interruption, he didn't question when Colin asked for the key to Lily Champagne's room.

Like most of the rooms facing the harbor, the French doors to the balcony were blown out, but the rest of the room was intact. He had no idea what he expected to find, but Victor may have left something behind. Something that would tell him where he took her.

He slowly walked the length and breadth of the small room, feeling like a voyeur. He avoided touching Lily's personal things but couldn't escape the lingering scent of lily of the valley sachet still clinging to her clothes. The note from Regla was under a glass inkwell and he read it again, suppressing a shudder. Victor was a monster.

The wardrobe was free of any sign of his presence and Colin knelt to peer under the bed. It was clear, save for a small, battered wooden footlocker. He slid it out. *Locked.*

"Damn him to Hell." He kicked it hard on the rusted latch, breaking it off, then squatted to open it. It turned out to be a treasure chest full of souvenirs of Victor's various conquests. Photos of his victims, wedding certificates, even a couple of obituaries detailing the suicides of two of his victims. Grim testimony to both Victor's power over women and their desperation at being abandoned. But nothing to suggest why he chose Lily or where he'd taken her.

Frustrated, he kicked the side of the locker this time, regretting it when pain shot up through the toe of his soft leather shoe. Cursing, he felt better knowing he'd caused some damage. The old wood panel on the side had fallen off, revealing a hollow spot between the outside and inside walls.

On his knees again, he pulled out a leather-bound portfolio to find a cache of incriminating evidence dating back to Victor's father's time at the Springfield Armory: plans and timetables, charts of the tides and maps of the South Carolina and Georgia coastlines, confirmed the suspected hiding place. He almost chuckled at the sight of the proverbial "X" marking remote location in the marshy wilderness between St. Mary's Georgia and Jacksonville, Florida. But there was nothing in the portfolio to indicate

Victor's buyers or his contacts with the Cuban liberation organization in Ybor City and Havana. Another dead end.

Furious, he ripped the lining out of the footlocker, gaining splinter and paper cuts for his trouble—until at the bottom, under several layers of floral paper, he found it. A map of Cuba with another X in a deserted area on the Eastern coast of the island, near Sancti Spiritus. It was rumored to be one of many camps used by the rebel army of free blacks, mulattos, native Indians, and outlaws now comprising General Máximo Gómez' Army.

It was roughly a two-day ride from Havana. Was that where Richard had been hiding all this time? Leaning against the bedframe in the middle of a room littered with the memorabilia of a lunatic, he wondered how much the rebels had paid for the thirty-year-old guns. Certainly not enough to provide the lifestyle Victor craved. And it was likely he owed money to his Mexican suppliers, who were more dangerous than the US and Spanish governments combined. Without the money to cover what was seized from the filibuster, Victor was a dead man.

And without Lily's trust fund, he had to improvise. Colin's theory about ransoming Lily now made even more sense. He knew only too well that a child's life was worth any price. And while her parents were traveling, her brother Clay likely knew how to contact them.

After seeing the mementoes Victor kept of nearly a dozen intelligent, wealthy women he'd robbed of thousands of dollars, it was clear that both he and Theodore Roosevelt had underestimated the man. It couldn't happen again. Lily had nearly died in Tampa. She may not be so lucky this time.

Stuffing all the documents into the portfolio to take with him, he shoved the footlocker back under the bed. He needed to find Harry Scovel. Despite George Bronson Rae's *braggadocio*, and Richard Harding-Davis' penchant for reporting fiction, no American knew Gómez and the rebel territory better than Harry.

CHAPTER 16

*L*ily woke up vomiting. She'd dreamed of being tied to a horse. Of a burning sun rising and setting, of her blindfolded body obeying orders while moving slowly, painfully through a tangle of roots, thorns, and branches. Sometimes she was mounted behind a man's body, but every time the fog in her mind started to clear, another sickly-sweet-smelling rag was pressed over her face.

This time was different. She was still surrounded by darkness, but the blindfold was gone. And though she felt as if she didn't own her body, she was on solid ground. Her ribs hurt as if she'd been kicked by a horse—or a boot—or both, and her mind was full of random images she couldn't trust as memories.

She took shallow breaths, counting slowly in her mind, *one thousand one, one thousand two...* until her head cleared enough to put together images of what had happened to her. It was Carnival, she remembered. Images of burned, mutilated bodies floating in the ocean foam became all too clear. Yes, the battleship *Maine* had blown up. She was with Colin and Frances. Then they disappeared and Victor grabbed her from behind. She remembered the noxious rag covering her mouth. Chloroform, she suspected. But how long ago? And where was she now?

Realizing she was untethered, she painfully moved her stiff limbs, beginning with her arms, to rise to her knees and feel her way through the darkness on all fours. The packed dirt floor was covered by a straw mat smelling of mold and damp sand as she measured the distance by the length of her arm. Three lengths away, she touched what felt like a wall of the sticks woven with palm fronds. Raising a head that felt heavy as an anvil to a tiny circle of light piercing the reed wall, she heard muffled voices in the distance.

Afraid to call for help from what may be her captors, the darkness in her mind called for her to come back, offering an end to her pain and a shield from the menace lurking behind outside. She ignored it. Pain meant she was alive. She anchored her fingers in the woven reeds, testing the leaden stumps her legs had become, and tried to stand. Biting her lips against the pain of each movement, she forced herself to her feet and leaned against the wall of her jungle prison. The tattered Carnival dress and petticoat hampered her progress as she stumbled along the curve of the hut to an opening.

Each halting step both terrified and strengthened her. The numbness in her once-shackled hands and hobbled ankles eased with the movement and her mind cleared. Ten tiny, stumbling steps later, she clung to the edge of a low opening to peer at small fire in a clearing. Beyond that lay a dense black void she'd never imagined. It smelled like the jungle surrounding Tampa but more intense and alive with noises she couldn't identify. It was as if the darkness itself was a creature stalking her—it's breath sour, musky, hot on her face.

She closed her eyes against the dizzying effects of the chloroform and realized a more frightening reality. It could be only one place. The untamed wilderness of Cuba. But where? The Eastern portion of Cuba was virtually under control of the *Mambises*, former slaves and people of mixed races, who had been fighting Spain for decades. She could be anywhere from Matanzas to Cienfuegos, or even Santiago de Cuba on the Southeastern shore. And if he'd taken her West, they could be in the wilderness of Pinar del Rio. A no-man's land of abandoned plantations and tiny villages, where most of the peasants and farmers had been herded into prison camps, their crops and homes burned to starve out the rebel forces.

A hot breeze carried the voices of the men around the campfire, and she recognized the dialect. *Mambises!* She took a deep breath, weighing their reputation by the Spanish as bloodthirsty savages, against the peasants' version of rugged heroes surviving in conditions no civilized person could imagine. A chill replaced the sweat drenching her body beneath the tattered satin gown and her skin itched from insect bites. Even her hair seemed to move of its own accord. But at least she was alone.

Was this Victor's punishment for confronting him? Was he selling her as a slave to the rebels? She watched the shadows of a dozen or more men clustered around the low fire. A few more were barely visible around the perimeter. Sentries, she surmised, and risked poking her head outside to better hear what they were saying.

They spoke in a crude mix of Spanish and native dialects, but she didn't have to understand all the words to recognize an argument in progress. From the oft-repeated word, "*gringa*," she assumed it was about her.

Instinct pulled her head back into the hut when she heard Victor's voice. Sharp against their soft patois, it startled the birds, but she couldn't follow his halting, mangled Spanish. She peeked out again and saw him stand, a tall, thin specter against the dancing flames, his arms flailing. Laughter followed him as he stomped in her direction.

She scrambled back to her pallet with an agility that surprised her and pretended to be asleep until he kicked her in the side. "Wake up, slut."

She moaned and forced herself to loll her head slowly in his direction. Then, as if only beginning to feel the diminishing effects of the chloroform, raised to lean on her forearms.

"Victor, why?" she croaked with a swollen tongue and cracked lips, until a dry heave left her gagging.

He grunted in disgust and pulled her up by the hair. "Why?" He spit at her face. "Because you ruined my one chance to finally get the life I deserve. I had a fortune in my hands, but you ruined everything."

Her mind screamed with the pain of literally hanging by her own hair, but she could only manage to groan. "I don't know…"

"No, bitch, you *didn't* know anything, but now you know too much." As quickly as he'd grabbed her, he let her go. Her head hit the rock-hard ground beneath her mat, and she closed her eyes against the white lights flashing behind her eyelids to hear her fate.

"But you can yet redeem yourself, my little Southern flower," Victor purred. "All you have to do is shut up and do as you're told—when I tell you to do it."

"But—" The flat of his hand again cut her off, and she again refused to cry out.

He squatted close, the smell of rum and sour stink of sweat from the once fastidious actor's body turned her empty stomach. "So, I see I have your attention. Now, here is what you are going to do," he began.

He stopped at the sound of approaching horses cutting through the thick jungle foliage. Then a shout rang out from the direction of the fire, followed by cheers.

"Don't move," he ordered and left the hut.

Lily again crawled to the opening, pulling her tangled mass of hair back from her eyes. The men around the fire rose at the riders' approach, then lowered their guns and cheered. With so many voices and dialects, she couldn't make out their words, but understood that someone of importance had arrived.

He dismounted just outside the fire, his back a silhouette as he faced the men. Standing next to his horse, he seemed slight in stature and wore the same clothing as the others—light homespun breeches, loose shirt, a bandana around his neck, and a woven peasant hat, but his bearing made him seem larger than life. While she couldn't hear his deep, low voice, she saw that everyone, including Victor, leaned toward him, hanging on his every word. A short time later, the campfire was banked, and the men retired, some to huts like hers, others to curl up on mats, covering their faces with wide-brimmed hats to shield them from insects. Fortunately, Victor never returned to her.

The night seemed endless until a lazy ray of sunlight poked tiny fingers through the loosely woven walls of her hut. She groaned and her empty stomach turned again, but this time, a few deep breaths controlled the convulsions. She opened her eyes to see Victor staring back at her.

"Get up. You have work to do."

She rubbed her eyes with hands that felt like sandpaper, feeling every bruise where he'd kicked and dragged her to this desolate jungle camp. She struggled to her feet. "Please," she pleaded, "I need a drink and to...to... relieve myself."

He blocked her way to the fresh, clean air of a new morning and nodded toward a stinking corner of the hut. Something snapped inside her at being denied the privacy to perform one of the most basic of human needs. A feral scream rose from her parched throat, followed by obscenities she wasn't aware she knew, as she kicked her surprised captor where it hurt the most.

She took the split second of his surprise to run toward the light, not caring if she met a bullet on the other side. She was almost to the woods when another arm wrapped around her waist, pulling her against rock-hard chest. "*Detener.*"

She understood the word, but it was the authoritative tone that made her stop. Seconds later, Victor stumbled out of their hut, sliding in the wet, sandy ground, Dangling inches above the ground from the man's grip around her waist, and facing Victor, Lily prepared to die, said, "General, sir. My apologies for the commotion. It seems my wife is displeased with the accommodations."

She struggled to take a breath. "No! I am not your wife, you monster! You kidnapped me!"

Waving arms covered with new and old bruises in all shades of the rainbow, she used what was left of the air in her lungs to hiss. "And you *beat* me while…"

"You bitch," Victor howled and lunged at her. She closed her eyes against the fist aimed at her face, but the blow never came. When she opened them, he was sprawled face down on the ground, arms behind his back, a large, very fierce *mambisa* sitting on him, a huge grin splitting his scarred face.

Her captor's grip loosened, and she was slowly lowered to stand alone. Swaying on her feet, she pushed back her filthy hair to face the one man that all of Cuba—and America—depended upon to free the island from Spanish domination.

General Máximo Gómez was taller close-up than he'd looked standing by his handsome Andalusian stallion. In his 70s, like Miss Barton, he looked ageless, but unlike her he also seemed fierce. Without an extra pound on his lean frame, he could have been forged from refined steel. His handlebar mustache was white against a face darkened by the fierce Caribbean sun, and his gray hair was thinning, but she remembered those turquoise eyes. She raised a hand to her pounding heart.

"Uncle Max?" was little more than a whisper, then she shouted, "It's me, Lily. Lily O'Grady."

Her breath came in short bursts. Perhaps there was a God after all. "My father is Patrick O'Grady. You came to Langesford when I was a child…to buy horses." He had a full head of dark hair then, and a dark mustache to match. She only knew him as Uncle Max. *Was he a soldier even then?*

His silent, penetrating glare kept her talking. "You taught me how to ride *a la gineta.* I wanted to learn *Doma Vaquera* but the pole was too long for me."

She ran out of breath and he stepped back, examining her in the early morning light. "*Ángel?* How can this be?" He turned to his men, saying in Spanish, "*Ella es una amazona con la voz de ángel.*"

Victor ignored the reference to the legendary female warriors, catching only the word for angel. "Yes, her voice is heavenly," he chattered. "She is very valuable. I am willing to sell."

Lily froze. How could Victor sell her like a slave to an Army? General Gómez' grip on her arm was the only thing that kept her from lunging at him, broken fingernails her only weapon. Looking back at the general, she pleaded, "Please, keep him away from me."

He told one of his men to tie Victor up in the hut, but when they turned, he was gone. "Leave him," Gómez ordered. "He is a fancy gringo, unarmed, with no food or water. Let the sand crabs and scorpions dine on him."

"Go to my tent," he told Lily. "You can wash, and my *medico* will see to your wounds. We will speak after."

"*Gracias,*" she said and cast a wary glance at the thick foliage shielding Victor. She felt him watching. He'd always be watching—until one of them was dead.

CHAPTER 17

*C*olin boarded the ferry to cross the harbor before dawn and catch the first train for Matanzas. He hoped the rebels he supported politically and morally had been considerate enough to refrain from blowing up more miles of track along the way. Even then, he had no idea how long it would take to reach the rebels' last-known camp near Cienfuegos. The fact that they were nearly impossible to locate was the key to their survival.

He chafed as the train stopped at nearly every village along the way. Victor was already more than twelve hours ahead of him and could have taken Lily virtually anywhere, including back to Florida, though he doubted it. Victor was already a wanted man there, and Colin had wired the Roosevelt the information from the footlocker. Likely the Wanted posters were already up in Key West, Tampa and the rest of the Florida coast. According to Scovel, Gómez was near Cienfuegos, halfway between Havana and rebel-controlled Eastern Cuba. His only hope was in how much Lily would have slowed Victor down.

Unfortunately, the rebels' latest raid on ten miles of track between Havana and Matanzas slowed his train to a crawl. It was early evening when he finally arrived in the city whose population had swelled to over fifty thousand, with refugees from Weyler's camps. While delaying his search until morning would be costly, tracking at night in the jungle could be deadly. He found a room and inquired about a guide to take him to Cienfuegos. Even riding hard, the hundred and forty-mile trip would likely take more than two days, but Colin was cavalry. He'd take an extra horse—two if he had to. Anything to avoid endless delays on the rails along Weyler's eight-foot deep *trochas*.

Too restless to sleep, he visited the hospitals, claiming to be a member of the Red Cross. He spent the evening and much of the night checking wounds and helping feed children too weak to feed themselves, until he fell onto a cot for a few hours of restless sleep haunted by visions of other hospitals, other wounds, and other dark-eyed, starving children.

In the morning, he searched out Scovel's contact, securing four horses and gear, then met a guide named Raphael Diaz at the livery. Diaz, a wizened old mulatto with matted gray-streaked hair, greeted him with a gap-toothed grin. Using Scovel again as a reference, Colin told him he was tracking a woman who had been kidnapped, offering him the going rate for a guide.

Raphael nodded enthusiastically and smiled. "No."

He assumed the old guide was afraid of meeting the much-feared rebels and was prepared to double his price if he had to. Instead, the scrawny man winked and fingered a scar along his left cheek, answering in broken English, "*Mambises* do not take women. And they move every day."

"We'll see," Colin answered. He dropped a few pesos into the man's dirty hand. "Where are they today?"

The man studied him through squinted eyes, then shrugged and counted his money. "Santa Clara. Two days on horseback."

As much as Colin wanted to saddle the horses and follow Raphael immediately, he wasn't stupid. In a world where there is no possibility of gainful employment, little food, and no money, scruples are hard to hold. And for every member of the resistance, there were three bandits. "You wouldn't know that unless you were one of them. What are you doing here?"

The old man's smile turned into a grimace. "My family. I hear they are here."

Colin's heart sank at the reminder of the human race's capability for cruelty. He thought of the people in the hospital, little more than breathing skeletons without even a bed to die on. Women, children, and the elderly suffered the most. "Did you find them?"

Tears pooled in Raphael's dark eyes. "No. My Maria and Pedro are with God now. They died for a free Cuba. I must go home now."

Colin recognized the special way a soldier says 'home'—as if it's a holy place. The place where remembered families live in peace and love. It was a fairy tale of course, but it had kept them going through the worst times. He gambled that while Raphael could easily lead him to a swamp or away from Gómez—he could take care of himself against a crippled, grieving old man. And traveling one day in the wrong direction beat four days based on old information. He'd ride behind Raphael, keeping his gun and knife, ready.

"Get me to Santa Clara in less than forty-eight hours and I'll pay you double," he said.

The old man bobbed his head, repeating, "*Si, Si.* I get you there pronto, *jefe.*" He frowned at Colin's white suit and spit-shined boots. "When we go?"

Colin picked up his old haversack, canteen, and bedroll, along with the battered medical bag. "Now. The horses are ready with all the gear we need."

Near dusk, he and Raphael kneeled beside a cold campfire set away from a small hut and a trampled plot showing fresh tent poles. Someone had camped there recently, but was it Gómez? And were Victor and Lily with them? He stepped toward the hut, stopping when Raphael's hand caught him. "Wait!"

"Why?"

The toothless grin reappeared. "Scorpions. They like the dark places."

Like Victor Champagne, Colin thought. Dark places and unsuspecting victims. He'd also met more than a few real scorpions and heeded Raphael's warning. "Well, I need to check it out. What do I need?"

The old man grinned and said, "Cinnamon."

"I don't have time to waste," Colin snapped and picked up a torch. "I'll burn the damn thing down, along with half the jungle if it means finding Lily…"

He stopped short at the look of understanding on Raphael's face when he removed his poncho, spreading it open on the ground. Tins, leather pouches, along with various lethal-looking knives were strapped inside. Sorting through them carefully, he pulled out a small snakeskin bag and tossed it to Colin. "Light the torch to set them moving and sprinkle the cinnamon ahead of you. But be quick. If they like a place, they fight back."

Not knowing if the old man was playing with him, Colin accepted that if he carried the cinnamon, there must be some basis to it. Opening his own kit with fresh, dry matches, he lit the torch, held it out in front of him, and bent low to enter, prepared to sprinkle the spice at any moment. But it wasn't the scurry of hideous, prehistoric spiders with claws that greeted him. It was the stench. Vomit. Lots of it. And dark stains of what could only be blood on the filthy grass matting. Holding onto the hope that it wasn't Lily's, he moved farther inside, toward a tattered, insect-infested mat on the floor. He bent when his light caught the edge of something white. Stooping low, he used a stick to raise a small linen handkerchief with tiny lilies of the valley embroidered along a torn edge.

"Son of a bitch!" sent jungle birds to flight. Raising the torch dangerously close to the low ceiling, he swore, "I'll cut you apart one limb at a time and feed you to the pigs."

Raphael's fingers circled his wrist, stopping him from tearing the hut apart and setting the jungle afire. "Who is she?"

Colin's arm went limp and he followed the old man back toward the sunlight. "A friend," he answered, knowing she'd become much more than that to him. Folding the handkerchief into his pocket, he took a deep breath. "What now?'"

Raphael had already given the tired horses food and water and laid his bedroll out on a mat of leaves under a spreading magnolia tree. He pulled a bag of dried beans and crusty bread from yet another pocket in his poncho. "We eat. And sleep."

Colin hadn't given a thought to his own hunger—or fatigue—until then. He nodded and opened his own canned rations. Handing his collapsible frying pan to Raphael, he gathered dry branches from beneath the tree to start a small fire.

"No!" Raphael shouted as Colin lit a match. He dropped it and Raphael crushed the ignited leaves with his own worn boot. "No fire. Smoke."

How could he have forgotten? He felt like a stupid "gringo" and contented himself with cold beans and hardtack before spreading his blanket under a royal palm. "At least we're close," he said. "Where would they go from here?"

His guide wiped papaya juice from his chin before answering. He pointed South. "La Granja in Santa Clara."

Colin looked at the sharp rise in the jungle floor and the thick foliage hiding any sign of a trail. "How long will it take?" he asked, but his companion was already sound asleep on the serape. Before he could sleep, he again tried to outthink Victor Champagne.

Why would he drag Lily into the jungle to a rebel camp? Was he going to sell her to the highest bidder rather than ransom her to her parents? There was no doubt she'd bring a good price. For the first time, he considered that Victor may just want to see her suffer for betraying him. The thought made him shudder. It was impossible to outthink a madman. When he couldn't think any longer, he closed his eyes.

The sun was barely a dull glow in the east when Raphael kicked him in the side. "Gringo," he said. "*Estás vivo?*"

"Yes," Colin grumbled, suddenly feeling every aching muscle in his body and every rock beneath him. "I'm alive damnit. Stop kicking me." I've gone soft, he thought. Time was when he could ride for two days straight, do surgeries in a makeshift tent, and rise to repeat it the next day, none the worse for wear. Still, he was barely over thirty years old now. Making a mental note to sign up for a men's athletic club when he returned to Boston, he scrambled to his feet. "How far?"

Raphael squinted at the rising sun. "Four, maybe five hours. In time for supper."

He felt Raphael's excitement about his homecoming and mounted his already-saddled roan. The horses were sure-footed in the steep terrain and they made good time, allowing for short breaks at freshwater streams. Colin marveled at Cuba's varied landscape; from seaside coves to dense jungle, and now giant rocks rising toward rugged mountains in a densely forested landscape. It was truly a tropical paradise—despite its bloodthirsty history.

Raphael stopped at a rise and Colin hurried to his side. "What's the—oh my stars," he said when he saw the trail below them. What looked like little more than a narrow path winding through lush vegetation and overgrown tobacco fields, led to a two-story house painted yellow and blue.

The trail was longer than it appeared from a distance, and the closer they came to the old stone plantation house, the more Colin respected the jungle's ability to reclaim itself. When the trail straightened, Raphael mounted his serape onto a mahogany tree branch and held it over his head. Now and then, he'd whistle or hoot like an owl, then pause for a response. When his sounds were returned, he signaled Colin to follow him past dilapidated tobacco-hanging barns toward the yellow and blue house that now just looked sad. But after two days on horseback and sleeping on the ground, any building with a roof and four walls looked like the Taj Mahal to Colin.

Though there were scars of neglect, the house was solid, the grounds and barns well-kept, with a few horses in the small coral. High walls covered by flowering vines enclosed a terraced English garden now gone to seed. But more surprising, women and children milled around the house and outbuildings.

"What is this place?"

"My home," he said with a sense of pride, Colin didn't expect. "Two years ago, the Generalissimo took over Eastern Cuba. We stay here… sometimes. Since the riots in Havana, the Spaniards are too busy keeping their cities under control and digging deeper *troches*. We are like the wind. Even when Captain-General Blanco toured the country, he did not find us. Now listen closely, you must do exactly…"

Colin stopped listening when a young white woman wearing a peasant blouse and brightly colored skirt came outside to stand under the sagging veranda roof. Two blonde braids circled her head. A moment later, she picked up a basket of newly washed clothes and joined the women hanging laundry on a line strung between two palms. He heard Raphael heading for the barn with the horses and stepped forward. Two steps later, something sharp bit into his back.

A wave of hot air smelling of tobacco and home-brewed Cuban rum breathed into his ear, "*No te muevas,*"

He obeyed the order to stay still, but the knife had already taken a bite of him. He raised his hands and said, "*Soy un amigo,*"

The brute didn't move. "Raphael," Colin called, hoping to catch his attention. Instead the blade traced a path along his spine, followed by a trail of liquid thicker than his sweat. He knew how easy it was to cut a spinal cord. One deep slice and he'd be paralyzed—or worse. Desperate, he yelled, "*Soy un menjenaro. Dónde General Gómez?*"

"*Detener!*" came from behind them.

The pressure of the knife receded, but the blood had already begun to stick to Colin's rough, homespun shirt. He refused to bow to the pain, telling himself that if he'd stood through ten lashes from a cat-o'-nine-tails, he could endure a scratch from a Spanish knife. Though he thought he'd go mad from the flies now swarming his wound, he didn't move while Raphael spoke to the sentry in a Cuban patois he couldn't understand.

He turned slowly when Raphael asked, "*Cómo éstas?*" His attacker was already out of sight and Raphael shook his head. "Americans," he said in only slightly accented English. "I told you not to move. If you want to stay alive, you must do what you are told."

He pulled up Colin's shirt. "Teo is very good with a knife. It is just a small slice along your spine. The skin is thin. It bleeds worse than it is. What is this about a message?"

It was a different Raphael who stepped in front of Colin. His back no longer bowed, he stood straight and his wet hair gleamed black instead of iron gray. And instead of a half-closed eye above a rough scar, both eyes were clear. Despite the ragged growth of beard, he looked like a soldier—one used to giving orders—and seeing them obeyed.

Despite the stinging gash on his back that burned like the fires of Hell, Colin straightened. "It's true. I have a message for General Gómez. From Harry Scovel."

Raphael's eyebrows raised. "*Cierto*? Show me."

Colin pulled a wrinkled letter from inside his shirt pocket addressed to the general and handed it to him. Raphael seemed to recognize the hand, then pointed toward Lily and said with only a slight Spanish accent, "Is that your lady friend? She doesn't look like a prisoner to me."

No, she didn't. What the hell had happened? And where was Victor? When they reached the veranda steps, Lily turned and saw him. The sheet in her hand fell to the ground.

"Colin?" she called and ran toward them, stopping short at his raised his hand. "I'm afraid I've had a little…accident," he said and turned around.

She gasped at the bloodstained shirt. "You're hurt!"

CHAPTER 18

"*Que paso?*" came from inside the house. Raphael straightened his shoulders as the commander of the Cuban rebels stepped from the shadows. Everyone talked at once, until he ordered, "*Silencio!*"

Major General Máximo Goméz y Baez, retired officer of the Spanish Army and inventor of the terrifying "Mambisa machete charge," subdued them with only one word and a look. He wore a fresh white military uniform, accented by the ever-present red cloth around his neck to cover a bullet wound from the Ten Years War that had never closed.

The general approached them, his tread so light it barely made a sound. He stopped in front of Raphael first, fixing his aquamarine eyes on the younger man's dark ones. Then he embraced him like a favorite uncle instead of the bane of the Spanish Army's existence. In deference to his American guests, the general spoke in English, "I fear your search did not go well."

"*Si,*" Raphael answered. He cleared his throat and looked heavenward when Gómez pressed a hand over his heart, asking God to give Raphael the strength to endure the loss of his wife and son.

Colin silently echoed the sentiment, hoping the younger soldier would handle the loss better than he did. For five years after her Winona's death, Colin could barely think of his wife without a gut-wrenching grief that threatened his sanity. It had faded to manageable levels in the last three years, allowing rare moments when he could smile at the recollection of her laugh, the moonlight glinting off her ebony hair, and the love in her bottomless dark eyes when she told him she was pregnant. He bowed his head when the two men crossed themselves.

The grieving ritual over, Gómez asked Raphael, "What do you bring from Matanzas?" Then he fixed an unsettling glare on Colin. "Besides a dandy gringo?"

Colin marveled at Raphael's transformation from crippled old man to professional soldier. Standing ramrod straight, his strong, gnarled hands no longer fidgeted in what must have been feigned tremors. He's a better actor than Victor Champagne, Colin thought. But then, Raphael's life likely depended on it.

"It's true I did not find what I had hoped for, sir," Raphael answered. "But I have information about the Spanish troops." He handed his commander the envelope. "And the gringo brings you a message from Señor Scovel."

The general nodded. "We will discuss this after you see to your men."

"Come inside," he told Colin, then waved at a young girl with café au lait-colored skin, ordering water for a bath, bandages, and fresh clothing for Colin.

Grateful for the hospitality, Colin admitted his back burned like hell, and his shirt pulled at the wound every time he moved. He didn't refuse Lily's arm around his waist, or her soft body as support when they climbed the steps to the open door.

"What are you doing here?" she said when they were alone.

"Rescuing you."

His heart jumped when she laughed—deep, sultry, her head thrown back, the slender curve of her throat begging to be touched. Though he'd never thought it possible, she looked more alluring in the loose-fitting peasant clothes than her expensive gowns. He felt the urge to pull her into his arms and carry her off on his exhausted horse, but right now he couldn't pick up a stone.

"You're welcome," he snapped.

He regretted it when she stopped laughing. "I don't mean to sound ungrateful for your Sir Galahad gesture," she said. "But thanks to the General, I am not a damsel in distress. At least not anymore. I made a huge mistake letting Victor catch me off guard the night of the explosion. It won't happen again."

She raised the hem of her skirt to reveal a lethal-looking blade sheathed in a leather strap around her calf. Impressed by both the knife and the slender curve of her leg, he also noticed rope burns on her ankles and wrists. Did she not understand that if Victor used chloroform again, she wouldn't have a chance to go for the knife?

"I'll agree on that point. Because you're going back home as soon as we return to Havana."

"I don't think so." She stepped away, leaving him to follow her to the kitchen. The Cuban girl entered from a side door, handing Lily a basin of water and motioning for him to lie down on the table.

Lily ordered, "Take off your shirt."

"Thanks, but I'll wait for the medic." He didn't expect a band this small to travel with a real doctor, but every camp had someone with medical experience, a midwife, dentist, or a seasoned soldier who had learned by trial and error.

"The medico is busy," Lily responded. "I know how to treat a scratch from a knife. Now take off your shirt."

"Do I have a choice?"

"Not unless you want whatever eggs the flies have already laid on your wound to start hatching."

She was right about the flies. Infection killed more soldiers than bullets, and flies, like scorpions, were the enemy of every living thing. He turned his back to her and unbuttoned his shirt, wincing when the fibers pulled away from the clotting blood.

Her gasp was low, but he heard it. He also knew it wasn't about the shallow gash from the guard's knife. But instead of asking about the jagged scars crisscrossing his shoulders and rib cage, she helped him lay face down on the wood table now covered with a sheet. Moments later, he felt a soft, warm cloth that smelled of…melon?

"What is that?"

"Prickly pear cactus juice," she confirmed. "I found some in the fruit cellar shortly after we arrived. It helps against infections. And there's no harm in smelling good while you heal. LaDonna, do you have any honey?" she asked the girl hovering outside his line of vision. When the answer was no, she asked, "Aloe vera?" Then said, "*Gracias.*"

He rested his cheek on a linen towel and under her soothing

ministrations, closed his eyes, realizing for the first time how truly exhausted he was.

"It isn't deep, for the most part, because of the...scarring," she said. "But it's long. About ten inches." Her voice sounded like an angel talking to him from a dream, until she said, "LaDonna, some whiskey please. And a needle and thread."

The sound of footsteps retreating and returning quickly told him the previous owners had left with their bar stocked. He bit his lip when Lily poured a good two fingers' worth over the elongated cut. It burned like a hot poker until she again rinsed it with the cool cactus juice, then pressed a fresh cloth firmly over the wound. Pulling it off, she said, "Just as I thought. It needs stitches. Hold your breath and don't move."

Before he could respond, she stabbed him with the needle and pulled the thread. "You're lucky I was never good at embroidery. My stitches are generous, but they should do the job."

"I'll thank you later," he ground out through gritted teeth.

"Teo is a butcher, an expert with a knife," Lily repeated Raphael's statement. "He could have severed your spinal cord with a tiny twist," she said while gently sponging away the blood oozing from his now-closed wound.

"I'm a doctor, remember. The chance of that happening is very remote."

"Even so," she argued, "The scar tissue may have deflected the blade."

He regretted his shortness when her gentle hand left him, and breathed easier when she returned, applying the miracle of aloe vera over the stinging stitches, and wrapping a strip of sheeting that smelled like fresh air over his back.

"Raise up a little," she said.

The touch of her gentle fingers brushing his chest as she wrapped the bandage around him was almost more painful than the wound and he felt a chill when she pulled away. The Sioux would have said it was the spirit of a loved one leaving him. Was Winona finally freeing him from his guilt and grief to experience the pleasure—and pain—of *feeling* again?

"I'm finished, *Doctor* Winters," Lily announced with an obvious sense of pride and more than a little pique. She steadied him as he pushed himself up to sit on the edge of the table.

"Where did you learn to dress a wound like that?"

Her smile lit up the room. "I was raised on a cotton plantation and horse ranch. The doctor was fifteen miles away. My mother lived with a medical missionary among the Comanche for a year and learned how to treat most of the injuries and illnesses on Langesford. I helped her."

Who *is* this woman, Colin wondered? A pampered Southern princess, gifted musician, and writer knowledgeable in tribal medicine. What would he learn about her next?

Raphael's entrance saved the awkward silence. He nodded to Lily, then shifted his gaze to Colin. "*Cómo estás?*"

"I'll live," he answered testily while pulling on a clean peasant shirt. "No thanks to you."

"I told you to stay. As a soldier, you should have understood there were sentries."

It felt like a thousand bees were building a hive on Colin's back. He needed a drink. Maybe two. Or three. "Soldier? What makes you…?"

"The General, he has friends in many places, and your name is well known for your valor in the American West, Major Winfield. You would be a Major-General if you had stayed."

Lily faced him. "You were in the Indian Campaigns? Is that where you got those scars? Are they from the Apache?"

"It's a long story," Colin answered. "And no, it wasn't the Apache." He turned to Raphael. "Where can we talk?"

Lily wouldn't be put off. "Don't think you're getting rid of me so fast. I know this is about Victor." She pointed at Raphael. "And I know him better than both of you. I can help."

Raphael's smile was patient. "*Si*, that is what the General said. He sent me for you…both."

CHAPTER 19

They entered the old plantation office single file, like children being called into the headmaster's office. Lily was impressed with Colin's tolerance for pain during and after her inexperienced and primitive medical treatment. Now, painful as it must be for him, he walked straight, like the soldier he apparently was. Why would he keep his heroism a secret?

General Gómez stood facing the only window in the room, his hands clasped behind his back. When Raphael cleared his throat for the third time, he turned and stared them all into submission before pointing to Colin and asking Lily, "Who is this man to you?"

Clearly, Colin's life depended on her answer. He'd treated her with a deference and respect she'd never seen from Victor, saved her life once, and at the bullfight, kept her from doing something that could have led to a firing squad. And he respected her dream of being more than Mrs. Someone. Now it was her turn to help him. "He is a friend."

The General's eyebrows raised. "What do you know *about* him?"

Not much, she admitted, but he'd risked his life to find her. She raised her chin. "I know he is an honorable man."

Gómez nodded gravely and turned to Colin. "Scovel's letter speaks highly of you. So many deaths from the explosion of the US ship. Do you know what that means?"

Colin winced as he took a deep breath. "I do...sir."

"Our...mutual friend...is convinced it was a Spanish mine. What do you think?"

"I am not an investigator, but the last I heard the cause is unknown. The ship was fully destroyed. We may never know."

Gómez' silence begged for more information and Colin added, "I think we all know that whether or not it can be proven, Spain is guilty in the world's mind. But I must say that in Blanco's absence, the Spanish authorities and staff St. Ambrosia Hospital did their best to treat the injured fairly, showing exceptional shock, sympathy, and support regarding the tragedy."

The old soldier then sighed. "So says Harry. Sadly, my old friend's message was old news before you arrived. Tell me why you are really here."

"For Lily," Colin answered without hesitation. "Our families are... distantly connected. She was kidnapped by a man pretending to be her husband. A swindler hoping to sell you Springfield rifles stolen from a US armory almost thirty years ago. They may look new, but they've been hidden off the coast of Georgia since they were stolen. Did I find you in time, or have you already bought them?"

The old general's gaze flickered to Raphael, who shifted on his feet and nodded.

Gómez turned and stepped behind a massive mahogany desk in a shadowed corner of the room. Taking the throne-like chair behind it, he motioned for Colin and Lily to sit opposite him. A glare at Raphael indicated he stay where he was.

"You are a man of healing," he addressed Colin. "What do you know of American gun smugglers?"

Tired, hungry and in pain, Colin stopped dancing for the general. "As you may already know, the smuggler is Victor Champagne. His real name is Lionel Carter. He's from Boston and as a young boy, helped his father hide the stolen Springfield rifles. Our government has reason to believe he has been negotiating with the Cuban Liberation Movement for them to purchase the guns—presenting them as new. He's also been swindling women for close to ten years—my sister among them—I assume for the money to recover the weapons and add newer ones to the mix. I'm working with the Assistant Secretary of the Navy to kill two birds with one stone, so to speak. I don't care if you already have the guns, but it would save us a lot of time if you'd just tell me where Victor is."

Lily gasped when General Gómez frowned and stood. What was Colin thinking by making demands on the commander of the Cuban rebellion? The man who could end their lives with just a nod. She could already see them blindfolded in front of the tobacco barn, facing a firing squad.

But guns were scarce and bullets even more precious. No, they'd likely hang them or slit their throats, leaving them somewhere in the barren tobacco fields for the scavengers to devour. After a long silence, a deep chuckle overrode the sound of her pulse throbbing in her ears.

"I have been fighting at Pinar del Rio. What makes you think I know the whereabouts of this man with many names?"

"Stop!" Lily shouted and stood, glaring at Colin, then the kind, gentle man she once called Uncle Max. "This isn't a game. Victor is a murderer, a thief, and a man who beats, drugs, and swindles innocent women." She nodded to Raphael. "And I suspect he swindled you into buying those old stolen rifles. We must find him…and kill him."

Stopping in the face of the general's frown, she realized how little control she had over her own fate and collapsed back into her chair. "If you'll pardon my vehemence, Sir."

After a long, painful silence he said, "Spoken like a true *amazona*, Ángel. Your rebel *generales* could have made good use of your valor. But death grows fat on valor. As the poet once said, 'Even in a hero's heart, discretion is the better part.' And until you take a life, you cannot imagine the burden you will bear for the rest of your life."

His words smarted, and even worse, both Colin and Raphael nodded in agreement, as if it was a burden the three men shared.

Outnumbered, she muttered a half-hearted, "*Perdóneme.*"

Colin brought them back to the topic at hand. "General, just know that no matter how Victor may have cleaned them up, in a fight, they're likely to kill more of your men than the Spaniards."

The veteran strategist who had survived more than fifty years as a soldier had a perfect poker face as he considered the information. An old grandfather clock ticked away the minutes as the afternoon sun poured through the window, heating the room until if felt like an oven. Lily felt perspiration drip down her back and between her un-corseted breasts, but neither Colin, nor Raphael broke a sweat—or eye contact with the General until he rose slowly and said to Raphael, "Tell him."

Lieutenant Diaz snapped to attention, saluted, and turned to Colin. "We…I…paid Champagne half his price in Ybor City after testing twelve of the Springfield guns. He delivered the Springfields ten days ago. The Mexican guns he promised were not with them and the sum we had already paid him covered the rifles. He was not happy, but he left, promising to return with the Mexican pistols and smokeless rifles. The next day, six men died when the guns blew up in their faces. Many more lie in the hospital barn here. Two of my men tracked Señior Champagne to Havana, where he stole the señorita.

"My men followed them for more than a day before taking them. She looked sick so they took them to our meeting place to wait for us. I was in Matanzas and they put them both in the hut. Champagne kept saying she was the daughter of a rich man in the US and would bring a great price. More than what we would pay him for the guns—if we set him free."

Raphael lowered his head to take responsibility for the gullibility and carelessness of his men. "When…Lily…ran to the General, my men were distracted, and Señor Champagne escaped—again."

"He's a master at deception," Colin said in Raphael's defense. "And a gifted magician, it seems. He's eluded trained Pinkerton and Federal agents for two decades. You should try chains next time."

"No," Raphael said. "The deaths of my soldiers are on me. As is the loss of our prisoner. I will carry the guilt to my own grave. But first, I will put Victor Champagne in his."

"You'll have to stand in line," Colin muttered.

"Behind me," came Lily, indicating a potential race to that end.

General Gómez slammed his fist on the desk. "No! A journey to vengeance ends with two graves. Must I remind you that we are fighting a war? Señorita Lily is safe, and we will test the rest of the guns another way." He looked at Colin. "And we will let the Americans deal with their traitor."

Lily couldn't believe her ears. "You mean you'll just let him get away? He's still here. I can almost smell him. Victor loves money, but he thrives on hate. And right now, he hates me more than anyone in the world." She touched Colin's arm. "We can flush him out."

"With you as bait?" he retorted. "No. If you won't go back to Georgia, you can stay in Havana. Aunt Clara and the Red Cross will keep you safe while I track him down. He can't hide in the jungle forever."

"No," Lily answered. "He'll follow me wherever I go. It will only put Clara in danger. "And my money helped him commit this crime. I'll stay here and help ease some of the pain it caused while *all of you* find him."

The General glared at each of them. "We may be called rebels, but we are soldiers, not assassins, bounty hunters or hostage-takers."

He stepped close to Raphael. "Command can be a curse. When good men die it is an added weight to the commander's shoulders. They were your men. And you are mine. I take responsibility for this tragedy. You are a competent leader, but you are an exceptional spy and tracker. Take Julio and another man of your choosing to track the demon down. Leave in the morning."

To Lily, he said, "Your father is a great friend of mine. I would not forgive myself if I let this man harm you. During your short time with us, you have proven very useful. You may stay if you wish." Then to Colin, "Please consider yourself a guest in my home. We will be pleased to have your assistance in whatever way you choose."

CHAPTER 20

Colin had learned to track from the Sioux and could follow a rabbit in a forest to its hole. But Cuba was more than a forest. He'd seen Raphael negotiate a jungle that hid the sun, the moon, and the stars. This was his land. He conceded that if Victor could be found, Raphael would find him.

Victor's guns were in the smaller tool barn and Colin followed Gómez there. Except for the ones the Spanish captured, they were nearly all accounted for. "Raphael is right," Colin admitted. "They look pristine."

"He is new to command," the old General answered. "As a spy, he should know that things are seldom as they appear. Now, he has learned that lesson the hard way."

What an amazing man, Colin thought, to recognize that no punishment would haunt the young man more than the faces of the men who died firing rifles he'd purchased.

They moved on, noting pits of rust inside more than half the rifle barrels, with some of the firing mechanisms completely rusted out. When the men pulled the triggers, the discharge would either delay or fail to eject, causing the weapon to explode in their hands. They enlisted men to set up a firing range to test the rest—from a distance.

With the General overseeing the tests, Colin moved on to the hospital barn where injured men in ragged clothes lay on grass mats. At least the roof was patched, and they were dry, he thought. Ten of the wounded men were casualties from the malfunctioning guns. Another forty from their most recent battle with Blanco's Guardia on the way back from Pinar del Rio. The remainder of the constantly moving rebel army had completed the goal of blowing up the several miles of track outside Matanzas that had delayed Colin's train. They also manage to recover all their wounded, saving them from a Spanish firing squad.

Lily joined him as he assessed the injuries, until Raphael came out of the main house to begin his search for Victor. A mestizo with a light complexion, he could easily pass as a native Cuban of Spanish descent. Bathed and shaved, his hair now fashionably barbered, and dressed like a gentleman, once in Havana, he would be welcome in any of Victor's favorite haunts.

Lily smiled at him. "You look so handsome."

Colin frowned. "I should go with you."

Raphael grinned back with teeth scrubbed clean of the blackberry dye he'd used in Matanzas. The man is good at disguises, Colin thought. But Victor was desperate. And when it came to men like Victor, desperate meant deadly.

"You would just slow me down, amigo," he answered, adding, "Do not worry, I will find him or die trying."

"That's what I'm afraid of," he muttered as Raphael swaggered away to one of Colin's rented horses. "And return my horse," he called out. "I don't want to be arrested when I get back to Matanzas."

Raphael raised his hand in acknowledgement before mounting the strong roan and looked up to the cloudless sky before kissing the cross he wore beneath his shirt. Then he leaned forward in the saddle and let the horse run.

"What are the odds?" Lily asked Colin.

"Slim to none," he replied as he led her back toward the makeshift hospital. "But eventually, Victor will find us."

Lily nodded and took his hand. "Then we'll get him."

He turned to face her, so close he could see the tiny gold flecks in her bright blue eyes. "Understand this," he said, trying to balance his anger with his growing desire. "There is no 'we' when it comes to Victor. *We* will see to these men. Then *I* will take you back to Havana. Where *you* will board a ship back to Tampa and take a train home to Georgia—where *you* will stay until Victor is safely in jail awaiting his execution for treason."

He expected her to argue, slap his face, or stomp away from him, but she stood perfectly still, lips inches from his, breasts rising and falling with each rapid breath. Forgetting for a moment that they were standing on the wrong side of the beginning of a war, he kissed her.

She stepped into his embrace, matching the pressure of his lips with her own, her tongue teasing his. There was a spark of the devil in her eyes when they separated.

"I want you to know that I am grateful for your *attempted* rescue and your chivalrous desire to protect me," she said. "But I am a grown woman who doesn't need your permission to go where I want or do anything I want. And I am not going *anywhere* until I find Victor—with or without you."

She smiled at his scowl. "I'm certain we will discuss this again, but right now, we need to work together to take care of these men."

A week later, they'd developed a rhythm to their care of the injured men, allowing the medic to join the others on a sortie to harass Spanish soldiers who now only half-heartedly guarded the ineffectual trenches and barbed wire fencing surrounding the cities.

Colin's back healed quickly, and he allowed Lily to take out his stitches. He'd begun to depend on her insights about both the wounded soldiers and the ailments of the women and children. She offered herbal solutions where many doctors would have used the knife and assisted him during a breech birth from a girl far too young to have a baby. When asked who the father was, she said simply, "*No se. Guardia.*"

Lily seemed to thrive in the rough territory, living on the simple fare of beans, rice, and the occasional wild possum and iguana—food totally foreign to them both. As in most Cuban communities, music was an important part of life. Though there was no piano for Lily to play, the membises, many of them former slaves, enjoyed the ageless spirituals she remembered from her childhood. In return they taught her the steps to Spanish and native dances. Colin was mesmerized by the way her body swayed to the sensuous rhythm of Latin guitars, maracas, and castanets—so different from the primal beat of Sioux drums.

They were both night owls, and when the camp went to sleep, with only the guards alert at their posts, they walked the perimeter, heads close, hands occasionally touching. They usually discussed the health issues of the remaining patients in the sorting barn. But on this night, the moon was full, and they wandered past the outposts, knowing their time was short.

As usual, Lily filled him in on the gossip from Santa Clara where some of the women went to trade their eggs and other goods. "There are rumors that the Spanish are pulling their forces back to the larger cities, waiting for the Americans to decide what to do about the *Maine,*" she told him. "LaDonna said the sailors who couldn't be identified were buried in Havana. The others were sent home. What do you think will happen next?"

He stopped and turned to her. "How do you do it?"

"What do you mean?"

"I mean, you spend most of the day at the hospital, help with the laundry, and teach English to the children before they go to bed—and still seem to know the latest news."

She laughed. "I listen." Then she repeated, "What do you think will happen now?"

"It's anybody's guess," he answered. "But the best bet is that once the dust settles over the graves, things between the two countries will likely heat up. Taking Cuba, Puerto Rico, Santo Domingue, and the Philippines from Spain will make America a force to be reckoned with."

"And Roosevelt a prime candidate for President," she added. Her eyes glittered in the moonlight. "How long do you think?"

He'd spent a week resisting the urge to pull her into his arms and kiss her again. To feel her breasts and hips against him. If he could keep her here in their little piece of paradise, he would, but now that most of the wounded had recovered, or were well enough to travel, the camp would be abandoned again. But where was Raphael? If he didn't return soon, there was nothing he could do to keep Lily from doing whatever she wanted, with or without him.

A small animal's screech in the darkness startled Lily. Colin pulled her to him, and she leaned into his embrace with a sigh. When their lips met, he forgot about US expansionism, Spanish imperialism, and their danger from both, becoming lost in her touch, her taste, and the amazing way her body fit with his.

She seemed to know exactly where and how to touch him, and they sank to the soft bed of blue-green and yellow Indian grass beneath a mahogany tree in a fallow field. She let him undress her first, and he took his time, surprised at the perfection of her body in the moonlight, and the halo of golden waves surrounding her head.

"Angel," he whispered as he removed his trousers, unashamed of his arousal.

His lips followed the curves of her body as he lowered himself over her until a hand against his chest stopped him. Her voice sounded husky among the high-pitched night sounds. "Your shirt," she whispered against his lips. "I want to see you as you see me."

"But…" The rest of his protest was forgotten as she raised his peasant shirt over his head. The same full moon that allowed him to see her in all her glory highlighted the rough landscape of his chest. Her sigh broke his heart, but while he expected revulsion, she traced them with her fingers, as if following a map to his heart. She surprised him by pulling him closer to taste them with her tongue. "Don't tell me how you got them if you don't want to…" she whispered when she lay back down. "But you should never be ashamed of scars. They're a badge of courage."

He brushed silky strands of hair from her face and kissed her forehead. "How did you get so wise?"

Her smile took his breath away. "I told you, I pay attention. Now tell me what you like."

He didn't need to. Every move she made, every touch of her fingers, made him feel like a boy with his first woman. But he didn't want to be serviced. He pulled away to lean on his forearms. "No, you tell me what *you* like."

For a moment, she seemed confused. "Why don't you surprise me?"

"My pleasure," he whispered against her lips as his fingers gently traced the bones of her face, then a path from her neck to the secret place between her thighs until she moaned with pleasure. When he reached beneath her hips and slipped inside her, she was ready. Warm, wet, and pulling him close while they rocked together, both slick with sweat and the scent of their own passion filling the air around them like the sweetest flower in the jungle.

Clouds had shrouded the moon, as if to give them privacy, when two short whistles from a sentry woke them. Two bursts warned of someone approaching the camp. Three was a breach, but there was not time to wait for the third. Breathless, Lily shook her hair like a goddess rising from the sea, rekindling Colin's passion, but there was no time. They had to get back to camp.

CHAPTER 21

*R*aphael rode into camp like the demons of Hell were after him, beating Lily and Colin back to the house. His sly smile under a moon now playing peekaboo with the clouds, told them they hadn't succeeded in putting themselves together as well as they thought.

"Hola," he said. "Enjoying the moonlight?"

His good spirits made them both hope he had news about finding Victor. For Lily, it was finding his dead body washed up on shore, half-eaten by crabs, while Colin hoped the bastard was in El Morro preparing for a firing squad. Neither was the case. Like the Devil or magician that he was, he'd disappeared as if into thin air.

He told them, "I bring a message from my half-brother, Ramon, for the General."

"Ramon?" Lily and Colin said at the same time.

"*Sí.* Captain-General Ramón Blanco and I share a father." He didn't seem inclined to explain further.

Lily had overheard from the few ragged men trickling in from a costly success at Cárdenas, that Gómez was rumored to be meeting with General Calixto Garcia about the possibility of the US declaring war against Spain. No one knew when he'd return. Did this message have something to do with that?

That evening, campfire talk painted America and Spain with the same brush—both greedy powers out to claim the riches of Cuba—at the expense of her native population. There was a shift in the social winds the next morning. Now, men who had been grateful for their medical attention and women who had worked at Lily's side washing bandages and soothing feverish foreheads, whispered behind their backs. As Americans, they were not yet enemies, but neither were they friends.

They ate breakfast with Raphael at the table where Lily had stitched Colin's back. She asked, "What does Harry Scovel say about the possibility war?"

His black eyebrow raised when she scolded, "I'm not stupid. I know the General has been working with him for years."

Raphael pushed his clean plate away and stood. "Scovel is devoting all of his attention to the *Maine* investigation, still favoring the theory of a sunken Spanish mine."

Colin nodded. "Harry sticks to his guns for sure, but when they know the truth, he'll report it either way."

Raphael's shrug was doubtful. "There is an uncomfortable feeling," he said, "of waiting."

"Like sitting on pins and needles," Lily offered.

"Or on a powder keg with the fuse lit," Colin added.

"Perhaps," Raphael said. "But there is a fever of discontent among the Spanish troops, and rumors at the Grand Palace of more soldiers on the way from Spain. My brother is most distressed that Weyler may return and destroy the progress he has made with the *reconcentrados*. He—"

"Progress?" Lily interrupted. "I toured Matanzas and Jaruco with the Red Cross. The conditions were beyond deplorable." Tears welled in her eyes. "People died waiting for the food your brother refused to distribute and held in warehouses for weeks."

Raphael flushed and Colin put a hand on Lily's arm. "Step down from the soapbox. You're preaching to the converted. He's reporting the news, not making it."

She gave Colin a harsh look while Raphael frowned in a way that suggested he should better control his woman.

"How is my aunt," Colin tried to defuse the tense moment.

"Señora Barton is working with the Spanish and Cuban officials to organize the distribution. She has visited many cities helping set up hospitals, orphanages and distribution centers."

Lily lowered her gaze, feeling guilty for whiling away her time with Colin, while the elderly Clara traveled the countryside getting things done. She turned to him. "We should be there with her. She's seventy-seven years old and can work circles around people half her age, including me, but she needs help."

He raised a hand. "And put you in the spotlight? You may as well put an ad in the paper telling Victor to come find you. No."

Her chair scraped the Spanish tile floor. "No? Did you just tell me *no?*"

"Your altruism and courage are commendable, Lily, but I ask you to take a moment to think of someone beside yourself for once. Please, sit down."

Her cheeks flushed as if she'd been slapped and she ignored him to remain standing. "What do you mean by that?"

He leaned back in his chair, warm dark eyes meeting ice-cold blue ones. "I mean I know what you're doing. You're putting yourself on the stage hoping Victor will show himself. But when you do that, you also put everyone around you in jeopardy. Aunt Clara, the nurses and doctors—and the innocent women and children in their care. Victor's father was a munitions expert. I'd wager he taught his son about bombs as well as guns."

Her determination weakened under his logic, but she argued, "No, his fight is with me." She frowned at Colin's cocked head. "And maybe you, but he'd never take the lives of innocents."

"Like my men who died shooting his faulty rifles?" reminded them of Raphael's presence.

She swiped at unwanted tears to surrender. "You found no sign of him then?"

"I didn't say that."

"What do you mean?" came from Colin.

"There were signs in both Matanzas and back in Havana. He's been amazingly public about the tragic loss of his wife to the 'savage' rebel Army who kidnapped her from her bed. He's comparing her treatment to Hearst's false story about the strip search of Evangelina Cisneros.

He winked at Lily, reached into his courier bag and pulled a week-old edition of her publisher's competitor. "I knew you'd be sorry you missed the story, so I purchased a copy of the *Journal* for you."

Her hands were shaking by the time she finished the fictional story of her capture, torture, and ultimate demise at the hands of savages claiming to be saviors of Cuba. Colin read it over her shoulder. "It appears we have no choice but to go back to Havana—together."

"And I will give you an escort," came from the open door.

The tired but regal commander of the Cuban Army stepped inside. He dropped his saddlebags on the freshly swept floor and dropped into a chair at the table, running his fingers through thinning gray hair. Lily jumped up to fetch him a plate of food while Raphael poured his exhausted commander a draft of Cuban rum.

"What word do you bring from Blanco?" he asked Raphael.

He handed his commander the sealed communication from Captain-General Blanco.

General Gómez ignored his plate of food to read the handwritten note sealed with a wax image of the Spanish crown. He emptied the mug of rum and set it down for a refill while three pairs of eyes stared at him. Then he laughed.

Rather than humor, it carried both irony and pathos. When he stopped, an oppressive, foreboding silence ruled the old kitchen. And while every mind screamed to ask what was in the message, every tongue was afraid to ask the question. Gómez signaled Raphael to fill all their cups with rum, raising his own in toast. "*Cuba Libre.*"

When the cups were drained, he rose slowly, not as an old man tired from his long ride, but as a warrior carrying the weight of the world on his shoulders. He squared his shoulders and took a long look at each of them. To Lily, he said, "Dark times are coming. It would be best for you to go home— to Langesford. But I know you will not."

He glanced at the innocent-looking parchment in the center of the table. "Instead, you will return to Miss Barton." And to Colin, "And you with her in the morning."

With a nod for Raphael to follow him, the great general left the room— leaving Blanco's letter on the table. Colin asked no one in particular, "What was that about?"

Lily picked up the letter and translated the formalized Spanish script aloud. The letter revealed that the Captain-General who had once offered a reward for Gómez, his generals, and any of his subordinates, was now offering him a commission in the Spanish Army to join forces against the US. In exchange, Spain offered true autonomy to Cuba.

She looked at Colin with a *Mona Lisa* smile. "My father told me Uncle

Max is a genius at strategy. When he plays chess, he sees the whole game in his head before his first move and has never lost a game. He'd have won independence long before this if America had supported him. He's an old man now and this is his last chance to free Cuba. You were in the Army. What do you think he'll do?"

Concern deepened the creases in Colin's forehead. "This isn't the first time Spain has offered autonomy, but I wouldn't trust McKinley any more than Blanco. But for Gómez, joining the enemy of his enemy may be his best bet to rid Cuba of the devil it knows—hoping for the best from the devil it doesn't. Either way, Cuba's dream for independence in our lifetime will likely remain only a dream."

Lily's heart broke for the generations of Cubans who had survived slavery, starvation, imprisonment, and oppression for more than three hundred years, and refused to surrender. She carefully refolded the official government document and placed it back on the table. She looked into Colin's worried dark eyes. "Then we need to help tip the odds in Cuba's favor."

He smiled at her. "The General was right about you."

"What do you mean?"

"You are both a warrior and an angel, with just a hint of demon mixed in. It could take a lifetime to figure out the ratio."

Now was not the time to talk of lifetimes, she thought. When for so many, there was no promise of even tomorrow. She stood. "No one knows the future."

CHAPTER 22

No one mentioned the letter when they bid General Gómez *adiós* in the pre-dawn stillness. Lily and Colin rode his rented horses while the other two carried precious beans, rice, and coffee grown on the hidden plantation. A leather pouch was filled with black-market tobacco to sell to the Spanish soldiers guarding the Matanzas *trochas* if needed. Raphael accompanied them on his own Andalusian mare, carrying an attaché pouch containing Gómez' response to the Captain-General.

They separated when Lily and Colin boarded the train for Havana. As always, the sun smiled on Cuba. There was little sign of the explosion's damage in the city, and even the newspaper offices had reopened. If not for the hulking skeleton of the once powerful warship rising out of the water, and the US Navy lighters carrying inspectors back and forth, it was hard to believe that the world had changed on the night of the explosion.

Colin had paid a month's rent at the Inglaterra for both their rooms and nothing had been disturbed in his, but when they opened the door to Lily's room, it had been ransacked. Lily gasped when she saw all her new clothes laid out on the broken bed, shredded with her own scissors. When Colin looked under the bed, the footlocker was gone.

They both turned to find, "*You'll pay,*" written in lip rouge on her mirror.

Colin put his arm around her, but he knew comfort wasn't what she needed. She needed Victor to be caught and punished for his crimes. Her clothes could be replaced. And he could pay for the repairs to her room. But they both knew she wouldn't sleep well again—anywhere—until Victor was in jail.

She surprised him by breaking their embrace to step away, hands on her hips, surveying the damage. "He's playing with me. This looks like an insane rage, but it isn't. When I recognized Uncle Max, he knew I'd be let go, and that I'd come back here." She raised both hands to her head, turning in circles to point at the message on the mirror. "Like an evil shadow, he'll follow me wherever I go. I won't know a moment of peace until he's dead."

Colin took her into his arms again. Her spine stiffened with a deep breath and she raised her head. "You give me strength,"

His body ached to comfort her right there, on top of her ruined dresses, then buy a ticket on the *City of Washington* for Tampa. But this was not the time. He'd loved another strong woman who had survived the hardships of a nomadic life and the constant fear of capture—only to die in her father's lodge.

He'd failed Winona, and even risking his life hunting renegades and outlaws couldn't ease his guilt. He refused to make the same mistake twice. Slowly, painfully, he separated from her. "You're right. Victor is playing with both of us. Perhaps it's time to join the game."

"What do you mean?"

"I mean you're right. We need to flush him out."

With a sweep of his hand, he explained. "Victor is a showman. This is his anticlimax, before the final act. He knows he's a wanted man. Fitzhugh Lee as well as Blanco have Wanted posters all over Havana and other major towns. And since the explosion, every boat entering or leaving any port on the island is inspected. Every passenger fitting his description is questioned."

"Then why haven't they found him?"

He looked back at the wrecked bed. "You said it yourself. He's a chameleon."

"*Perdónome*," came from the open door where the concierge wrung his hands nervously. "We are sorry, Señora. At the Inglaterra, we pride ourselves on the safety—and privacy—of our guests. We are happy to offer you another room, free of charge, for as long as you wish."

Colin spoke before Lily had a chance to accept. "No. She has a place."

He led her away from the curious man and told her, "I learned this morning that Aunt Clara has secured a residence for her staff and Red Cross personnel."

He felt her stiffen, but she remained silent. They both knew she needed a safe place. It was true that anything and anyone leaving any port in Cuba was being searched. The only cargo that hadn't been opened were the caskets of the *Maine* victims. But the funeral transport had sailed more than a week ago. Where was Victor hiding?

Lily answered, "I know you're trying to protect me, but you said yourself that using the Red Cross as a shield is wrong. We need to make Major-General Lee aware of Blanco's plan to form an alliance with the rebels. Perhaps President McKinley will offer Gómez more financial support rather than a military intervention."

The Devil and the deep blue sea, she thought. It seemed Shakespeare was right that, "misery acquaints man with strange bedfellows."

"Indeed," Colin surprised her by agreeing. "But for the time being, you'll be safest with Aunt Clara and her staff at her residence."

With nothing left to salvage, including the gun she'd hidden under the mattress, Lily couldn't argue. She'd never feel safe at the hotel again. They closed the door on her past with Victor and spent the afternoon shopping for new clothes suitable for a secretary or nurse. Drab, Lily thought, in somber black, gray, or white. Something appropriate for a woman whose husband was missing—and for tending the poor and destitute population living in the streets.

She was speechless when they approached the new home for the Red Cross nestled in the old walled part of the city. The serene beauty of the Jorrin estate rivaled any of Georgia's stately mansions. Everywhere Lily looked, gardens bloomed with flowers she'd never seen. There was even a little river lined by palm, banana, and coconut trees. Finding such peace and quiet inside the tumultuous city seemed miraculous.

Clara greeted her as if she were a lost child. "You poor dear," the seasoned nurse, diplomat, and emissary comforted. "There is so much evil in this world." She squeezed Lily's hand. "But so much good as well. After all, the good Lord sent you to me with your talent, dedication, and quick mind."

With a mischievous smile at Colin, she added, "And the voice of an angel."

Fighting to control her emotions kept Lily from saying that she was anything *but* an angel. "You are too kind."

The older woman's laugh surprised her. "I only do what must be done," she answered. "The Lord provides the rest."

Lily was surprised at Clara's faith and ability to laugh after all the sickness and horror she'd witnessed in her life. Perhaps laughter *was* the best medicine —after aloe and alcohol.

Clara introduced her to the new staff as Lily O'Grady and led her to her room on the second floor facing East, with a view of the gardens. It was beautiful, serene, and safe, but she missed the banter of women in the camp, the camaraderie as they went about their daily chores of laundry, cooking, and tending the children and wounded.

"I have other news," Clara told her. "A gentleman returning to Spain has offered us a lovely home in the city for the orphanage and Consul-General Lee has requested us to staff it. It is well appointed, with rooms enough to fit two hundred children. There is also a large area for them to play, even a swimming bath. All for the nominal sum of just over one-hundred dollars a month."

Children, Lily thought. Her monthly flow had come in Santa Clara, so she knew she wasn't carrying Victor's child, and she had only been with Colin twice at the rebel camp. But what if she was carrying his? She felt guilty. Carrying the child of a wealthy Boston Brahmin couldn't compare with the burdens borne by women struggling to keep themselves and their babies alive in Cuba. Or those poor motherless orphans.

"Now that you have a larger staff," she asked, "could I possibly work and stay at the orphanage?"

Clara's face split into an ageless smile. "Of course, dear," she said. "Your sweet temperament and musical talents will bring great joy to the children."

Colin had entered the room in time to hear Clara's acceptance. "What did I miss?" he asked and frowned when Clara told him the new orphanage was on Tulpin Street near the center of old Havana, not far from the newspapers, the palace—and the cable office.

"I think you'll be safer here," he told Lily.

She bristled at his authoritative tone. "And I think I will be of more help to Clara at the orphanage. I will also be closer to the train station if she needs me to accompany her to the other hospitals."

The world-renowned nurse/diplomat interceded on Lily's behalf in what was fast becoming a stalemate. "Now, Colin dear, it's clear her talents will be well served there, and in emergencies we can tap her as a nurse." Her smile was coy when she placed her hand on her great-nephew's arm. "Truth be told, she'll also likely never have a moment alone. And I would be ever so grateful if you lent a hand at the hospitals. We can travel together. Won't that be wonderful?"

CHAPTER 23

"*Spain Preparing for War with US*," hit the headline of the *World* a week later with the news scoop that the Governor-General had solicited Spain for more troops, as well as General Gómez' support in case of a US invasion. The paper outsold Hearst's *Journal* and earned Lily a regular feature in foreign news coverage.

By mid-March, the city was buzzing with talk of war. Harry Scovel's daily reports on the progress—or lack thereof—toward a final resolution of the cause of the explosion of the *Maine*, fueled the continued rumors of Spanish sabotage. While never officially confirmed, Gómez' refusal to join forces with Spain became obvious with increased rebel attacks on the trains to fortified cities and Spanish camps.

As American papers promoted rumors of war, more extreme groups in Washington pressed their congressmen to annex the entire island, effectively goading the Spanish Empire into a fight. Theodore Roosevelt was the biggest voice, using a skewed interpretation of the Monroe Doctrine's "Manifest Destiny," to claim the US had a duty to exercise its rights as international police, judge, and jury in the Western Hemisphere.

Before settling into her role at the orphanage, Lily accompanied Clara and Colin on a return visit to the hospitals in Matanzas, Artemisa, Jaruco, and Cienfuegos. The number of deaths were diminishing with the influx of supplies, medicines, and food from the Cuban Relief Network of New York.

The four tons of food in the warehouse at Las Fosos had been distributed, with fifty more tons on the *Fern* waiting in the harbor, and donations from as far away as Kansas on the way.

She left the group after Artemisa to move into the orphanage. "Sister" Bettina, the head nurse and wife of Dr. Lesser, one of the Red Cross surgeons, met her at the door. A petite woman dressed in black, Sister Bettina had assembled a small staff of nurses charged with the care of two hundred orphans, from infant to twelve years old. She greeted Lily with a smile of welcome and after settling into a room shared with Ailish O'Malley, an Irish nurse from Boston, Lily set to work. She did everything from laundry and changing diapers, to serving food. And since she was fluent in Spanish, she was assigned to teach English and music to the recovering children.

Colin returned from Cienfuegos a week later to find Lily finishing a piano lesson with a young boy around six or seven years old. He watched them together for a short time, smiling at her blonde head bent over the child's dark one. He cleared his throat. "I'm sorry to interrupt."

Her smile lit up the room and Colin's heart beat fast when their eyes met and she answered, "We're nearly finished."

She looked down at the child and said in Spanish, "Pedro, it's a beautiful day. Why not go outside and pick some new flowers for the centerpiece tonight?"

He turned awkwardly on the piano bench, his left leg angled oddly below the knee, his foot twisted nearly backward. He reached for a primitive crutch to stand, smiled brightly at Colin and lurched past him to do Lily's bidding.

"What happened to him?" Colin asked when the door to the yard slammed shut.

Tears glittered in her eyes. "A year ago, he kicked a Guardia who was beating his mother. The monster picked him up and threw him like a toy. He fell against a wagon, breaking the leg in several places below the knee. There was no doctor to help him, and it healed…like that."

Colin stood by the window facing the play yard as the boy hobbled out to where a few other boys played stickball. The ball headed toward him and with surprising agility, he hop-limped to an angle where he could hit the ball with his crutch. The other boys picked up the game, leaving him to slowly turn toward the lush gardens at the other end of the yard.

"He's an amazing boy," Lily said.

The fresh scent of lilies of the valley filled Colin's senses and he leaned in to steal a kiss. "I can see that. You, Sister Bettina, and the others have done an amazing job here, in a very short time. Especially with their injuries and illnesses. Aunt Clara said they were the ones no one thought would survive."

She nodded. "They're all fighting hard to live. Most only need food and care to fight the fevers and regain their strength." She sighed. "But for each one out there, there are five more fighting to live. And I worry about the wounds that will never heal. The ones inside them."

She turned from the window. "But that's not why you came. You look troubled."

He smiled and pecked her cheek. "You're a witch to read me so well."

"No more flattery," she chuckled. "Get to the point."

"You should go back to the US," he said. "You can see for yourself that the Spanish presence here is more apparent every day with...incidents... against American civilians becoming more prevalent. If you won't go home to Georgia, Tampa should be safe. It's rumored to be considered as a key port in case of—"

"In case of what? War?" Her sudden anger cut him short. "I read the newspapers too. I know the risk."

Gone was the soft, gentle woman who wept over the plight of sick, orphaned children. The *amazona* had returned with eyes blazing, jaw set, and hands on her hips. But he wouldn't give up that easily. "If you're so well informed, then you should know Congress is considering a blockade. Once that happens, there won't be a way out. The Tampa Bay Hotel would welcome you back in an instant and you could still report for Pulitzer."

Tears of hurt and anger filled her eyes. Since returning to Havana, their time alone together had been limited. It was almost as if she'd imagined the magic of their night under the mahogany tree and the few stolen moments before they left the rebel camp. What they'd had together was not a fleeting moment for her. His touch, his voice, and the feel of him inside her had changed her.

He didn't say it, but she knew it changed him too. There were times in the hospitals when they seemed to read each other's mind. But now and then, even in her presence, he seemed to go somewhere else in his mind—

became someone else. And sadly, no amount of subtle inquiries could loosen his tongue enough to tell her why.

Now, he was pushing her away—again. Away from Cuba, where she'd finally found a purpose for her life. Away from him and their complicated relationship. She wouldn't give him that pleasure. She stared at him until he blinked first. "Do you believe I would willingly leave people who need my help to sing for my dinner at an over-decorated, decadent monument to wealth, power—and war?"

She spread an arm toward a stack of fresh sheets for cots in the Jaruco hospital. "My body may be at risk here, but my heart and soul are much safer with the children, Clara—and you."

"But Victor…" he protested.

"He's gone," she snapped. "Or he isn't. It doesn't matter. One day, he'll pay for what he's done. We have more important things to do…here."

Focused on those guarded, dark-brown eyes, he seemed to float toward her. "I don't deserve you."

Stepping into his arms felt like coming home and she whispered, "Tell me what haunts you."

Again, the sound of someone clearing their throat forced them to part. It was Ailish, her roommate. The young Irish widow had lost both her husband and daughter in a Boston tenement fire. She carried the scars of her own injuries on her neck and arms as a constant reminder of her loss. But when looking into Ailish's warm, olive-green eyes or listening to the musical lilt in her voice, the physical deformities disappeared.

"Sorry to…uh…interrupt," she stammered, "but there's been an accident…in the yahd."

Colin and Lily both spoke at once, "What happened? Who is it?"

"Little Pedro. He fell tryin' to catch a ball."

They ran outside to find Sister Bettina carrying the boy back to the house. Colin took him from her and followed Ailish upstairs to Dr. Lesser's examining table where Lily washed a thin line of blood trickling down from a scrape on his twisted knee.

Through it all the child never made a sound or shed a tear. With the wound washed and salve applied, Colin examined the badly healed old breaks. His gentle fingers traced the line of the original injury. "It was broken in three places," he said. "You're a very brave boy."

His fingers pressed against the misshapen foot and Pedro winced. "You have feeling in this foot?"

"*Si*," he said, squirming to get down from the table. "I okay. My *muleta*?"

Ailish handed him the crutch after Colin lifted him down and steadied him on his good foot. He watched the tilt of the boy's head as he hop-skipped down the hall and balanced on one leg to open the door to the room he shared with six other boys. Colin called after him in Spanish, "Stop using your crutch to kick balls."

"What did you mean about feeling in his foot?" Lily asked.

"What?" he asked as if bringing his mind back…from somewhere. "Oh, his ankle. Yes. The breaks were clean, and the nerves are still alive. He's young. A good surgeon could reset the breaks. His muscle tone is weak, but with new strength therapies, it could be improved. Maybe get him off the crutches."

"Can you do it?" Sister Bettina asked.

He sighed at what seemed an impossible dream and shook his head. "I've set freshly broken bones, stopped bleeding, and sewn flayed skin together, but nothing this complicated—or on a child. And I haven't practiced in quite some time.

Her eyes shining with both disappoint and hope, she answered, "My husband is a general practitioner, but he may know a specialist. Though not in Cuba, of course."

He shrugged. "Even if it succeeded, it would be extremely painful and take a long time to heal properly. Children are resilient. He seems to manage well enough."

He answered Sister Bettina's disappointed nod with, "I really should go." Then to Lily, "Frances is back. They invited us to dinner at the Inglaterra. Are you free?"

"Ah, say yes, Lily girl," Ailish encouraged her. "Ye're only young once. We've not so many wee ones now, with families and friends from the villages claimin' 'em on a reg'lar basis." With a wink at Colin she added, "I willna' wait up."

That evening, they met the Scovels at a table on the patio facing the harbor and ordered drinks. Frances lowered her voice. "Public sentiment in favor of war has grown," she said. "Back in February, someone…"—she winked at her husband—"…leaked a letter from the Spanish ambassador,

Enrique Dupuy de Lôme, to his friend in Cuba, calling McKinley coarse, weak, and a low politician."

"I know," Lily and Colin said at the same time.

Chastened for delivering old news, Frances turned to Colin. "Your friend Theodore Roosevelt is in his glory, spouting his nonsense that saving the Western Hemisphere from Spain is America's destiny and all that blah, blah, blah." She drained her rum. "If you ask me, he's building a platform for his own election for President one day."

Unable to defend his friend's warlike bent or his political aspirations, Colin shifted in his seat.

"And what of the *Maine* investigation?" Lily changed the subject.

Harry ordered a refill of his Bacardi rum from the hovering waiter and waited for him to leave before answering, "Oh, Spain blew up the *Maine*—or someone acting on behalf of Spain. Naysayers are pointing to an explosion from the ammunition magazine, but there's no doubt in everyone's mind—though they won't admit it—that if it was from the magazine, someone lit the fuse."

He paused when the new rum arrived and took a drink. "Spanish messengers, visitors, and prominent loyalist citizens had been all over that ship at one time or another. It wouldn't take much to smuggle a few boxes of nitroglycerin in with the champagne deliveries and tuck it away for later." He leaned toward them, lowering his voice. "There's another theory that it could have been one of our own people, anxious to goose McKinley into taking a stand."

"Well, that's a twist," Colin admitted. "How would they do it without blowing themselves up?"

Harry shrugged. "Every war has its martyrs. And at this point, it doesn't matter. Spain is the most likely culprit, though they'll never admit it."

"According to the Yellow Press."

Lily put her hand on Colin's arm. After all, her column was in one of those papers—and Harry was their friend.

He gave her a stern glance but ended the conversation by conceding, "It may be a mystery that's never solved. And nothing moves a country's economy ahead like a war. My only hope is that if America steps in, it respects the native population."

Harry looked puzzled and Frances coughed into her napkin, but Lily knew what he meant. Her sister-in-law Elena had told her enough about the final, horrifying fate of the Southwest tribes at the hands of the invading US Army.

Harry's nod seemed like an after-thought. "I suppose so, but it all comes down to money, doesn't it? There are fortunes to be made from tobacco and sugar, not to mention tourism once there's peace. They'll need cheap labor."

Lily held her tongue at the omission of self-government.

Frances again changed the subject. "So, you two, tell us about the wonderful work Clara Barton is doing. And Colin, I understand you are related to her."

Lily smiled at her diplomatic friend. A well-known reporter in her own right, an adventurer who braved the Klondike in winter—and now a mediator.

"Sadly, much of Aunt Clara's time is spent touring politicians through the hospitals," Colin said. "And even more sadly, after Senator Proctor visited the hospitals and presented a lengthy letter to Congress detailing the horrors of the trenches and fortified cities, it's become an attraction for visiting politicians."

Lily nodded. "Two more senators, the head of the New York Cuban Relief Committee, his wife, and several other functionaries have recently arrived. Clara's weariness and frustration over entertaining them is starting to show. She could be negotiating with Lee and Blanco about opening the fields outside the *trochas* for farming and housing instead of being a tour guide."

"I've reluctantly volunteered to take her place on that trip," Colin told them. "She has a meeting scheduled with Lee and Blanco next week."

"That's wonderful," Lily squeezed his hand under the table. "I wish her luck—and you too. Try to be patient with the bureaucrats."

He turned sad, soulful eyes on her. "It won't be easy. I'm meeting them tomorrow. We'll leave early for the ferry and the train to Matanzas. It seems to be the only city with sick and starving people of interest to the politicians."

Harry rose as Colin and Lily stood for the walk back to the orphanage. "I'm too keyed up to turn in," he said and kissed Lily on the cheek. "I hear Davis and Rae are back for a few days. I need to probe their assessment of the climate in Washington. It seems to change with the weather, so to speak."

Frances smiled at his pun and rose as well. "I'll go with him and make sure he doesn't get into any trouble."

Lily and Colin exchanged glances. No doubt the Scovels would report what they learned to Gómez. Lily was glad Harry worked for Pulitzer instead of Hearst's yellow rag, but he walked a thin tightrope, receiving and dispensing information to and from the Americans, Spanish, and rebels. She hoped he could keep his head low long enough to survive.

CHAPTER 24

*L*ily settled against Colin's arm, his body strong and warm beside her as they walked slowly in the sultry air cooled by fresh ocean breezes. The streets were quiet now as people prepared for Holy Wednesday and the city's annual, though officially illegal, Good Friday reenactment of the Passion of Christ, down the Paseo del Prado. Tulpin Street appeared far too soon for Lily's preference. They stood for a moment beneath a street lantern on the corner. "Let's go in the back way," she whispered. "The night is so lovely. I hate for it to end. How long will you be gone?"

He stepped into the shadows cast by the building and pulled her close. His lips followed a path from her lips along her neck to whisper, "Too long."

She opened her lips to him, pressing against the hard length of him. How could she have possibly confused the drama that surrounded Victor for love? Lunacy, she thought. She'd been blinded by his charm and bewitched by his promises to fulfill her every dream. Instead it had been nonstop chaos, spiked with alternating euphoria, depression, drama, and temper tantrums.

There was mystery with Colin, to be sure, but his strength—and his virtue—were constant in his soft voice, honest eyes, and gentle touch. She couldn't remember a time she'd heard him raise his voice, even when facing Victor's rage.

Now, in the shadows of the mansion, his dark eyes caught the moonlight and his kiss showed her how much he'd miss her. They kissed again, longer this time, their bodies fitting against each other with a familiarity gained from their few trysts in his room at the Inglaterra. But it wouldn't happen tonight. She shared a room with Ailish, and he'd leave before dawn. They separated slowly and painfully.

"I'll miss you," Colin's warm breath whispered against her ear. "But before I go, we need to talk."

Her heart raced with the hope that he'd finally share what happened in his past that kept him from pursuing a future with her. But she was no longer a daydreaming schoolgirl, and after being ruined by Victor, she had no fantasies about making a good marriage—especially to the son of one of Boston's royal families. Though Colin denied his desire for politics, if he changed his mind, her baggage would only weigh him down.

Truth be told, at times it felt freeing to think that she would make her own future. All she hoped for was that somehow, in some way, Colin would remain in her life. It would never happen if he didn't let go of whatever was haunting him. She reached up to caress his clean-shaven cheek, feeling the muscle in his jaw jump at her touch.

"I will wait for you."

They walked together in silence to the side kitchen door, both surprised to find it unlocked. Colin snapped his wrist to drop a derringer into his palm. "Stay back."

Rather than argue that her new gun was snug in a specially sewn pocket in her gown, she did as he asked. She was only a breath behind him, straining to see through the wavy old glass window where a shadow crouched in a chair, his back to the door. She followed Colin's step inside. The smell of the jungle was heavy in the room, the man's shirt torn, a dark stain running down the sleeve.

Colin pressed a gun at the back of his head. "Don't move."

The man obeyed. "Don't shoot. Por favor. *Necesitamos ayuda.*"

"Stand up. Slowly," answered the man's plea for help and Lily lit a lamp across the room.

The intruder's strained, painful attempt to stand confirmed he was hurt —badly—as did the dark stain on his shirt and an equally dark puddle on the flagstone floor. When he raised his head, Lily's hand went to her mouth and Colin dropped the gun to his side. "Raphael?"

He brought the lantern to the table while Lily pumped fresh water into a basin. As she had so many times in Cuba's makeshift hospitals, she dowsed a clean towel into it and handed it to Colin.

"It's not too bad," he reassured Raphael. "Needs stitches and it looks like you lost a fair amount of blood." He handed his friend the flask he carried in his pocket and Raphael took a long swig. When he handed it back, the wounded man could only manage a wan smile.

"What happened?" Colin asked.

Their friend's speech was slurred and barely audible. "Outside Jaruco. The Guardia caught me inside the *trochas*."

Raphael never got caught. He could move with the stealth of a cat, and just as fast. And he knew six ways in and out of every city—with or without wires.

"We didn't hear about any skirmishes," Colin said, though it didn't mean there weren't any. Sadly, the country had become accustomed to guerilla warfare in the last two decades, with only a brief respite during the so-called armistice. It would be impossible to report every engagement.

"No skirmish," Raphael answered. "I received word that my wife and son were sent to Jaruco after Matanzas."

"Did you find them?" Lily whispered. The fact that he was wounded and alone didn't offer much hope.

He looked up, not bothering to hide his tears. "They were there, but again, I was too late. A year ago, before Weyler was removed, one of his men attacked Maria. My son fought him, but the punishment for fighting is death." Grief beyond measure shone from his reddened eyes. "He was only six years old. I should have known."

Lily's tears dripped into the pool of blood at their feet. She could barely breathe, let alone speak to his grief. And if she could, there were no words in any language to comfort him. Colin was silent too, but instead of grief, his face darkened, and his jaw set as if fighting a rage that threatened to consume him. His hand trembled when he took a small sip from the flask before handing it back to Raphael.

He emptied it and swiped his chin with his good arm. "They are in heaven now," he said, wincing as Colin dressed and bandaged his wound with a torn dish towel. "They are in heaven now. Their suffering is over." His black eyes reflected the lamplight. "We must stop the killing of innocents."

He took a deep breath to gather the strength to continue, "Gómez is in Havana. He sent me to find you." His voice faltered, "But I delayed, searching for the man who killed my family. He will never hurt anyone again."

Lily touched his feverish forehead. "The General would never judge you for that…"

"It looks like the bullet went through the meat of your arm. How did you get out?" Colin interrupted.

"I took too long in the killing, and someone came for him. I escaped but the new wire slowed me down. They shot a wild volley and one hit me just as I slipped through. They are lazy, the Guardia, and bragged that they would come for my body in the morning. I used palm leaves to stop my blood and kept to the jungle, eating bananas and papaya. It was two days ago. I don't think they followed me."

"You'll be safe here," Colin said.

"How did you find us?" Lily choked through her grief and anger.

Exhaustion, loss of blood, and whisky took their toll on the injured man. Raphael's eyelids fluttered and his voice slurred as he said, "I didn't know you were here. It was by the grace of God I found the Red Cross House."

He looked up at Colin. "And by the same grace I found you. We need to go to the General. I am late already." He moved to get up, then fell back in the chair. With a beseeching look at Colin, he said, "It isn't far. Help me…please."

Anger replaced Lily's horror. While Ramon Blanco was not Captain-General when his half-brother's family was imprisoned, he was a prominent Spanish officer under Weyler. He could have freed them with just a word.

Colin cleared his throat and shook his head. "You won't get to the corner without rest."

"There is no time," Raphael growled. "It is not far. Help me there."

"Where?" Lily asked.

"Better you don't know," they answered in unison. Colin helped Raphael to his feet, then kissed Lily hard on the mouth. "I love you," he said, and turned to brace his friend against him as they left the kitchen to disappear into the darkness.

CHAPTER 25

*L*ily put her back into the job of cleaning the kitchen after they left. Filling a bucket with water and taking a fresh towel to the blood on the floor, she fought tears of grief for Raphael's loss, and anger with Colin for leaving her behind. Three buckets later, Sister Bettina appeared in the doorway.

She looked down her prominent, hooked nose and said, "I thought I heard voices. *Male* voices." She squinted in the semi-darkness and noticed the wet floor. "What on earth are you doing?"

Lily stood, hiding the bloodstained rag behind her back. "It was Dr. Winfield, walking me back to the hotel. Panic made her ramble, "We had dinner with…friends. I couldn't sleep and came in here for a glass of warm milk before bed and…spilled it…on the floor. It would attract rats if I left it."

Breathless at the multiple lies, she picked up the bucket to throw the pink wash-water out into the yard, stuffing the stained towel to the bottom of the dirty linen bin. "My, it is late, isn't it? I'm so sorry for disturbing you."

Bettina's pale gray eyes narrowed in revulsion at the thought of spilt milk. "I'm so glad you cleaned it up," she said. "And you do look tired. You should get some sleep."

The older woman left the room and Lily admitted her fatigue, but it wasn't so much from the active day and long evening—or even finding Raphael. No, after only three months in Havana, she was tired of war and rumors of war, of hatred and suffering. Most of all, her heart ached for the many people in Cuba who had lived with it for generations. Knowing Ailish would be snoring in the bed next to hers, she lowered her head onto her arms before falling into a fitful sleep.

Ailish found her that way in the morning, exclaiming, "Miss Lily!"

She raised her head, grimaced at the stiffness in her arms, and rubbed her eyes at sunlight streaming through the open window. She rose slowly, surprised at the stiffness in her back. "I was…cleaning. I must have nodded off."

"Cleaning? Is that what you call it? I heard voices down here last night. One was a man. Was it that lovely Dr. Winfield?"

Their room was above the kitchen and Lily thought that for a wealthy man's mansion, the ceilings were amazingly thin. "Ailish!"

The wit of an Irish sprite brightened Ailish's scarred face. "We all know you're smitten with him. Your eyes light up every time he steps into the room —and his for you." She lit the stove for tea and sat next to Lily. "He's a good man. An old soul, we Irish would say. But there's something inside o' him that's holdin' him back. A demon he must fight himself. You jest have to hold on."

It takes an old soul to know an old soul, Lily thought. But to her, the poor Irish widow was all heart. And after all the tragedy in her life, still a romantic. She let Ailish think she was pining for Colin and admitted that maybe she was.

Where was he? He'd left with Raphael hours ago to find Gómez. Raphael had said it wasn't far. Perhaps, rather than disturb her, he went back to the Inglaterra. Then her thoughts turned ugly. The Guardia prowled the streets at night, beating vagrants and drunks in dark alleys. Maybe they were arrested. Maybe they were already in El Morro Castle. No, she couldn't let her thoughts go there. He was scheduled for another early train and Clara hadn't inquired about him. She told herself he was fine.

It was Clara who returned three days later, exhausted but exhilarated that Mr.

Klopsch, the chairman of the New York Relief Committee, would now oversee the distribution activities. She visited the orphanage the day after her return, pleased with their efficiency and the orphans' improving health. "You do a wonderful job with the children," she told Lily. "Music is a great healer, and with your help, they are making strides with English."

Lily smiled, but sadly knew the meaning behind her words. Speaking English could help them if America won the imminent war with Spain. And since nearly all were orphans, the publicity about their plight was attracting offers of homes from communities across the US. But what kind of homes?

Ailish had told her about the orphan trains from the slums of New York City during the War. Tens of thousands of real and perceived poor orphan children were placed on trains and virtually auctioned off as white slaves for Midwest farmers starving for cheap labor. Yet another form of slavery she thought, praying that "her" children would be spared that injustice.

"Thank you," she answered. "Hopefully, your work with the governor to open farming again will reunite them with their families or friends."

"From your lips to God's ears." The older woman's sigh was tired. And with good reason. It was her third marathon tour of the hospitals within the month. "Sadly, both the Consul-General and Captain-General have concerns about the rebels threatening the safety of the former *reconcentrados*—"

"That's ridiculous," Lily interrupted, then realized Clara wasn't dealing with an emperor. Someone comfortable with his power to make decisions. Rather, she was dealing with functionaries and politicians, concerned foremost with their own reputation and potential for advancement. It made them very good at seeing that nothing was ever actually done. "Can you go to the President?"

Clara smiled and nodded. "I sent the telegram this morning. But with the direction of rhetoric going on in Washington, I have little hope he'll bother with the issue. We will, however, stay our course."

"I admire your faith," Lily said, surrendering to the older, wiser woman, but she couldn't hold her concern for Colin any longer. "Where is Colin? I thought he was traveling in your stead."

The older woman's hand settled over hers. "He neglected to meet the party at the ferry, so we took the later train. Perhaps something else came up suddenly."

Lily's mind raced. Had something happened while taking Raphael to meet Gómez? Her thoughts again went to the castle by the harbor. "What do you think happened? I hope he isn't hurt."

Clara patted her hand. "No, I'm sure I would have heard if something had happened to him. He is a grown man. He's traveled extensively and made many friends. And he is always willing to help someone in need. Perhaps such an occasion arose short notice."

"Yes, of course," Lily agreed, knowing just how true it was. "Even at his own peril."

"Whatever do you mean, dear?"

She'd gone too far and struggled to recover. "Oh, nothing. I'm just surprised he didn't advise either of us about his change in plans."

Clara wrapped an arm around her shoulder. "Not to worry. Like a cat, Colin has nine lives. He can take care of himself."

Lily wondered, between the Army and Cuba, how many lives he'd already used and knew in her heart that something had happened to them. But what? Colin wouldn't abandon the wounded man, even if the Guardia had found them. She fought off panic by convincing herself they'd know if something had happened to a prominent American.

"I have other news," Clara said.

Wonderful. Lily thought. Anything to take her mind off Colin, Raphael, and the future of her orphans. She smiled. "Good news would be welcome."

"Indeed, it would," Clara agreed. "And this may be, in the long run. I've been asked to visit the Red Cross headquarters in Washington, regarding preparations in case of a conflict. I'm sure you've heard the rumors."

"Who has not?"

"I'll be leaving on Sunday aboard the *City of Washington* for Tampa, then take the train to Washington. Hopefully, my work will be done in a week or two and I'll be back to consider further expansion of our health efforts among the *reconcentrados*."

"Sunday? But that's only a few days away. You should rest. And there's so much we want to share with you about the orphanage."

"I'm so glad you take such an interest, my dear, but bureaucracy rules the world. You and Sister Bettina are perfectly capable of managing the orphanage, and Mr. Elwell will be there to scold me into pacing myself. Pray that events do not change all of our plans."

Lily agreed. According to the papers, all of America was suddenly outraged over atrocities that had been going on in Cuba for generations. It was only after Americans lost property and fortunes that they adopted a moralistic stance against Spanish rule. She had no doubts that the robber barons were looking to regain their losses by bilking the native Cubans of what should belong to them.

CHAPTER 26

Colin and Raphael turned left from the orphanage, toward the Tulpin train station. It was past midnight now, a time when night-dwellers and thieves ruled the streets. Thanks to his Spanish blood, Raphael was tall, with broad shoulders from a lifetime of hard living. And while Colin's own broad shoulders carried nearly all his friend's weight, it was slow going. They stopped to rest beneath the dim circle of light from a streetlamp three blocks from the orphanage and Colin checked Raphael's bandage.

An off-duty Guardia approached them, his uneven gait testifying to a night spent drinking. They held their breath as he looked them over, then spat at their feet and turned at the next corner. "It looks like the bleeding has stopped," Colin said. "But you need a change of bandage, some food, and rest."

"It is not far," Raphael panted.

"Stay where you are," came from the alley behind them and Colin turned, expecting to be arrested for loitering after curfew. Instead, a hooded figure moved closer, his face hidden in the shadows, a pistol in his outstretched hand. It exploded in a flash of light and what felt like a cannonball struck Colin's chest.

Raphael's voice repeating, "*Levántate mi amigo*," and his tugging on Colin's shoulder confirmed he was still alive. He moaned and tried to lift his head, falling back when the streetlight moved in circles above him. He closed his eyes and counted to ten. When he opened them, the world seemed stationary enough to lean on his right elbow.

Raphael sat beside him. "I thought you were dead." He touched his wounded arm and his hand came away bloody.

Colin propped himself up against the lamppost. "I feel like I was hit by a train. What happened?"

"A gunman," Raphael puffed. "He came from the alley and shot you. I went for him and his second shot grazed me. I hit my head on a brick when I fell. When I came to, he was gone."

The two wounded men assessed each other. "That's one unlucky right arm you've got there, Colin panted. "It doesn't look bad."

"A scratch," Raphael agreed. "But your jacket. There's a hole above your heart." He made the sign of the cross over his own. "But no blood."

"What?" Colin looked down at scorched hole above his breast pocket. While it was difficult to breathe, if he'd been shot there, he wouldn't be alive to wonder about it. He pulled the jacket open to reveal a gash across his upper chest from left to right. It had bled through his shirt, but like Raphael's wound, not bad enough to worry about.

He examined the charred hole in the pocket that had carried his watch since the belt chain broke during his search for Lily. Winona gave it to him when she told him she was pregnant. The young artist, Frederic Remington, was visiting Fort Meade and painted a miniature portrait of her for the case. He felt inside. The pocket was empty.

"It appears my watch saved my life." He found his wallet in his right pocket. "The crazy bastard took my watch instead of my wallet."

"Good thing," Raphael said. "If we want to get to Gómez, we'll need everything you have and then some. For now, I'd say we need a little help from a friend of mine. She's on the way."

They clung to each other, staggering like drunks to keep their balance for two more blocks, then turned onto what looked like an alley. But it wasn't an alley. It was an ancient street, now blocked off by more impressive, modern buildings fronting the Prado. Chipped and broken adobe walls revealed old stone foundations. Tiny wooden doors shuttered shotgun-style tenements. The dim light inside came from candles behind dingy glass windows. Colin looked up at yesterday's laundry still hanging from crisscrossing lines strung between rooftops above the narrow pathway. He turned to Raphael. "What is this?"

He was already knocking on the door next to a tiny window niche illuminated by a red-painted lantern. One, one-two, one, he knocked three times, as if in code. "You can't be serious," Colin whispered in Raphael's ear. "A whorehouse?"

A thin line of red-tinted light stabbed the darkness as the door creaked open. Raphael spoke a dialect Colin didn't understand to a light-skinned mestizo with a scar running down the side of his cheek. It dragged the line of his mouth into a permanent frown as he nodded and stepped back. Colin forgot his pain as he beheld a place that could only have come from the book, *The Arabian Nights.* Multicolored scarves hanging from the low ceiling created tiny little dens where laughter and other obvious sounds of delight spilled outside. He whispered, "What the hell?"

"*Silencio,*" Raphael told him with a jab that shot pain through Colin's chest.

After a few more whispers, the doorman led them through a long hall to the back, where a woman nearly six feet tall, wearing a long, red silk robe, greeted them. Colin looked closely and saw a line of stubble along her jaw. "What is this place?"

Raphael smiled despite the spreading stain on the bandage covering his wounded arm. "The best-kept secret in Havana."

It seemed that a rebel named Raul Garcia, also known as Rosalita Estaban, wore many hats in the hidden world of Old Havana. He served a clientele that few cared to admit existed—while concealing an underground communication chain with General Gómez and his army.

"Make no mistake," Raphael warned. "Rosalita demands complete loyalty—but she offers the same to anyone in trouble."

Fascinated by this man presenting himself as a woman in order to run a wide-ranging intelligence operation, they followed Rosalita to a small room in the back of the house. A moment later, two young women dressed as Arabian handmaids brought fresh water and bandages. Rosalita dismissed them, professionally dressing both their wounds and offering them a warm tea with a bittersweet taste, a plate of dates, dried meat, and a fruit Colin couldn't identify.

"Fig," she said in an undisguised baritone. "It will give you strength."

He'd barely heard her response when his eyelids grew heavy. When he woke, he didn't know if it was morning or night in the windowless room lit by a tiny lantern. Raphael was gone and he felt like he'd been kicked by a horse. The skin above and below the bandage wrapped around his bare chest, was already turning purple, but he could take a deep breath without gasping.

Otherwise naked, he rose slowly and stood. Along with underwear, a fashionable white suit and shirt, complete with waistcoat and cravat, lay across the foot of his cot, He touched the fabric—a better quality than his own tailored suits from Boston. Who *are* these people? he wondered and dressed as quickly. He stepped into the hall to find Raphael already dressed in a clean peasant shirt and homespun trousers. His twice-wounded arm was in a sling and now washed and shaved, he was so pale, he'd scarcely be taken for a mestizo. It was obvious he wasn't going anywhere.

"Hurry," Rosalita ordered in a deep, authoritative voice. "The Guardia is on high alert for rebels and American spies. Follow me."

Big, scarred hands clapped at Colin's dumbfounded stare. "*Prisa!*"

Raphael stayed back while he followed the vivid orange gown along another narrow corridor and down several steps to an ancient, hand-hewn door. Rosalita knocked twice, stepping back and motioning for Colin to enter.

He didn't move. "What is this?"

The door opened wide, as if to answer his question. "It seems we meet again, Doctor Winfield."

"What the...?" he muttered when General Máximo Gómez ushered him into a small room furnished with the barest essentials, including a lone lantern sitting on a fruit crate.

"Sit down, please," the general asked and pointed to a three-legged stool. "There isn't much time."

Colin did as he was asked, leaning toward the man seated across from him, so close their knees nearly touched. Realizing he'd entered a world he knew nothing about, he recognized that he was in too deep to walk away. He'd already aided and abetted an enemy of Spain. They could only kill him once. "What do you want of me, Sir?"

The old man once again produced a sealed letter. "I have a dispatch to be hand-delivered to your President McKinley. It is of utmost importance that he receives it as soon as possible. I have a filibuster boat waiting for you in a cove east of the harbor. Rosalita will take you there."

Colin thought of Lily. She'd worry about him. "My apologies, sir, but I have other pressing business to take care of...here."

The old man nodded. "Ah yes. Señorita O'Grady. She has grown into a woman a man cannot easily forget. But some things are more important. This cannot wait. Peace—or war—rests on it. I am certain she will understand."

Colin wasn't so certain, especially since he'd disappeared after telling her he loved her.

The General stood. Looking down at Colin, his light eyes reflecting the candlelight. "The Spanish governor has requested that I join him if a war with America is declared. As you may know, I have declined his invitation. Since then, we have repelled the Spanish at Majagua and are not far from a victory over Spain."

He leaned closer. "I need you to carry a message to your President, assuring him that we do not need American soldiers to complete the victory we have nearly won. We need only the aid of their warships to keep the Spanish Navy out of the harbor. If he agrees, Cuba will rid itself of the Spanish curse."

Colin wiped cold sweat from his forehead. "But why send me all the way to Washington when you can reach him through Fitzhugh Lee? He has a direct communication cable to the President."

The general paced a tight circle around Colin. "Isn't it obvious? Lee is a buffoon. He's likely to regard it as a slur upon his ability to manage the US presence here. He would bury it." He snorted and raised a hand, as if to God. "But you are an American hero from a prominent family. While others carry the tale that we are like helpless children rebelling against a cruel parent, you have seen our determination and ability to outmaneuver the Spanish with your own eyes. The President will listen to you."

He was right. McKinley was a veteran of the Civil War and in no hurry to sacrifice more young men, this time to a war on foreign soil. He had offered Colin the job as his personal physician and advisor, but he'd declined. Now, the crowds were following Theodore Roosevelt's call for war. Rather than sharing his misgivings about his country's colonial interests in the Western Hemisphere with the leader of the Cuban resistance, he saluted the general. "I'll do what I can, sir."

CHAPTER 27

On March 27th, Lily saw Clara Baron and the always-attentive Mr. Elwell off on the launch taking them to the *City of Washington* and their trip to Washington D.C., hoping they'd return quickly with good news. As always, she turned her back to El Morro Castle. What sounded like the staccato sound of gunfire was carried by the breeze. It's just your mind playing tricks on you, she told herself. And a reminder of why she couldn't report Colin missing to the Guardia.

His danger was real. Is that why he'd told her he loved her? Did he know when he left with Raphael that it could be his last chance to tell her how he felt? Tears of regret filled her eyes for not saying she loved him too. Because she did. And now, he may never know. But today was not a day to think of that. Instead she clung to the hope that Clara Barton could successfully serve as an intermediary between Spain and the US—for the sake of the innocent people of Cuba.

Clara returned on April 6, just days before the Easter holiday. None of the news was good. The President had kept Clara waiting for more than an hour, and while he was receptive to her request to be allowed to remain in Cuba, he denied it on the grounds that the Red Cross did not wait for the guns; it followed them. And it appeared that wait wouldn't be long. Washington was readying for war. Rumors about calling for a volunteer army had yielded more volunteers than they could handle.

The order from Washington for all Americans to leave Cuba on April 9, came the day before Easter Sunday. They had barely twenty-four hours to pack their belongings before boarding the *City of Washington* and the *Olivette*, with support from the Hearst's famous yacht, the *Vamoose*, filibusters, and other private boats.

Clara broke the news to her staff and administrators in her office at the Jorrin home. White mariposa and butterfly jasmine were in bloom outside her window, and the singing birds created a sense of peace and harmony at odds with the threat of war lurking beyond the manicured lawn. "I have called you here," she said, her voice low, eyes shining with unshed tears, "to tell you that in the interest of the safety of all Red Cross personnel on the island, our leadership cannot put our civilian volunteers or staff unnecessarily in danger. Should you decide to stay and continue helping the Cubans rehabilitate the *reconcentrados*, you will not have the support of the Red Cross."

"Impossible," Lily protested, ready to stay alone at the orphanage, if need be.

Clara ignored her outburst to explain to the group, "Of course, the final decision is up to you, but after the boats leave tomorrow, there will be no way out until either hostilities or negotiations are complete. Understand that you have all done an exceptional job here, but until—if—war is declared, the Red Cross will *follow* the guns wherever we are needed. In the interim, the Cubans must manage with the resources we have already provided."

Silence reigned as forty people weighed the risks of staying in a hostile country without diplomatic support from the Red Cross—or the protection of the US government—against their own fears and those of their families and friends at home.

Lily couldn't abandon the children or leave without knowing Colin was safe. She spoke first. "I will stay."

"I am not surprised, Lily," Clara answered and looked at Ailish, already nodding her head to stay with Lily. "I'm certain many of you with few ties to the States feel the same, but please understand that this may be your only chance to leave the island safely. I urge you to comply with the order until your services are once again needed."

While it was obvious that all the staff and volunteers wanted to stay, concern for their families convinced them to return home. Clara turned to Lily. "Fortunately, the number of children at the orphanage has been greatly reduced. I have Captain-General Blanco's assurance that the few too ill or disabled to be placed in homes will be taken care of by the Cuban staff."

Lily's heart broke at the thought of little Pedro. He would never be claimed. What would happen to him? "But there are rumors the Captain-General may be replaced. If so, and Weyler returns, the starvation will return —and the brutality."

"We will do what we can," Clara assured her. "And come back as soon as possible. Until then, we pray for the safety of the innocents."

While Lily believed in the power of prayer from people like Clara, she put more faith in action. She drew Clara aside after the meeting. "Take one or two of the children with you. They'll be safe and when this is over, they can come back."

Clara's blue-veined fingers covered Lily's shaking hand. "You know I can't do that, dear. The Spanish will be monitoring the departures closely. The Red Cross cannot be found taking Cuban children without authorization."

Lily paced the room. "Then what good are we if we leave now, when we're beginning to make progress and war is only a rumor?"

"A strong rumor, Lily. The moment war is declared, we will be unauthorized citizens of an enemy of Spain, and considered prisoners of war, subject to imprisonment and/or execution."

Tears fell from her eyes as she squeezed Lily's hand. "And the punishments will be most harsh for those who have been reporting negative information about Spain to US newspapers."

"What do you mean?" Lily asked, knowing if what she said was true, it would be her worst nightmare.

"I mean, it's well known that you work for the *World*. The other reporters were notified that if they stay, it will be at their own peril."

"I haven't received such notice."

An eyebrow raised at having her information questioned, but Clara's voice remained even. "Perhaps they assumed that as a woman, you wouldn't need notice."

Lily rested her hands on the back of a chair, struggling to draw breath. "I intended my articles to foster diplomatic negotiations and encourage financial support for the Red Cross and native forces. I never meant to incite war."

"Of course not, but you must be aware that salacious rumor is more appealing than truth. Readers love drama, and with the new cables, news is spread nationwide, nay, worldwide, before it can be confirmed or disproved. Others have not been so discreet in their reporting."

Lily collapsed into the chair. Clara was right. While it would be folly to think Spain's weakening Army and decaying Navy could defeat the US, despite its small and untrained volunteer Army, if it happened, there would be no safe place for an American journalist to hide.

Clara offered, "Your friends, the Scovels, have booked passage on the *Olivette.* Frederick Remington has already left, and his friend, Mr. Harding-Davis, is rumored to be traveling with us on the *City of Washington.* Even Consul General Fitzhugh Lee will sail with us. If anyone knows when it's time to jump from the frying pan before it catches fire, they do."

She tugged Lily's unresistant hand. "Come with us, dear. We've done all we can for now. When the time comes, we will return. I promise."

"When the time comes." Lily couldn't hide the sarcasm in her voice. "You mean when war is declared, making even more people suffer and die. And what if Colin is still here? What if he's wounded…or worse? I can't go until I know he's safe."

Clara didn't have to respond. The tears in her eyes said it all when she nodded. "We are all soldiers in our own way, my dear. We serve when and where we are needed most. And as for Colin, he's survived more than you know. If he's here and thinks you stayed behind because of him, it will only make his mission more difficult."

"Mission? What—"

"Please think it over," cut her off. "I'll need your answer for our booking as soon as possible. We leave for the ships early tomorrow."

"Not until I know what you meant by 'mission.' What is Colin involved in?" And what other secrets had he held from her?

Clara smiled. "So tenacious. I wish I'd had you with me in Turkey." After a long moment of consideration, the older woman returned to her chair behind the desk. She folded her hands together on the clear desktop. "I think it's time you understood some things about my darling grandnephew."

Lily acknowledged her defeat when the woman told her that the man she loved, but did not know at all, was in Washington, apparently on a special mission from Gómez. She also recounted the tragic deaths of his Sioux wife and child in a miscarriage while he was on patrol. Tears filled Lily's eyes over the fact that he blamed his absence for their deaths. But while her heart melted for the tragedy in his life, she still smarted that he wouldn't tell her himself. And if he'd committed to a life of solitude, why did he tell her he loved her—then leave?

Relief that he was safe fought with hurt and anger that he hadn't tried to reach her or given Clara a message. She sighed in defeat. It seemed there was no need for her to stay. Even Ailish, who had no family to mourn her, had agreed to leave.

"I appreciate your generosity and confidence in me," she conceded. "But I'll pay my own way. Will you book a single cabin for me? It seems I have a great deal of thinking to do."

Clara's intelligent eyes narrowed. "Does that mean you will be leaving us when we reach Tampa? What will you do?"

Only sheer determination gave her the strength to respond. "I may be young, but I can make my own way in the world. It seems Colin has made his choice. Now it's time for me to make mine. If I could, I would take all the children at the orphanage with me, regardless of the consequences, but I know I cannot. In Tampa, I will continue to write about the atrocities committed by Spain against the people of Cuba—until I can come back."

"Well said," Clara answered with a sad smile. "But I will pay for your booking. As a token of my appreciation for your help."

An hour later, Clara's carriage dropped Lily off at the nearly deserted orphanage, with only Sister Bettina and Ailish watching over a half-dozen children still clawing their way back from death's door. She was weeping at the kitchen table when Pedro hopped in with the new crutch Colin had purchased for him.

"Why are you crying?" he asked in nearly flawless English.

If Pedro could smile through all the pain and loss he'd suffered, perhaps there was hope for the world after all, she thought. Fortunately for him, Father Augustus at the venerable Church of the Holy Spirit had claimed the bright six-year-old for the boys' choir.

"I'm going to miss you all so much," she choked, pulling him to her. "But when I return, I will find you, I promise."

Accepting her statement at face value, he tugged her hand. "Come to your room. A gringo man came. He said he was your friend. He left something for you."

Her heart fluttered. *Colin?* Had he returned for her? If so, why hadn't he waited for her? Her head pounding from the emotions of the day, she trailed behind the lame child. When they stopped in front of her door, Pedro said, "The man said to close your eyes."

Her stomach lurched. Victor had told her that every time he prepared his climax. She never saw him fully naked in the light. Please God, don't let it be him. She sighed. "I'm tired, Pedro, and not much in the mood for guessing games."

His guileless little face fell, and she pulled him close. "While I'm pleased that I had a visitor, you should be very cautious when talking to strangers."

"Oh, he isn't a stranger. He talks to us when Ailish takes us to the park. His name is Victor and he brought you a present."

She swayed on her feet as her lungs refused to fill and her heart fought to beat.

"Aren't you going to see?" the little boy asked the statue she she'd become.

"In a minute," she told him. "Thank you for bringing me the message. I...I think Ailish might need you downstairs. And be careful on your way down."

She waited until she heard him talking with Ailish, then reached inside her clutch for the gun she'd bought from a street vendor. She'd tested it once, satisfied it would fire when needed. Letting out a long breath, she rested her free hand on the knob and slowly turned it.

The door opened with barely a sound and she pressed it all the way open until it touched the wall. Keeping her back against the door and the gun pointed in front of her, she slowly stepped inside. Sweat trickled between her breasts and the tight sleeves of her dress stuck to her arms, but the closet-sized room, crowded with two beds, a nightstand, and a tiny open wardrobe, was empty.

Shaking, she dropped the gun into her pocket and sat on her rumpled bed, opposite Nora's neatly made quilt. Forcing herself to breathe deeply until her frantically beating heart slowed, she saw that nothing had been disturbed. Though relieved, it didn't lessen the threat that Victor was still in Havana—and knew where she lived—until tomorrow.

The afternoon sun glinted off something on Ailish's Irish Chain quilt. She leaned over the small space to see a fine gold watch and broken chain with a fancy "W" hanging from it. She remembered the broken chain and watch Colin carried in his breast pocket. She wanted to lunge for it, but her feet refused to move. Instead, she fell to her knees and slowly reached the distance between the beds for it. It was a double-faced watch, opening from both sides.

Her fingers shook as she studied a deep dent in one side, making it difficult to open. She used a hatpin to force it open, revealing a shattered face and a badly scratched inscription. She turned it over and recoiled from dark spots spread across the back cover. It opened more easily, and tears filled her eyes when she saw the scratched miniature of a lovely, dusky-skinned girl with jet-black hair and shining, black eyes. *Colin's wife?*

She couldn't scream. Couldn't breathe. Couldn't move. Then she saw the note on the quilt. "*I warned you*," was written in Victor's painfully familiar Baroque script, and signed with an oversized "V."

She dropped the watch when Ailish stepped into the room cheerfully announcing, "It's time for supper. We have cake… What's the matter?" addressed Lily's frozen silence. She went to her side and after one look at her devastated face, pulled her into her arms. "What happened, *anamchara?*"

Normally the Irish endearment cheered Lily, but nothing could console her now. And Ailish was an innocent. She mustn't know what happened, or Victor would kill her too. She slid the watch into her pocket with the gun and choked back her sobs to pull away and lean against her bedframe. Brushing away tears of anger and loathing, she answered, "Nothing. I'm just sad to leave."

Ailish stood, hands on her hips. "We all are, but this is something different. It's that man, isn't it? Colin? Did you hear from him? Is he staying?"

"No," she choked. "He's gone."

Ailish again squeezed her tight. "Oh, my sweet dear. He left you here alone. Though I didn't see it in him, some men are just plain bad." She stepped back. "He's not worthy of your love, and you have a life to live. Now get yourself in order and meet me downstairs in five minutes for our going-away party with the children."

Still struggling to catch her breath, Lily choked. "A life to live. Yes." Though she couldn't conceive of a life without Colin, or of living with the guilt that she was the reason for his death. Her fingers caressed the cool muzzle of the derringer in her pocket. Somehow, she had to lure Victor into the open—where she could kill him.

CHAPTER 28

Somehow, she survived the endless "last" supper. After hugging each child until they squealed for breath, she tucked them in and went to bed herself, spending a sleepless night listening to Ailish snore. Only the innocent sleep that soundly, she thought, knowing she wouldn't rest a full night until Victor Champagne was dead.

On Easter Sunday morning, she delivered Pedro to Father Augustus after the sunrise Mass, reaffirming that she would be back as soon as possible. The remaining half-dozen children were left to the care of two Cuban nurses when a carriage from the Red Cross headquarters pulled up to take Lily, Ailish, and Sister Bettina to the harbor.

It was already teeming with Americans obeying President McKinley's mandatory evacuation order. Small boats and private yachts that had once served as filibusters smuggling goods between the two countries, joined launches running back and forth between the two White Star ocean liners bound for Tampa. Combined, the *City of Washington*, and *Olivette*, had a capacity for nearly 1500 passengers. With the others, they could easily carry out the evacuation in one trip, but from the crowded launches sitting low in the water under the weight of the passengers and their belongings, it would take most of the day to board.

The Red Cross party stood together, and Clara encouraged them to be patient and brave in the face of an uncertain future while they waited for a launch big enough to carry them all together. Most had several bags and a steamer trunk or two, but Clara and Mr. Elwell were seasoned travelers, carrying only a carpetbag each. Lily also traveled light, hiring a Cuban boy to pull her battered little trunk while she carried a carpetbag and Royal typewriter in her arms.

Recalling the horrific night of the *USS Maine* explosion, she felt exposed on the open pier, even surrounded by Red Cross staff. While the others seemed entertained by the hustle and bustle of the busy port, she kept her back to the water, and her anxious gaze on the crowd, looking for a man who could make himself invisible.

The sun was beginning to lower in the western horizon, tinting the clouds in shades of orange and blue when they finally stepped off the launch onto the deck of the *City of Washington*. The Red Cross staff disbursed to their staterooms to prepare for departure, and Clara attended a meeting in one of the many salons.

Lily's stateroom was on the port side of the ship, one level above the promenade deck. She noted that Victor would have to be a spider to reach it from the outside, and the size of a four-year-old to climb through the porthole window. After locking the door and putting the desk chair securely under the handle, she opened the window and filled her lungs with air smelling of both the sea and the bustling port city.

Exhaling slowly, she felt safe for the first time since finding the watch. It lay like a rock in her pocket with the gun, but she couldn't bring herself to open it again. Perhaps tomorrow, she thought, and lay down on her neatly made bed.

Three steady blows of the ship's horn woke her, signaling that it was finally backing out of its berth to sail through the channel into open water. She rose and straightened her skirt to brave the promenade deck and bid *adios* to the ancient fort that haunted her dreams. It occurred to her that Victor was likely on this ship, or one of the others, but her purpose wasn't to hide from him. Not anymore. If he was aboard, there would be nowhere for him to run from her.

She watched Havana Harbor become smaller with every churn of the ship's three massive engines. "I'll find you Victor," she whispered to the open sea. "And I'll kill you or die trying. I promise."

With the El Morro castle behind them, she wound her way through the crowd to the railing. The breeze picked up, carrying the scent of Victor's

Rowland's Macassar Oil hair cream to her. Someone bumped her and her feet slipped on the mist-covered deck. Only the waist-high railing kept her from falling overboard while a deep voice growled, "You should be more careful."

She froze a second too long after recognizing the voice and when she turned, all she saw was the crowd of other passengers, their gazes fixed on horizon. She noticed one man with Victor's build in a well-tailored dark suit and bowler hat, stroll away with a self-satisfied strut. In the moment it took her to reach into her pocket for the gun and take a breath, he was gone.

Be calm, she told herself. He wouldn't push her overboard in broad daylight on a deck crowded with gawking passengers. And she shouldn't have been so close to the railing. Whoever he was, he was right. She should be more careful. And she'd keep an eye out for the man with the bowler hat.

Ailish knocked on her door later in the day, inviting her to join the Red Cross for supper. She pled a headache, promising to meet them for breakfast. Once, during the long night, she thought she heard the rattle of the latch on her cabin door and held her breath, hoping the chair would hold if Victor used one of his tools to jimmy the lock. And if the chair didn't hold, the gun was under her sheet, pointed at the door.

"Lily," came from the other side, sounding so much like Colin that she sat up. Willing to take the chance to see his smile, touch his face, and have him tell her it was all a nightmare, she even pushed back the sheet. But Victor was also an accomplished mimic. If Colin was aboard, Clara would have told her. A long minute later, she thought she heard a heavy sigh and soft footsteps fading down the hall.

There was no mimicking Ailish's Irish lilt the next morning when she knocked on her door with a breakfast tray. "We missed you again," she said. "I worried you was ill. Ocean boats can be a trial for some."

Lily smiled at her concern and invited her friend inside. Ailish sat in the vanity chair while Lily ate her poached eggs and toast. "How are ye doin?" the young widow asked.

She surprised herself by returning the smile. For the first time since escaping Victor in the jungle, she was finally not afraid. He'd kill her, or she'd kill him. It was that simple. In the meantime, she'd live her life, albeit carefully, without fear and without endangering anyone else.

She set the tray aside and stood in the narrow room to embrace her dear friend. "I am fine," she said. "I'm taking your advice and starting over. Living my own life."

Ailish beamed. "Miss Barton gave us the rest of the trip to relax and prepare our next steps," she chattered. "I've decided to stay on with the Red Cross. Me an' a few others'll be stayin' with her until word comes fer us to go to Key West. For Cuba, you know. An' if war is avoided, she's offered me a position assisting Mr. Elwell."

Lily hugged her. "I'm so happy for you!"

Excitement colored the Irish girl's pale cheeks. "We stop in Key West later today. Miss Clara has asked me to go with her to meet the Naval commander. I may be busy the rest of the day and wanted to make sure you'll be fine—alone. Have you given thought to what you'll do? You know there will always be a place for you with us."

"We'll see," Lily answered, knowing she had to separate herself from Ailish and the Red Cross to keep them safe. And even if she went home to Georgia with her proverbial tail between her legs, she would place her brother and his family in danger. It would be easier to disappear in New York, but she didn't want to disappear. She wanted to be alone to flush Victor out.

"I'm thinking of my options," answered Ailsih's questioning gaze and she remembered Colin's suggestion about the Tampa Bay Hotel. It suddenly seemed like a good idea. It would make it harder for Victor to catch her alone and give her the advantage of seeing him first. She brightened. "Maybe the hotel will hire me to entertain."

Clara approached her that afternoon and announced, "We have decided to make our interim headquarters in Tampa. While we're there, we could still use your valuable organizational and writing skills. Mr. Elwell and I will have plenty for you to do until…things…are determined. Please say you'll consider it."

How could she refuse? They'd had word that military leaders were already congregating at the hotel. Victor wouldn't dare harm her or Clara in a hotel full of generals. Tears again threatened to flood her eyes as she nodded her agreement, knowing that if diplomatic efforts failed, they could be only weeks from returning to Cuba.

Once in sight of the Florida coastline, Clara held a brief prayer meeting before they docked. As a lapsed Methodist with a father who attended church on Christmas and Easter, and a mother who wove Comanche spiritualism into her theology, Lily had an ambivalent relationship with religion. But considering the miracles Clara had accomplished on battlefields and at negotiating tables, it was clear that God rarely said no to Clara Barton. While Clara and her cadre of nurses and administrators prayed for peace, Lily prayed for the courage to kill Victor when the opportunity presented itself.

As the ship approached Port Tampa, Lily and the others sang "Amazing Grace" to acknowledge that unlike the more than three hundred crew members of the *USS Maine,* they had come home safely. For most of the Red Cross volunteers, it was the beginning of a longer journey to their homes ranging from New York to Oklahoma. More good-byes. More tears. More doubt about an uncertain future.

Safely ensconced in the center of the remaining members of the Red Cross contingent, Lily watched everyone leave the ship, searching the crowd for the man with the bowler hat. He wasn't among them, and no one else who disembarked bore any close resemblance to Victor. Either he was never on the ship, or he was still onboard, disguised as a crew member.

She hoped she'd been overly cautious, but something in her bones told her to keep her guard up. In the meantime, there was safety in numbers. They took the Plant train the nine miles to Tampa. Until either war was declared, or the Red Cross was dismissed, she would hide in plain sight, surrounded by people who cared about her.

Except for Colin. The thought made her knees weak.

The boardwalk leading to the hotel reminded her of when she and Victor arrived and his promise to make all her dreams come true. Instead, his promises had burst like champagne bubbles in the air. Now, little more than three months later, while the scent of gardenias and confederate jasmine still perfumed the thick, humid air, Victor wanted to kill her—perhaps even more than she wanted to kill him.

Clara stopped the group just shy of the stairs to the hotel's rambling grand veranda, furnished with rocking chairs and tables, most of them already occupied by fashionable men and women sipping tall, cool drinks.

"We will be staying on the third floor," Clara told them. "I'll check us in. Please stay together until our rooms are assigned."

Lily wasn't part of their group and would have to book a room of her own. The higher rooms on the fourth and fifth floors were more expensive, and though the risk was greater on the ground floor facing the courtyard, she hoped there was one there. She could set some sort of alarm on the window and door.

While she was thinking, the others had moved on. As she reached down to pick up her valise, a tanned male hand covered hers. Too shocked to scream, and unable reach her gun, she raised her foot, stomping the heel into the toe of his soft leather boot, then spun around to punch him in the chest. It was something her brother Sean, a notorious brawler in his younger years, had taught her.

"Oww!" The man in a white planter's suit and Panama hat bent over, one hand on his knee, the other pressed over his heart. While he took short, labored breaths, her own breath caught in her throat when she recognized the suit. But white suits were common in the South. Even Victor owned one. As much as she wished otherwise, it couldn't be Colin. Her hand slid into her pocket and gripped the gun.

She felt, rather than saw, the group on the veranda watching them and the man was still bent over. She hadn't punched him that hard. Oh, God. What if he was an old man trying to help her? Still cautious, she rushed to him, pressing her gun into his side. "Stand up."

He obeyed, albeit slowly, raising his free arm to remove the Panama hat. Clara screamed, "Colin," and flew like a big black bird toward the injured man.

Colin? "No," Lily whispered when he faced her. She stood frozen in place, unable to even lower the gun.

He dropped the hat and rubbed his chest with one hand, raising the other to signal Clara to stop. "Lily, it's me, Colin," he said and pried the derringer from her hand.

"But you're dead."

Clara turned to her flock, saying, "Everything is fine. Just a misunderstanding. Move along. We have a schedule to keep. She turned to the other gawking train passengers. "Give them some privacy please."

Lily followed him to a bench near a fountain, and collapsed, unable to speak through her sobs. A quick look inside his shirt told him that though his battered chest was still intact, it was mad as hell. "It's alright, darling," he consoled. "I can assure you, I'm fine."

But *she* wasn't. Her heart was beating too fast. She couldn't catch her breath and could barely speak. He dipped his handkerchief into the fountain, pressing it against her forehead and cheeks, encouraging her to take deep breaths until her color returned.

He smiled when her eyes cleared. "Didn't Clara tell you I was in Washington? Whatever made you think I was dead?"

She opened her reticule to pull out a handkerchief and dabbed at her tears. "You left with Raphael and didn't come back." She hiccupped. "Clara said you were in Washington, but then Victor came to the orphanage and... and..." She blew her nose. "And he left a note on my bed saying he'd warned me." Dipping back into her purse, she held out his watch. "This was on top of the note."

"Oh no," he whispered, caressing the damaged surface of the watch etched with two crossed arrows. Tears magnified his eyes before opening the back, followed by a sigh of relief when he touched the tiny portrait.

Lily's heart broke again when his finger traced the scratches on the inscription as if it was a holy relic. *He's still in love with his dead wife.* She couldn't compete with a ghost. Blinking away her pain, she said, "I am so sorry for hurting you. I thought you...were...him. We should go in. Clara will want to know what happened to you."

"There's no time for that," caught her attention.

"What do you mean?"

"I was shot a few blocks from the orphanage. That watch saved my life, though I had no idea Victor fired the gun. Then I was called away by General Gómez to deliver a message to President McKinley. I met Raphael in Havana and gave him McKinley's response. But it seems the President chose to deliver it more publicly. I was aboard the *City of Washington* and stayed low in case Victor was too. I thought I saw him once or twice, but he's quick."

He cupped her chin in his palm, forcing her to meet his gaze. "I'm so sorry I let you worry this way. How did you know it was my watch?"

"The 'W' on your broken watch chain. Clara had told me about your wife's miscarriage. I assumed the portrait was hers."

He stiffened, "My wife's miscarriage?"

"Yes, she didn't want to tell me, but...the circumstances...you know. I refused to leave when the evacuation order came, because I thought you were...somewhere...in Cuba."

He closed the watch and put it back in its place over his heart. "I'm so sorry for causing you such worry," he said as if to an old friend, not the woman he'd professed to love. It cut like a knife when he changed the subject. "I suppose I'll need to offer my services to the President. But I'd like to talk with you before I leave. I need to explain...what I said before I left...with Raphael."

Her hands fluttered in the air like a startled bird. "No. No, you don't have to explain anything. It was a very tense time. After seeing your wife's portrait, I understand."

His kiss surprised her. "No, you don't. I meant what I said to you," whispered against her ear. "I'll let you settle in and meet you in the dining room in an hour."

CHAPTER 29

$\mathcal{C}$olin avoided questions about his reason for being in Tampa while dining with the Red Cross team. He declined dessert, but instead of retiring early, waited for Lily to eat her lemon ice and meet him in the Greek Garden, amid statues of ancient Greek gods and goddesses, strategically draped with loincloths.

He paced the flagstone path near the statue of Athena, goddess of wisdom and war, rehearsing what he wanted—needed—to tell Lily. He wasn't supposed to fall in love with her. She was simply another one of Victor's victims. A spoiled socialite looking for Prince Charming. But when he heard her sing and saw the courage it took to hang from a single cable, he couldn't forget her.

It was a different kind of love than he'd had for Winona. With her, it was as if their souls had reunited from other lifetimes. He felt her deep within him every time he looked into her eyes and still felt her sometimes, in the call of her totem, the great horned owl. Like the owl, she could see beyond the masks that humans wore and call out their lies and deceit.

As if in response to his thoughts, he heard the familiar call from a nearby Banyan tree. He looked up just a few feet above his head, and for an instant he saw Winona's face reflected in the fabled hunter's golden eyes. It looked down at him for a long moment, then stretched its wings. Colin felt a chill at hearing what sounded like, "good-bye," when the great hunter harnessed the ocean breeze and flew toward the crescent moon.

Still shaken, he turned at the sound of light footsteps on the cobblestone patio. *Lily.* She moved with the grace of a ballerina, her lavender gown floating above the tops of her silver evening slippers, reminding him of an angel floating on invisible clouds.

"Colin?" she whispered, and as much as he wanted to pull her into his arms, he remembered the pain he'd suffered the last time he surprised her. "Here," he said, stepping from the shadows. His voice sounded high, like an adolescent boy at his first ball and he cleared his throat. "By the fountain."

She found him quickly and smiled up at him, her eyes bright. Then she was in his arms. They kissed until they both ran out of breath. Her heartbeat was fast against his chest, her tears felt like ice melting against his cheek. He pulled back. "You're crying. Did I hurt you?"

Tears darkened her silk bodice. "Yes, to both." She sniffled, brushing at her cheeks. "You could have cabled me. Or asked Clara to let me know you were safe." She looked up at him, anger replacing the happiness of their reunion. "I thought you were dead! Why won't you be honest with me?"

Her slap coincided with the clap of cymbals climaxing Tchaikovsky's "1812 Overture" and he touched his stinging cheek grateful she hadn't punched him in the chest—again. "I didn't want to put you and the children in danger."

Her arms folded across her breasts like the wings of a vengeful angel. "I've been in danger since the day I met you."

"Well before that, if you recall," he countered. She shook off his hand on her elbow intended to guide her to the bench in the shadows and seated herself. Obviously, she wasn't going to make it easy. "Well, tonight I'm an open book," he said. "What do you want to know?"

"First, tell me about your wife."

It caught him off guard. Was she jealous of a dead woman? "Clara told you, she's dead. It's a long story that we don't have time to go into right now. More important, I think you're right about Victor following you, whether on the *City of Washington* or another boat."

The diversion seemed to work. Her arms relaxed at her side and she turned to him. "Yes, that's what I'm hoping."

"What?"

"Shh," she answered, and used his own diversion tactic against him.

"We'll talk about Victor later. You seem to know nearly everything about me, but I know virtually nothing about you. I trusted Victor on blind faith and look what happened. Tell me everything about your life, including your beautiful wife—and what really happened to her—or leave me alone."

So, his aunt wasn't as good a liar as he thought. It was late and the orchestra was ending the night with another rousing finale of patriotic songs. A few dancers walked through the garden on their way to the bar to celebrate the evening's entertainment. They'd soon be shrouded in a darkness lit by only the stars and a quarter moon. Perhaps it's fitting, he thought. He wouldn't be able to see her revulsion.

"But you already know," he said, lowering his voice as the caretaker snuffed the nearby lanterns.

"No, I know what Clara told me and I know she wouldn't lie. I believe your wife and unborn child are dead, and you feel responsible, but I also know there's more to the story. I want...*need* to know who you were, in order to trust my love for who you are now." She took his hand in hers and said, "Take your time."

He looked up at the clear sky and put his faith in a shooting star. "I knew enlisting in the Army Medical Corps was a mistake with my first assignment at Fort Abercrombie in North Dakota. A small band of peaceful Lakota Sioux were camped along the river nearby. Winona..." he paused to swallow, "...it means 'first daughter', and a few other Sioux women did laundry at the fort. We...well...it was as if we were two halves of the same person."

His voice broke and Lily relented. "I'm so sorry. You needn't go on."

He thought of the owl. "No! It's been eight years. It's time to set her free."

He kissed Lily's hand. "Her father was a clan elder. In '89, rebels in the Sioux camps were furious about their agent swindling them out of nearly forty thousand acres and breaking it up into six tiny, uninhabitable reservations—no doubt intended to starve them out. In the fall, Chief Sitting Bull convinced them that the Ghost Dance would make them strong enough to destroy all white men.

"Winona and I had been married in a tribal ceremony the previous year, and she was seven months into her pregnancy when Chief Sitting Bull was murdered, I was out tracking a few young Sioux hotheads who'd stolen some cattle and her father, Chief Spotted Elk, gathered his people to set out for the

Pine Ridge Reservation; but they were on foot, and slow. They stopped to camp at Wounded Knee Creek for the night.

"We were on our way back with the Sioux boys when we saw smoke and followed it to find the Army, outnumbering the Sioux by four to one, annihilating the camp with Gatling guns."

His hand gripped hers as if it was all that held him to the present, while their tears fell like hot summer raindrops onto his skin. "Winona was visiting her sick father and went along when they left. She was...murdered...with the others."

"I'm so sorry..." Lily sobbed into his chest. "So, so sorry that it happened, and that I made you re-live it."

But he wasn't finished and looked up at the Banyan branch where he'd seen Winona's totem. "I didn't know she was there until that night in camp, when the men, still bloody from the slaughter, celebrated their victory. I heard one brag about shooting a pregnant woman shielding an old chief with only one ear. The bastard felt he should get paid double for killing two 'prairie niggers' with one bullet."

Lily pulled away to stare at him, stricken silent by the glow of the memory in his eyes. His voice lowered to a monotone, as if he was telling a story that had happened to someone else. "I volunteered to verify the dead when they burned the bodies and chose him to go with me. When we found...them, I cut off his nose, and forced it into his mouth. And while he was still alive, I stripped him, slit open his stomach and threw him on the funeral pyre."

His moan silenced the garden and Lily fought her disbelief, horror, nausea, and sympathy for the man who had taken an oath to do no harm. She slipped her hand into his and whispered, "I would have picked a different organ to feed him."

He pulled away. His eyes, though swollen, shone clear again in the moonlight. His touch along her cheek was light. "No, you wouldn't."

He stood, cupping her chin in his palm. "I'm unrepentant when it comes to what I did to him, but I'll carry my guilt into Hell for leaving Winona alone. I understand if you never want to see me again. Just know I won't let an animal like Victor Champagne hurt another woman I love. Even if I die trying."

She stood too, moving his hand to her lips. "You've done nothing but try to help me," she said. "I was a fool to fall under Victor's spell and was careless at the harbor. And I was jealous of a woman you loved with your heart and soul. But Victor is arrogant. He thinks he killed you. Sooner or later, he'll get careless."

She kissed Colin's tear-stained hand and glanced around the now-deserted garden. "This is no place to discuss it. Where is your room?"

"Are you sure?"

"Really? After all we've been through together, are you concerned about my reputation?" Her yes narrowed. "Or is it yours? If it's your aunt you're worried about, I think she already knows."

He pulled her close. "You may have the courage of a warrior," he said, his voice hoarse with emotion. "But you have the heart of a saint."

She looked up and kissed lips that tasted like tears. "I'm sure I'll have to remind you of that one day."

His suite was on the fourth floor, with its own full bath and a separate sitting room. As painful as it was to confess that he'd butchered Winona's murderer, somehow, he felt lighter. As if the burden had flown off with the owl he'd seen in the garden. Not free of his sin, but somehow innocent...forgiven. But with the forgiveness, he also felt ...empty. He'd carried the burden for so many years, without it, he felt a little lost.

He opened the door and led Lily to the divan in the sitting room, turning on an electrified chimney lamp before nodding toward a combination Victrola and bar. "Would you like a drink?"

"Sherry would be nice."

The nervous quiver in her voice told him that as much as she'd tried to take the horror of his story in stride, she was still shaken. Was she having second thoughts about being alone with him? He wouldn't blame her. He crossed the room, poured himself a Kentucky bourbon, and handed her the wine.

She set it on the marble-topped tea table and looked up at him. "There is more, isn't there?"

He set his own drink down to join her. Without touching her, he said, "I think Winona and I both knew there was no future for us. Perhaps it made the flame burn even hotter. But as the end of my enlistment approached and her pregnancy advanced, she became more agitated. She said she had dreams and worried for our child. Though it broke her heart to leave her homeland, she begged me to finish my tour in the East. But I waited. I had to take out one more patrol. And when I came back, everyone in the world I loved was dead."

He looked up at the painted sunset on the ceiling to avoid the judgement he imagined in her gaze. "If I'd listened to her, we'd have been on our way to Baltimore to finish the last two months of my enlistment at Fort McHenry."

Lily put her hand over his and they sat that way for a several minutes, fingers intertwined as if their lives depended on it. "If 'ifs' were 'ises,' we'd all have a wonderful time," she whispered.

A thick brown eyebrow raised. "What do you mean?"

"My nanny Chloe used to say that when I complained about not having my own way. I finally understand what she meant. We weren't put on this earth to have a wonderful time. You were doing your duty, and Winona was doing hers by caring for her father. We can't change the past."

She cocked her head and his hand felt cold when hers returned to her lap. "But you're not finished yet."

How could she know him so well after such a short time? "No, I'm not." He stood to pace. "I took an oath to do no harm when I became a doctor, but from the moment I joined the Army, my entire life became a violation of that oath. I had to atone."

"Colin, it wasn't…"

His raised hand kept her still while he stared out at the jungle beyond the manicured lawns. "After Wounded Knee, I did my best to get killed by volunteering for every dangerous assignment I could find, from South Dakota to New Mexico."

He turned to face her. "I fought in some of the bloodiest battles near the end of the Indian wars and survived without a scratch. "Then I went back home to Boston to find that my sister had tried to drown herself in the coy pond. Our gardener pulled her out before any damage could be done, but as soon as she recovered from that, she tried to hang herself from the second-floor landing. The railing broke and she landed on a divan, suffering only a few bruises. Now she stays in her room, a shell of the brilliant and vibrant woman she once was.

"Searching for Victor gave me a purpose back then, but truth be told, I never expected to find him. Amanda had family to take care of her and while he took her money and a big chunk of her pride, she survived…physically."

He returned to stand by Lily but made no effort to reach out. "Then I found you. Despite Victor's threat, you are the best thing that could have happened to me. I began thinking of a future with you the moment you corrected me about your name—after just falling from a ceiling. But my timing was bad. If McKinley bows to the pressure to declare war, I'll likely be called back to active duty as an officer or a medic. I don't deserve, or want, either option, but I can't refuse—and Victor is still out there."

She sipped her unfinished sherry and rose to step into his arms. They stood that way for a long time, just holding each other.

To Lily, it would always be her wedding night. Even the night she'd given her virginity to Victor's practiced lovemaking couldn't compare to the passion, tenderness, and connection she felt with Colin. They'd made love since that first time under the mahogany tree, but this time they were two people who finally knew each other's secrets and sins—and accepted both.

Colin undressed her, and she undressed him. For a long time, they lay together on the feather-tick mattress, naked and silent, listening to each other breathe, feeling the heat of their bodies and the rhythm of their heartbeats. She marveled at the sinewy strength in his arms and traced the scars on his chest. The newest one, caused by Victor's bullet, was still pink and ragged. "These old scars," she asked. "You said they weren't from the Apache. What are they from?"

He caressed the soft fullness of her breasts and kissed her. "I disobeyed orders to pull a woman and child from a burning lodge. I was nearly court-marshalled for my insubordination, but the woman and child survived—if you can call living on the desolate San Carlos reservation surviving."

"And the ones on your back?"

He was silent a long moment, then sighed, "Cat-o'-nine-tails. Twenty lashes."

"Why?"

"For burying my wife and child."

Unable to comprehend man's cruelty to his fellow man, she pressed, "Do they still pain you—physically?"

"No. They remind me that I'm still alive, though I haven't understood why—until now."

He raised to his elbows, just short of touching her, as the moon's glow highlighted the strong angles of his features. Then he slowly moved over her, his fingers caressing her face, her breasts, her stomach, stopping short of the part of her that throbbed the most for his touch. Hovering over her, his body testified to his passion.

She opened for him, taking a breath when his tongue touched her… there, then raised to kiss her lips with the taste of her own body on his tongue. In the next moment, he entered her, leaving the past in the past and the future to fate. For those precious moments, there was no threat of war. No fear of Victor hiding in the shadows. Indeed, Lily wouldn't have minded if he was. Then he could see how a real man loved a woman, and how much love she could give to the *right* man.

After, they lay breathless and moist in the warm, humid air, dozing as the moon slowly gave over the night to the light of a new day.

CHAPTER 30

The early morning call of a mockingbird from the edge of the jungle woke Lily. She kissed the burn scars on Colin's chest and breathed into his ear, causing one sleepy brown eye to open. "It's dawn," she whispered.

His body stirred against her and hers throbbed in response, but the sun was fully up. "You have the early train and I have a meeting with Clara at nine o'clock." Suddenly concerned about propriety, she worried, "I must get back to my room. I hope no one is up yet."

He tilted his head. "Regrets?"

The hurt in his voice touched her and her long kiss gave him her answer. "Never. But you have a train to catch and I have a reputation to maintain."

"For now," he said, trailing a finger along the line of her cheek. "If you're willing, when I return, I'd like to make an honest woman out of you."

The man she loved more than her own life had just asked her to marry him, but instead of feeling giddy, she felt angry. She rolled off the bed, naked in the rays of the early morning sun as she faced him. "I *am* an honest woman, and there's no need to march me to the altar after a few rolls in the hay, so to speak. And now, when you're leaving and there's a war coming, is *not* the time to talk of marriage."

He looked stunned and more than a little miffed at her censure.

"But understand this. "I will be here—or anywhere else you need me to be—when you return."

Pulling the dress over her naked body, she gathered the rest of her clothes into a bundle and kissed him on both cheeks before carefully opening his door, stepping barefoot into the hall and sprinting down the service stairs to her room.

While men could dress in a few minutes, women took much longer. Even now, when dresses no longer dragged the ground and bustles had replaced hoops, there was still the corset to manage, the camisole, the stockings, and the tedious task of shoe-lacing. Not to mention hairpins and hatpins. Lily was ten minutes late for breakfast with Clara and her departing friends.

In the distance, the morning train's whistle confirmed that Colin had again stepped out of her life. Hopefully it wouldn't be for long. She wished him a safe trip, a successful effort to avoid war, as well as a speedy return, before turning her attention to the latest news and gossip swirling around the breakfast room.

"Plant has asked President McKinley to protect Tampa," a gentleman with a newspaper at another table said loud enough for the Red Cross table to hear. *Politician*, Lily thought, but she kept an ear tuned to his voice while politely nodding to her companions.

"I hear Fitzhugh Lee will be arriving soon, and Sigsbee from the *Maine* as well," again rose above other conversations, catching the room's attention. He tossed his paper onto the table and stood, telling his companions, "Mark my words. Tampa will become a hub for the war."

Lily would have followed him if Colin hadn't already filled her in on the latest news from Washington. The gentleman was correct. The hotel would soon be inundated by military officers.

She realized that Gómez' request to negotiate US support for the rebels in the form of money and munitions was doomed from the start. America would never play second fiddle in a war so close to home and with so much at stake. She recognized the sad irony that stories about it could make her career.

The departing members of the Red Cross group opted to take the midday train to Gainesville for their connections east and west. The heat of the day hadn't yet set in when they gathered in the lobby amid hotel guests headed for golf courses and sightseeing tours. Those remaining enjoyed the air circulating from electric ceiling fans in the lobby and the shade on the veranda. When they set off for the depot. most of the rocking chairs were already claimed by those inclined to spend the day people-watching

She recognized two new arrivals. Author/journalist Steven Crane looked frail next to Frederick Remington the famous artist and illustrator for Hearst's *New York Journal*, who was already sketching the social and military celebrities.

"Mrs. Champagne," startled her and she turned to see Richard Harding-Davis standing by his friends, motioning for her to join them. Impeccably dressed in a gray suit, white shirt with a high collar, and perfectly aligned tie, his brand of charm didn't quite ring true to her. She forced a smile when he gushed, "What a wonderful coincidence."

He remained standing when she declined his offer of a chair. "I'm so glad you and your husband got out of Havana safely," he said. "I was in Ybor City last evening, following up a story, when I chanced upon Victor. He never mentioned you were staying here. Will we be honored by another performance, if not on stage, at the piano?"

She didn't hear anything after Victor and Ybor City.

"Mrs. Champagne, you look pale. Are you unwell?" Davis asked, repositioning the empty chair. "Shall I send for a doctor? I believe I saw you chatting with Dr. Winfield yesterday. Perhaps he's free."

Angry at her reaction to the mere mention of Victor's name, she snapped, "No!"

Heads turned at her exclamation and she opened her fan. "It must be the heat," she said. "I'm afraid I left my parasol in my room. Not to worry, I'm fine, though I doubt I'll have time to entertain. I'm working with Miss Barton." His eyebrows rose at her admission of taking a job and she added, "Victor has...other business...in Ybor City." She smoothed her skirt, smiling as brightly as she could manage. "If you'll excuse me, we're seeing some of the staff off on the train. I don't want to miss them."

The three men, all standing now, nodded politely and she walked briskly to catch up with the Red Cross group, her mind chanting, *he's here. I was right. He's here. He's here. And I'm alone.*

But wasn't that what she wanted? Colin was safe. Victor didn't know he was alive. He also didn't know she was aware he was in Ybor City. She patted the derringer in her purse and scanned the shrubbery for Victor.

They reached the station well ahead of the second and final departure of the day and joined other passengers to sit on benches in the shade. Clara chatted with Sister Bettina, who was returning to New York with her husband to await word for their return to Havana. Lily looked for Ailish and stopped short when she saw her chatting with a man near the tracks.

Fear gripped her as she recognized the distinctive tilt of Victor's head, his hand innocently resting on the woman's back as they leaned over the track toward the approaching train. Her heart racing, Lily called, "Ailish!"

It startled the man, and Ailish stepped back as Engine Two roared past them.

Breathless, Lily took her friend's hand, gently steering her away from the tracks—and Victor. She huffed, "I…thought I'd missed you."

"Me too," Ailish exclaimed and embraced her.

Lily took a deep breath to calm herself. *Would Victor really have pushed Ailish in front of the train?*

In the confusion of hugs, bags being moved, and packages dropped while the crowd all pressed to board at the same time, Lily realized her purse was missing. Clara, Mr. Elwell, and the remaining staff had turned to go back to the hotel, and she returned to where she'd said her last good-bye to Ailish. But instead of her purse lying on the platform, she found Victor's leering smile. "Missing something?"

He wore a stylish white suit, complete with a fine silk vest and a gold watch chain with a "C" hanging from it, attached to the pocket of his waistcoat. She had no doubt he was mocking Colin's style of dress and thanked God he'd taken the early train. His sly smile widened when he dangled her black velvet bag from his fingertips. "Forget something?"

She damned herself for forgetting what a talented pickpocket Victor was. Cursing herself for a fool, she answered, "It seems so," to the smile she'd once found so charming. Her calm surprised her. It was as if she'd gone cold inside, impervious to fear, or even anger. Not surprisingly, he pulled his hand back as she reached out for the bag.

She stepped back, refusing to play his game. "I see you made it out of Cuba without harm. Perhaps you really are a magician."

He circled her slowly, reminding her of the sequin-clad matador at the bullfight. She remained still, even when he stepped behind her, so close she could feel his breath on her neck. One step later, he was in front of her, far enough away to ward off a blow, but too close to offer a chance to escape. With the train disappearing into the distance and Clara's group too far ahead to call for help, perspiration beaded under her hat, but she refused to blink as he loomed over her, pure evil shining from his amber eyes.

"I see you noticed my fine suit and gold watch chain," he oozed.

When she didn't respond, he taunted, "He was so easy to kill, you know. He and the greaser. They were standing under the streetlamp, for God's sake. I was only going to follow them, but I took it as a sign. Sadly, my aim was too true. Your lover never knew what hit him. I wanted my face to be the last thing he saw."

He stepped back to bow. "But we take the opportunities when we see them—don't we, darling?"

She finally saw the madness in his eyes. Maybe it had been there all along. Thinking of the matador, she reasoned that Victor thought he'd stabbed her where it would hurt the most—without killing her. Why, she wondered? To throw her in front of a train and claim it as an accident? If so, he'd missed his chance. And they were standing on a public boardwalk. He couldn't be that mad.

Finally realizing his arrogance as his weakness, she tugged her purse from his hand, stepping back onto the walk. "What do you want of me, Victor—or Robert—or is it Lionel Carter?"

He took two steps toward her and she took two steps back. Her hand slid into her empty purse and she wished she'd had the foresight to move the derringer to her pocket.

The cruelty in his laugh made her flesh crawl. "We could go on like this all day, Lily," he said. "So, I'll answer your question. I want fifty thousand dollars. The amount I lost for the confiscated guns—doubled for the pain and anguish I've suffered because of you."

He circled her once more, and this time she joined in his dance, refusing to relinquish eye contact.

"The Spaniards caught me, you know," he sneered. "Sent me to that damn castle, but I bribed a guard with what little I had left from Gómez' deposit on my guns. A few misfires and Diaz refused to pay the rest."

His sly grin only made him look even more depraved when he said, "I waited in the filthy back alleys of Havana for weeks for you to come back. We'd have talked sooner, but you were falling all over the 'good' doctor and clinging to that old hag from the Red Cross."

"You're insane," she hissed. "I don't have that kind of money, even in my trust fund, which you very well know I can't access. And if I could, any withdrawals of more than a thousand dollars must be approved by my father until I'm thirty."

She refused to cringe as his finger ran the length of her cheek and he changed the subject. "I see you've let your hair grow back to its natural blonde. It makes you look cheap—but then maybe you are. If you can't draw on your trust, I suggest you find another way to come up with the money. His hand squeezed her breast. Considering all the millionaires strolling these grounds, I'm sure you can think of something."

He caught the hand she raised to slap him, squeezing her wrist until she thought it would break. With a nod toward Clara's distant back, he smiled. "Your elderly friend Miss Barton seems very frail. She's such an important person, it would be very sad if something happened to her."

She stepped on his boot, causing enough discomfort for him to release her wrist, but he was too close to hit him hard enough to cause any harm. "Don't you even think about hurting her. If she so much as stubs a toe, I'll see you hang."

His gold eyes burned into hers. "I'm through playing now. You no longer amuse me. You have two weeks to pull the money together. And don't run. If you do, I'll find you and I'll kill you—slowly and painfully."

He stepped back, offering a mad, two-finger salute to his fine silk hat. "Until later, my love."

She stood stock-still until he hailed a cab and climbed in. Back to his cave in Ybor City, she assumed. Or maybe a berth in a Port Tampa bawdy house. *Two weeks.* It would be mid-May. Her parents weren't due back until August, and she refused to even think about conceding to his extortion. He'd kill her even if she paid him a king's ransom. It would never end until Victor was in jail—or one of them was dead.

CHAPTER 31

*A*s much as she hated to admit it, Victor's sudden appearance, threat, and disappearance shook her. Wondering where and when he would appear next, and how she'd deal with his impossible demand, consumed her and she barely noticed the now-crowded veranda filled with new arrivals, many of them wearing uniforms. Lost in her thoughts, she jumped at the sound of her name screeching from across the lobby. She looked up in time to see a woman in a hotel maid's uniform swoop toward her. The halting gait and big smile with a few missing teeth told her who it was.

"Willie!" she cried in return and they embraced in the middle of the marble foyer filled with millionaires and millionaire want-to-bes. She noticed that hotel guests frowned at their undignified and socially unsuitable public show of affection and pulled away, worried Willie might put her new job at risk by accosting a guest.

The older woman caught on and curtsied saying loudly, "Yer room is ready, ma'am."

"Well, it's about time." Lily did her best upper-crust socialite impersonation before following her down a short hallway to an empty sitting room.

"We're so glad you're safe," Willie exclaimed, breathless from her run down the stairs and across the lobby. "We heard you was stuck in Havana."

She leaned close. "Where is that bastard husband o' yours? Don't tell me he deserted you among all them wild jungle heathens."

Lily controlled her pique at the unjustified and insulting description of the Cuban rebels. Like most Americans, Willie had no idea what it was really like to live as a peasant in Cuba. And as thrilled as she was to see her friend, she couldn't tell her about Victor. Instead, she answered, "It's a long story. I'm fine. Victor is…gone. I'm using my given name, O'Grady."

Willie nodded, her wise eyes showing she'd read between the lines. "Aye, that's good. O'Grady suits you. And ye look well. There's a bloom in yer cheeks and yer hair is back to the sunny blonde it was afore…*he*…made ye change it."

Lily didn't correct the errors in her compliments. Any flush on her cheeks was because of Victor's threat, and she was at least ten pounds thinner than in December. And while her natural honey-blonde hair was coming back, she hid the dyed lengths in a chignon, or under a hat. In short, she bore very little, if any, resemblance to the voluptuous Lady Liberty of only a few months ago. Instead, she changed the subject. "More important, how are you still here? And where are Merlyn and Esther—and her dogs?"

The older woman planted her hands on a waist that had thickened in the last four months. "We all stayed. We knew ye'd be back and couldn't desert ye." Responding to Lily's doubtful expression, she confessed, "Truth be told, Victor took our money so we couldn't pay our bill. We're workin' off that, an' the damages."

She took Willie's hand in hers. "I'm so sorry you were left with that. I don't have much money right now, but I can wire what's left in my account in New York to help pay off some of the debt. It was my fault, after all."

Willie's arthritic fingers squeezed hers. "No! None o' it was yer fault. It was the best thing could happen to us. We was all has-bins, and ye know it. I'm happy makin' beds and mendin' fancy clothes. Sometimes I help dress the ladies or arrange their hair. An' the tips are good."

She leaned in. "Merlyn…it's his real name, ya know. Well, he's a night porter. In the daytime, he gits a little extra doin' magic shows fer the kiddies. They love him, but who knows what hijinks they'll get into when they git home."

Lily was surprised she could still laugh. And once she started, she couldn't stop until the tears of laughter became a torrent of pent-up emotions. Willie held her until she calmed. She dried her eyes and blew her nose in Willie's handkerchief, saying, "I'm so sorry. It's…just…well, I'm so happy things worked out for you two. What about Esther and her dogs?"

Now, Willie's eyes glistened with tears. "She let her babies out one night and they chased a gator what wandered through the garden. Stupid mutts, the gator ate all four of 'em."

Lily gasped and the older woman patted her shoulder. "But Esther is doin' okay. She cares fer the rich ladies' little mutts and teaches 'em parlor tricks. The hotel pays her a little an' she does fine on tips. We all git room and board and pool our tips so's we kin live together when we're old someday."

Lily's eyes misted again. "I'm so happy for you all. But I still intend to pay off that debt. And I have some news of my own."

"Ahem," came from the doorway, where Georges stood, arms folded across his chest. "You got nothin' to do, Willie?"

She turned and gave him a clumsy curtsy. "Sure do, boss. Them beds on the third floor ain't gonna make themselves." She winked at Lily. "Merlyn an' I git off work at six, and Esther finishes her dog walks at three, afore the gators git hungry. If ye kin git away, we kin meet at the old tradin' post. It's a tavern in town. We kin toast a pint or two."

Meeting at a tavern was out of the question. After what nearly happened to Ailish, and Victor's threat about Clara, she didn't want to put anyone else close to her in danger. "I'd love to, but I have…work…that will keep me busy here. If you have a day off, maybe we can meet in the garden—during the day?"

Willie's eyes narrowed at the obvious ruse. "Sure thing."

The days were filled with activity for the reduced Red Cross staff as they drafted letters seeking funds and supplies and Clara repeatedly requested permission to return to Cuba. In a rare visible moment of frustration, she shared that she had been trying for years to convince the military that the mission of the Red Cross was to move *with* the troops, not follow them at a safe distance. She sniffed and tossed yet another condescending letter from the Chief Army Medical Officer who insisted that civilian doctors and nurses, specifically women, should be used only to support the meager and under-trained Army staff, onto her desk.

"Most Army physicians haven't even seen a war," she grumbled. "And the ones who have, haven't read a medical journal in decades. They'd be of more service as butchers than surgeons."

On April 25th, the US declared war with Spain, and Clara pulled Lily aside. "We may be leaving soon," she said. "President McKinley has finally granted my request for a ship. The *USS Texas* is in New York being fitted out with sixteen-hundred tons of supplies for Cuba. It may take a few days, but when it sails, we'll meet it in Key West. I've been authorized to oversee the organization and distribution in Cuba."

It was both wonderful and terrible news for Lily. Clara had been her surrogate grandmother for months. She was a counselor, guardian, and mentor to whom she literally owed her life. But she couldn't go with them. Her only solace was that Clara and the others would be safe from Victor in Key West.

But sadly, it was just as Colin had feared. Though no shots had been fired yet, they were officially at war with Spain. Her heart sank at the thought that he would be called back into the service of his country—with the President choosing his role. Would it be physician or warrior—or both?"

She embraced her benefactress. "That is wonderful news. I'll miss you all so. But I cannot go with you."

The old woman's smile was kind. "I know, my dear, and I've come to think of you as the daughter—or perhaps granddaughter—I never had. I will miss you and Colin, but we will be doing God's work as we oversee the food distribution to the Cuban nationals. Our government doesn't give them the credit they're due. The doctors and nurses on the island are fully qualified. It's only food, facilities, and medical supplies they need. Hopefully we can get to them before there's a blockade. Have you decided your path yet?"

Lily reviewed her options. She'd already decided that going home to Georgia would endanger her family. Victor would follow her anywhere. "I have a small income from my books and articles," she told Clara. "Perhaps I can be of service as a translator for the Cuban volunteers already pouring in from Ybor City. I'll be fine."

Clara smiled and patted her arm. "I'm certain you will, darling. You are a very independent woman."

The compliment meant a lot coming from the septuagenarian founder of the International Red Cross. "How long do we have together?"

It wasn't as long as she hoped. Clara and her entourage boarded Henry

Plant's steamship, *Mascotte,* on the 29th of April to meet the *Texas* in Key West. Both Lily's mentor and her job were gone, and the country was readying for war. The only word she'd had from Colin was a short letter telling her the President had requested he remain in Washington to discuss a special assignment.

Still, she wasn't alone. She had Willie, Merlyn, and Esther. Even Georges seemed part of their motley crew, and with three-thousand troops already camped at Tampa Heights and rumors of thousands more on the way, she'd have little time alone.

She let Georges know she'd be happy to entertain as a pianist in the lavish ballroom, dining room, or even the lobby. She'd learned the hard way that the best way to learn the latest news—and reactions—was from America's rich and powerful elite.

CHAPTER 32

On May 1st, Lily responded to a second short letter from Colin telling her he'd been asked to train a new group of soldiers for Theodore Roosevelt. He had resigned as Assistant Secretary of the Navy and proposed an elite fighting force of volunteers from the West who he touted as well-prepared for the hostile climate and type of combat the Army would face in Cuba.

The band of cavalry veterans, Texas and New Mexico Rangers, frontiersmen, Buffalo Soldiers, and ranchers from the Western territories had taken on the nickname, "Rough Riders," from Buffalo Bill's Wild West shows. He'd leave for San Antonio, Texas, in mid-May. He hoped to visit Tampa along the way.

Excited about seeing him again, she wrote:

It has only been a week since Clara's departure and as you predicted, Tampa has been overrun by the military. Within days of the declaration of war, volunteers began arriving by train. More than fourteen thousand already, in camps surrounding Tampa. Some of them sleep in tents on the beach, others in the sand itself. They seem woefully ill-prepared, and rumors are that it is only half the expected increase in Tampa's population from only a few hundred souls.

I go to the post office once a week and have seen the decline in order. Horses run in the streets and guns are fired into the air by exuberant soldiers. I fear for what the streets might be at night, with so many idle soldiers waiting for their time to go to war. Perhaps some of the many officers lounging on rocking chairs, drinking wine, and dining on eleven course meals—the price of which could feed most of the orphans in Cuba—should spend more time with their men to restore order.

How I miss your ability to see through to the heart of matters and find order in chaos. Though I am a member of the press and would put my life on the line for the truth, I am disappointed in the behavior of many of my colleagues. Numbering more than one hundred, they stalk the corridors, listening at doors, and shadowing dancers at evening balls. Sadly, it seems that if they can't find a story, they invent one. Davis, Remington, Crane, and George Rae have claimed a table on the veranda, watching it all over tall glasses of sweet tea. Harry arrived only yesterday and looks very tired. Perhaps his fevers have returned. The officers now occupy two entire floors of the hotel, with only a few wives in the mix.

Despite the circumstances, I happily await your visit. Yours always, Lily

There was so much more she wanted to write, but there were rumors about Spanish spies stealing correspondence from Tampa and other key military cities. More than noisy ballrooms and crude bars outside town, the post office was the hub of the tiny frontier-style city. Soldiers gathered to mail and receive letters, openly discussing their lives in the camps. What better way to learn what was really happening in the war effort than from the very men who would fight it? It sparked an idea and she struck up a conversation with Mr. Monahan, the postmaster.

"Gettin' busy around here," he said after stamping her letter. "Afore long, with all them mucky-mucks out at the hotel sendin' an' gettin' letters, I'll need me a runner. But all the fit young boys 'round here joined up. The rest ain't worth spit."

He paused to do just that, with perfect aim at the copper spittoon in the corner. He was right that the troops, outnumbering the combined populations of Tampa and Port Tampa by three to one, had taken over the towns, as well as the sleepy villages surrounding them.

"I'll do it," she volunteered.

Bushy gray eyebrows raised in both surprise and amusement. "Ain't no job fer a lady."

"On the contrary, sir. I live at the hotel and have a bicycle. I can gather the outgoing mail and bring it here, returning with the incoming mail. It will keep the commotion down. And if you're busy, I can take mail and help sort it."

He stood firm until she said the magic words, "And you don't have to pay me."

"When can you start?"

"Now, of course."

From there she went directly to the *Daily News* to offer her services in providing weekly updates on camp life—without having to visit the overcrowded, unsanitary, and unruly camps. The publisher was familiar with her work for Pulitzer and offered her the same rate.

Pedaling as fast as she could on the rutted sandy road back to the hotel, she studied the faces of men in unwashed wool uniforms lounging on the boardwalk, swatting flies and carefully stepping over horse dung in temperatures approaching ninety degrees. Mr. Monahan had told her that by June, when the sea breezes stilled and the humidity settled hot and thick on every surface, mosquitoes would descend on them in cloud-like swarms to suck their life's blood.

"It's the same in Cuba, I've heard," Monahan said. "If they wait much longer, this Army will die of fever before they fire a shot."

She remembered Colin had told her, "Waiting is the worst part of war."

It was another reason she was happy to take the courier job. She was tired of waiting for Victor to come out of his hiding place. If he was watching, she wanted him to know she wasn't afraid of him—thanks to yet another derringer in her duster pocket. More than once, she thought she saw someone his size dart into an alley. But she couldn't be sure. How frustrating for him, she thought. That the tiny Gulf Coast town was thronging with government officials and men wearing guns—while he was a wanted man.

Three days later, she parked her bicycle and walked up the stairs to the meandering veranda, acknowledging nods and smiles from those who enjoyed her evening piano performances and patriotic sing-alongs. Richard Harding-Davis again invited her to join the growing group of journalists at his table. She again declined, citing the dust clinging to the hem of her white, sailor-style dress with navy trim.

Georges waved her over to his desk when she approached the hall to her room. She was surprised at the gregarious host's grim expression and noticed an official-looking document in his hand. Her blood ran cold. Thank God it wasn't a telegram. Nothing good ever came from a telegram. She put a hand on his arm. "What is it?"

"I don't know, miss, but Major-General Shafter's man asked me to give you this."

Shafter, a Civil War veteran from Michigan, had recently been promoted to command the 5th Army Corps of volunteers, including Colin's Rough Riders. Since his arrival, she'd seen the three-hundred-pound general a few times, sitting in the rocker Henry Plant had custom-made for him. She opened the note and looked up at Georges. "He wants to see me. As soon as I return, it says. On the verandah. But it doesn't say why."

He winked. "I don't know, but best not keep him waiting. It's approachin' dinnertime. You could be the main dish if you wait too long."

She smiled through her worry. "I think I would cause him a grave case of indigestion."

Conscious of her unkempt appearance after the bicycle ride, she shook the hem of her skirt and hastily re-pinned her hair under a jaunty sailor-style hat in preparation of having tea with one of the most powerful men in the hotel. Twenty minutes later, she stood at attention on his left side while he rehashed yet another Civil War battle with his former enemy, General Fitzhugh Lee. She cleared her throat and said, "Major-General, Sir."

Lee stood to greet her and removed his hat. He looked like a Southern planter in a tropical white suit, his white hair parted neatly in the middle. "A pleasure to see you again, Miss O'Grady." He smiled. "Or is it Mrs. Winfield by now?"

A flush warmed her already sticky body. "It's O'Grady, sir," she answered and turned to General Shafter. While Lee was a man of generous proportions himself, he seemed dwarfed by his enormous companion, who remained seated.

"I apologize for the hasty invitation," a gravelly voice came from beneath a thick gray handlebar mustache. "But these are extreme circumstances, wouldn't you agree?"

At her nod, he stretched an arm wearing more braid than she'd ever seen on one uniform. "This shouldn't take long. Please, be seated."

He flagged a waiter and ordered her a sweet tea, then leaned toward her as much as the space between his belly and the table would allow. "I'm told you worked with Miss Barton to set up the relief efforts for the *reconcentrados*."

She nodded and he continued, "I admire the woman very much. It took a great deal of courage for the Red Cross to accomplish what they did in Turkey."

"Thank—"

He held up a ham-sized palm. "I didn't ask you here to flatter you. I asked for you…Miss O'Grady…because you are in a unique position to be of service to your country."

After leaving her speechless, he explained, "I am acquainted with your father, Representative O'Grady. He is an honorable man. I'm also told you speak Spanish."

She stopped herself from saying, *yes, sir* to answer, "Yes. I am fluent in the language. What do you need from me?"

When Shafter smiled his eyes nearly disappeared into the folds of his face, becoming tiny blue specks in a mass of sunburned skin and a thick neck overflowing his military collar. He cleared his throat. "We have reason to believe that information about our troop movements and camps have been finding their way to Havana. We suspect a Spanish loyalist disguising himself as a Cuban in Tampa. The post office there serves us and Port Tampa, so the only way to get word in or out is through there."

"Shouldn't you be talking to the postmaster?" challenged the commander of the 5th US Army.

His flushed deepened at her audacity. "Once mail has been stamped in by the post office, it is protected. We need to see his messages before they're processed—and his incoming mail before he sees it."

The smile that split his enormous face reminded her of a Halloween jack-o-lantern. "I'm told you are a very enterprising young woman and your message delivery service is very popular, after only a few days. Perhaps you can strike a 'friendship' with him to discover his contact and his purpose."

Gooseflesh rose on her arms while a flush heated her face. She leaned toward him to whisper, "Are you suggesting I become a spy…sir?"

He smiled at her audacity. "My apologies if there was ever any confusion, Miss O'Grady, but that is exactly what I…we…are asking you to do."

Lee took over then. "What my colleague means is that since you spend considerable time at the post office, you could perhaps strike up a conversation with this man and find a way to intercept his mailings. We would then be able to determine who is corresponding with him. Of course, your mission would remain among the three of us only. Whatever you discover, take it directly to Major-General Shafter. We simply must keep this information from leaving Tampa."

For reasons having nothing to do with the fact that Shafter was a Yankee, she didn't trust him. But he was Colin's commander. She turned to him. "I want this 'conflict' to end as quickly as possible too, Sir. I'll be happy to help in any way I can…within limits."

The next morning there was a line in front of the post office and a haggard Mr. Monahan struggled to both receive and distribute the day's mail to a room crowded with Negro soldiers wearing clean blue flannel uniforms.

"Buffalo soldiers," Colin had called them. A name of honor bestowed by the Western tribes for their curly hair and courage in battle. Lily cleared her throat behind the tallest, broadest one with a sergeant's insignia on his arm.

Without turning, the big man said in a deep baritone, "Wait your turn, son. Cain't you see the man's busy?"

"Excuse me," she tried again.

He turned then and took off his hat. "Pardon, miss," he said in a softer tone. "Is there somethin' ah can do for you?"

Heads turned and his men followed his example by taking off their hats and parting like the Red Sea to create a path for her. Was it instinct or training from parents who had likely been slaves? Either way, she was grateful. As a white woman, she should have gone immediately to the now-open counter, but something about the sergeant's voice held her in place. She looked up to see big, sea-green eyes in an ebony face.

She took a deep breath. "Grover? Is that you?"

He pulled away when she reached out to touch him. Thirty years after Emancipation, it was still unheard of for a Negro to touch, or be touched by, a white woman in public. She should have remembered that.

Now at a safe distance, he cocked his head. "Miss Lily?"

"Yes," she answered the son of her beloved Chloe, and Lester Hawkins. They were one of twenty families of former slaves who accepted forty acres each to stay at Langesford after the war. Five years her senior, Grover had saved her life when she jumped into the Ogemaw River during rainy season to save a puppy caught in the current. She gave him the fine, red-bone hound in exchange for his silence, and he proclaimed himself her protector for life.

But more than his size and his loyalty, it was his voice that made him stand out. Changing early into a deep baritone, he was a big attraction at the Jeffers County Fair. Every year, his rendition of "Amazing Grace" and other favorite hymns had emptied white wallets for the orphans supported by the Jeffers Negro Baptist Church.

"What are you doing here?" they said in unison, and suddenly became the center of attention in the crowded little building.

A wide, proud smile lit his face. "Quartermaster Sergeant Grover L. Hawkins, at your service, Miss Lily." He motioned to his men. "We are the 10th Cavalry, here to free the Cubans from slavery."

If anyone could, she believed it would be Grover, but while Negroes had shown uncommon skill and bravery during the War and after, in the Indian Campaigns, they were generally relegated to support functions, with the so-called "glory" going to their white comrades.

A white man stepped into the building. He frowned at her and the smiling black giant in disgust. She realized that if he reported Grover for accosting a white woman, he could be court-martialed, or worse. She raised her voice so the man could hear. "It's good to see you doing well, Grover. I'll tell my father you have made a fine boy of yourself."

Grover smiled and lowered his gaze to grovel. "Why, thank ya, Miss Lily. Ah appreciate your good will."

The man gave them both a wide berth on his way out and Grover escorted her to the counter, where a shocked Mr. Monahan stood, tobacco juice dripping from his open mouth. "Sergeant Hawkins was one of my father's…people," she muttered, ashamed for not being able to call him her friend.

At just past noon, "*Por favor*," came from the other side of the counter. Lily leaned forward to see a shock of black hair belonging to a Cuban boy whose head barely reached the top.

"*Hola, Peudo ayudarte?*" she offered her help.

He seemed thrilled to hear his native tongue and answered in Spanish that he had a letter to post, then skipped out after proudly handing her his two cents. When the door banged shut behind him, Monahan said, "That's strange."

"How so?" Lily asked, though she doubted the boy knew how to read, let alone write a letter—or have the coins to post it.

"Comes in every Tuesday to post a letter. And on the fourth Tuesday of the month, picks up the incoming mail from a rented box."

"He must be a messenger," she offered, her skin prickling with curiosity. "Have you asked him who he works for?"

It seemed like a logical question, but Monahan's face puckered like he'd just eaten some bad fish. "I don't speak greaser,' but a man can wonder."

"I suppose so." Her heart raced. Could the spy be using the child as a courier?

She ached to retrieve the child's letter she'd just dropped into the bag of outgoing mail, but not in front of the postmaster.

"It's been a long morning, sir," she said. "Why don't you take a break before we close? I'll clean up."

The short, stout Irishman patted a wispy circle of white hair along the back of his head and smiled. "What a lovely lass you are. I must say, I believe I could use a pint after all the hoopla from those new colored troops." He handed her the door key. "Put it under the azalea pot by the shed when yer done."

Surprised that a US postmaster would use an azalea pot as a place for his key, she reasoned that until recently, few people felt the need to lock anything in a town with fewer residents than the hotel had guests. She returned his smile. "I'll do just that Mr. Monahan."

"Call me Ira," was followed by the tinkle of the little bell on the top of the door as he left.

She pulled the boy's letter from the top of the outgoing mailbag. It was addressed to a man named Carranza in Montreal, Canada. Why would someone in Tampa exchange mail with a Spaniard in Canada—using a little Cuban boy as a courier? Perhaps General Shafter was right about the spy. She lowered the shades on the two front windows and put the *Closed* sign on the door before lighting the little cookstove to boil water in the tin teapot. While it heated, she reached for the keys to the numbered boxes.

Stealing private mail was a crime, so she told herself she was intercepting the letter—*for* the government, and if it was correspondence between Spanish spies, it would be unpatriotic *not* to open it. If it wasn't, she didn't trust General Shafter to protect her so she decided to see if there was any incoming mail *from* Senor Carranza.

She opened fifteen of the twenty boxes and found nothing but personal correspondence. Letters from home, addressed with feminine handwriting, smelling of lilac and rose sachet. It was getting late and when the tea pot screamed, she stopped opening boxes to steam open the boy's letter.

What she found confirmed General Shafter's suspicions. There were photographs of Army tents, boxcars filled with weapons and supplies, even the horse corral of the 10th Cavalry. The spy's latest report, no doubt. Her heart beat fast and she could hardly breathe in the warm, steamy back room. She jumped and nearly screamed when someone pounded on the locked door and a dark shape pressed against the shaded window. "Let me in," a drunken voice slurred. "I gotta piss."

She crouched beneath the counter until the drunk was gone, then tiptoed over to finish opening the numbered boxes. She struck pay dirt at number nineteen, where three envelopes, all with a Canadian postmark on a modern, gummed envelope waited to be claimed.

They were from Montreal, addressed to a man named Carter. Her heart raced at seeing Victor's real name on a spy's letter, and she considered replenishing the coals in Ira's tiny cookstove to open them. But he could return any moment. There was one more week before the boy retrieved the contents, so she decided to take the lot back to the hotel to properly steam them open and reseal if they turned out to be personal in nature.

She opened box twenty to make sure she didn't miss anything and saw that everything was in place. With her little reticule too small for the letters, and the derringer filling her pocket, she unbuttoned her blouse, placing them between her chemise and shirtwaist. She moved the teapot from the cooling stove and like a thief in the night, left through the back door, locked it and placed the key under the azalea pot before climbing onto her bike.

She forced herself to pedal at her usual pace while keeping a careful eye out for anyone following her. A block from the post office, she saw the boy talking to a tall, lean man with dark hair. Even from a distance in the midday heat, she shivered at seeing Victor.

He was focused on the boy, but his profile was clear. Her bike swerved in and out of a rut in the sandy road, nearly crossing the path of a mounted soldier. He managed to pull the fine chestnut out of her way while she fought to keep the bicycle upright and her skirt out of the spokes. The soldier's angry curses echoed in her ears, and the fear that Victor had seen her gripped her heart as she sped back to the hotel.

She left the bicycle at the servants' entrance and rushed inside, going straight to the kitchen to heat another pot of water to melt the thin layer of mucilage sealing the expensive envelopes. As soon as it started to whistle, she took it from the stove and bolted to her room, locking the door. Her heart raced and sweat beaded on her forehead as she sat on her bed, holding each envelope over the steaming pot.

The letters opened easily, each one revealing a bank draft for fifty dollars. The last one had instructions about providing additional information and where to send it. While the bank draft was in American currency, the letters were in Spanish. Apparently, Victor had picked up the language during his time at El Morro.

He'd told her he bribed a guard to escape, but these letters proved he'd made a different agreement with his captors. One far more dangerous than swindler or gun runner. Now, Victor was a traitor and a spy.

She rose on shaking legs to fill her tub with lukewarm water and undressed. Twenty minutes later, hoping General Shafter wasn't at luncheon, she dressed carefully in a mauve afternoon dress, complete with corselet, flower-topped hat, gloves, and parasol. With the letters tucked into her beaded bag, she opened her door to climb the grand staircase to his second-floor office.

CHAPTER 33

*M*ajor-General Shafter showed no emotion as he listened to her translate the letters, sniffing at her suspicions about the identity of the spy. "An actor, you say. You can't be serious, gir...Miss O'Grady. I understand the man is a cad, but we have every reason to believe this operation is being run by highly skilled spies from Spain. We will send men to Montreal immediately, as well as conduct a search for the boy to find his employer..." He glanced at an envelope. "Mr. Robert Carter."

"It's an alias...sir," Lily tried to explain. "He's used many of them, including Victor Champagne. His real name is Lionel Carter. He's a swindler and gunrunner. Check with Mr. Roosevelt. I understand he is under your command. Or Dr. Colin Winfield, also under your command. Victor used that alias to swindle Colin's sister."

She saw only bemused impatience in Shafter's cold eyes when the door opened and the General rose. "Thank you for your service Miss O'Grady. It seems we will no longer need you. Major Kennedy, please show her out and authorize the standard payment for an informant, payable to Miss Lily O'Grady."

She ignored Major Kennedy's outstretched arm and turned back to the General. "But I saw him talking with the boy. And I think he saw me. He'll come after me."

He turned his back to her and waddled to the window overlooking the

Greek garden. "I suggest you contact the local constabulary about this *personal* threat. In the meantime, I have a military campaign to run."

"I will pray for our soldiers," she said to his broad backside. "For protection from the enemy within."

She gave Major Kennedy a withering look before pulling her skirt away from the prospect of touching his spit-shined boots, and sailed past him, back straight, head held high. She was on her own. Once Victor concluded that she'd stolen his mail, she wouldn't be safe in Tampa—or anywhere. She had to find him before he found her—again. What had her sister-in-law Elena told her about hunting? Yes, *Be the hunter, but think like the prey.*

Midway down the stairs, she heard voices raised in the lobby, with guests and military officers scurrying to the open front doors. The sound of church bells being relayed throughout the city filled the air and she rushed toward the front desk, shouting to Georges, "What's happening? Is there a fire? Where?"

"The post office is aflame!" he shouted above the din.

The post office? After she'd only just left it? "How?"

"Old man Monahan," someone said. "He went out for a drink and came back to a bonfire. The place was closed. Nobody hurt."

Relieved that Mr. Monahan hadn't been injured, and certain the coals were out in the cookstove, she knew exactly who set the fire. Was Victor pretending to be the drunk at the door? It wouldn't have mattered. There was no lock Victor couldn't pick. He must have checked his box after talking to the boy. But if General Shafter didn't believe Victor was the spy, it wasn't likely he'd believe her when she accused him of burning down the post office.

When the alarms finally stopped and people crowded both the staircase and the elevators to return to their rooms, she turned toward the wide Moorish doors, stopping in mid-step.

"Colin," she whispered.

His white suit was singed, covered with soot and ash. Only the threat of Victor lurking in the shadows stopped her from running into his arms and never letting him go. It would be like putting a target on his back.

He found her from across the lobby and apparently sensed that something was wrong. "How nice to see you again, Miss O'Grady," he said a little too loud.

"I wasn't aware you were coming…today," she answered, while her mind screamed, *Are you hurt? What happened? It was Victor who set the fire!*

"It's a quick trip to review the area before leaving for San Antonio. I'm meeting with General Shafter."

"I wish you luck," she said with undisguised acrimony. "I've recently had dealings with him and find him quite…difficult."

He nodded. "Yes, I served with old Pecos Bill in Texas when he commanded the 10th Cavalry out of Fort Davis."

He didn't look thrilled about seeing him again, but she recognized the unit. "Is that the colored cavalry unit? The one they call Buffalo Soldiers?"

His eyebrows raised. "How did you know that?"

"I know someone in it. Master Sergeant Grover Hawkins. They're here. I saw him this morning at the…post office."

"You were…" He looked around at the thinning crowd and took her elbow to guide her to a quiet corner. "I need to clean up and I'll be with Shafter the rest of the day. But we need to talk."

"Wait." She caught his hand and stepped close. "You need to know that Victor set the fire. I told Shafter he was a spy, but he doesn't believe me."

The doubt in Colin'a eyes hurt, but she couldn't let him go without telling him, "I found letters…from a spy in Canada, in a post office box. Addressed to Robert Carter and…"

"There you are, Colonel, sir," came from the stairs. Major Kennedy approached them quickly and saluted his superior officer. Ignoring Lily, he said, "I see you've been helping with the unfortunate fire. General Shafter asked to see you as soon as you arrived."

Colin returned the salute and his voice lowered. "Of course, Major."

He turned to Lily. "I've been invited to a reception this evening with General and Mrs. Shafter and his staff. I dare say, she would be pleased to have some feminine company. I'd be honored if you would accompany me."

Dining with the behemoth General was the last thing she wanted to do. They had to find Victor, but she owed it to Colin. She aimed her brightest stage smile at Major Kennedy. "I would be honored to be the General's dinner guest, Colonel Winfield."

His brown eyes glittered with humor. "I'll see you at eight."

An evening storm came up from the Gulf of Mexico that evening, drenching the opportunity to walk together after the tedious reception with too much food and wine—especially for the obese General Shafter and his generously proportioned wife, who talked too loudly and laughed too long at her husband's ribald jokes. His staff followed suit, of course, but Colin simply looked pained.

Lily assumed the meeting had not gone well, and when the interminable meal was over, they both begged off joining the others in the salon for more wine and idle chatter. Rather than risk using the elevator, or the stairs past a second floor literally crawling with correspondents and the third with US military, they stepped outside to use the servant entrance to Lily's first-floor room.

He left her before dawn to return to his room and met Richard Harding-Davis on his way down to breakfast. "Ho," Davis said, "I heard you were here. Had dinner with General Shafter—and the lovely Mrs. Champagne." He nudged Colin. "I never took you for a man who likes to play with fire."

Pompous ass, Colin thought. He never liked Davis. He considered the man, with his saccharine romantic novels, exaggerated exploits in the Turkish wars, and dandified costumes, to be an imposter, turning the horrors of war into romanticized chivalry to justify his own conceit. He faced Davis. "What do you mean?"

"Whoa, boy..." Davis raised his hands in the empty hallway. She's a catch alright, but a married woman. And her husband is in Ybor City. Rumors are Champagne's playing both sides of the fence."

Colin repeated, "And what do you mean by that?"

Davis smiled like the famous Cheshire cat in Lewis Carol's fantasy, *Alice in Wonderland.* "I may look like a fop my boy, but I know people—everywhere. A lector friend of mine at the Havana-American Cigar Factory told me he's been making overtures to the Cuban Liberation people about new Remington rifles. Trying to save his reputation, I suppose, after the fiasco with Gómez. And I heard from Shafter's chatty assistant that he may be sending intelligence letters to a Spanish spy in Montreal."

The elevator door opened, and Davis paused to doff his hat to Mrs. Shafter and her attractive young niece.

Colin considered that he may have misjudged the man—and Lily. He didn't doubt Victor was looking for quick cash in the form of a "deposit" by showing off a few new rifles with the promise of more that didn't exist. He decided to take a chance on Davis.

"Champagne's real name is Carter," he said. "He's wanted for fraud up and down the East Coast, by the Army for selling stolen guns, and by Gómez for selling him ones that blew up in his men's faces. What else do your 'sources' tell you about Champagne and the Cuban Liberation Army?"

Davis cocked his head. "Well now, I can't give away all my information, can I? How do I know you won't spill this to a lovely blonde reporter?"

"You don't. I'm a special attaché for President McKinley. Carter is the centerpiece of several investigations, but he's slippery. If you know anything that can help me find him, your country will be *very* grateful. Let's take the stairs."

Gratitude is a wonderful thing for a reporter with political aspirations, and Davis fell for it, hook, line, and sinker. "Oh, so your coziness with the wife is a ruse? Very clever."

Colin fumed at his leering grin and pat on the back, but they were almost to the lobby. He didn't have much more time before entering the crowd. "Just tell me what you know."

"A little testy, aren't we?" Davis sneered. "Could it be you became attached to your mark? But then you *are* an amateur at the game of intrigue."

"I can have you arrested for fraternizing with the insurgents," Colin snapped. It was an idle threat, but Davis raised his hands in surrender.

"Alright. No need to get surly, my man. When I finished with my informant, I stopped at a dive in Ybor City and saw Champagne chatting it up with the man who replaced Enrique Dupuy de Lôme as Spain's ambassador to the US. It can only mean one thing. He's double-dealing. I want the exclusive."

Colin nodded. "Agreed. When can you set up a meet for me with your cigar maker?"

Davis raised his hands. "What? No. You've got US Army written all over you. It could get my man killed."

Colin couldn't argue with that. He was raised for the military. "You may be right. And Champagne knows me. But I have someone who can fill the bill. He's Governor Blanco's half-brother and General Gómez' right-hand man. Victor's guns killed several of his men."

Davis' raised eyebrows showed a measure of respect for the man he'd derisively called "the good doctor," referring to those who stayed behind the line of fire. "Who is it?"

"Well now, I can't give away all my information."

Davis gave it some thought, apparently recognizing that he could be forced to turn over his sources—or be accused of treason. "What do you want me to do?"

"Get Victor to meet my man at the Red-Light tent in Last Chance Village. Tell him he's a buyer from General Garcia."

They separated in the lobby and Davis stepped onto the veranda to take his usual seat at the table behind Shafter's rocker. Colin nodded as he left the hotel to walk to Tampa, musing over whether to tell Lily about their plan. Hopefully, he could arrest the bastard tonight and still make his train for San Antonio in the morning.

The walk calmed him as he marveled at the changes to the sleepy little town in just a few months. The former cluster of tumble-down, unpainted storefronts was now replaced with half-constructed brick buildings. Tarpaper shacks had been torn down and replaced with frame homes, including a few mansions under construction to compete with the opulent standard set by Henry Plant. A few of the main streets were even paved, with sidewalks and drain sewers. As if overnight, cigar stores and restaurants had opened among the pines and palmettoes, serving the hot, thirsty hotel guests taken over by the bicycle craze.

After nearly being run over by two of them, he turned off the street where the shell of the post office still smoldered under the early summer sun. Rumors had it that the fire started with a kerosene-filled bottle thrown through the front window. A young Cuban boy was seen running away moments before flames erupted.

Fortunately, the damage was limited to the reception area. Local fire volunteers, with soldiers from the Negro Cavalry regiment, had it out before the mail was destroyed. He was impressed by the teamwork displayed between the white volunteers and the sons of former slaves using only buckets and an old hand-pump tanker pulled by an elderly horse.

It was a short walk to Tampa Heights and Colin turned down Florida Avenue to have a look at the 5th Infantry, the first of General Shafter's troops to arrive. Since then, tents had spread out like a blanket for nine miles, east and south, toward Ybor City, Desoto Park, and Palmetto Beach, threatening to overrun Port Tampa.

Part of the purpose for this trip was to scout a location for his Rough Riders to camp. So far, it looked like a thinly wooded, sandy area about a half-mile west of the hotel would fit the bill. It was high ground with a little grass, and palmetto trees to shade the horses. And close enough to the hotel to keep an eye on Lily, he thought, though he had no idea how long they'd be there.

Satisfied about his choice of a camp, he rented a rig for Ybor City a few miles northeast of Tampa. After Raphael recovered from his wounds, Gómez sent him to investigate Victor's activities from the Cuban side in Florida. He was working in the cigar factory that served as a hub for both rebel and loyalist underground activities.

Davis' informant was the lector who read newspapers and books aloud to keep workers' energy up and conversations down. Most of the papers, both anti-and pro-Spanish, anticipated the declaration of war, and workers had been disappearing for weeks to volunteer as guides and spies for the American Army. Word had reached Washington that a thousand Cuban ex-patriots were waiting to serve.

He sat at a table in a nearby café until the noon whistle blew and hundreds of employees poured out of the three-story factory for their twenty-minute lunch break. He knew the exit Raphael would take and smiled when Davis, wearing common laborer clothes, passed a note to a man in a white shirt and tie.

Colin paid a street urchin to do the same with Raphael. Both notes read: *"The Red-Light, Last Chance Village. Ten o'clock."*

Raphael nodded from across the street, scratched a match on his heel to light a hand-rolled Havana-America cigar, and then turned it to the note. A few doors down, Colin saw Davis' man do the same. Wishing he had one of their cigars, he pulled a simple cheroot from the jacket pocket that had once held his watch and followed Davis to Fuedo's Taberna.

They struck a plan over a bottle of rum. The lector would arrange a meeting between Victor and Raphael at the tent tavern in Last Chance Village, a tent city constructed on the beach to serve the bored and randy soldiers. Raphael, who Victor had never seen in Cuba, would pose as an old friend of José Martí. He'd offer to buy the guns for ten-thousand dollars—after testing the product at a remote location along the Hillsborough River. Then Colin would arrest the bastard.

"You realize you could be court-martialed—or worse—for doing this without authorization," Davis warned.

"I have authorization," Colin lied. His authorization was voided when Theodore Roosevelt resigned his position as Assistant Secretary of the Navy. But if he succeeded, General Shafter would be more than happy to take credit for it. He raised his glass to Davis. "To acting now and asking for forgiveness later."

Davis raised his own and returned the toast with, "I hope she's worth it."

At ten o'clock that night, according to plan, Colin and Davis, disguised as privates in the 11th Infantry, sat in a darkened corner of the Red-Light Tavern, one of dozens of tent bars and brothels set up on the beach outside Port Tampa. The bar was made of wood planks on top of whiskey kegs, and girls in low-cut dresses flirted with customers. The canvas doors were open to the street where black women fried chicken on clay stoves beneath large umbrellas stuck in the sand.

Colin ordered a one-two punch, whiskey chased by a beer. Davis drank straight-up whisky and dealt cards, as they chewed cigars and tossed money back and forth between them. From their vantage point in a dark corner of the old circus tent, Raphael and the lector's negotiation with Victor was going well.

It was close to midnight when Victor stood and Raphael touched a finger to his forehead, signaling they were headed to the guns. Colin and Davis waited until the three men were outside before following. There was no hurry. They knew the destination.

Once outside, they waited by the tent to keep their distance, when a woman's scream rose above the music, singing and shouting of drunk soldiers with nothing to do. It was followed by the shrieks of a terrified child—and gunshots. Tents emptied out and bodies blocked Colin's view of Raphael's white hat. Another shot rang out and chaos erupted when the crowd cleared to watch as a white soldier dangled a Negro child from one arm, daring his comrades to test their marksmanship by shooting through the sleeve of the boy's sleeping gown.

The mother was in hysterics and a half-dozen Buffalo Soldiers of the 10th Cavalry were incensed. When someone managed the feat and the child was freed, they opened fire, forcing their way into bars and brothels they weren't allowed to enter, and shooting their way out. White soldiers chased them, stealing as much whiskey as they could carry along the way.

Colin and Davis joined the officers of the Second Georgia Volunteer Infantry to quell the riot. But when the whites, who greatly outnumbered the Buffalo Soldiers, began beating them, they switched sides. Raphael returned while they were herding the last of the injured men from the 10th to the safety of the Red-Light tent.

"Where's Champagne?" Colin shouted in the confusion.

"Took off like a rabbit when the shooting started. I chased him but got run over by the biggest, blackest man I ever saw. When I woke up, Champagne was gone. The lector too."

As dawn lightened the sky, the leader of the Georgia volunteers appeared at the front of the tent, carrying a lit torch. "Send 'em out, Private," he ordered Colin.

Instead of sending a dozen beaten and bloody Negro soldiers out to be murdered, Colin stepped out, unarmed. "It's over," he shouted. "And it's *Colonel*, Sergeant. 5th Army. I'm a doctor. Those men need medical attention. Go find blankets and cots—now!"

The confused crowd had begun to disburse when Colin saw Victor Champagne. He tipped a finger to his bowler hat, still in place after hours of shootings, fires, and chaos. Colin jumped from the boardwalk and was nearly run over by an ambulance from Port Tampa. When it passed, Victor was gone—again.

He fumed. It would be useless to follow him into the dark corners of Port Tampa or Ybor City. He could pose as a soldier or steal a boat and hide in one of hundreds of hidden coves by nightfall. And the Rough Riders were waiting for him in San Antonio.

"Tough break, old man," Davis said.

Colin threw his hat on the muddy, rutted road and stepped on it, then sat on an empty keg outside the tent. "That's the understatement of the year. Champagne is a lunatic. He kidnapped Lily in Cuba and tried to kill me."

For once, the unflappable Richard Harding-Davis seemed floored. He pulled up another keg. "What are you going to do?"

"I honestly don't know. Roosevelt and the Rough Riders are in Texas and I'm in charge of training them. I thought we'd have Victor in jail last night and I have to leave—today."

"I've heard about the Rough Riders," Davis said with a new tone of respect. "A rough lot, I understand. And *you* are training them? Will wonders never cease? I can't tell you how much I envy you."

Colin was too tired to be mocked and took a hard look at the man who had stayed with him to defend the men of the 10th Cavalry and see to their welfare when things settled down. Davis had fought like a soldier, not a reporter. He took a chance. "I have to go, but Lily is alone, and Victor won't give up. I'll be back in a few weeks and I need your help."

Davis' blue eyes sparked with amusement. "Are you asking me to watch over your sweetheart while you go off to be a war hero?"

As much as he loathed the idea, he had to admit he was. "In a way. I need you to keep an eye on her. You're a terrible flirt, but a married man. I shouldn't have anything to worry about, right?"

Davis shrugged. "I confess to both. But if I dallied, I have to say your woman is a bit…bold…for my taste. I also don't think I'm exactly her cup of tea."

"Not even close. All I'm asking is that you keep your eyes and ears open. And when we finally catch Victor, the offer of an exclusive story is still open."

"It's a deal," Davis answered. "On all counts."

CHAPTER 34

*L*ily hadn't seen or heard from Victor since Colin left for San Antonio, but she continued to carry the derringer in her pocket and kept her daily schedule at the repaired post office, helping Mr. Monahan, interviewing soldiers and often helping them write letters home. It frustrated her that Pulitzer edited out the more graphic details of her report about the riots and the heinous conditions of the camps, specifically rampant disease, and violence in the tent cities.

"It isn't what the country wants to see," he told her on the telephone following the riot. "They want parades and soldier heroes, not sick, hungry men who signed up to fight a foreign enemy...and got dysentery, yellow fever, and typhus instead."

The delayed train carrying the Rough Riders to Tampa finally arrived on June 3rd, coinciding with the soldiers' first payday in two months. The town was overrun with drunken soldiers, laughing, singing, and shooting guns into the air. From the hotel, it sounded like the Fourth of July fireworks.

"May I walk with you?" Davis asked as Lily stepped outside on her way to meet Colin. She stopped and smiled. He'd been strangely attentive since Colin's departure, but never stepped over his boundaries as a married man. She'd even come to enjoy sparring with him over politics and economics, as well as their energetic discussions about women gaining the right to vote. She was for; he was against.

But she wasn't in the mood for banter or debate today. She'd taken special care with her toilet. Willie had expertly cut off what was left of her bleached hair—the last evidence of her life with Victor. Now, instead of a veil or chignon, she wore a jaunty little hat that showed her natural, sun-kissed curls to their best advantage.

"If you must." She answered Davis more sharply than she meant, and they set out at a pace tediously slow for her racing heart. At the first sight of smoke from the steam engine, she let him have the advantage when he pulled out his notepad to scoop the unheralded arrival of the most famous volunteer cavalry in the US Army.

If reports of the Rough Riders' journey east through the former Confederate states being greeted by bands, flags, and cheering crowds were true, it was another world in Tampa. In the chaos of the first payday in three months for nearly thirty-thousand volunteers, the arrival of a thousand more men went unnoticed. Even Major-General Shafter didn't bother to meet them.

She worried they wouldn't have much time together before he left for Cuba. Supplies, guns, animals, wagons, and equipment had been slowly moving from the camps to stockpiles along the docks in Port Tampa for more than a week. She and Davis had watched the chaos, shaking their heads at equipment sitting uncovered during the rainy season. Animals balked at rough handling, and freight, once loaded onto the few ships in the harbor, was unloaded to make room for other items.

"If Clara was here, they'd be loaded and gone by now," she'd told Davis.

He'd nodded. "There is much to be said for the woman's ability to organize a project."

"The Red Cross is far more than a project," she argued. "Leadership is a trait most women share, but rarely have the opportunity to show. Men are too busy thinking about glory and stature to be efficient. They easily lose sight of the details." She smiled up at him. "And we all know the devil is in the details—as demonstrated by Spain's colossal underestimation of our fleet in the Philippines. I hope the easy victory there and the male propensity toward arrogance won't lead to our own undoing if Spain fortifies its efforts to retain Cuba."

Davis' response was drowned out by a shrill whistle and the rumble of the arriving train. Lily caught her breath when she saw Colonel Colin Winfield, commander of the renowned Rough Riders, standing in full dress uniform by the open door of the first car. She waved and smiled, surprised at his frown when he saw her. Stepping back from a sudden burst of steam, she realized she was clutching Davis' arm. She dropped it, but Colin had already passed.

The cars were still moving when the other doors opened and a mass of men in Western gear leaped toward freedom in the bright sunlight. One trim cowboy with a black leather vest stopped and stared at Lily. Her heart skipped a beat and her pulse pounded in her ears. She pushed Davis aside to run to him. "Sean!"

Her oldest brother smiled and caught her up in his arms, swinging her around like a child. Indeed, she felt seven years old again and her favorite brother was swinging her onto her first horse. "What are you doing here?" she asked, breathless, a thousand questions running through her mind. "You're a US Marshal. What about Elena? And the children. How many are there now? Two?"

His laugh rose above the conversations of the men milling around as if they'd landed on the moon. "Three," he said. "In January. A girl. We named her Rosa, after Sam's wife."

She remembered Rosa Contrereo, the Mexican wife of Sean's best friend —also a New Mexico Ranger. Rosa was a former brothel owner with the proverbial heart of gold who helped nurse Sean back to health after the great train wreck outside Pecos, Texas, in '84.

"How is Sam?" she asked.

"Retired now. Said he's too old for war, and after nearly falling into a paddle wheel as a youngster, he keeps a safe distance from water."

Lily's laugh was interrupted by, "What have we here?"

Sean stiffened to attention and Lily turned. Colin grinned at them but made no move to embrace Lily. She understood. He was her brother's commanding officer. He also had a thousand men and a trainload of horses and supplies to unload—with no apparent means of transportation for any of them in sight.

Suddenly miffed, she faced Colin, her hands on her hips. "Why didn't you write me that my brother was a Rough Rider?"

"Everyone loves a surprise," Colin answered, his eyes shining with the affection he couldn't show.

"Don't leave me out of this," Davis interrupted, notepad in hand. "Who might this be?"

After the introduction, he asked, "The Sean O'Grady from Georgia who was wanted for murder back in'92, then uncovered a notorious land swindle scheme in New Mexico? He faced Lily. "Why didn't you tell me your brother was famous?"

Then back to Sean. "I think I still have an old Wanted poster from when I wrote for the *Denver Post*. You were the inspiration for my first book, *My Buried Treasure*."

Sean's unusual gray eyes darkened with dislike. "It was a long time ago. And I am familiar with your books Mr. Davis, but there's no romance in thievery and murder."

The famous novelist flushed at the shortened version of his name and fidgeted under Sean's steel-colored gaze. "I suppose not, but everyone likes a good story."

"Sorry, I'm not much of a reader," ended the conversation.

Colin saved the awkward silence to tell Sean, "It looks like they forgot we were coming, Lieutenant. Have your men unload the horses and pack as much as they can on them. Then assemble the equipment under guard while I find transportation. I'll check with Command at the hotel and meet you here in an hour."

Lily's jaw dropped when her brother, the family rebel-turned-lawman saluted and turned on his heels to follow orders.

"I think I'll stay around and watch," Davis told them and followed Sean.

"Don't you want the story?" Colin asked Lily when she took his arm.

"You are the only story I want," she purred, longing to press her body against his and kiss him until they both ran out of breath. But while she'd stopped using Victor's name, she was still recognized as a married woman, albeit one who had been abandoned. She hated being the subject of pity but appreciated the respect she was shown for her courage and independence.

"I haven't seen Sean in five years," she said as they strolled to the hotel. "When can I visit him in the camp?"

"Not a good idea. They're a rough lot, though it seems there's a better code of honor among the Rough Riders than the untrained rank and file. I'm having dinner with Teddy Roosevelt and Major-General Shafter this evening. I was hoping you'd be my guest, along with your overly protective brother."

She would have kissed him right then if they hadn't been within sight of the hotel veranda. Instead, she exclaimed, "Wonderful. Even if I have to listen to Mrs. Shafter prattle about their grandchildren."

His arm slipped around her waist and pressed her against his side. "I'm sure you'll charm them both—again—and Teddy will adore you."

They spent a half hour on the veranda, drinking cool glasses of lemonade while Colin waited impatiently for permission to see Major-General Shafter. He excused himself when Major Kennedy finally allowed him to visit Shafter's office, now on the main floor. Lily rose too, anxious to tell Willie and Merlyn about finding her brother with the Rough Riders.

She unlocked her door and threw her hat on the bed. Again, she thought she smelled the scent of Victor's Bay Rum cologne. Then it was gone. She checked the window. The tiny row of colored glass ornaments on the sill hadn't been disturbed. And Bay Rum was a common scent for men. It must have come from the nearby garden walk. Shaking off a sudden chill, she whispered another of Chloe's wise sayings, "Stop looking for shadows in the sunlight."

She reminded herself that this was a wonderful day. Colin was back, even if for a short time. He'd spend as much time as he could spare with her and there was the bonus of seeing Sean again. Pushing worries about Victor and war out of her mind, she hummed as she loosened her hair and opened the wardrobe to change into her bicycle dress for her daily trip to the post office.

This time the smell of Bay Rum assaulted her and instead of finding her crisp, freshly laundered dress on a hanger, she saw Victor's leering face. Too shocked to scream, she stepped back, nearly falling onto the bed behind her. Trapped, and knowing from bitter experience, that cowering would only encourage his cruelty, she straightened her back as if there was a wall behind her instead of a soft feather mattress.

"How did you get in here?

He didn't move. "I thought Henry Plant would have better locks in the jewel of his hotel empire. A ten-year-old could have picked that lock."

While he bragged about one of his many nefarious talents, she sidestepped toward the foot of the bed. "Get out before I scream for help. You're a wanted man, and the hotel is full of military officers."

"I doubt that," he hissed, taking a slow, almost graceful step out of the wardrobe. "I'm sure you picked this room for its privacy. Probably for your whorish trysts with the good doctor." Hot, moist breath smelling of rum made her eyes water.

"Yes, you could scream, but most of these rooms belong to the maids. They won't be back until well after supper is served."

The smile disappeared, while a long, thin finger caressed her cheek. "And where is your hero now? Oh, yes, seeing to his beloved cowboys. I saw him during the riots in Last Chance Village, you know. Had a good shot, but there were too many witnesses."

The afternoon sun caught his gold eyes until they glowed with hatred, while she went cold inside. He wasn't there to collect his blackmail money. He was already a fugitive and could only be hanged once. He'd kill her this time.

"I'm not afraid of you," she lied and batted away the palm that cupped her chin. "Don't touch me."

He grabbed her by both wrists before she could lower her hand to the gun in her pocket. "Or what? You'll scream? Not if you want to stay alive. And if you want your brother to stay alive, you'll do what I say. Now strip. I want to see you on your knees—naked before me. Begging for your brother and your lover's lives."

"Never!"

He pulled her toward him, then pushed her back across the bed, leaning over her, one hand squeezing her throat. Her vision blurred and she knew if she passed out, he'd take her. And when she woke, he'd kill her. "Wait," she croaked. "I'll give you the money. Sean brought it with him."

The pressure on her throat loosened, but his knee between her legs slowly moved upward, while his other hand tore at the front of her dress. With both his hands occupied, she wrapped her left arm around his shoulder and writhed as if with pleasure—while her right hand slipped into the hidden pocket in her skirt.

Quicker than a cat, he clamped onto her wrist. "What kind of fool do you think I am?" he sneered, raising his free hand in a fist above her.

"*Don't!*" she screamed, turning her head before his blow crushed her face. Instead, it glanced off the side of her skull with most of the force hitting the iron headboard. He howled in pain as blood trickled from his knuckles. "Whore!" he screamed. "I'll take you alive or dead and leave you in the swamp as alligator food."

She shifted her body enough to find the trigger on the derringer as he put his full weight on top of her. Without knowing where the gun was pointed and knowing she could kill herself instead of him, she pulled the trigger. Pain shot through her hand and her thigh felt like it was on fire, but she was still alive.

She opened her eyes and met a startled, one-eyed glare from half a face awash in blood and gore. Then Victor's body fell on top of her.

She lay there a long moment, his weight crushing her and what was left of his head staining the pillow next to her. Then she screamed for help. When Willie found her there and froze in horror at the grisly scene, Lily shouted, "Get him off me."

Boots running on the tile floor echoed from the hallway while Willy tugged at Victor's sprawled legs. "Halt," rose above Willie's wails and Lily's moans. "Stand down," Colin ordered the half-dozen officers behind him and entered the room. Willie fell into his arms in hysterics while the men crowded the doorway, struck dumb at the scene of a dead man with half a head lying on top of a bloodied woman in a white dress.

He passed Willie off to Major Kennedy and rolled Victor's body off Lily, into the space between the bed and the armoire. "Darling," he whispered to her wide, panicked eyes while he checked her pulse, then shouted, "She's alive."

Willie fell to her knees, praising the Lord while Colin pulled Lily's other hand from the blackened pocket of her dress. A four-inch pistol, still in her grip, fell to the floor when she moaned.

"Don't move," Colin e whispered, and dropped the bloodied pillow over what was left of Victor's face on the floor. She clung to him with her good arm, sobbing into his chest while he whispered over and over, "You're safe, the bastard is dead."

CHAPTER 35

*W*hile it was impossible to keep the horrific death of a suspected spy and gun runner from making the newspapers, Henry Plant's relationships with the local press and Lily's friendships with the correspondents kept the hotel out of it. Instead, they reported that Victor Champagne, aka Lionel Carter, met his end in a back alley in Last Chance Village—likely in a falling-out among thieves. Georges St. James at the front desk, answered the rumors of a woman screaming in the first-floor hallway with the story that an alligator had slipped inside through a door carelessly left open.

Colin took Lily to his room while the hotel closed hers for repairs from the 'alligator attack'. She lay on top of his bed wearing one of Esther's satin robes, while he tended to the powder burns on her hand and thigh. "Try to keep them open to the air as much as possible. And keep applying the aloe," he repeated his instructions from New Year's Eve.

"I know," she said. "I think we've been through this before. Only this time, I understand the meaning of 'burns like hell.' I'd rather a broken rib than a burn."

"You're lucky that little gun didn't blow up in your pocket. And it was pointed in the right direction. If you must carry it, I suggest you keep it in your purse."

"I lost two guns that way." She smiled as if she'd been injured from a childhood prank. "Perhaps I should wear a holster under my duster."

"It would be safer," he agreed, missing the intended humor.

He paced, grappling between his love and concern for Lily and his duty. With Victor gone, she'd think she was no longer in danger and wouldn't *stay* in the hotel. With thirty-thousand randy men spoiling for a fight within a mile of her, she'd be in danger anywhere off the hotel grounds.

"Just say it," she finally snapped, tears brimming in her eyes. "You're leaving."

He knelt beside her pressing her uninjured hand in his. "As much as I want to be at your side—always, I'm needed at the camp with my men. We're still training, and unlike the other officers, I intend for as many of them as possible to come back from Cuba."

"But do you have to spend the nights there? I don't think I have much of a reputation to protect anymore and don't want to be alone…tonight. I'll ask Willie to stay with me."

He touched her battered face and kissed her split lip tenderly. "Roosevelt will be in camp until his wife arrives midmorning tomorrow. If you need company, I can manage tonight."

She tried to sit up, then pressed her good hand to her swollen cheek and lay back. "When will you show me the camp?"

"Don't even give it a thought," he warned. "I don't know if you have a concussion or not. You need to lay still and let your body rest."

"I'm fine," she ground out. "I'll feel better in the morning. And it's a short ride. It will help take my mind off…what happened."

The determination in her voice told him if he didn't agree, she'd try to go on her own. He tried using logic. "We're not set up yet and while it's high ground, we'd have to go through Tampa Heights, which is basically a sewer. I don't advise it—yet. We'll be here a while. Once it's habitable and you feel up to it, I'll take you."

"I'll be ready tomorrow," she answered as if she hadn't heard a word. "I've heard stories of the dire conditions in the camps and seen some of the men in Tampa. I've also heard that the tiny hospital in Port Tampa is woefully unprepared for cases of yellow fever and typhoid, and the longer the troops stay, the worse the chaos seems to get."

He marveled at her excitement to see living conditions that would send any white woman of her social standing to her smelling salts. But if it took her mind off her injuries and the trauma of killing a man, he'd do it. He stroked her thick, sun-blonde hair. "You may be aware that our military has shrunk considerably since the…"—he couldn't label the wholesale slaughter and near annihilation of North America's indigenous people as a war—"… end of our Western expansion.

"Most of our leadership hasn't seen a war in thirty years. Rough Riders aside, the volunteers are mostly college boys with family connections to Washington or starry-eyed farm boys looking for some excitement. Frankly, I haven't noticed any concerted effort to train them for war. And the thought of leading a virtually untrained volunteer Army into jungle warfare and certain slaughter infuriates me."

Lily's good hand found his. "But your oath. I understand why you did what you did after your wife's…death, but you've found your calling again. I saw you with the wounded in the rebel camp and with the sick in hospitals. You're a healer, Colin. Not a killer."

"Yes," he admitted. "I only took the Army commission because that's what the second son does in my family. And it got me out of Boston. And…"

"You mean Winona," she finished. Tears filled her eyes. "But I'm not Winona. And I'm not pregnant. I can take care of myself."

"So you've said, many times. It's taken me eight years to admit I'm still a doctor," he said, perhaps more to convince himself than Lily.

"A healer," she corrected.

He smiled at the word. "Perhaps, but I've negotiated a way to serve my country and my calling."

"What do you mean?"

"My time in the rebel camp and with Aunt Clara reminded me how much I missed…healing people, not just patching them up to go back to battle. When I met with the President, I committed to commanding the Rough Riders through their training, with the agreement that when they land in Cuba, I will turn command over to Roosevelt and go with them as Chief Surgeon for the 5th Army Corps."

She winced when she tried to smile. "That's wonderful, but doctors don't carry weapons. You'll just put yourself in more danger. Is that what you want?"

Again lingered in the humid air. His finger caught a tear as it began its descent down her battered face. "No, darling. That's not what I want. And I fully expect to carry a loaded weapon if I need to reach a wounded soldier. You have my word that I intend to complete this commitment, return in one piece, and leave the military forever."

His thumb smoothed her bruised brow. "Maybe then you'll finally agree to marry me."

Joy lit her good eye before she repeated, "Now is not the time to discuss this. We're at war." Her voice quivered when she added, "At the moment, I'm not much of a catch. I may even be charged with murder."

He pulled her close. "Over my dead body. The authorities are aware that Victor had threatened you, as well as his other crimes. I'm sure they will be more than happy to close the book on him. And by the way, there's an outstanding reward for the capture of anyone involved in the armory robbery, as well as a bounty for spies—dead or alive. You could come out of this a very rich woman in your own right, with a line of suitors out the door. I'm hoping to hold a place in the front of the line."

He kissed her un-battered cheek. "Rest now. The bruises will fade. I've ordered supper sent up to you and when Willie recovers from her vapors, she'll sit with you until I come back. The danger is over now. Victor is gone for good."

He turned to a tea table and offered her a cup of something that didn't smell like tea.

She asked, "That smells amazing. What is it? You're not trying to drug me, are you??"

"Wild black cherry tea," he said with a mischievous smile. "And a little boiled root bark. Try it. It's delicious. You'll sleep like a baby with no ill effects in the morning, I promise."

～

She woke to the gray light of early dawn, feeling the heat of another body next to hers. Colin, she knew, recognizing his even breathing and male scent. He faced her, hair tousled, the lines of worry and pain in his forehead smooth in slumber. She couldn't resist touching a lock of his chestnut-colored hair.

She was surprised that she'd slept a wink after killing Victor and shuddered at the memory of seeing the shock in his dead eye after blowing half his face off. Gómez had warned her that taking a life leaves a wound in your soul that, like the hole in his throat, never fully heals. He was wrong. In Victor's case, she felt better already.

Colin sensed her movement and opened his eyes. "Good morning, sunshine," he said and held his new pocket watch up to the dim light. He leaned on an elbow, facing her while she traced the burn scars on his chest. Scars from saving a mother and child.

He lightly kissed her bruised lips, tracing a path down her neck while his surgeon's fingers easily opened the tiny buttons of her nightdress. Her hand stopped him.

"Wait. I don't want you to see me…like this. I'm hideous."

"No, you're beautiful. Especially now. All I see when I look at you is your beauty and your courage." He reached over her to the jar of aloe vera and showed her that a man and woman can make love with just their fingers, lips, and tongues.

Too soon, they couldn't ignore the golden light of dawn. Lily stretched, still feeling the relaxing effects of the wild black cherry and root bark tea while he slid from the sheets, gloriously naked in the sunlight. Even Victor's tall, trim body couldn't compare to the power packed in Colin's slighter, more compact physique.

She watched him dress, his movements swift but not hurried. Athletic, she thought, imagining him riding his horse into battle. It wasn't the first time she'd seen him naked and appreciated his physique, but this time, knowing they had only a few more days together, she wanted to remember everything.

"How are you feeling?" he asked while buttoning his shirt.

"Now? Wonderful," she answered, then raised her good hand to her cheek. "But I must look like a monster."

He pulled it away. "You're beautiful. The bruises are turning a lovely shade of mauve, by the way. It makes your eyes shine brighter."

"No, *you're* beautiful," she whispered.

He kissed her neck and chuckled. "It's the tea. Settle back in and Willie will bring you breakfast at eight. Theodore and I will be having luncheon with Edith. If you're up to it, please join us at one o'clock. And *if* the camp is in order, we can visit it after. For now, just rest."

Her hand flew to her battered face. "But I can't be seen in the dining room…like this."

"It was your idea, remember?" His voice softened then. "Even so, bruises and all, you're the most beautiful woman in this hotel. I know you must feel like you've been thrown off a horse into a pile of hot coals, and I still think you should rest in bed for a couple days, but I know you won't. Just promise me you'll take it easy on that leg."

"I promise," she said. "I'll see you at one o'clock."

Taking a soothing, rosewater sponge bath and reapplying the aloe vera to her powder-burned thigh and singed hand, she took her time preparing for luncheon with the former Assistant Secretary of the Navy and his wife. Edith Roosevelt must be a saint, she thought, to put up with her husband's grand ambitions, boasting, and wild rhetoric. All while raising five children of her own and one from his previous marriage.

She applied a fresh wrap around her leg and determined she could hide the burn on her hand with a glove. And on the street, she could cover the bruised side of her face with a veil, but she couldn't eat through a veil.

Willie came to the rescue with her pots of stage makeup. "This'll do the job," she said, dropping it all onto the vanity. A moment later she was stirring up a mixture of flesh-colored cream to smooth over Lily's bruises. "Remember yer an actress?" she prattled. "Ye kin plead a trip-and-fall, or that you fell off that bicycle contraption yer so fond of."

She's right, Lily thought, attributing her lack of strategic thinking to the residual effects of Colin's tea. The trip-and-fall story would cover all her injuries, even the one on her hand, which could easily be labeled a scrape. Still, it grieved her. "Yes, more lies," she answered. "They're like snowballs, you know. Once they start rolling, they get bigger and bigger."

Willie faced her. "Don't beat yerself up. Victor ain't—wasn't—worth it."

"But I don't want to embarrass Colin in front of Lieutenant Roosevelt and his wife. I lived in New York when he was Police Commissioner. For all his quirks, it's a better city for his government commission on crime."

"Diversion," Willie said.

"What do you mean?"

"I learned it from Merlyn. Keep 'em occupied with somethin' else. A man likes nothing better than to hear compliments about himself and I hear Mr. Roosevelt likes praises almost as much as his own voice. And any mother I've known would miss a three-legged donkey with a top hat to brag about her little ones. Jest keep 'em talkin' an' you won't have to 'splain a thing. But if they ask, keep it simple. Say ye fell an' change the subject."

She turned Lily to the vanity mirror. "There. Have a look."

"Oh, my stars," she exclaimed. "You can hardly see—well, any—of the bruises." She patted the skin beneath her right eye in amazement. "There's a little puffiness but if I sit in a shadow, it will be barely noticeable."

She stood to hug Willie and put on a jaunty lavender, boat-shaped hat with the brim turned down on her bad side and a closely woven lace veil to shield her from the dust and sand on their tour of the Rough Rider camp.

Luncheon was brief and Lily thanked her lucky stars that Major-General Shafter's gout prevented him from joining them. In contrast, she found Roosevelt and his stunning wife to be most pleasant. Colin saved her from her well-rehearsed lies by saying, "I see you're doing well after your fall yesterday. Mr. Plant has already seen to the torn carpeting on the stairs."

And Willie was right about Lieutenant Roosevelt loving the sound of his own voice as he recounted his many adventures hunting wild game in Africa and the West, including trapping the mountain lion he'd brought with him from San Antonio. Lily wisely held her disgust at killing innocent creatures or caging them to show off as prizes.

"Mrs. Roosevelt," she interjected when Theodore stopped for a sip of sparkling water. "How on earth do you manage six young children?"

Colin winked when Edith Roosevelt's face lit up to share the trials of mothering, maintaining a menagerie of wild animals, and a husband with unbounded political ambitions. Shortly after a light desert of key lime pie, they boarded a hansom cab for the ride to the Rough Rider camp.

"You are quite an accomplished actress," Colin whispered as he helped her into the cab.

"I wasn't acting with Edith," she whispered back. "She's amazing. If only her husband would notice."

Theodore again monopolized the conversation on the way to the camp, romanticizing the American intervention in Cuba. Arriving at the Rough Rider camp, he leaped out of the cab first, shouting, "A splendid camp. Bully, absolutely bully." He turned to the ladies. "Don't you agree?"

Colin answered for them. "It is indeed. At least for the short time we'll be here. Others haven't fared so well for the long term."

"Tut, tut, old man," Teddy told the commanding officer who would soon hand over the reins of leadership to him. "It will all be forgotten once we've achieved our victory."

He turned to Lily. "O'Grady...are you related to Representative Patrick O'Grady?"

"Yes, he's my father. He's—"

Met him once," cut her off. "A good man. Sean too. A true warrior. Come, you'll want to see the horses."

Lily was grateful for the use of one of Willie's canes while they walked to a crudely constructed corral. The sight of so many fine, high spirited Mustangs and Mustang/Morgan crossbreeds, along with a few Andalusians, tugged at Lily's heart. It had been too long since she'd ridden an amazingly graceful Andalusian, or run full tilt on a strong, agile Mustang.

"Beautiful," was all she could manage.

"Ah, there you are," Theodore said to a man wearing the blue flannel shirt, buckskin breeches, and the Rough Riders' signature navy blue and white polka dot bandana.

"Sean," Lily called when he raised his head and removed his slouch hat. She limped up to him, again throwing her arms around his broad shoulders. "I'm so sorry I missed supper last night. The vapors, you know. They come on unexpectedly sometimes."

He steadied her on the uneven ground and lifted her chin. "Vapors? You've never had the vapors in your life, Lily Pad. I heard what happened. Colin practically hog-tied me here. If the bastard wasn't dead, I'd have done it myself."

"Shush," she whispered, glancing at Roosevelt to make sure he hadn't overheard. "You taught me to shoot, remember?"

He smiled and lowered his voice. "You always learned fast."

Conscious of Roosevelt's pique at not being the center of attention, she straightened her hat and turned to him. "I would love to see your own horses."

She couldn't resist comparing the set-up rows of tents, grassy corral, and carefully planned wastewater facilities in the Rough Rider camp to the filthy conditions in the other camps—or the irony that while tents shielded Roosevelt's horses from the sun, men in other units slept in the open.

The politician's face split into a toothy grin. "Bully! Right this way." He cleared his throat, preening like a peacock. "I'm sure you'll agree that these are the finest mounts in the cavalry, perfect for our splendid expedition. Let me introduce you to Little Texas and Rain in the Face."

She was duly impressed with his choice of mounts, as well as the surprisingly orderly camp for what many considered "uncivilized" Westerners. And though he took credit, she saw Colin's touch in nearly every part of it. But her patience ran thin when he boasted about his grand scheme to make the US a world power.

"With Admiral Dewey's embarrassingly easy victory in the Philippines, Cuba is all that remains to rid Europe's influence from the Western Hemisphere," he announced, comparing it to a walk in the park.

All Lily could think about was that two of the men she loved most in the world were both going to war.

After their tour, she and Colin visited the other units of the 5th Cavalry. "They've been here quite a while," Colin explained. "With little or no planning, few supplies, and basically no supervision after arriving, they've overused the latrines and contaminated their own drinking supplies. I'm meeting with their medical officers to see what I can do to help."

"But I hear there's typhoid in some of the camps. And yellow fever. What if you're infected?"

"Typhus can be avoided by good sanitation," he said. "And I survived yellow fever in New Orleans during my training. I'm immune."

"Are you sure? I was in New Orleans with my mother one summer and we heard of people having it more than once."

"It's rare enough to support the immunity theory," he said sharply enough to worry her.

CHAPTER 36

*F*our days later, Colin received notification for the troops to leave. If the weeks before the order were a chaos of loading, unloading, and reloading ships from railcars and wagons, the final boarding of men and horses was horror. Units wandered the depots and docks, not knowing which train to take and no idea what ship they were supposed to board.

The Rough Riders were told at the last minute to leave their horses behind, along with more than a third of their men, because of inadequate space on too few ships. Since Colin wouldn't be free of command until they landed in Cuba, the responsibility to inform them fell to him.

He pushed past Major Kennedy to confront Major-General Shafter at his desk. If he wasn't so angry, he'd have laughed at the obese general stuffed behind a delicate French desk. Instead, he stood over his commanding officer and pounded his fist on the lady's *secretaire*. At this point, even the threat of court-martial wouldn't convince him to lead seven hundred cavalrymen on foot against an army of thousands armed with smokeless Mauser rifles.

"I want the Cubans," he demanded. "And Lieutenant Raphael Diaz to lead them. A hundred men from the excluded units are indispensable, especially the New Mexicans. And since you've literally cut our legs out from under us by leaving our mounts behind, I want the two Colt automatic guns Roosevelt's friends, Stevens, Kane, and Tiffany, gave us. "We'll also need at least a third of the horses, medical tents, and supplies. If you won't do that, you can be the one to tell them they spent weeks training and traveling across the country to live in a vermin-infested swamp—for nothing."

Shafter's face reddened like an overripe watermelon, and his beady eyes bulged to the point of exploding. His hands twitched as if he considered shooting Colin on the spot, but his gun was across the room. Instead making the trip, he rested his sweaty forehead in his hands.

"Command let us down," he said. "We don't have enough ships or supplies to send all the volunteers. Hell, we don't even have proper boots for most of 'em."

The man disgusted Colin. Shafter and more than a few of the old Civil War veterans were bordering on senility and he felt no remorse in pointing out, "The time to pass the buck is past…sir. My…our…men are leaving without the tools to do their jobs. I won't send them to slaughter, and neither will you."

He pushed a freshly prepared document in front of his commander. "Now please write those orders…Sir. With the hastily scrawled order to add the additional men, three hundred horses and the rapid-fire guns to the Rough Riders unit in his hand, Colin didn't bother to hide his disgust. "I'll see to my men now."

He now faced the odious task of informing four of his twelve troops that they would be left behind. Their reactions didn't surprise him. They were all good, loyal soldiers who had trained their hearts out for the mission. Most were angry and many of them wept at the news. As for the others, those who would leave their well-trained mounts behind, mourned the loss.

While Troop F from New Mexico was one of the excluded groups, two dozen men, including Sean O'Grady, were pulled to accompany the main body, along with the Cubans, under Raphael and Captain Luna, a Spaniard descended from one of New Mexico's first Spanish settlers.

"But why Sean?" Lily asked after Colin killed her relief over Troop F's exclusion. "He shouldn't even be here," she argued. "He's older than most of the men and he has a family—and a new baby."

"The choice was his," Colin argued. "He's a natural leader. He has amazing tracking and law enforcement skills and knows how to take orders as well as how to give them. We both know he'd go crazy waiting it out here —despite your lovely presence, of course."

But the determination in her eyes and the weight of her argument melted his resolve. He was close to granting her wish, when she sighed. "You're right, of course. Sean has survived being a lawman for ten years." She stabbed a finger into Colin's chest. "But I'm holding you responsible for his safety. I've already told my brother that I hold him responsible for yours."

She stepped back and took a deep breath. "I don't know which of you will have the hardest job because I know you won't wait in the medical tents for the wounded to come to you and Sean will want to be at the front of every battle."

Colin pulled her into his arms, knowing it could be the last time he'd feel both her strength and her softness. "I promise," he whispered against her cheek knowing it could be a hollow promise. Factoring that both he and Sean had used up far more than one cat's nine lives, would their luck run out in the jungles of Cuba?

After being stalled in the open water off the coast of Florida for more than a week, due to a miscommunication from Washington, the *Yucatan* landed at Daiquiri west of Guantanamo Bay on June 23rd. Consistent with their departure, the landing onto crumbling docks was a fiasco of confusion amid nearly impassable high seas.

Unfortunately, Colin's medical supplies had been misappropriated by another unit and while he had tents, there were no cots, sheets or blankets, and very few bandages. Most of the few hundred horses they'd been able to load drowned after being whipped into jumping from the transports and forced to swim to shore. Roosevelt's horse, Rain in the Face, was one of the casualties, but his chestnut gelding, Little Texas, survived.

As evening darkened the roiling sea, the *Yucatan* retreated into deeper, calmer waters. Colin and Theodore stood together on the sandy beach of Cuba's Guantanamo Bay, surveying the result of the chaos and shameful waste of supplies, arms, and horses. Colin observed, "If this is a sign of what's to come, I'd say we're in for a rough time,"

He turned from the sea toward the wooded ridges surrounding the sandy bay that had protected mariners from summer hurricanes for centuries. Ridges that could easily have made the disorganized landing party a tempting target for the Spanish. He told Theodore, who had assumed command during the landing, "A few hundred men from the bush up there could have finished us off in no time."

"You can thank Generals Castillo and Garcia for that," came from behind them.

No longer his commanding officer, Colin greeted the man with, "Raphael."

"How so? Lieutenant Diaz?" Roosevelt asked, already assuming his role of command.

Raphael nodded toward a half-dozen ragged, exhausted Cubans watching the chaos as their friendly invaders attempted to set up camp. "The rebels have been fighting skirmishes for two weeks to keep the Spanish resistance low for your *long-awaited* arrival."

Roosevelt nodded. "Your men look done-in. It looks like we got here just in time."

Raphael bristled, and Colin frowned at the new commander's arrogance. He surveyed the Cubans who, even barefoot, could run circles around any of the American Army units. One tall mestizo stood out from the rest and he recognized the man who posed as Rosalita in Havana, wearing a filthy, torn peasant suit. His straw hat was in tatters, his long face scarred with a fresh wound.

Raphael led them to the exhausted rebels, explaining, "They will stay just ahead of the Spanish and keep them busy so we can place our men. But we need to move fast. Now that we're here, the Spanish will dig in at Santiago. The El Camino Royale is clear to Las Guásimas, but there's no telling how long it will remain so."

"Bully," Roosevelt said to the exhausted men without shaking their dirty hands and strode off to oversee the placement of the tents for the Rough Riders and the 10th Cavalry.

Raphael stepped up to Colin. "Your friend will get himself and many of his men killed. He is what you Americans call a 'Glory Hound'."

Colin nodded. "That he is. And a politician. Keep your people low and watch your back. Cuba will need good men to govern them—if they get the chance."

They both looked back at Roosevelt, one hand resting on his holster, the other waving in circles as he shouted orders no one could hear over the surf. Colin shook his head and looked at Raphael. "It's likely we'll be the first on the trail in the morning. Are your men ready?"

"They are always ready. And your men seem ready for war, but in their flannel shirts and canvas pants are they ready for Cuba? If they sleep on the beach tonight, warn them about the sand crabs."

"Yes, sir." Colin saluted and shook his friend's hand.

On their first full day in Cuba, the young Army discovered how deadly war can be. They were only a few miles along the El Camino Royale, a fancy name for what was little more than a wide path along the shoreline leading to a Spanish stronghold reported to be in the nearby village of Guásimas. Against Raphael's intelligence that the Spanish hadn't yet withdrawn to Santiago, they left under the command of the elderly Confederate General, Joseph Wheeler. Three miles in, they spotted a dead Spaniard left as a marker by the Cubans to identify the Spanish line.

Despite the warning, General Wheeler ordered a frontal attack, separating the Rough Riders to both sides of the road when he shouted the charge, "We got the Yankees on the run."

The Spanish Mauser repeating rifles with smokeless powder made it nearly impossible for artillery to locate the enemy, but by the sheer force of numbers, the Americans pushed the Spanish back. Of the seventeen American soldiers killed, seven of them were Rough Riders. One, a Harvard graduate, earned the dubious honor of being the first to fall, and Roosevelt gloried in the fact that the Rough Riders had carved their place as leaders in battle on their first day in Cuba.

Colin and one attendant saw to the fifty-two wounded soldiers at an abandoned farmhouse and sent the ambulatory wounded back to Guantanamo. Knowing that if not for the support of General Castillo's Cuban troops, the numbers would have been much higher, Colin thanked God that the enemy's larger force had chosen to retreat to Santiago, rather than stand and fight.

They received orders a week later to move toward the fortified city of Santiago and deploy at the base of Kettle Hill in the surrounding San Juan Heights. Colin left the Rough Riders under Roosevelt, and the 10th Cavalry under Major John J. Pershing, to set up a hospital with only three small tents and no cots. The rains had already begun, and he knew better than to line the sand floor with blankets—even if he'd had them.

He ordered a pit for continuous fires to boil water for drinking and surgery, and gathered up what little flour, rice, and potatoes they had for food. Their supply of bandages woefully slim, Colin turned to his only orderly. "These are the worst conditions I've ever seen. Even in the West, we had cots, sheets, and bandages."

"We're too far ahead of the supply line," the young Negro from South Georgia drawled. "With no mules or wagons, we's in a world o' hurt…Suh."

Colin nodded. "I couldn't have said it better, but we will make do as best we can. These are good, strong men. I know it's hot but set those kettles to boil and keep them filled. Don't drink or touch the wounded with anything that hasn't been boiled first. And wash your hands after handling a wound. I'm going to find a detail to gather palm leaves for a floor."

CHAPTER 37

*L*ily joined the throngs of people seeing the soldiers off without knowing which ship carried the Rough Riders. It didn't matter. The sight of seventeen thousand soldiers crowded into forty-two boats crowded with animals, arms and supplies, filled her with fear—and anger. Besides being outnumbered by the Spanish eight to one, they carried weapons far inferior to Spain's. And she thought whoever decided they should wear flannel uniforms to a tropical jungle ninety miles south of Key West should be shot. Perhaps Colin was right that more than the Spanish Army, their biggest threats were the climate, insects, infection, and disease.

Georges St. James raised a hand to her when she returned to the hotel that now seemed empty and abandoned. Even Richard Harding-Davis and his inseparable pals, Steven Crane and Frederick Remington, had found ways onto the transports.

"Hello, Georges," she said with a forced smile.

"Miss Lily," he answered without meeting her eyes. "Now the Colonel and the troops is gone or goin', the manager is wonderin' when you are plannin' to leave."

It didn't surprise her. While few knew what really happened in her room, the manager was right to worry that word would get out. And a nearly deserted hotel had little need for an entertainer. She reached for Georges' hand and tried to sound convincing. "No matter. I plan to follow the ships to Cuba—somehow."

"Are you crazy?" came from Willie, who was passing by to the laundry. Georges echoed the sentiment. "War ain't no place for a young lady like you."

"I have to," she said. "I'll go crazy staying here, even as a guest. I heard Miss Barton's Red Cross ship is still in Key West—waiting for the fighting to begin. I'll leave on the earliest boat available."

She hugged them both as if it might be their last and left to send the cable. By noon, she passed Harry Scovel, who was also trolling the docks for an available vessel. He greeted her with open arms, and she went straight to the point. "I assume you're planning to follow the ships. Have you found a boat?"

"What makes you think that?"

Hands resting on her hips, she said, "We don't have time to dance, Harry. Clara Barton is expecting me in Key West. I must get there quickly, or I'll miss my only chance to report on the wounded for our mutual boss."

His head cocked. "Are you crazy? This is a real war. It's no place for a woman. Even Frances is staying on the home front—for now."

"Lookin' for a boat, folks?" came from behind them and they turned to find an old salt rubbing his bristled cheek.

"No," Harry said.

"Yes!" Lily overruled him. "But only if it's safe. Do you know one?"

He sneered at Harry. "Ah see the missus runs the ship. Follow me."

Without bothering to correct him about their marital status, they followed him to a surprisingly fit filibuster named *The Three Friends*. "She beat the Hearst's *Vamoose* five years straight," he bragged. "Wouldn't be runnin' her like a ferryboat, but the war put me outta business. Cap'n Napoleon Bonaparte Broward," at yer service."

Lily fought a smile at his fanciful name and Harry began the negotiation. How fast and how much for Key West?"

With a little haggling, they settled on what Lily considered highway robbery. Harry winked. "Not to worry. It's on our boss. Pulitzer will pay anything to get ahead of the *Journal*."

Even before the declaration, the two newspapers were at each other's throats, including cutting their newspaper prices to two cents a copy. But while Pulitzer still tried to tell some semblance of the truth, Hearst had gone completely "rag" to fabricate stories like the fictional strip-searches and execution of women prisoners at El Morro.

"When can we sail?" Lily asked the old smuggler.

"Tide goes out at two," he said, his shrewd gaze noting the age difference between Scovel and the much younger Lily.

"We'll be here," Harry answered for them both and paid Captain Broward a quarter of the rental. "You'll get another quarter when we board, and the rest when we land in Key West—before nightfall."

The old man counted the money. "A fair deal, mate. Ye'll watch the sun set over a tall drink in Key West Harbor."

Lily checked out of the hotel and hugged Willie again, then Merlyn, and Esther. With Georges behind the counter, safe from her second bone-crushing embrace, she held out her hand to him. "You know there is no way to thank you for all you've done for me."

His wide, black eyes brimmed with tears when he clasped her hand. "Jest come back safely with that man o' yours and I'll be happy."

With no way to guarantee that, she nodded. "Me too."

Harry tapped her on the shoulder. "We better get a move on."

Captain Broward was pacing the dock and nodded his approval when they arrived carrying only one bag each. "Was feared ye'd slow me down loadin' trunks an' the like. Make me late."

"I wasn't born yesterday, *mate,*" Harry muttered and led Lily across the narrow gangplank, ordering Broward, "Cast off."

The former tugboat refitted with a filibuster's powerful engines, were ready and the jolt nearly knocked them both to the floor as the bow raised and it turned into the receding tide, leaving white caps in its wake.

After the suffocating heat of Tampa, the fresh sea wind and spray invigorated Lily as she prayed the *Texas* was still in port. Fortunately, Captain Jack was as good as his word, landing a half-hour before the sun set on Key West.

Her prayer was answered at the sight of the *Texas* still moored in deep water outside the port, and Clara met them with open arms. "I was thrilled with your wire," she told Lily. "Many hands make light work," she said. Harry left them to take care of his own business while Lily hugged Ailish, then Sister Bettina, who had rejoined the mission when war was declared. At dinner aboard the ship, she confessed, "I couldn't stay behind and read the newspapers, when I could be there with my husband, helping the wounded.

And even with Mr. Elwell, and Ailish, Clara will need me to keep things organized."

Lily visited Clara in her cabin after dinner and the president of the Red Cross filled her in on their activities since being "grounded" in Key West. Pride sparked in Clara's eyes. "We've not had a dull moment. With the Spanish sailors wounded on the ships we captured offshore, and the training injuries in our own Navy, we've honed our triage skills. Though I am sad to say we won't be allowed to dock in Havana and unload our supplies for the civilians, we will find ways to use them for our men. I understand the departure from Tampa was most disorganized, and many tons of food and medicine were left behind in favor of loading the men."

Her voice lowered, "A losing proposition from the start, I fear. As a veteran, President McKinley should remember that an army runs on its stomach, and that healing the wounds and getting soldiers back on their feet bolsters morale and the fighting capability of the others. I tried to convince him, and every officer who would listen to me, to let us at least sail with the transports, but as you see, we were not successful."

"I thought the troops were landing at Havana," Lily said. "If not there, where?"

"We received word that Admiral Cervera has moved his ships and is now at the port of Santiago. We are sailing for Guantanamo Bay in the morning."

Lily's heart raced at how close she'd been to missing her chance to help Colin and Sean, especially now that Roosevelt was commander of the Rough Riders. "I'm anxious to serve in any way I can," she said to Clara's knowing gaze. "Will we be near the front lines?"

She squeezed Lily's hand. "Do you mean near the Rough Riders? Yes, I'm thankful to say, though I fear our commanders, with exception of Colin, are woefully unprepared for what they will face."

They left Key West on June 20. Six days later, after stopping in Guantanamo Bay, Harry disappeared. On his own mission, Lily assumed.

Sadly, the troops had left Guantanamo after a costly engagement at Las Guasimas. The *Texas* steamed on to Siboney, a tiny village not far from Santiago where they had to anchor offshore. The next morning, Lily rose just after dawn and stood on the deck, wondering where Colin and Sean were in the massive jungle. Through the morning mist, she saw the shadowed outlines of men trudging along a trail that twisted like a snake over a hill toward Santiago.

Both the Cuban and American hospitals were already set up on the shore and she anxiously scanned the approaching launch. Of the two medical officers aboard, neither was Colin. At tea, the doctors seemed thrilled to have the Red Cross supplies but were adamant that female nurses stay aboard the ship, telling Clara, "A field hospital is no place for a woman."

Lily held her breath as Clara rose to her full, though diminutive, height. "Well, that's odd," she said in an imperious tone. "Because I have spent the better part of my life in them—during war *and* peace."

The surgeon flushed and stood, no doubt to assert both his size and authority. "Well, not in my hospitals, Miss Barton."

Having no choice but to accept his dictum, at least for the moment, she walked with them to the launch. As they stepped onto the ladder, Clara had the last word. "You will regret your decision soon enough, sir. But not to worry, we will be here to help."

The Cuban doctors arrived in the wake of the departing American boat —with a very different attitude. Perhaps because they were used to women standing beside their soldiers, Lily thought. They were thrilled by Clara's offer of help, inviting her to join Dr. Lesser's tour of their hospital.

Lilly, Ailish, and two other nurses accompanied them. Near the end of the day, after cleaning and organizing the meager Cuban supplies, Clara grinned. "It seems the American hospital has reconsidered their decision and has requested our help, including that of our female nurses."

The next day, the first refugees from Spanish-held Santiago arrived at Siboney with news that the fighting had begun. Lily asked one of them, "Are the Americans wearing blue-dotted bandanas?"

"*Si*," the exhausted man answered. "*En la parte delantera. Loco gringos.*"

Her heart sank. They were at the front line and she agreed with the refugee. They were indeed crazy. She wondered if they were the men she'd seen on the ridge. "Roosevelt's weary walkers," they were called, because only their commander enjoyed the luxury of a mount. As much as she wanted to blame Roosevelt for using them as a shield, she knew her brother and the Western volunteers weren't the sort to let others fight their battles. She could only pray that Colin had the sense to let the wounded come to him.

"Are you alright, dear?" Sister Bettina asked.

Lily jumped. "No. I mean yes, of course. It's just that…"

"I know, dear, War is indeed a hell on earth."

Late in the day, the wounded, some nearly dead on their feet, began arriving on stretchers or were carried between the walking wounded. Lily scanned the face of every man, both hoping and dreading to see either Colin or Sean. Darkness fell and she couldn't look anymore, as the dead boy-soldiers arrived, their bodies already ravaged from sand crabs and vultures.

The wounded who managed to make it down the hill without assistance reported they'd been without food for nearly three days of sporadic fighting. Now fed, but still weak, they helped in any way they could. And while Lily did everything from washing and feeding patients, to assisting the exhausted surgeons, she asked everyone, "Have you seen Lieutenant O'Grady or Dr. Winfield?"

One young man who looked barely seventeen said, "Last I seen Lieutenant O'Grady, he was on his way over to help Roosevelt out of a fix he got himself into at Kettle Hill. An' if'n you mean that crazy doc flittin' all over the battlefield with only his little black bag, I wish I had his guardian angel. He had his hands full with the ones too bad off to move."

She leaned against a tree and took a deep breath, knowing that at least the day before, they were both alive. Clinging to that hope, she tried her best to ignore the stories of the heavy toll taken from Spanish snipers using guns with smokeless powder, aimed for their officers.

"I need a little help," jolted her from near panic.

"I'm here," she shouted, jumping up to face a tall Negro soldier in what was left of a bloodied dark blue flannel shirt. He leaned on a broken tree branch, blood from a wound in this thigh following a slow trail down his leg. He swayed a bit and smiled. "Miss Lily?"

She looked up at his amazing green eyes, cried, "Grover!" and threw herself toward him. She held most of his weight against her body as she led him through the maze of wounded and sick men. She screamed for assistance through blinding tears until Dr. Holman ran to her and helped the wounded man onto a bloody canvas sheet on the ground.

"No. A cot," she insisted, knowing that infections were killing more soldiers than bullets. "

A small hand touched her arm and Ailish's calming voice said, "There ain't no cots, darlin'. This will have to do for now. Let 'em set him down an' keep his leg raised on your lap. It'll keep it clean and slow the blood whilst I get some water."

Color and rank made no difference at death's door as Cubans, Buffalo Soldiers, officers, and infantry men lay side by side on the ground or filthy sheets, suffering from fever, malaria, mortal and secondary wounds. The worst were treated first.

Lily saw that Grover was laid on the cleanest edge of the filthy canvas, his leg propped on an empty medical supply box. "I'll get you a doctor," she promised.

He shook his head. "I'll wait my turn. Bullet went right through. Looks worse 'n it is."

Relieved, she sat beside him, moving his bloodied leg from the hard box to her moderately clean apron. He sighed and closed his eyes as the throbbing eased.

Knowing no one could sleep amid the chaos of doctors and officers barking orders and men crying and screaming with pain, she asked, "What is happening up there? Did you see Sean?"

Eyes still closed, Grover's head swayed back and forth. "No, ma'am. 'Tween our smoke and the Spanish bullets, wasn't no time to sightsee. One thing about them Mauser rifles," he said, his lips barely moving. "Bullets is small an' sharp. An' dang they's fast. If there ain't nothing major to stop 'em, they go right through."

"Stay with me, Grover," Lily shouted as his words became slurred and his voice dulled. "Don't you dare die. I'm ordering you."

Ailish touched her shoulder and set a bucket of clean warm water in front of her. "Let him sleep. Take this towel and clean the wound to see the damage." She looked up the hill. "There's more comin'. I'll be right back."

Lily dipped the clean piece of muslin into the bucket and washed the wound until the water turned pink. Grover was right. The bullet had gone right through the fleshy part of his thigh. But the exit hole was bigger than the entrance wound.

"Needs stitches," Ailish said while supporting a man using his belt as a tourniquet above a shattered knee. "We're low on catgut, but I have a spool of silk thread in my bag. I already boiled it so it's clean."

"Can you do it?" Lily asked.

"No," Ailish surprised her. "I got the arthuritis in my fingers and Doc Lesser wants me. You'll have to do it."

Lily had watched and helped numerous surgeries involving sutures, and stitched the shallow knife wound on Colin's back, but this was much worse. What if her needle struck an artery, or her stitches were too big to stop the bleeding? She looked around. All the exhausted surgeons were busy, and while Grover's bleeding had slowed, it was still oozing through the muslin.

"Hurry," Ailish shouted from several feet away. "He can't afford to lose more blood."

Lily left him to retrieve the spool of red silk thread and a pack of needles. Her hands shook as she cut a long length and threaded a needle, but it steadied when it approached the wound and she took comfort from Ailish's massive understatement, "It's like mending a rip in an apron."

"It's *nothing* like mending a rip in anything," Lily muttered. It was a deep wound in human flesh. She wiped her forehead with the now-bloodied sleeve of her uniform. "I'm so sorry," she told Grover as she pierced the flesh on both sides of the cleaned wound.

He surprised her by chuckling. "Miss Lilly, this ain't nothin' but a scratch. I was stabbed with a Comanche spear in New Mexico. Went clean through my side. Had to break it off and ride back to the fort with it still in there."

He kept up a steady banter of what she hoped were greatly exaggerated stories of wounds and battles until she rolled back on her heels and they both examined her work. "Great job," Ailish told her, flying by like a guardian angel on another errand.

Grover joked, "I especially like the little bow you put on the end," while Lily wrapped a clean bandage around his thigh. She was admiring her handiwork when he rolled onto his good leg and pulled himself up with a fallen branch from a mango tree.

She scrambled to her feet screaming like a fishwife. "What are you doing? You need to rest. Don't you dare turn away from me Grover Hawkins! Where are you going?"

He turned slowly and smiled. "Back to the front, Miss. My men need me. And I got a cocky New Mexico Ranger to keep in line."

"What do you mean? Do you mean Sean? Is he alright?"

He shrugged. "Last I saw, he was chasin' up that damn Kettle Hill like the divil hisself was after him."

So, Sean and Colin were together—at Kettle Hill—yesterday. And the fight was still going on. "You're not going anywhere soldier," came from Dr. Lesser. He ordered, "Now sit down," and Master-Sergeant Grover Hawkins lowered himself gently onto the hard-packed sand.

The doctor leaned on one knee to open the bandage and examine Lily's handiwork. He smiled at the bow on the end and winked at her, saying to Grover, "You have some right fancy stitching there, young man, but you don't want them to break."

With a glance at the wine-colored water in the bucket and Grover's bloody trousers, he said, "Looks like you lost a lot of blood. If you can walk with that branch, go to the mess for some food and take a blanket to one of the small tents on the East side of the hospital for a little lay-down in the shade. Keep your distance from the fever wards. If the wound is still clean in the morning, we'll change the bandage and you can go back."

The surgeon cut off Grover's protests with, "You're no help to your men if you collapse on the way there."

A wary look at the latest ravaged body being carried away prompted Grover's, "Yessir."

Lily wagered he'd be gone after a hot meal and a short nap, taking what he could carry from the mess tent back to San Juan Heights.

Dr. Lesser faced Lily. "We need to gather what supplies we can to take up to the front in the morning. We received an urgent message from General Shafter. The field hospital there has no supplies or food. The situation is dire. There's no time to waste."

"I'm going with you," Lily said.

"Take me too," came from Ailish. "And me," from Dr. Lesser's wife, Sister Bettina.

CHAPTER 38

The morning of July 4th dawned clear for the first time in days. The night before, Mr. Elwell and his staff fought darkness and heavy seas to land supplies without a dock. Once onshore, ambulatory soldiers loaded two four-mule wagons. But Elwell and his men were in no condition to drive stubborn mules with overloaded wagons up the winding trail to San Juan Heights.

Lily was looking for volunteers when Grover caught up to her. Less than twenty-four hours after being shot through the thigh, he walked with barely a limp. "I hear yer lookin' for drivers."

She squinted up at him. "I know what you're doing Grover, but you can't go back into battle yet. You need at least another day to rest that leg and replenish your blood."

His eyes rolled heavenward. "Lord, save me from well-meanin' women. With all due respect, Miz Lily, I ain't stayin' here to catch a fever an' die, whilst waiting for my leg to heal. You sewed it up real good, and I'll be sittin' on a wagon all the way to the top." He motioned to another Buffalo Soldier. "This is Toby. He grew up with mules. Knows how to get 'em to move."

"But his arm is in a sling. How will he drive four mules?"

Grover laughed. "I got one leg an' two arms and he gots two legs an' one arm. Twixt the both of us we kin manage a bunch o' dumb as stumps mules."

"We'll take you both," Clara spoke up from behind them. With a stern glance at Lily, she said, "They're all we have. Our doctors and nurses have their hands full here. And I can drive a mule team."

All jaws dropped at hearing the tiny old woman offer to drive four mules up a muddy, rutted hill.

"All due respect, ma'am," Grover ventured. "You can't..."

"I can help her with the mules on the second wagon," Ailish piped up and smiled at their shock. "My da' hauled coal through Boston with a wagon bigger'n this an' four o' the meanest mules on earth. I rode with him since I was old enough to climb up to the box. 'Twixed us, we'll have enough arms and legs for all the wagons. Right, Toby?"

The lanky young man from Georgia nodded enthusiastically. "Sure can, Miss. All's I need is a good whip for crackin' over their heads an' we'll be there afore you know it."

With no ambulance or other transportation available, Lily and two other Red Cross nurses bounced inside the wagons amid bales of hay protecting the supplies. Both the mules and drivers struggled uphill in muddy clay that sucked the wagons down to the wheel hubs. Four hours later, they pulled up to the First Division Hospital of the Fifth Army Corps near the battlefield. Clara reported to General Shafter, who greeted her from a cot in his tent, feverish and suffering an attack of gout.

Lily and the nurses stood speechless at the bleak horror surrounding them. The flat landscape was hard-packed sand, offering no drainage, and the only vegetation consisted of sparse patches of long, spindly wild grasses. A few small pieces of canvas the size of tablecloths spread over low-hanging branches of scrub trees offered little relief from the sweltering sun. Soldiers suffering from open wounds sat on palm leaves or the hard-packed sand, watching insects feed on their blood. Most shocking of all were the hundreds of men fresh from the battlefield or the operating tables, lying naked on the ground, with no sheets to cover them.

Clara's group marveled at the lack of complaints from the naked, wounded men who hadn't seen food for nearly four days. Instead, courage and gratitude greeted them when they were offered simple gruel. Some soldiers even cried with gratitude, and as night fell, though still naked and bloody, they remained uncomplaining.

Lily asked everyone she saw if they'd seen Colin and was frustrated at their bleary-eyed shrugs. Finally, one soldier with both arms in slings nodded north, toward the three hills guarding the Spanish port city of Santiago.

"He comes and goes."

It broke her heart to be so close to Colin and not see him, talk to him, or touch him. All night long, the lanterns inside the surgical tent cast ghastly shadows of the remaining two doctors bending over patients with bone saws and surgical instruments. Before retiring to the dog tent she shared with Clara, Ailish, and Bettina, she found a bolt of cotton cloth in one of the wagons. It wouldn't keep the men warm, but it would cover their bodies and shield them from the insects.

A hazy dawn brightened the sky and the women rose, still wearing their mud-caked clothes, to step into the already stifling heat. "They're coming," someone called, pointing to three men stumbling toward the camp. It was followed by cheers of, "They made it!"

"It's the last of the wounded," someone else yelled, and recovering soldiers, many of them half-naked and on crutches, rushed to help.

The only one Lily could identify from the distance was Grover's tall, strong body on one side of a wounded soldier and a smaller man in ripped and bloody clothing on the other side. As they approached, she recognized Colin as the other ambulatory man. He and Grover stumbled from exhaustion but didn't seem to be wounded.

The man between them hung limply, his arms over their shoulders, shaggy dark hair hiding his face, feet dragging along the muddy ground.

One man from the camp dragged his own stretcher to help, and men from the hospital tent arrived to lay him gently onto it. Colin and Grover collapsed on the ground nearby. Their clothes were nearly as ragged as many of the patients and covered in blood. Lily hovered outside the edge of the crowd of injured men cheering at the escape of the last three men alive on the battlefield. Her heart leaped at knowing Grover and Colin were safe, then fell. Where was Sean?

She pushed her way through the crowd to reach Colin, stopping short at the litter. The wounded soldier's face was bearded and bloody, but his eyes were open. Quicksilver gray eyes that could only belong to her brother, stared up at the cloudless Caribbean sky.

The stretcher bearers stopped in their tracks when she screamed, "Sean!" and fell to her knees beside him. With a cry that many compared to an Irish banshee, she bent over his body, calling her brother's name until those glazed eyes turned to her and an unrecognizable hoarse whisper said, "Stop the keening, Lily Pad, I'm not dead yet."

"Ma'am, we need to get this man to the surgery," one of the litter bearers told her and she stood, not knowing whether to go to the man she loved, or to follow the brother she adored.

"What are you doing here?" came from behind her in what was little more than a growl. *Colin.*

It wasn't what she'd expected. She'd imagined running into his arms, kissing his weary eyes, caressing his sunburned face. She never imagined meeting brown eyes darkened to nearly black with anger. He didn't reach out to her, so she stood her ground. "I came with your aunt—to help."

"But you're not a nurse. You're a journalist. A noncombatant. You could have been killed." His weary gaze surveyed the field of wounded and sick. "Or worse."

Forgetting they were surrounded by an audience of interested soldiers with nowhere else to go, she stared him down. "You should know by now that I can take care of myself. And I can help here."

"She's right on all counts," came from Grover. "With all due respect, Sir, she sewed my leg up right proper after one o' them Mauser bullets shot through me. Used fine silk thread that held tight. I couldn't a found y'all without it."

Colin turned back to her. "Is that true?"

"The wound was clean and Dr. Lesser was busy. The thread was Ailish's. Red was all she had."

He managed a weary smile. "Ah yes, your favorite color for sewing."

Fists on her hips, she switched roles. "And why were *you* on the battlefield instead of in the surgery? You were supposed to stay behind the lines, not be a target for Spanish sharpshooters."

He led her away from the men gawking at them. "I couldn't leave wounded men on the ground, and Sean is the best shot in what's left of the Rough Riders. He saved my life. Grover found us last night at dusk, and while he and I rounded up the last of the wounded, Sean tracked down the snipers by following the flare of their guns in the dark. He got the last one, but not before the sniper shot him in the shoulder."

"Will he be alright?"

"He's lost a lot of blood. I won't know until I get him on the table. At best, it will be a long, painful recovery."

"You can't operate. You're exhausted."

"We're all exhausted," he said, reaching out to touch her face. "And I thought you were safe in Tampa."

Ignoring the surrounding men, Lily kissed him. When they parted, she asked, "Where is Raphael? I heard he and his men were here."

Horror, grief, and exhaustion reflected from his eyes and his voice broke when he said, "He didn't make it. On the second day, he created a diversion to draw fire away from Roosevelt and his men who were surrounded on Kettle Hill. Raphael and half his men died, but it helped turn the tide. He saved a lot of Rough Riders' lives, including Roosevelt's."

Lily fell against him. He swayed on his feet as he held her a moment, then stepped away. "I have to see to Sean. Since you're so very good at fancy sewing, are you up to helping?"

Doubt gripped her stomach. All the others from the Red Cross were more than occupied. But what if she made a mistake that killed her brother? "Do you think I should?"

"I trust Grover's reference. And an extra pair of steady hands is always welcome."

They reached the tent to find three ambulances and a wagon with more supplies. Once emptied, they were loaded with as many wounded men as they could hold and were headed back to the hospitals on the beach by the time Lily and Colin had washed and entered the surgical tent.

Sean was already on the table. His filthy clothes removed, a clean sheet of the muslin from their wagon covering him. Colin told her, "Doctor Fischer's patient needs to have that leg wound closed, and you seem to have experience."

"But…"

Dr. Lesser touched her arm. "I can help here. Your brother wouldn't want you to see him like this."

She made sure she was close enough to hear the two doctors assess the damage from the small, fast, Mauser bullet. "He was lucky," Dr. Lesser said. "It went straight through the shoulder muscle. The bone may be nicked but it seems solid."

While Dr. Lesser stitched the wound on both sides with strong catgut from the new supplies, Collin found Lily pacing outside the tent. "Barring infection," he said, "Sean may feel a twinge before it rains, but he'll recover. Now we need to make sure fever doesn't get him."

Dr. Lesser joined them. "The hospitals in Siboney are filled with more fever victims than wounds," he said. "And many of these men shouldn't be moved. We brought a hundred cots and have enough fresh sheets, water, and food to last a few days."

"Can we keep him here?" Lily asked. "I know you and the others need to go back. We can move him to our dog tent, away from the others. I'll stay with him. When I found the bolt of cotton for sheets, I also found some mosquito netting."

The older man shrugged and looked to Colin. "It seems she's thought of everything, son. You need the help and it's her brother."

"Stop talking to me like I can't hear you," Sean croaked from inside the surgical tent and they stepped inside. His eyes were glazed with pain from the un-anesthetized surgery, but his voice gained strength when he said, "My legs are fine. I can walk…to Siboney…on my own."

He moved to rise but couldn't resist Colin's restraining hand. "If you're so fit, Lieutenant, I can use you here, even one-handed, to help with the others."

Two days later, they emptied the camp of the last of the wounded. In Siboney, they heard that while they'd been at San Juan Heights fighting to take Santiago, the Navy had been pummeling the armed blockhouses in the hills above the hospital tents. Most of the town was in ruins, but the hospitals on the shore were safe.

CHAPTER 39

$\mathcal{T}$he Red Cross left for Santiago on July 18th and Lily stayed behind with Ailish to tend the remaining seriously injured and fever patients, including Colin, who had succumbed to a malarial fever. Fortunately, they had ample quantities of quinine to treat the intermittent bouts of fever and chills until a ship came for them.

The Rough Riders had lost nearly half its enlistment, including a hundred dead from fever in Tampa. Roosevelt wrote letters to Washington and found a way for their survivors to be among the first shipped home. Lily hugged Sean before he boarded the transport ship to a hospital in Montauk, New York.

"Kiss Elena and the children for me," she said caressing his cheek.

"Kiss them twice," Colin added. "Once for me." He shook Sean's good hand. "It was an honor serving with you, Ranger."

Sean chuckled and saluted his superior officer, answering, "It's just Sean. I think I'm getting a little long in the tooth to traipse all over the mountains looking for desperados. Elena's been after me to settle down. And now that the territory of New Mexico has fought a war for the United States, maybe I can help it become one."

After seeing them off, Colin wired his resignation to Secretary of War Russell Alger, and they boarded the *Olivette* to join Clara and her group in Havana.

"Colin, you look well," Clara exclaimed after their short time apart.

"As do you," he answered, when in truth, they both looked like they'd walked through hell and back.

Lily felt the old woman's bones when she hugged her. "Clara, are you well? Shouldn't you be returning to Tampa?"

"In due time," she answered. There was an edge to her voice, as if the suggestion had been posed too many times to tolerate. "Our original mission here was to distribute food to Havana. When war was declared, our supplies went to the military. Secretary Alger has commissioned another ship with food for us to complete our original mission. I will return to the United States when the goal has been accomplished."

As if recognizing the disappointment at their upcoming separation in Lily's eyes, she added, "Truth be told, I have lost so many of my little family to illness and other duties, I could use some help."

"It would be my honor to help you, Auntie," Colin said and looked at Lily. "For both of us, I'm sure."

"That went without saying," Clara chided and looked at Lily. "I am so grateful for the service you've offered thus far, but I know nursing isn't what you've planned for your future."

Lily swallowed hard. "Sometimes other things are more important than our little plans."

On their third day in Havana, they received word that the steamship, *Comal*, with 1200 tons of food and supplies, arrived. Unfortunately, it couldn't be handed over to the Red Cross to distribute because the ship carried no authorization to do so. Then Clara fell, injuring her eye.

"You look like death warmed over, Auntie," Colin told her. "I share your disappointment, but you need to go back to Tampa. We can stay here and work with the Army and Spanish officials to straighten this out. I guarantee the food and supplies will not go to waste."

Lily touched Clara's arm. "You've done more for the world than humanly possible. And your work isn't finished. You're needed in Washington to testify to the blunders and needless sacrifices suffered during this war. Let us deal with the Spanish and see that the supplies go to the people meant to have them."

Clara's head bowed to cruel reality and she boarded the *Clinton* on September 3rd, leaving Colin and Lily among the few American military and civilians remaining to evacuate the Spanish officials and help set up the new government.

"You should have gone with her," Colin said when the *Clinton* put out to sea.

"How can you say that after all we've been through together? And with all there is still to be done?"

His finger lifted her chin to kiss her. "Because I love you. We have no idea how the Cubans will react to American occupation instead of the immediate self-rule we promised. Or how long it will take to help them create an independent government of their own. It might not be safe here…"

"I'm not Winona," came out before she realized the pain it would cause him. She reached for his hand, but he pulled away. "Oh, Colin, I'm so sorry, I didn't mean…"

"Yes, you did," he said softly. "Is that why you won't marry me?"

"Can you deny she's still in your thoughts?"

"What about Victor?" he countered. "Can you tell me he isn't always in the back of your mind? Is that why you can't trust me?"

She stepped back. "How can you say that? I came to a war zone because of you."

"And for your brother. And for a story."

The accusation felt like a slap and she raised her chin to glare at him. "If you believe that, then you don't know me at all. Victor is dead. The war is over. You saved the lives of hundreds of soldiers to repay your debt for taking the life of one murderer. What will it take for *you* to trust *me*?"

"Lily, I didn't mean…"

She turned her back to him and raised a hand to hail a taxi to collect her few belongings at the Inglaterra and left to do one more thing before booking passage on the next ship out. It was a short walk to the Church of the Holy Spirit. Father Augustus was still there, though like most everyone, he looked thin and weary—and older. After the usual pleasantries, she said, "I've come for Pedro."

The smile she suspected he used for children, old people, and women faded as he looked over her shoulder. "And where is your husband?"

"My…husband…is not here. I came to fulfill my—our—wish to adopt the child."

The priest led her to his office. "I am afraid that will make things difficult, Mrs. Champagne. I cannot release a child to one parent, let alone an American woman—and one who is not a Catholic. You must understand that I am concerned about the boy's immortal soul. He seems happy here and has shown an exceptional talent for music. He is also most helpful to me."

She refused his offer of a chair and lost the fight to control her temper. "Are you certain that you are refusing me out of concern for Pedro? We both know his angelic voice will change as he grows, and he is a mestizo. No matter how he studies your bible, he will never be accepted into seminary. Or are you refusing me because he is such a 'help' to you?"

While she prayed the good priest wouldn't abuse the child, Pedro would still grow up as little more than a slave to the Catholic Church. "I appreciate your care and concern, but when I left him with you, we agreed that I would return for him."

She placed both hands on the priest's desk and leaned toward him. "With or without my *husband,* I am here to claim the boy as my son and give him the life he deserves."

"I'd listen to her if I were you," startled them. Lily turned and Father Augustus jumped to his feet. "Oh, you must be Mr. Champagne, sir," the priest groveled to Colin, dressed in his full-dress uniform. "I had no idea you were an American officer."

Colin pressed his advantage. "Please prepare the adoption papers immediately. My…wife…uses her maiden name for business transactions. You have my permission to put the custody agreement in the name of Lily O'Grady."

He placed a twenty-dollar Liberty Head gold piece on the cluttered desk —a small fortune in Spanish currency. Father Augustus scooped it up and called for an altar boy to find Pedro. Then he sat down to write up the adoption agreement before the crazy Americans changed their minds.

Lily turned to Colin. "How did you know I'd be here?"

"Because I *do* know you. I know you're headstrong and independent, beautiful and tender, and above all, loyal. And because I love you."

He guided her out of the priest's earshot. "Yes, I loved Winona, but I'm not the same man now," answered the doubt in her eyes. "Not since I saw you dangling under the dome at the Tampa Bay Hotel."

She didn't resist when he pulled her to him and whispered, "When you left me, I realized that without you in my life, I have no life. Our time together—and apart—has taught me what I really want to do, but it won't be worth anything unless I'm with you."

"And what is it you want to do with your life?"

"I want to open a free clinic in New York for immigrants, children, and veterans."

"That's wonderful, but you know nursing isn't what I want to do with *my* life."

A smile flirted with the corners of his lips. "Yes, I know. You're a crusading reporter. It's one of the things I love about you."

"And Pedro?"

"He's a very special little boy. I'd be honored to help you raise him—if you'll let me."

Father Augustus cleared his throat and waved the completed adoption certificate in the air. Colin went back to him and read it, then frowned.

"Is something wrong?" the priest asked, his voice high, bordering on panic.

Colin handed the document to Lily and she caught her breath. She looked up and asked Father Augustus. "Pedro Diaz? Are you sure?"

Color returned to the priest's face. "Of course," he said condescendingly. "The boy knows his own name."

Lily and Colin spoke together. "What is his father's first name?"

"Raphael," came from the doorway behind them.

They turned and Pedro screamed, "Señora Lily!" The joy in his eyes turned to fear when he saw Colin's American uniform. "Señor doctor?" he whispered, looking as if he might bolt.

Lily dropped to her knees and held his shoulders. "It's safe, Pedro. We're going to take you to America."

"America?" He dropped the crutch and fell into her embrace, pressing his face against her to hide happy sobs.

Lily stepped away to cover his face with kisses. "It's over, darling," she said through her own happy tears. "You have a new family."

Pedro pulled away and looked up at Colin towering over them. "*Con él?*"

"*Sí,*" she answered. "With him. God Willing."

Still on her knees, she looked up at Colin and took his hand in hers.

"Lily, what are you doing?" he asked, looking confused and more than a little concerned.

"Shh. I have something to ask you."

"Then stand up."

"No. I have to do this," she said. In front of the puzzled boy and a very shocked priest, she asked, "Colin Winfield, will you make an honest woman of me and be a father to this child?"

Joy lit his face when he pulled her to her feet. "I will."

His kissed her and reached his hand out to Pedro. The boy hesitated until Lily nodded, then placed his small, dark hand on top of theirs.

Colin put his other hand into his pocket, pulling out a tiny velvet box and holding it out to Lily. "Only if you promise to never take this off."

They stepped back as she opened the box to reveal a bed of white silk holding a silver ring with a band shaped like the leaves of a lily of the valley surrounding a blue sapphire that matched her eyes. Happy tears filling her eyes, she answered, "I promise."

Colin picked her up and swung her around, then put her down and did the same with Pedro, who squealed with delight and flopped onto the floor by his crutch.

The priest was staring at his gold coin when Colin turned to Lily. "Alger approved my discharge today, and the *Oregon* is leaving for New York in the morning. I've booked a double cabin for the three of us."

Her jaw dropped. "But the *Comel* and its cargo?"

"The Spanish and American governments are taking it over. Aunt Clara won't be happy, but she understands politics. At least the people will get the supplies they need."

He kissed her forehead and dropped another gold coin onto the priest's desk. "You need to marry us. Now."

EPILOGUE

1900

*P*edro held the door open as Lily pushed a baby carriage through the doors of the Winfield Clinic on Lenox Avenue, a few blocks from Harlem Hospital. It was a glorious spring afternoon in New York City, thanks to brisk western breezes pushing the smoke and clouds from the city out to sea. At three o'clock, only one patient from the surrounding Jewish and Italian immigrant neighborhoods waited to see him.

Lily straightened her hat and smiled at a pregnant woman and another, older one who was likely her mother. Both returned her smile and she noted that the pregnant girl's olive complexion glowed with health, thanks to Colin's information about diet and natural, herbal medicines.

"Is he busy?" she asked Ailish, who served as Colin's nurse, receptionist, and accountant.

"In between," she said, nodding to the two waiting women. "And you look fit as a fiddle," she told Pedro, who had endured several surgeries at Johns Hopkins Hospital over the last eighteen months. "I see the cast is off. How does it feel?"

The nine-year-old blushed at her attention and mumbled, "Much better…Miss Ailish. They said it could be my last."

Lily smiled proudly at his nearly flawless English, adding, "It came off last week. His doctor recommended taking it slow, but Colin feels that after more than a year of surgeries, and months in casts, he should try to exercise as much as possible."

Ailish nodded for the mother and her pregnant daughter to go into the examining room, then asked Pedro, "How is it going?"

"I don't use the crutch except for stairs," he answered proudly.

Lily warned, "Just don't try to jump rope or play kickball—yet."

"I will be careful, *Madre*."

Her heart warmed every time he called her 'mother', though she and Colin would never replace Raphael and Maria Diaz. They didn't want to. Maria was a martyr to Spanish domination and Raphael had died a hero, saving American lives. She saw the same courage and integrity in Pedro's eyes and loved him as much as she did her six-month-old daughter, Rose.

The Italian mother-to-be approached Ailish for her next appointment, stopping to coo over Rose fussing in the pram. "*Bellisimo.*"

"*Grazie*," Lily answered in rudimentary Italian.

"What have we here?' came from behind them and Pedro walked toward Colin with only a slight limp.

"Great job," he said. "How far today?"

"Ten blocks here," the boy answered with a sense of pride in his voice.

"A half-mile. Great job, but don't overdo. I'm working in my lab the rest of the day and could use some help." He looked at Lily. "Walter Reed says we're close to proving the theory that yellow fever is from infected mosquitoes and not contagious."

"That's marvelous."

"Yes, but now the real work begins to find a vaccine that will protect against it." He sighed. "It could take decades."

Her gloved hand rested on his arm. "You've said that finding the cause is halfway to finding the cure—and you're young." She picked up a fussy Rose, kissed her blonde curls, and handed her to her father. "I have a favor to ask."

Rose settled into Colin's shoulder and quieted. He smiled at his wife. "And what adventure are you embarking on now, my love."

Taking a moment to kiss the three people in the world she'd give her life for, Lily answered, "Something I've put off for far too long. The National

American Woman Suffrage Association is meeting this afternoon. Susan B. Anthony is passing the suffrage torch to Carrie Catt. Besides fabulous stories for my column, it's time I took part in gaining women the right to vote."

She stroked Rose's cheek. "For future generations of *amazonas.*"

THE END

❧

Coming soon!
Book 4 of the Langesford Legacy
The Story of a Lifetime, takes the reader to 1964, as the Langesford family is again forced to fight for their Legacy—and their lives.

❧

Don't miss out on your next favorite book!

Join the Satin Romance mailing list
www.satinromance.com/mail.html

THANK YOU FOR READING

Did you enjoy this book?

Tell the world and leave a review at the site from which this book was purchased.

DID YOU KNOW THAT LEAVING A REVIEW...

- Helps other readers find books they may enjoy.
- Gives you a chance to let your voice be heard.
- Gives authors recognition for their hard work.
- Doesn't have to be long. A sentence or two about why you liked the book will do.

ABOUT THE AUTHOR

Doris Lemcke is a Michigan native and writes historical and contemporary fiction about strong, intelligent women caught in a web of, *Love, Lies and Family Secrets*. Now living in Southeast Michigan's beautiful Ann Arbor area, she's continues to write fact-based and fast-paced historical and contemporary novels.

Fascinated by American history since childhood, she researches her novels through authentic journals, letters and contemporary accounts for authenticity. *Rebel Treasure*, book 1 of *the Langesford Legacy Series*, introduced one of Georgia's founding families during the South's "Reconstruction" period; Book 2, *White Mountain Spirit* takes them through the tragedy and triumph of America's Western Expansion; Book 3, *Champagne Promises*, showcases America's "Splendid Little War" with Spain in 1898, and *The Story of a Lifetime* tests the strength of the old family during the turbulent Civil Rights Era of the 1960's.

An avid quilter, she compares writing a book to making a contemporary quilt. Both involve, "Connecting bits and pieces" of colorful elements together—in ways that inspire "the eye of the beholder" to see history in a new way.

For more information:
www.dorislemckebooks.com
Doris@DorisLemckeBooks.com

~

Eager to hear what's next for Doris Lempke?
Join her mailing list!
www.dorislemckebooks.com/contact.html

facebook.com/Doris-Lemcke-Author-177898622282712

ALSO BY DORIS LEMCKE

WITH SATIN ROMANCE

The Langeford Legacy Series

Rebel Treasure

White Mountain Spirit

Love, Lies and Family Secrets Series

Legacy of Lies

www.ingramcontent.com/pod-product-compliance
Lightning Source LLC
Chambersburg PA
CBHW020817260626
47169CB00003B/712